A
SENSE OF SIN

A
SENSE OF SIN

ELIZABETH ESSEX

BRAVA

KENSINGTON PUBLISHING CORP.
www.kensingtonbooks.com

BRAVA BOOKS are published by

Kensington Publishing Corp.
119 West 40th Street
New York, NY 10018

All Kensington titles, imprints and distributed lines are available at special quantity discounts for bulk purchases for sales promotion, premiums, fund-raising, educational or institutional use.

Special book excerpts or customized printings can also be created to fit specific needs. For details, write or phone the office of the Kensington Special Sales Manager: Kensington Publishing Corp., 119 West 40th Street, New York, NY 10018. Attn. Special Sales Department. Phone: 1-800-221-2647.

Brava and the B logo are Reg. U.S. Pat. & TM Off.

ISBN-13: 978-0-7582-5156-5
ISBN-10: 0-7582-5156-4

First Kensington Trade Paperback Printing: April 2011

10 9 8 7 6 5 4 3 2 1

Printed in the United States of America

To Joanne Lockyer,
for patience, friendship, and
extraordinary insight.

CHAPTER 1

Dartmouth, England, 1794

"Delacorte? You're looking remarkably bloody-minded for a ball. Even for you. Are you planning to dance with whomever you've set your sights on, or thrash them?"

Rupert Delacorte, Viscount Darling, ignored the amused remark of his friend Hugh McAlden and concentrated on his quarry. It should be a difficult thing to hate a woman one had never seen before, but Del looked across the expansive ballroom at the beautiful woman descending the stairs and reckoned he'd manage just fine. Because hate her he did. With a cold, implacable fury that seethed deep within him, burning unabated throughout his long year of mourning, like molten lava hidden beneath an icy mountain, until, at long last, the time had come for justice.

No matter what, no matter the consequences or social carnage, he was going to make her pay for her misdeeds. His deep-seated sense of justice demanded it. He was going to ruin her elegant, effortless life just as surely and as ruthlessly as she had ruined Emily's.

"Haven't decided." Del tossed back a small measure of brandy to swallow the stinging taste of bitterness that always rose in his gullet at the thought of Emily, his adored younger sister.

She had been his anchor, his compass. Without her, he had come unmoored, adrift and without purpose. For a year, he had rashly and stupidly tried to blunt the pain of Emily's loss with liquor, fornication, and a recklessness that might have seen a lesser man to his grave. But nothing had helped.

Emily was dead. And it was the fault of the woman across the room. Celia Burke.

The drink of potent liquor sent small licking tongues of fire through his chest, feeding the flames of his ire. He would permit himself only one, small drink. He couldn't afford the continued self-indulgence of blissful, drunken oblivion. Not since he had received the bloody blackmail letter and found out about Celia Burke.

The mere thought of her betrayal nearly sent him howling with rage. No wonder he looked bloody-minded. He felt murderous. That carelessly scrawled demand for his money and his silence had overthrown all his beliefs, all his love, and all his hopes. That one letter had obliterated all the letters that had come before, and left both his past and his future in tatters.

Del had not known who she was when he first laid eyes upon her, but he instinctively didn't like her. He distrusted beauty. Because beauty walked hand in hand with privilege—unearned privilege. And she was certainly beautiful. Tall, elegant, with porcelain white skin, a riot of sable dark curls and deep dark eyes—a symphony of black and white. She surveyed the ballroom like a queen: haughty, serene, remote, and exquisitely beautiful. Beauty had a way of diverting unpleasantness and masking grievous flaws of character. It was not to be trusted.

Her name was confirmed by others attending the select ball at the Marquess and Marchioness of Widcombe's. It wafted to him on champagne-fueled murmurs in the hot, crowded room:

"Dear Celia," and "Our Miss Burke." Others seemed to call her The Ravishing Miss Burke, as if it were her title and she the only one to wear that crown.

The Ravishing Miss Celia Burke. A well-known, and even more well-liked local beauty. She made her serene, graceful way down the short set of stairs into the ballroom as effortlessly as clear water flowed over rocks in a hillside stream. She nodded and smiled in a benign but uninvolved way at all who approached her, but she never stopped to converse. She processed on, following her mother through the parting sea of mere mortals, those lesser human beings who were nothing and nobody to her but playthings.

Aloof, perfect Celia Burke. *Fuck you.*

By God, he would take his revenge and Emily would have justice. Maybe then he could sleep at night.

Maybe then he could learn to live with himself.

But he couldn't exact the kind of revenge one takes on another man—straightforward, violent, and bloody. He couldn't call Miss Burke out on the middle of the dance floor and put a bullet between her eyes or a sword blade between her ribs at dawn.

His justice would have to be more subtle, but no less thorough. And no less ruthless.

"You were the one who insisted we attend this august gathering. So what's it to be, Delacorte?" Commander Hugh McAlden, friend, naval officer, and resident cynic, prompted again.

McAlden was one of the few people who never addressed Del by his courtesy title, Viscount Darling, as they'd known each other long before he'd come into the bloody title and far too long for Del to give himself airs in front of such an old friend. With such familiarity came ease. With McAlden, Del could afford the luxury of being blunt.

"Dancing or thrashing? The latter, I think."

McAlden's usually grim mouth crooked up in half a smile.

"A thrashing, right here in the Marchioness's ballroom? I'd pay good money to see that."

"Would you? Shall we have a private bet, then?"

"Del, I always like it when you've got that look in your eye. I'd like nothing more than a good wager."

"A bet, Colonel Delacorte? What's the wager? I've money to burn these days, thanks to you two." Another naval officer, Lieutenant Ian James, known from their time together when Del had been an officer of His Majesty's Marine Forces aboard the frigate *Resolute*, broke into the conversation from behind.

"A private wager only, James." Del would need to be more circumspect. James was a bit of a puppy, happy and eager, but untried in the more manipulative ways of society. There was no telling what he might let slip. Del had no intention of getting caught in the net he was about to cast. "Save your fortune in prize money for another time."

"A gentleman's bet then, Colonel?"

A *gentleman's* bet. Del felt his mouth curve up in a scornful smile. What he was about to do violated every code of gentlemanly behavior. "No. More of a challenge."

"He's Viscount Darling now, Mr. James." McAlden gave Del a mocking smile. "We have to address him with all the deference he's due."

Unholy glee lit the young man's face. "I had no idea. Congratulations, Colonel. What a bloody fine name. I can hear the ladies now: *my dearest, darling Darling.* How will they resist you?"

Del merely smiled and took another drink. It was true. None of them resisted: high-born ladies, low-living trollops, barmaids, island girls, or senoritas. They never had, bless their lascivious hearts.

And neither would *she*, despite her remote facade. Celia Burke was nothing but a hothouse flower just waiting to be plucked.

"Go on, then. What's your challenge?" McAlden's face housed

a dubious smirk as several more navy men, Lieutenants Thomas Gardener and Robert Scott, joined them.

"I propose I can openly court, seduce, and ruin an untried, virtuous woman"—Del paused to give them a moment to remark upon the condition he was about to attach—"without ever once touching her."

McAlden gave a huff of cynical laughter. "Too easy in one sense, too hard in another," he stated flatly.

"How can you possibly ruin someone without touching them?" Ian James protested.

Del felt his mouth twist. He had forgotten what it was like to be that young. While he was only six and twenty, he'd grown older since Emily's death. Vengeance was singularly aging.

"Find us a drink would you, gentlemen? A real drink. None of the lukewarm swill they're passing out on trays." Del pushed the young lieutenants off in the direction of a footman.

"Too easy to ruin a reputation with only a rumor," McAlden repeated in his unhurried, determined way. "You'll have to do better than that."

Trust McAlden to get right to the heart of the matter. Like Del, McAlden had never been young, and he was older in years, as well.

"With your reputation," McAlden continued as they turned to follow the others, "well deserved, I might add, you'll not get within a sea mile of a virtuous woman."

"That, old man, shows how little you know of women."

"That, my darling Viscount, shows how little you know of their mamas."

"I'd like to keep it that way. Hence the prohibition against touching. I plan on keeping a very safe distance." While he was about the business of revenging himself on Celia Burke, he needed to keep himself safe from being forced into doing the right thing should his godforsaken plan be discovered or go awry. And he simply didn't *want* to touch her. He didn't want to be tainted by so much as the merest brush of her hand.

"Can't seduce, really *seduce*, from a distance. Not even you. Twenty guineas says it can't be done."

"Twenty? An extravagant wager for a flinty, tight-pursed Scotsman like you. Done." Del accepted the challenge with a firm handshake. It sweetened the pot, so to speak.

McAlden perused the crowd. "Shall we pick now? I warn you, Del, this isn't London. There's plenty of virtue to be had in Dartmouth."

"Why not?" Del felt his mouth curve into a lazy smile. The town may have been full of virtue, but he was full of vice. He cared about only one particular woman's virtue.

"You'll want to be careful. Singularly difficult things, women," McAlden offered philosophically. "Can turn a man inside out. Just look at Marlowe."

Del shrugged. "Captain Marlowe married. I do not have anything approaching marriage in mind."

"So you're going to seduce and ruin an innocent without being named or caught? That *is* bloody-minded."

"I didn't say innocent. I said untried. In this case, there is a particular difference." He looked across the room at Celia Burke again. At the virtuous, innocent face she presented to the world. He would strip away that mask until everyone could see the ugly truth behind her immaculately polished, social veneer.

McAlden followed the line of his gaze. "You can't mean— That's Celia Burke!" All trace of jaded amusement disappeared from McAlden's voice. "Jesus, Del, have you completely lost your mind? As well as all moral scruples?"

"Gone squeamish?" Del tossed back the last of his drink. "That's not like you."

"I *know* her. Everyone in Dartmouth knows her. She is Marlowe's wife's most particular friend. You can't go about ruining—*ruining* for God's sake—innocent young women like her. Even *I* know that."

"I said she's *not* innocent."

"Then you must've misjudged her. She's not fair game, Del. Pick someone else. Someone I don't know." McAlden's voice was growing thick.

"No." Darling kept his own voice flat.

McAlden's astonished countenance turned back to look at Miss Burke, half a room away, smiling sweetly in conversation with another young woman. He swore colorfully under his breath. "That's not just bloody-minded, that's suicidal. She's got parents, Del. Attentive parents. Take a good hard look at her mama, Lady Caroline Burke. She's nothing less than the daughter of a Duke, and is to all accounts a complete gorgon in her own right. They say she eats fortune hunters, not to mention an assortment of libertines like you, for breakfast. What's more, Miss Burke is a relation of the Marquess of Widcombe, in whose ballroom you are currently *not dancing*. This isn't London. You are a guest here. My guest, and therefore Marlowe's guest. One misstep like that and they'll have your head. Or, more likely, your ballocks. And quite rightly. Pick someone else for your challenge."

"No."

"Delacorte."

"Bugger off, Hugh."

McAlden knew Del well enough to hear the implacable finality in his tone. Hugh shook his head slowly. "God's balls, Del. I didn't think I'd regret so quickly having you to stay." He ran his hand through his short, cropped hair and looked at Del with a dawning of realization. "Christ. You'd already made up your mind before you came here, hadn't you? You came for her."

Under such scrutiny, Del could only admit the truth. "I did."

"Damn your eyes, Delacorte. This can only end badly."

Del shrugged with supreme indifference. "That will suit me well enough."

It was called blackmail, though the letter secreted in Celia Burke's pocket was not, in actuality, black. It had looked innocuous enough: the same ivory-colored paper as all the other mail, brought to her on a little silver tray borne by the butler, Loring. It would have been much better if the letter had actually been black, because then Celia would have known not to open it. She would have flung it into the fire before it could poison her life irrevocably. The clenching grip of anxiety deep in her belly was proof enough the poison had already begun its insidious work.

"Celia, darling? Are you all right? Smile, my dear. Smile." Lady Caroline Burke whispered her instructions for her daughter's ears only, as she smiled and nodded to her many acquaintances in the ballroom as though she hadn't a care in the world.

Celia shoved her unsteady hand into her pocket to reassure—*convince*—herself the letter was still there. And still real. She had not dreamt up this particular walking nightmare.

She released the offensive missive and clasped her hands together tightly to stop them from trembling. She had no more than a moment or two to compose herself before the opening set was to begin.

Blackmail. The letter, dated only one day ago, was clear and precise, straight to the point.

> *Celia Burke, we know what you did in Bath with Emily Delacorte. What we know, if we were to share it, would ruin you. We will tell all if you do not deliver the sum of three hundred pounds within a fortnight. We will contact you then. We will be watching you, Celia Burke.*

They could be watching her now.

Her heart began hammering against her chest like a violent,

mistimed clock as she glanced around quickly. So many faces. So many strangers. She could feel a pain, like hot acid etching its way through her chest, closing off her breath and choking the air from her lungs.

Paranoia. That's what her friend Lizzie Marlowe would have called it. A false judgment based on current, unsettling events. Lizzie knew all sorts of big, impressive words, though she had never been sent away to school like Celia. Lizzie had felt paranoid when she first moved to Glass Cottage with all its strange goings-on. But Lizzie, the one person in whom Celia could have confided, the one person Celia would have trusted to help, was gone off with her new husband, taking all her forthright advice and decisive thinking with her.

"Celia, dear, you must smile. Young men need to be encouraged! We cannot disappoint your aunt and uncle Widcombe by appearing unhappy with the company. You look lovely. Let me see you smile." Lady Caroline's voice was growing insistent but not yet impatient.

Celia caught sight of her ashen reflection in a mirror and pressed her palms up to warm her pale cheeks.

It did no good. Her hands had gone cold.

How on earth had this happened to her, of all people? She was innocuous Celia Burke, not some exciting, wild creature who invited censure. She had always lived a life of quiet, orderly compliance and good sense that even her own mother despaired of marrying her off, despite her supposed beauty.

Poor mama. Celia had tried her very best not to disappoint and upset her mother's plans for a grand match, but they were quite untenable. Despite her supposed beauty, and despite Lizzie having given her the nickname by which she was now known throughout all of Dartmouth, Celia was never going to be a diamond of the first water. Or even the second. Not at all. Because her own beauty held no appeal for her.

She had learned to value other characteristics, in herself and in others: loyalty, companionship, and intelligence. Not things she had found in great abundance amongst Dartmouth society's young lordlings. The sort of young men her mother and aunts invariably favored seemed to care only for pretty appearances, or for horses with pretty appearances. Such men would make terrible husbands, and she would make any and all of them a terrible wife.

Celia's dream of perfect marital happiness was with a different sort of man. A man of action and determination, a man who earned his place in the world through his own daring and resourcefulness. But such men did not attend balls in Dartmouth, and even if they did, they were far beyond her awkward abilities.

She drew a long wistful breath at the thought.

"Celia!" Her mama's voice grew sharp.

"Yes, Mama." Celia turned away from the mirror and pinched her cheeks to flood color back into her face. But there was little hope for it. The evening was going to be awful. Her mother was a veritable terrier when it came to ferreting out a single untruth, let alone a whole letter of them.

Celia would be ruined one way or another.

Her mother was halfway to working herself into a fine glower over Celia's lack of enthusiasm. Lady Caroline Burke did not like to have her plans thwarted by anyone, least of all her apparently scatterbrained eldest daughter.

But Celia was not scatterbrained. She was, as her father so kindly put it, everything sensible, but often preoccupied, and tonight she was entirely occupied with her imminent, total, and complete ruination.

Ruination was a word that encompassed rather a lot, but Celia knew exactly what it would mean to her. She would be repulsed by her family, rejected by society, and unable to make a marriage—any marriage. It would be the end of everything she wanted. She *had* to keep from being ruined—there was simply no alternative.

The Ravishing Miss Burke, they called her. The great local beauty. How disappointed the Marquess's guests would be. She didn't need to consult the mirror to know she was not in good looks. She looked tense and guarded. And no wonder. She *felt* tense and guarded, hollow and brittle from the effort of holding herself together. There was no one with whom she could share the letter. No one she could ask for help. No one who cared about the truth.

She was completely and utterly on her own.

CHAPTER 2

Celia pasted on a pleasant smile, turned back to the ball-room, and stood as still as possible for her mother's inspection. Bains, Celia's maid, had done her job well and Celia's appearance, from her carefully, elaborately curled hair to her elegant gown, could not be faulted. Bains had chosen to dress her in a white silk gown, in the up-to-date style of a simple chemise dress. Lovely floral embroidery on the flounced neckline and sleeves in deep, vibrant silver, blues, and pinks complemented the Turkish blue satin sash at Celia's waist and managed to make the most of her fair complexion and dark hair.

"There. I told you, you look lovely. Absolutely perfect." Lady Caroline's happiness was thus restored.

If only Celia could restore her own happiness and composure as easily. Where was she to obtain three hundred pounds, when she didn't even have three?

"Celia, attend to me, please! I shouldn't have to remind you how important this ball is. It is the only ball your aunt and uncle will hold at Widcombe Court all summer and it is imperative you show yourself well as the niece of the Marquess and Marchioness. There will be no dancing with vicars and the like this evening, do you understand? Your beauty and connections entitle you to higher ambition, my dear girl, if you would but throw off your awkwardness. You ought to have grown too old for this woeful shyness. You are beautiful. You dance well. All you have to do is hold your head up and smile. It is not too much to ask."

"Yes, Mama." It was not too much to *ask*, though it had always seemed too much to accomplish. For the hundredth time in the past month, Celia wished her friend Lizzie was there. Lizzie would know what to do. Lizzie always had.

But Lizzie was gone off with her new husband, Captain Marlowe, on his ship. She was undoubtedly giving the French no end of trouble, but could not help Celia one bit.

So Celia would have to learn to help herself. She would have to get through this night. She would have to hold her head up and dance with young lordlings, who saw her as nothing more than the architecture of her face. She would have to whisk herself out of the ballroom for a moment of peace and solace when her mother was otherwise occupied.

And, she would have to find the money somehow, somewhere, without anyone else being the wiser. She would have to get herself out of the hideous, tangled web of lies and deceit. She would have to cope.

Because it wasn't only her reputation at stake, but Emily's as well. Lady Emily Delacorte had been Celia's friend and mainstay during the interminable year she had spent away from home at Miss Hadley's school in Bath. Emily had made school bearable. Emily had made study fun and had convinced Celia she had more to offer than just her face. That she had talents and ambitions worth pursuing.

But Emily was dead. Celia had failed her when Emily had needed her most. And so Celia wasn't going to fail her again. It was the very least she could do to serve Emily's memory.

"And you will not dance with any of that Glass Cottage

set." Her mama was still instructing. "Now that Mrs. Marlowe has gone away, there is no call for you to be seen with those naval officers. They are an entirely too common lot."

"No, Mama." It had done no good to tell mama she had only a passing acquaintance with the officers who were still in residence at the Marlowe's property. The only one she knew by name was Lieutenant McAlden, and she went out of her way to avoid him and his forceful, blunt ways.

"Your cousin, Ronald, is, I think, old enough to dance with you credibly. You may lead out the first dance with him."

"Oh, no, Mama, please. Ronald is not yet fifteen." *Anybody but Ronald.* Like any spoiled, gawky boy of his age, Ronald's chief mode of communication was insult. And like any particularly obnoxious younger relation, he knew just what to say and what to do to embarrass his cousin Celia.

"He is your uncle's heir. He will be the Marquess someday. You will dance with him."

"Of course, Mama." Celia spoke quietly with all the appearance of compliance. But she would not suffer Ronald without putting up some resistance. With her mama, most times the indirect approach was best. As Lizzie would say, the easiest way into the house is through a back door.

"I only hope he has grown taller since the last time I saw him. I would hate to tower over him so awkwardly and put him into one of his tempers. His short height did make me seem so *very* tall last time. Gentlemen do hate it when they appear so very short in comparison."

"Do you know, now that you mention it, I don't believe your aunt will allow him to dance yet. Fifteen is too young to be in company still, I find. We will look elsewhere for your first partner."

Celia would certainly look elsewhere—to her uncle's small, private book room off the library. Familiarity with the house was one of the blessings of relation and Celia knew the time spent among her uncle's extensive collections of books would afford her the only real moments of peace and pleasure she was likely to have all evening.

The Marchioness of Widcombe, Aunt Margaret, came bearing down on Celia like a galleon under full sail. "Celia, darling, you look marvelous. You must come and meet some of my guests."

Her aunt was nearly as ambitious for Celia as mama. Between the two of them, there would be no peace, but at least there would be less time to give herself over to anxiety. It was wholly disconcerting, the relentless fear. And wholly new. She had never had occasion in her life to be afraid before. Until now, there had been nothing in her life to be frightened of. She had never known want, poverty, or sickness. She had been loved and cosseted—indeed her mother's maneuvering and chiding came from love, from wanting only to secure the best possible future for her daughter.

As a result, Celia had no skill, no experience with which to combat the constant roiling in her belly, the squeezing in her lungs.

"Stand up straight, Celia. And smile, dear," her mama instructed. "Smile."

"Yes, Mama," Celia murmured again, all compliant obedience. But compliance and obedience had become an unsafe habit, dulling her ability to think and act for herself. It was a habit she could no longer afford.

Celia's mother had taken her usual station at the top of the dance floor, much like a general surveying the field of battle, ready to make her strategic pronouncements about how Celia was to be best deployed. There was no chance of a reprieve. Lady Caroline Burke would not relent. As she so bluntly put it, Celia could no longer afford to indulge in a young girl's awkwardness. Awkwardness simply would not do.

Celia knew all the rules. She must stand up straight and proud and show herself to best advantage. She must be sweet and accommodating to all, but only dance with the right people. She must say the right thing to each person she met, but know to whom she must speak. Her head ached with the wealth of contradictions. People, and their rules and games never made any sense.

If she were very lucky, her mama would be feeling extremely picky about the quality and quantity of the evening's eligible gentlemen—not that there was a superfluity of the species in Dartmouth—and she wouldn't have to dance above once in four sets.

The possibility of having to dance with a stranger—with *the* stranger—whoever was blackmailing her, struck her. He could be right there in her aunt's ballroom. Celia glanced around the room, trying to act circumspectly, at the same time taking measure, trying to identify who might be the threatening stranger. She'd lived in Dartmouth all her life, but she felt as if she hardly knew the place.

Everyone seemed to be watching, and waiting, for something.

She felt frozen and stiff with fear. Only a few minutes into the ball and already her face felt as if it would crack in two.

At the touch on her arm Celia whirled and came face to chest with a rather large blue uniform—Lieutenant McAlden in all his looming, naval glory.

The Lieutenant was an extremely large man of rugged handsomeness and overwhelming masculine presence. He had, from the first moment of their acquaintance, intimidated her. Wearing his naval dress uniform, he was nothing short of unapproachably splendid. He bowed correctly, but very stiffly. "Miss Burke."

He was ill at ease, she realized, with the polite formalities of the ball. She returned a curtsy. "Lieutenant. It is a pleasure to see you here this evening." She spoke automatically, with polite, expected words. Then she realized she actually meant it. Despite the fact his cool, almost stern demeanor normally made her feel awkward and tongue-tied, she was warmed by the recognition that he was nearly as uncomfortable at the ball as she. It made him seem much more human. "You look quite resplendent in your uniform."

"You are too kind. Will you do me the honor of the next dance?"

A small bolt of shock winced through her, but only a small shock. She supposed she had, in the course of the evening, begun to grow accustomed to the sensation. In this case the shock was the result of knowing the Lieutenant did not normally, under any circumstances, care for dancing. She was too curious at his behavior to think of refusing.

It certainly was a day for firsts.

Celia shot a glance at her mother, but decided she would chance it. "I would be honored, Lieutenant."

"It's Commander now, actually." He indicated some distinguishing article of gold braid upon his uniform.

Normally, Celia liked nothing better than a defining characteristic, some particular thing that helped her sort a person apart from the rest. But she had long ago classified McAlden as *homo periculus x territus*, a terrifyingly dangerous man, even before she knew anything of his distinguished naval service.

"As a result of our last, successful mission." He was explaining his promotion. "The business out at Redlap Cove."

"I congratulate you, Commander."

"I thank you, Miss Burke."

They took their places in the set, and spent a companionable time dancing without ever once being required to talk. As a consequence, for the first time all evening, Celia began to relax enough to almost enjoy herself.

But Commander McAlden was not. His fierce scowl had deepened.

"Commander McAlden, I fear you are not enjoying this."

"Not at all Miss Burke," he lied politely. "It is only . . . I am not a comfortable dancer."

"Then you have already been kind enough by dancing with

me this much. I beg you would let us retire from the field before we are completely routed by Roger de Coverly."

Relief cleared his face. "You are too kind."

"You must not think so," Celia demurred. She had her own
selfish reasons to leave the floor: escaping the regard of her
mama and whoever else might be watching and looking at
her with antagonism. She clasped her hands behind her back
as they walked towards the terrace. The Commander would
undoubtedly fare better out of doors. He was too big, even for
a ballroom. "Perhaps it is only that I must save myself from
being seen with a man who appears to be grimacing while he
is dancing with me." She smiled to show she meant it only in
jest.

The Commander was immune to even her best smiles. "I
apologize. I am not a comfortable dancer," he repeated. "I
don't dance often enough to be at ease."

"Pray don't apologize. I know it was only out of kindness
that you asked me to dance, so it is only fair that I return the
favor and do you the small kindness of retiring in turn."

"You *are* too kind," he insisted, then shook his head, rather
like a frustrated, angry bear. "This will not do. I must warn
you. You'll be eaten alive."

She felt instantly frozen and numb, stunned by the instant
return of her panic. The letter! What could he know of it? "I . . .
I beg your pardon?"

"May I have your permission to speak plainly, Miss Burke?"

Her heart kicked up, hard and erratic inside her chest. She
hardly knew what to expect. "Please do, Commander."

"I must tell you"—he ran his hand through his hair in a gesture of frustration and annoyance—"I fear the world may not
be an entirely safe place, Miss Burke. Not even here. I would
caution you to guard yourself."

She stepped back from him abruptly. How on earth was
Commander McAlden, one of the most single-mindedly steadfast men of her acquaintance, mixed up with the blackmail?

"What"—she swallowed—"do you know?" Her voice was nothing but a tremulous whisper.

He shook his head again, like a big, angry bear. "Honor prevents me from . . . I can . . . only say you must be careful."

"Of whom?"

"Of unworthy men." With that he bowed and abruptly walked away—leaving her in a world turned upside down.

Del advanced to the edge of the dance floor. His friends, Lieutenants James, Gardener, and Scott, ranged behind him like a pride of lions at the edge of the savannah, garnering all the attention. Even in a backwater like Dartmouth, his purposefully uncivilized reputation was well-known. People turned to look and speak behind their fans.

He had worn his scarlet Marine Forces uniform in defiance of custom, even though he was no longer a serving officer. The brilliant red of his coat, alongside the deep blues of the navy men, stood out like a beacon. His presence could not be missed. And so, when James began to talk of an adjournment to the library for a glass of Widcombe's best brandy, he left them behind, and began to stalk her.

Del moved through the crowd slowly, pausing here and there to speak when he was acknowledged. He let his eyes wander, noticeably looking for her, before he politely excused himself to move on, so everyone might watch, take note of his passage, and wonder to whom he was going. So everyone might make conjectures and bandy his filthy reputation about until he moored up next to her, snug and familiar, as if they had long ago been introduced and were more than acquaintances. As if they were intimate.

He would smile at her in a way that would tell he had seen everything there was to see beneath that concoction of silk and embroidery draping her frame and been very pleased, indeed. Her reputation would be linked—and tarred—with his. The mere fact of his notice, his singling her out, would stain

The Ravishing Miss Burke's porcelain reputation before he even had to charm her into relinquishing the last of her good name.

As he prowled closer, the whispers began. He heard snatches of his denouncement from every quarter, especially from the Gorgon's group of matrons.

". . . ought to keep to London. He and his friends act in the most scandalous fashion."

". . . reputation quite beyond the pale. This past year, when he ought to have been in mourning . . ."

". . . carousing in public with sailors and ruffians of all sorts . . ."

"They say he delights in prizefights! The other night at the Heart of Oak tavern, dreadful place on the waterfront, they say he fought . . ."

"Though he *is* a Viscount, he doesn't normally move in polite society."

". . . heard of one drunken rout out at Glass Cottage . . ."

The Gorgon herself, Lady Caroline Burke, was one of the few to actually meet his gaze. She gave as good as she got, fixing him with a gimlet, disapproving eye. "I'll have nothing to do with the likes of him, Viscount or no. Libertine, that's what he is. He ought know he's not wanted here, amongst civilized people."

Oh, but he was definitely *wanted* there. By any number of women who were at that very moment casting looks as sharp, delicate, and subtly dangerous as fly lures in his direction. Angling they called it. Del lowered his chin and smiled through half-closed eyes at their flutterings of eyelashes and knowing, come-hither smiles. He had not spent all his time since he had arrived in Dartmouth thinking only of vengeance and retribution. The local ladies had been more than accommodating and deeply appreciative of his diligent attentions.

But, he gave the ladies no more than a knowing smile and a passing glance. He was saving his lethal brand of charm for The Ravishing Miss Burke. He was stalking her like prey through this heated jungle of silk and feathers. He would track her down and ruffle that carefully preened plumage of hers. He would pin her down with nothing but his eyes and his words, and devour her.

But he was too late. McAlden had stolen a march on him and was dancing with her. Maybe even warning her. But Del could turn it to his advantage. McAlden's reputation was not as a libertine or a ladies man. Quite the opposite, but he was still known as a dangerous and not-altogether civilized man—who never danced. His dancing with Miss Burke might not shake her reputation, but it would certainly stir it up a bit. The Viscount Darling's own presence beside her would finish the trick McAlden's dancing had started. She would be talked about.

Del kept up his steady path through the crowd, still pausing here and there to speak, until the music came to an end with a smattering of applause. He stepped to the edge of the dance floor to intercept them, but his quarry had flown. Celia Burke was nowhere to be seen.

A few moments ago she had been floating above the dance floor, a beautiful, untouchable ice princess, her dark eyes unlit, her face bearing the slightest of smiles and her arched brows giving her a haughty demeanor. But, she was gone. She had thwarted him.

The Ravishing Miss Celia Burke. *Fuck her.*

With a hunter's instinct, Del turned towards the far end of the room, where glass-paned doors led to the ubiquitous terrace and country garden. He knew McAlden would need air after the purgatory of dancing. Perhaps he could find Miss Burke attempting to amuse Hugh, languidly fanning her pale, haughty cheeks in some conveniently darkened corner. Yet, as he strolled across the flagstones and down the gravel paths, neither Miss Burke nor McAlden was anywhere to be seen.

Damn her for a clever jade. He would have to regroup. Del turned his feet and his thoughts back towards the house. His friends should have already found the Marquess of Widcombe's stash of smuggled French brandy in the library—somewhere across the house in the opposite wing.

If he went back through the ballroom, there would be more censorious looks and disapproving stares. He found he was no longer in the mood for them. He felt thwarted and caged—in the mood to bash heads together the way he had at the local Heart of Oak tavern three nights ago. Best to avoid the ballroom altogether.

He set off across the inner courtyard to the wing opposite the ballroom that housed the library. The curtains were drawn and the outer doors locked. He might have gone on, rattling doors until he was heard, but he noticed a window open to the evening's breeze at the very end of the wing. A lamp was lit inside. In the warm glow of the light, it looked to be a part of the library—perhaps the Marquess's personal book room—with a desk and a chair, most likely giving into the library. If he couldn't have Celia Burke, at least he could have a decent drink while he pondered his next move.

CHAPTER 3

Celia was beyond hesitation. Every pair of eyes felt unfriendly, every stranger a threat. She tried to catalogue and keep track, separating them into their respective identifications of relations, friends, acquaintances, and others—those who were unknown and therefore unclassified, their characters and motives a mystery to her—until the ballroom felt close and constricted, and she couldn't stand the scrutiny any longer.

She skirted the dance floor and hurried in the general direction of the ladies withdrawing room before ducking out of sight into the servants' corridor. Thank God the ball was at her uncle's estate, and she could find her way without assistance. She knew Widcombe Court almost as well as she knew her own house.

In another moment, she was safely hidden behind locked doors in her uncle's book room, leaning against the table to catch her breath. It was a small room with bookshelves, a single table, and one armchair before the fire, but it had always felt safe and comfortable, a place where she could read her uncle's collection of the *Philosophical Transactions of the Royal Society* without fear of detection or interruption. Even cousin Ronald never thought to look for her there.

Celia sat down and drew another calming breath. She had to get a hold of herself and her runaway fears. She had to rise to the challenge. If not for herself, then for Emily's sake. Resolution steadied her.

What on earth could Commander McAlden have discovered that he was not willing to say? Unworthy men? His warning was vague at best. According to her mother, *most* men were unworthy.

Celia reached through her skirts into her pocket and pulled the wretched piece of paper out to study anew. Emily had taught her to observe the many minute facets of life. Everything—people, animals, plants, insects and even clouds—almost everything under creation had something, some characteristic that set it apart from the rest of creation. It all depended upon how closely one looked.

She schooled her heart to beat more slowly so she could look. And think. And approach the blackmail logically. She read the terse note again.

We know what you did in Bath with Emily Delacorte.

The implication was chilling, more so because it was a lie. The blackmailer could not possibly know what they had done, because they had *done* nothing. Their work—the collecting, cataloguing, and drawing of plant specimens—had been undertaken with the utmost discretion, and with concern for the reputation of the school and their beloved headmistress, Miss Hadley, lest her establishment be labeled a haven for bluestockings.

But the letter was not referring to science. Its filthy implications were about Emily and the reason she had died. And how she had died. That she had drowned herself over a love affair with Celia.

A wave of dark, bitter guilt and shame washed over Celia,

pushing her momentarily under, leaving her chilled to the marrow.

It was all so cruel. She had never suspected, never seen any indication Emily had felt such unrequited passion. Surely if Emily had felt so deeply as to kill herself, there would have been some sign, some word. But try as she had, for over a year, Celia could recall nothing. She had loved Emily as a sister and been deeply grieved and horrified by her death.

But most important, Celia could not fathom how anyone else could have knowledge of such a thing. The suicide note found in Emily's room was known only to Celia, Miss Hadley, and Emily's father, the Earl of Cleeve. At the Earl's direction, Miss Hadley had put it about that Emily had died of a putrid fever, had closed the school immediately, and sent the girls home for the rest of the term.

Miss Hadley would never attempt to blackmail Celia with a threatening, anonymous note. The idea was preposterous. When she looked at the paper with a more analytical gaze, the writing, while clear and steady, lacked the elegant flair of Miss Hadley's hand.

The thought prompted Celia to cross to the low cupboard and extract a quill, paper, and ink. If she could identify all the unique characteristics of the letter and list them down, she might be able to discern the hand behind it. Of course, even if she could discover who was blackmailing her, it did not follow she could make them stop. And it certainly wasn't going to get her the necessary funds. But at least it gave her a semblance of order and control. It was a start.

Miss Hadley's school was situated in Bath and the note mentioned Bath specifically. The blackmailer had to be someone from Bath, or at least someone who had been there at the same time Celia and Emily had attended school.

Celia turned her attention to the pen strokes. Again, she doubted it was Miss Hadley's, nor was it the cursive style Miss Hadley's pupils were taught. It was what Celia could only characterize as a strong hand. Not elegant, but not heavy on the downstrokes like her father's style, nor quite like that of his secretary, Mr. Hodgkins, whose pen strokes were always very precise. All told, the blackmail note didn't seem feminine. For some reason, she had already conceived of her blackmailer as a man—as *He*.

Celia moved the note closer to the lamp and noticed the quality of the paper as the light shone against it. She held it up before the lamp and, lo and behold, she recognized instantly the paper's watermark. It was that of the Dartmouth stationers Asquith and Sanders. Her mother purchased papers from them on a routine basis. So did all of Dartmouth society.

Illuminating facts, but hardly revelatory: a man who had been in Bath more than one year ago, or knew someone who was, who bought paper in Dartmouth's most exclusive stationer for the purpose of blackmailing her. That left half the gouty population of Devon.

Then there was the money. Three hundred pounds seemed like a monstrous amount of money. At least to her. And to whom else? Who else would think it a large amount of money—the kind of money a lord's daughter would be able to put her hands on? Not one of the lordlings. They wagered such sums carelessly and routinely. She had heard them, at card parties and on the edges of dance floors, wherever there were two or three of them gathered. Wagering was part of their way of life.

Celia had never held more than five pounds in her hand at one time. And now she was to get three hundred. It seemed impossible. What little allowance she had of her own she spent on paints and heavy paper. Her mama paid the few tradespeople from whom she bought materials for dresses out of her own funds set aside for the purpose. Her only assets were her clothing and jewelry, but she knew from Bains that castoffs had good value at the rag traders down near the quay. It was another good start. In the morning she would confer with Bains and see which of her clothes they might part with most easily.

The thought of taking action steadied her somewhat.

Celia looked at the letter again, worrying and chewing on her lip, until the paper was covered in shadow.

Del climbed through the window, only to find himself enveloped in scent. Not the comfortable rich tones of paper and leather bindings, but a garden full of summer jasmine and citrus with something else uniquely the scent of woman.

Somehow, he knew before he saw her. Celia Burke.

"Oh!" She jumped up—quite literally, jumped out of her seat at the table—and in the process managed to upend a pen and an inkwell all over herself. She flailed, trying to catch the thing but then hid her ink-covered hands behind her back, looking at first frightened, and then entirely guilty. She was flushed and discomposed, with her mouth open in a horrified little *o* of surprise. A huge, black ink stain dripped down the front of her dress. Not at all the serene ice princess of the ballroom.

Had she been waiting for him? Seeking him just as assiduously as he had been stalking her? Had she engineered this moment to catch him off guard?

He *was* off guard, damn it to hell. Here was his first opportunity to intimidate her, though there was no audience of dancers to see his interest in her and set her reputation on its ear, and all he could think—although *think* was not the operative verb—was how intoxicating she smelled, even covered in ink. And how much more incredibly beautiful she was close up.

How . . . *real* she appeared.

It had been one thing to think badly of her from across the room. At a distance, she had appeared like a doll, untouched by any humanity. But up close, up close she had dark smudges under her wide, dark eyes and bruised, bitten lips. Lips that were the color of summer plums. Lips still before the full flush of ripeness. Lips that looked as though they had never been kissed.

Del fought the urge to shake off the thought like a wet dog. *Damn his eyes!* He had no business looking at her lips. He had no business noting the dew-soft texture of her skin, or the dusting of freckles hovering just below the translucent surface, nor the depth of her dark, almost black eyes. Eyes the color of the stormy North Atlantic, fathoms deep.

He had not expected her to be so beautiful and so human. He had certainly not expected his body to react so strenuously to her appearance without asking his brain for permission.

The luminous, fey creature in front of him was the bluestocking friend of Emily's letters, the girl he had fallen in love with, not the coldhearted woman he had conceived in the wake of the blackmail demand. He had forgotten those long-ago feelings, pushed them aside from the moment he had received the blackmail letter.

But he would be foolish to trust her appearance. Emily had done so. Emily had thought them two peas in a pod. Until it was too late.

He stared at her without a lucid thought in his head. Maybe the stare would work all alone. Maybe she could feel the weight of condemnation in his eyes.

He marshaled his voice into a harsh command. "How did you get in here?"

"*I* used the door," she answered quietly. She gestured with her ink-splotched hand, a small economical motion, but she kept her watchful eyes focused on him the way one might keep a wary eye on a stray, wet dog.

Points to her for perception. Damn right, he bore vigilant watching. As did she.

After her guilty start, The Ravishing Miss Burke seemed to give way to a rather thorough, wide-eyed curiosity. Her dark eyes scanned over him, as if she were examining him for flaws in his confirmation, like a horse at a country fair. She was, in that moment, every bit the scientist Emily had thought her, noting his characteristics, cataloging his individuality, if only as a means to distinguish him from the myriad of other sandy-haired English gentlemen standing about. So determined and serious. And ink stained. And flushed and lovely.

Not at all as he had expected.

"What are you doing here?" He wondered how had she planned their encounter, when he had chosen to go to the library only on the spur of the moment.

Her dark eyes became wider, if possible. "Reading."

Her voice was so low and soft, tentative even, he had to turn his head slightly to catch the words. A small, reasonable feminine voice. His own blunt demands sounded crass in comparison.

All he had seen, when he had looked across the ballroom, was a woman he wanted to crush and humiliate. But from less than two feet away, he could hear the uneven, fragmented cadence of her breathing and smell the beguiling scent that rose off her. Up close, the combined effect of her beauty was all the more stunning for the strength of personality it revealed. She was the wondrous girl of Emily's letters. The girl radiated wonder and intelligence. And something even more dangerous. Innocence wreathed her the way incense clung to a nun.

Del backed away, fumbling for the door. He had to get away from her, he had to think things through before anything happened, before they were caught in a compromising situation. He wanted to ruin Celia Burke, yes, but he did not want to spend the rest of his life married to her.

She shot out her hand to forestall him. "Forgive me, you must be Viscount Darling."

He moved away before she could reach him. "*Must?*" He drew himself up to his full height, for the haughty effect, and to keep from being touched by her. And to keep from inhaling any more of her scent, or feeling the intensity of her regard.

She seemed not to notice anything he did. Her eyes continued to search his face. "You are Viscount Darling, are you not? I should introduce myself. My name is Celia Burke and I was at school with your sister, dear Emily. How strange you should come when I was just this moment thinking of her."

He reacted before he could control himself. His head reeled back as if he'd been slapped. Her words had been a blow. How dare she even pronounce Emily's name?

"Miss Burke," he managed. His voice sounded cold and abrupt even to his own ears. He had nothing of his usual, lethal brand of charm, he had nothing of the self-possession with which he had originally started his ludicrous passage across the ballroom towards her.

"I know it is not done, sir, as we have not been introduced," she continued on, "but I could not let you pass without giving you my deepest, most heartfelt condolences."

Every sound, every sensation faded and there was only her voice, soft and low, and her words. Condolences had been few, and only from his closest friends. Even his family could not bear to speak of his sister's death. His father had seen to it that Emily had not been declared a suicide, but her death had nevertheless been hushed up. No one had spoken of her, and no one had approached him in the intervening months with anything like condolence.

And yet this *betrayer* presumed to speak to his pain. It was all he could do to stand it. "We have not been introduced." His brain was beginning to work but so was his uneven temper.

"No, sir. I do apologize for my impetuous behavior but I felt I could not let you pass unnoticed. I am Miss Burke, Celia Burke, and I was a great friend of your late sister."

"Ah, yes, The *Ravishing* Miss Burke." He arched one eyebrow at that, indicating he found her sadly lacking in the ravishing department, and wasn't about to be put off by the fact that she was clearly everyone's favorite. She had chosen to tangle with him. He would let her do so at her peril. "One wonders how you came to be ravished, but it's no wonder if you're secreting yourself in closets, accosting men, and waiting for opportunities for assignations. You ought to be more careful. You'll make yourself an easy target for blackmail."

Her face registered his hit: an instantaneous recoil of her head, a dramatic paling of her skin, and the startled parting of her lips. But she did not run away in tears as she ought. Though clearly shaken, she spoke.

"Your very great pardon, sir. Perhaps you would be so kind as to tell me how I have offended you?"

It was an elegant little volte-face.

That she refused to be sensible of the danger into which she was putting herself made him irrationally angry. Did she not understand he was on to her filthy little game? Did she not comprehend her mistake in tangling with him? He stepped closer, so he could tell her in no uncertain terms exactly what he thought of her. But that moment brought him close enough that her scent wafted across his senses and ensnared his brain. That scent, something beyond just the light note of fragrance she wore, was like the answer to a question he had forgotten he had asked.

What do you want? The answer was, *this woman*.

He was acting completely irrational, he knew, but he inhaled again, deeply, his body commanding him to find more of the bliss that burst within his chest like an opiate, heady and intoxicating, knocking him off center.

He tried to force himself to act rationally and logically, as if that would give him armor against the feeling that the deck had turned to water beneath his feet. All he could think was that she smelled like the Garden of Eden, all fresh temptation.

His body, his senses would not let go of her *rightness*.

What had he been about to say? He had called her ravishing and she was, entirely. She had ravished *him* somehow, without a word, without him knowing how. Without his bloody, god-damned consent.

Del straightened and armed himself with his newfound knowledge. The little hothouse flower of a girl was the most dangerous woman he had ever met. He did the only sensible thing to do when faced with overwhelming enemy forces. He turned smartly on his heel and made his retreat.

That had not gone well. Celia realized Viscount Darling had just given her the cut direct. How strange, when *he* had been the one to burst in on *her*.

Yet, she was not sorry she had spoken to him. Her memory of Emily had demanded it. The knowledge of the close relationship Emily had shared with her brother had prompted Celia to speak. Emily had shared her letters from her brother, to ease their homesickness at school. At least Celia had been homesick, missing her family and her friends from Dart-mouth. Emily had not missed her own home and family in the same way, but she had spoken constantly of her older brother, Del, and had read every letter of their secret correspondence out loud.

And Celia had fallen in love with him, that faraway, daring, adventurous man.

When he appeared, it was as if she had conjured him out of fantasy. She would have known him anywhere, he looked so much like his sister. The same blue eyes and golden blond complexion, all sunshine, open sky, and far-off, adventurous places. Of course, Emily had been willowy where the viscount was tall and broad, and undeniably feminine where he was all unbridled masculinity.

It stung, his out-of-hand rejection of her approach to him. More than stung—it hurt deeply. She had meant to be kind. She of all people knew the loss he had suffered. She knew from his letters how much he had loved his sister. How could she not speak to a man whose feelings, whose hopes and joys she had come to know as well as her own?

But she didn't know him so well, after all. He was no longer the white knight of her schoolgirl infatuation. He was a blackmailer. Her blackmailer. He could not have stated his involvement any more clearly. How could he have become so different, so unworthy, so cold and uncaring? How could he have come to hate Emily's memory so much, he would betray the love and affection she had so freely bestowed upon him?

It was a question without an answer, a pain with no antidote.

She would be the sorriest of friends if she would let him tarnish either her memories or her future in so callous and highhanded a fashion. He was not going to bully and blackmail her. She would not allow it. She had talents and intelligence. She would use them.

She would be obedient and compliant Celia Burke no longer. She would be resolute. She would become daring.

But at the moment, she was covered in ink. Her gown, which Bains had worked so hard embroidering, was ruined. Her mother was going to poke and prod and chide her over the incident.

Fifteen minutes spent arranging their hasty departure bore her out.

"Celia Augusta Burke," her mama began as she was handed into the coach by Celia's father. "You will kindly tell me where you disappeared to. And, oh my God, child, what in heaven's name have you done to your gown?" Her grammar was slipping along with her elaborate feather headdress, crushed against the brocade, upholstered roof of the carriage.

"I spilled ink. You don't need to upbraid me for my stupidity. I feel quite bad enough about it as it is. I've already thanked Papa for his kindness in cutting his, and your, evening short and allowing me to go home. I'm very sorry."

"Oh, Celia." Her mama heaved a long-suffering sigh. "And I suppose your gloves as well?"

"No, they survived quite unscathed. I had taken them off before I had my fateful encounter with the inkwell and Aunt Margaret's housekeeper was kind enough to find me lemons from the orangery with which to bathe my hands and bleach the stains out of my fingers."

"At least you had the presence of mind to do that. But this is what will happen when you keep disappearing."

"Now, Caroline." Lord Burke spoke up to ease Lady Caroline's temper.

"Oh, well. Although, I don't suppose you could have chosen a more opportune or auspicious moment. The Vile Viscount Darling, Rupert Delacorte, graced the ball with his scurrilous presence. I don't know what could have possessed my sister-in-law, the Marchioness, to invite him. I daresay he was up to absolutely no good. He quite looked like the cat amongst the pigeons, he and the rest of that rather disreputable Royal Navy bunch out at Redlap Cove."

"Mama, please. You know very well Captain Marlowe and Lizzie have gone off on one of his ships and the Lieutenant— no he's Commander now—*Commander* McAlden is in residence at Glass Cottage to see that the free traders don't dare come back to Redlap Cove. Viscount Darling was in His Majesty's Marine Forces. It makes perfect sense he should know both Captain Marlowe and Commander McAlden."

Lady Caroline's owl-sharp eyes narrowed. "How do you know so very much about the man?"

"I don't," Celia covered. "I was at school with the viscount's sister, Lady Emily Delacorte. You remember."

"Be that as it may, I forbid you to know anything about him. You are not to so much as speak to him, under any circumstances. You are to give him the cut direct."

How ironic Viscount Darling had already done the same. "I'm sorry, Mama, but I already have. Spoken to him."

"What?" The exclamation was nearly a screech. Celia grabbed onto the leather carriage straps in case the horses bolted.

"I could hardly have avoided it, Mama. He found me quite by accident. But as I said, his late sister was a particular friend of mine from Miss Hadley's in Bath. It would have been strange, not to mention rude, not to offer my condolences."

"There was no reason for you to speak to him. He is a libertine. He is a rogue and a gambler. He is not seen in polite society."

"Then you had best speak to Aunt Margaret about her guest list, rather than me."

"Celia Augusta Burke! What has gotten into you?"

Celia closed her eyes on a sigh. She knew exactly what had gotten into her—or rather under her skin. Viscount Darling and his wretched blackmail.

Celia had never been the sort of child to make trouble or sail against the tide. It was only after the tumultuous events of a year ago that she had begun to grow out of her terrible awkwardness—thanks to her studies and the steady application of Lizzie's outrageous affection. It was Lizzie who had teasingly given Celia the title The Ravishing Miss Burke. If Lizzie said it, all Dartmouth had decided it must be true.

Having people think she was beautiful had not mattered in the least. At least, not until Viscount Darling, the one man in all the world whose good opinion she had thought she wanted, had burst in upon her and looked at her with such infinite disdain. As if he were a lion and she was too skinny a Christian to bother killing. Not worth his time. The lion image suited him well. He had all but prowled into the bookroom, with the same rangy, swinging stride as the great lion pacing in its cage at the traveling zoological exhibit, all tawny, ferocious hunger, and pitiless, searching eyes.

As a lion, Viscount Darling ought to have an unruly, golden mane. Yet, his shining blond hair had been cropped brutally short, like new-mown wheat lying upon the ground, as if he had no time to waste upon the vanity of poetic, tousled locks. But even cropped short, in the candlelight his hair had been luminous, like the halo of a fierce martyred Christian. Or a pale, avenging Renaissance angel.

She had recognized him instantly because he looked so much like Emily, who had always appeared lit from the inside by the saintly glow of inner passion.

"What would you have had me do, Mama?" Celia lowered her voice and spoke softly to hide the strange feeling of restless, confusing disappointment. "Should I have cut him? Would that be the gracious, ladylike, Christian behavior you are always urging me to? I thought not. But you needn't worry. We exchanged only a few words. I offered my condolences, and he did not seem pleased by my sentiments."

"I imagine he was rude. He is no credit to his family, poor people. Careless, ratchety young man, that's what he is," Lady Caroline opined. "Ran away from his family to enlist, of all things, though he is the heir. No respect for what's proper. He could have been dead for all they knew. Then suddenly he turns up, like a bad penny, straight from the Marine Forces where he had been the whole time. Years it was. Although they do say, he became an officer."

"A Colonel, Caroline," Lord Burke pointed out. "A position of rank and respect."

"That is as may be. He is not an officer now, no matter what coat he wears. He is a careless, heedless libertine who drinks and gambles too much, and is too often found in the company of"—she looked at Celia and censured her language—"people of questionable morals. He is not the sort of man with whom Celia should associate, I'm sure you'll agree."

What a curiously careless lifestyle for a man engaged in blackmail. *He* ought to know better.

But it gave Celia ideas. Daring, adventurous ideas.

CHAPTER 4

"Have you given up this infernal idea of yours about Miss Burke?"

Del could tell Hugh McAlden was still deucedly tetchy on the topic. He wouldn't even pass the ale across the breakfast table at Glass Cottage, the remarkable, huge house perched near the cliffs at Redlap Cove, which McAlden was minding for Captain Marlowe.

"No, but what's it to you?" Del reached across for the pitcher himself. "You harboring a secret *tendre* for The Ravishing Miss Burke?" The sudden unease in his gut was merely anger, nothing more. Nothing to do with disappointment or useless jealousies.

McAlden, damn his eyes, was neither flustered nor amused. "Don't be any stupider than you can already help."

"You seem to take a particular interest in her."

McAlden shrugged away the suggestion, but his expression remained serious. Two parallel lines had etched themselves into his forehead. "It's not particular on my part. She's a nice girl, but she's Mrs. Marlowe's *particular* friend. God help you if *she* finds out about this."

"She?"

"Captain Marlowe's lady. Miss Elizabeth Paxton, as was,

Lord Paxton's daughter. If she gets wind of your plan, or if, God help you, you actually accomplish the ruination of Celia Burke, you'll be lucky to escape with your life. She doesn't forgive or forget, that one. And she won't rest until she tracks you down."

"Then we've a great deal in common."

"Hmm. It gives me an idea." McAlden eased himself back in his chair and smiled behind half-closed eyes. It was a look that spoke of pleased satisfaction.

It was a look, Del thought, of a man in love. He sat up straighter. "Ah. Now, I begin to see. It's not Miss Burke you're harboring a secret fondness for—it's the absent Mrs. Marlowe." It was a capital revelation. Del could drink on Hugh's tab for months if he played it right.

"Oh, no secret at all. I am all open admiration for Captain Marlowe's very fine wife. She's a woman of admirable, uncommon qualities. She's got a very long arm, a dead eye, and an uncanny ability with a wicked fowling piece. Not entirely housebroken, our Mrs. Marlowe." McAlden's grin curved up the entire side of his face. "Do you know," he mused, "I think I *shall* write to tell her what you're up to. It seems only fair. She can be counted upon to even out the odds. I reckon she'd take great pleasure in blasting a few holes in you."

"Don't interfere, Hugh."

"Christ, Del, someone's got to. It's not right. Furthermore, it's simply not *you*."

"Isn't it?" Del pushed away from the table. "You have no idea."

"Then tell me," McAlden insisted, leaning forward on his elbows. "Explain yourself like a man. Your dislike of Miss Burke, who from all accounts wouldn't harm a flea, is"—he searched for the word—"irrational, a mania almost. Not at all the kind of logical, soldierly, and even gentlemanly behavior I would expect from you."

"Gentlemanly? Does not a gentleman seek to revenge a wrong?"

"On Miss Burke? What on earth could she have done to wrong *you*?"

"Not me. My sister, Emily."

McAlden's mouth turned down in surprise before he sat back and crossed his booted ankle over his knee meditatively. "Didn't know you had a sister. Didn't know you were the bloody heir to the Earl of Cleeve and a Viscount to boot either, so it's hardly surprising."

"No." Del hadn't shared his family story or name with any of his shipmates or fellow officers. He'd been obsessed with the idea of earning his way on his own merit. McAlden knew almost nothing of Del's past but that portion of his history they had shared aboard His Majesty's Frigate *Resolute*.

"So what does your sister Emily have to do with Miss Celia Burke?"

"Emily was at school with Celia Burke. At Bath. They were friends by Emily's account. Particular friends. Until Celia Burke betrayed my sister."

"Betrayed? Doesn't square with what I know of Miss Burke, but women are unpredictable creatures."

"Exactly what Emily thought."

McAlden took a long, meditative breath. "So you're going to publicly ruin Celia Burke as a revenge for a betrayal?"

"You needn't worry about it becoming public. I'll be quiet enough."

"Then a private revenge only. What does your sister say to that? Does she know what you plan?"

"No, she knows nothing. She's dead. Emily killed herself. Threw herself off a bridge, I've come to find out. Because of the rumors. And it is *that* woman's fault." He jabbed his finger onto the wooden tabletop. "I will not rest until I have served her some of the same rough justice she gave Emily."

*   *   *

The money was an impossible amount. Simply put, Celia had almost none. The small wooden chest containing what amounted to her life's savings contained only one guinea, given by her grandmother on her last birthday, and three pounds in sovereign coins with assorted shillings and pence. A grand total of four pounds, four shillings, and a ha' penny.

A pittance compared to how much she needed. She had some small pieces of jewelry she might take to a pawnbroker, but most would be missed if she did not wear them. Still, if she had any hope of coming up with the money, she would have to part with some of the pieces. There was no other hope for it.

Bains would no doubt object to find she was not to be given Celia's cast-off clothing, but there were rag traders down on the quay who gave good money for clothes like hers. Celia would have to appeal to her.

She rang for Bains and laid out her plan in characteristic straightforward fashion, giving in to only a little falsehood. She could not bring herself to tell Bains the real reason behind her need for the money. Bains was loyal, but not to a fault. If she knew, she would feel compelled to tell Celia's mama. Thankfully, Bains only raised her eyebrows but got to the business at hand.

"We can't sell all of them, miss. And not round 'ere. These gowns of yours'd be recognized, sure as day. I'll 'ave to get 'em down to Plymouth, somehow. Happens my sister'd do for you, as she goes down there time to time on a market day. She'll get a fair price for 'em. But not that 'broidered silk, miss. I 'broidered that with gilt and silk thread, I did. You sell that, an' your lady mother, Lady Caroline'd know straight off it were missing. Ruint as it is, I'll cut up and rework that one."

"All right. I'm sure you know best. How much do you think they will fetch?"

"Can't rightly figure it, miss, but my sister Suzann'll get you all she can."

"Thank you. We'd best go through the jewelry as well."

"You keep those lovely pearls Lady Caroline and Lord Thomas gave you 'pon your come out. And that cross, too. You part with those and they'll be no end o' trouble. Jig'll be up right quick."

"Thank you, Bains. I know this will be a loss for your pin money, but I'll make it up to you. I will. Now let's bundle these up and be off to your sister's, before my lady mother makes other plans for my day."

As it turned out, the lady had. Lady Caroline called out from her parlor as Celia and Bains made for the door.

"Celia? Where are you off to? I had thought to visit my cousin Harriet. You know her ball is only days away."

"Yes, exactly. We are on our way to the town, Mama. I thought to look at some lace for my gown for Lady Harriet's ball."

"How nice you're finally taking an interest." Her mother gave her a genuine smile. "I believe I shall accompany you. What a wonderful summer for balls we're having, to be sure, but you must look your very best at Cousin Harriet's. Some of her guests will be coming from London," she added meaningfully. "Though why anyone would want to live in London all the year round, especially in the summer, makes no sense."

Celia felt Bains dig a thumb into her ribs from behind. "No! I mean, I'm taking the pony trap. It's already at the door and . . . and Bains and I need to get there at the earliest possible—"

Bains piped right in on cue. "Mr. Morris, he did say as he could only hold that lace so long, miss, as there was others wanting it, though he'd rather sell it to you. Devon bobbin lace that is. Very fine."

"Yes, of course." Lady Caroline could only agree with such mercenary, if mercantile, logic. "If *you* are known to wear lace from Morris's establishment, then all the other young ladies will be mad for it and he'll sell twice as much. Canny man."

"Yes, Mama. So we had best be going straightaway. You may trust between Bains and me, we'll do very well. That last gown Bains made up was quite lovely—the embroidery alone . . ." She realized it was perhaps not an auspicious time to remind her mother of *that* particular gown. "We'd best be going." She gave her mother a kiss on the cheek and let Bains hustle her out to the waiting pony trap.

"That was a near run thing, miss."

"Yes." Celia took up the reins and clucked the pony onward, away from Fair Prospect, as the house was called, with relief. Her mother would have insisted upon all the pomp and circumstance of a liveried coach with a full complement of servants, but the pony trap suited Celia's country ways and her preference for a more low-profile approach to Dartmouth. Low profile, meaning invisible. Celia pulling up in a pony cart outside of Bains' sister's cottage would not be remarked upon, whereas a coach and four in the lane behind the village was sure to draw more than one eye.

"How much shall your sister be able to get? I should like to get at least fifty pounds."

"Fifty pounds? Lord bless me, miss! You'll be lucky to get a few pounds a dress, and that if Suz bargains hard." At Celia's astonished, crestfallen expression Bains added, "Bless me, child, you've no idea at all, do you?"

Celia blinked back the foolish heat building behind her eyes. Bains was right. She had no idea. "No, I don't suppose I do. I'm sorry."

"Don't be so hard on yourself now, miss. Lord bless me, but if I had ever got fifty pounds selling your castoffs, I'd have no reason to work now, would I?"

"No, I suppose not."

It came to Celia just how little she knew of the world, even the little that lay between the gates of Fair Prospect and the town. She was completely and utterly ill-equipped for dealing with the present circumstance. Her own maid knew the value of a pound far better than she. "If you don't mind my asking, Bains, if it's not too personal a question, how much do you earn in wages?"

"Well, I'm a ladies maid for you, so I get fourteen pounds per annum in wages, plus room and board and the pin money that comes from castoffs and what not. I've skills, haven't I, what with hairdressing and the dresses I make for you. The only ones to earn more are Fells, your lady mother's maid, and Lagman, who does for your father, Lord Thomas. Personal servants earn the most. I save most of mine, now our mum's gone. I've been saving up so I can have my own shop some day and make dresses. But I don't half mind working for you, miss. You're a rare treat of a young lady, you are. Never an unkind word, and that's worth mor'n wages, I can tell you. Here now, miss. Are you all right? I hope I haven't put you out of countenance with what I said?"

"No. Not at all. You were right. Quite right."

But she still needed the money. She had to have something with which to bargain when she dealt with Viscount Darling.

She thought about her drawings. Celia had nothing of the work she and Emily had completed before her death in Bath, but she had a full year's worth of specimen drawings completed from her own work in Dartmouth. She had hoped to expand her study farther afield, throughout Devon, but she had not yet got very far. Publishing such a work, if it was even good enough for publication, would have to be undertaken in London. How was she to get there?

It was altogether impossible.

Unfortunately, the town, with its steep, narrow streets and busy shoppers, forced Celia's attention to driving. She and Bains did have buying to do as well as selling. Her mama was expecting Celia in a new gown for the next summer ball.

Unlike most young ladies of her acquaintance, Celia

wanted as little as possible to do with the process of selecting material and making up a new gown. Not that she didn't appreciate the finished results, for it was always better to look fashionable rather than invite censure by appearing ill-dressed, but she had never felt less like spending money on something so frivolous as bobbin lace. Another beautiful ball gown was not going to improve her marriage prospects as much as the lack of blackmail money was going to ruin them.

She knew she was fortunate, beyond lucky, to have Bains, who liked nothing better than to design and make Celia's gowns, and bargain hard with the tradespeople. Bains was more than excellent—she was inspired and tenacious. Lady Caroline, who knew the value of a skillful servant in more ways than one, had always paid without a quibble, for whatever materials Bains wanted. Celia did everything she could to assist her in bargaining the draper down, so she might save at least a few more precious pennies for her paltry war chest.

They concluded their business at the drapers warehouse in no time—without Lady Caroline to contradict or second-guess her Bains was very decisive—and were headed past the booksellers, when Celia felt a light touch at her elbow.

For a moment, her heart skipped and started within her chest. She had to take a breath before she was ready to face whoever had touched her arm. She could think of only one possibility. Rupert Delacorte, Viscount Darling.

She turned with some surprise to find a petite young lady, smiling up at her. Miss Melissa Wainwright, a former friend from her days at school.

"Oh, my! Melissa, what a lovely surprise. I have lately been thinking so often of school and dear Miss Hadley's. How are you?"

"Dear Miss Burke, do forgive me for imposing myself upon you." Melissa's cheeks were pink with a pretty blush.

"Goodness, it is no imposition to greet an old friend. You will call me Celia, I hope, just as before. I am so very glad to see a friendly face." Melissa was not exactly Lizzie, but then Celia was simply glad to have any ally at all. "Has it really been over a year since we last saw each other in Bath?"

"Yes, I believe it was. A year ago Easter or so. Everyone left school so suddenly."

"Yes. But you must tell me what brings you to Dartmouth and how long you plan to stay."

"I am happy to say I have achieved a small independence and I thought to establish myself in a lovely, smaller city, where I already had some acquaintance."

"And so you have, and I am very glad for it. It is always a pleasure to see a friendly face. Have you come lately from Lincolnshire, or have you been traveling elsewhere? I have read Holbeach is a very handsome village."

"Fancy you remembering the name of my little village. I can scarcely remember it myself. I have not been there for many years."

"So you have traveled. How lovely. And have you been to London?"

"I have not. My fortune is not such that it will allow London living, and I have no acquaintance there."

"But you cannot have come to Dartmouth all alone?"

"No, indeed, I have my companion and chaperone, a lady of sterling reputation who will give some respectability and companionship to my small establishment. She is just there." Melissa gestured towards an older lady with the lace cap and the dun-colored gown. "Mrs. Turbot."

Mrs. Turbot did indeed look every last, myopic inch the respectable companion lady, with her lace cap under her bonnet and her modest, but well-made clothes.

"How lovely for you. May I become acquainted with her?"

"You honor me," Melissa said with another becoming blush.

They had not been great friends at school, but Celia took a moment to notice how fresh and pretty Melissa was—a petite, vivacious doll of a girl. Once established in Dartmouth, and with the help of hostesses like Lady Caroline, Melissa would soon find herself much sought after at parties and balls, even if she did not possess a large dowry. Even a small independence, as Melissa had said, would be made to serve. Certainly she was pretty and sweet enough to make some young gentleman set aside matters of birth and fortune.

Strange, how confident she could be about Melissa's future, when her own felt so uncertain. But Melissa had Celia to ease her way through any difficulties, while Celia had no one she could burden with her cares.

She was giving in to self-pity. Melissa had come to Dartmouth, or at least come from Bath, at some point, entirely on her own. The girl who had no one else in the world to rely upon had learned to rely upon herself in a way Celia never had.

It struck her with all the force of a cold dash of water how selfish, not to mention how naive and protected, she had been. How she had taken everything and everyone completely for granted. How she had taken Bains' pin money from her hands and *asked* her help to do it. How sorry for herself she had felt at the first uncomfortable sign of misfortune.

How she had almost let the arrogant, disdainful, Vile Viscount disorder her life to such an extent she began not to recognize herself. That was certainly enough. She would stop her whining. She would take action and rout him yet.

CHAPTER 5

The Summer Solstice Ball was held at the home of Lady Harriet Renning, a cousin of Celia's mother who had an exquisite jewel box of a house with extensive grounds in Dartmouth, where she often held very good concert evenings. Celia was in no way musical—she did not even sing—but she had great enjoyment in listening, and was an appreciative audience. She was therefore a favorite of her cousin Harriet.

It was small relief to Celia to know she would be amongst mostly family, though there were still a number of others, including guests from neighboring estates. Some were strangers to her, but they were fewer in number than at the Widcombe ball and thus far, Viscount Darling was not among them. She'd had two days and two nights in which to accustom herself to Emily's brother blackmailing her, and the idea no longer shocked, though it still rattled her greatly.

Celia had sent a request to Lady Harriet, asking if she might do Celia the very great favor of extending an invitation to her friend Miss Wainwright. Cousin Harriet had been generous enough to do so, and Celia hovered as inconspicuously as possible near the entry to the ballroom, so she might see Melissa in, and introduce her to Cousin Harriet herself.

When Melissa finally arrived Celia went to her immediately, holding out her hands in greeting. "Melissa!"

"Dear Miss Burke. How kind you are to receive me yourself."

Celia squeezed Melissa's hands in her own. "Please, you must call me Celia. But now you must prepare yourself for a great squeeze—my relations are both extensive and voluble! Come let me introduce you."

They began with Lady Harriet and her husband, Lord Renning, but Celia's effusive greeting of someone unknown to her mother earned her an imperiously raised eyebrow that bade her come immediately.

"Come, will you let me introduce you to Mama?"

"You honor me." Miss Wainwright was all blushing appreciation.

"Mama, may I have the pleasure of introducing you to my dear friend, Miss Melissa Wainwright of Lincolnshire? Miss Wainwright and I were lately together at Miss Hadley's School in Bath."

"Ah, yes. Miss Wainwright. A pleasure." Lady Caroline acknowledged Melissa's curtsy with a regal nod of her plumed headdress.

"My mother, Lady Caroline Burke."

Lady Caroline was gracious, and did Melissa the further kindness of introducing her to some of the other matrons, hostesses all. Melissa was thus assured of her share of invitations in Dartmouth society for however long her residency.

"Miss Burke, I must thank you for the generous—"

"Oh, no, it will not do. Please, you must call me Celia." She linked her arm with Melissa's. "We were not so formal at school, were we?"

"No, we were not, but I have found, for a woman of my . . . background, living in the world bears little resemblance to the wonderful, protected days we spent at Miss Hadley's School."

Celia had never minded that Melissa was most likely the

natural daughter of a gentleman who paid for her schooling anonymously. She had no other parent or relations, but Celia gave no particular importance to social status. She had been enough influenced by Lizzie and her radical ways of thinking to admire self-made people, and she had long ago learned to judge people on the content of their character before anything else.

"I loved my place there," Melissa continued. "But perhaps it was because I did not have family in any place so lovely as Dartmouth to come home to. How you must have missed it. You left school so suddenly, before anyone else."

Celia had her pat answer. "My term there was almost up and my parents were concerned . . . they required me home." She put on her best smile and changed the subject. "Where is your Mrs. Turbot? I should very much like to be able to introduce her to some new acquaintance as well."

"That is very good of you, Miss Burke. I am quite flattered you should put yourself out so for us, for me. We were not the best of friends at school."

"Nonsense. If we were not then, we should be now. We are grown up and have put away childish things. Your coming has made me useful in a way I very much want right now."

"Useful? Why ever should a woman as rich and beautiful as you want to be useful?" Melissa gave a light laugh. "I am sure I have spent my whole life dreading being useful. Mrs. Turbot must be useful, but I had much rather be decorative. Would not you?"

Celia smiled at the compliment, but stuck to her point. "Then purposeful. I desire above all things to be purposeful."

"Well, my only purpose is to find a husband." Melissa glanced sideways at Celia. "I fear I shock you by speaking so boldly of my ambitions."

"Not at all. I do not condemn ambition in a woman. Rather the opposite."

"And you? What is your ambition, Celia?"

"This evening, it is to draw as little notice as possible."

"But that is quite impossible. You are too rich and you are far too beautiful. It is impossible not to notice you. Indeed that military man cannot take his eyes off you."

Celia turned to see Commander McAlden propping up the doorway to the card room. "Ah, the very person. Come Melissa, should you like to be introduced? Commander McAlden is with the Royal Navy and is quite the local hero."

But Melissa was looking rather more like she would prefer having a tooth pulled than being introduced to a common officer. "Oh, my dear Celia. I hope I give no offense, but I had rather higher ambitions than a mere naval officer."

Celia could not help but be wounded for Commander McAlden's sake, but if Melissa was truly that shallow, she was not worthy of him. "Then let me introduce you to Mr. Harrington. He has a lovely estate in Somerset. Five thousand a year, or so my mama says."

When Melissa was happily dispatched to dance with the amiable Mr. Harrington and his more amiable five thousand, Celia moved quickly away from the dance floor in search of the Commander. He was kind enough to be waiting for her in the corridor.

"Commander?"

"Your servant, Miss Burke. Do you care to dance?" He bowed smartly, but wore a look of determined politeness.

She took pity on them both. "No, I thank you." She lowered her voice. "But please, you know we must talk."

"Yes," he nodded in agreement, though his forehead was lined with a scowl. The Commander led the way down the corridor that paralleled the ballroom, where they might speak privately while still being in public.

Celia looked about her for prying ears before she spoke. "I hope you can imagine my topic, Commander."

"I can."

"You left me with a dreadful state of anxiety, in which I

have remained ever since. Because I fear your warning can only have referred to Viscount Darling."

"He has been my friend, Miss Burke, through fire and water, but I cannot condone what he does. He has forgotten himself as a gentleman."

"Yes, that I understand, but, can you tell me why? Why me?"

"He set the bet, he says, because of his sister."

The note said he knew what she and Emily had done, and he would tell everyone and ruin their reputations. He would threaten to blacken his own sister's name? It made no sense. But what had McAlden just said? "A bet? He has already made it public with a *wager*?" Her voice was an incredulous whisper.

Celia felt her stomach drop into her slippers. It was infamous. Outrageous. He was blackmailing her *and* making it public?

The aristocratic bastard. Her mama was right. Celia could recognize nothing of Colonel Delacorte, the man of Emily's letters, in him. He *had* grown careless of other people. He *had* become just as heedless and ratchety as her mama had accused. *Wagering* with her reputation. And his sister's. "Of all the unmitigated cads. How dare he?"

"It was a private wager. Between only the two of us. I beg you would believe me, Miss Burke, I did not agree to take the bet. For his sake, I must tell you I don't believe he will ruin you in reality—physically." Commander McAlden's ears turned red, and his cheeks grew high spots of color in his embarrassment to speak of such a thing. "I think he rather means it . . . metaphorically."

Celia felt a flush flame across her cheeks and down her neck and chest, and knew she must be as red as he. But she could not afford to be anything less than resolute. "You must explain yourself, Commander."

The Commander looked back up the corridor and lowered

his head to speak quietly. "He was very clear. He meant to seduce and ruin you without once touching you. Those were his
exact words, so he must mean to toy with your emotions, to
engage your heart, and then abandon you. But without ever
once touching you. He was very clear. Miss Burke? Miss
Burke, you're not going to faint on me, are you?"

"Well. I only wish I could." Though her legs did feel a bit
rubbery. She sat abruptly in a chair along the wall. "I'm too
sensible."

"Shall I get you a glass of water perhaps, or wine?"

"Yes, please." She wanted to be alone. She wanted no one,
not even Commander McAlden to witness her distress and her
humiliation.

Her impression of Viscount Darling had been exact. He *did*
think she was too skinny a Christian to bother eating. He
couldn't even deign to seduce her properly so she might have
gotten some enjoyment out of her ruination. If she ever saw
him again she would slap him. She would slap him so hard her
hand would leave a print across his face like a marker that said
this man is a cad.

A footman brought her a glass of sherry on a tray. Perhaps
the Commander was too afraid to find her crying to return.
Well, she wasn't about to cry. She was too shocked for that.
And too angry. She tossed the sherry down in a single, fiery
bolt, and gasped for air. Goodness! No wonder they called it
liquid courage.

But the warm, glowing sensation inside was heating her resolve.

She'd like to teach Viscount Darling a thing or two, to show
him he couldn't use people so carelessly. He couldn't use *her*
so carelessly. By heaven's name, she was The Ravishing Celia
Burke and he would do well to remember it. She had talents
and ambitions that were not about to be stopped by some arrogant, self-important lion of a lordling.

Let him roar and pace in his cage. The Christians weren't

without their armor. Strength came from knowledge. *Per Scientiam Vires*. Now that she knew his strategy, she could combat it. Her strengths were honesty and openness. If she used the truth, all the guile in the world would not help him. He would have nothing to combat such weapons.

Resolved, Celia rose, shook out her skirts, and marched back to the ballroom.

"Why look at you, Celia, you're all alight!" Melissa's smile was mischievous. "Where have you been and with whom? Are those roses of love in your cheeks?"

"Not at all. I rather fancy it must be anger. How does it look on me?"

"Rather glittering." Melissa retreated an uncertain step. "But tell me you are not angry with me, surely?"

"No, not at all. It is nothing. We must have you back at dancing so you can continue to take Dartmouth by storm. We must keep up the introductions so the young men won't take me to task for neglecting them." So she could leave Melissa to her ambitions and go on and pursue her own. She was about to take Melissa across the room into a group of young bucks when Melissa put a hand on her arm to halt her.

"Miss Burke? Celia?" Melissa's face had taken on a rather pinched, green look, as if she might suddenly cast up her accounts. "I am not intimate with Dartmouth society, but is that by any chance the Vile Viscount? What is he doing *here*?"

Celia turned. It was indeed Viscount Darling. And he was coming straight for her.

Del had not been invited, but that had never stopped him before and it had not stopped him this evening. The Viscount Darling came from a long line of men who knew their way around a hostess.

"My dear, Lady Harriet," he had confessed as soon as he crossed the lady's marble threshold, "I throw myself on your mercy for my mother's sake. She particularly recommended you to me as a most sympathetic friend." Lady Harriet Renning was an old friend of his mother's and he would take every advantage of the connection.

"Viscount Darling." She looked him up and down critically with the frankness only an older woman who had enjoyed her youth and been happy ever since could carry off. "I had heard you were about the town, though I have not had a letter from your mother in some time. I have written to her, of course. Such a dreadful loss for a mother. But she might have warned me of your arrival among us here in Dartmouth."

"You are too kind, my lady. But you must not be too severe upon my mother. The Countess does not yet know I am come to Dartmouth. I have only just written her of my residence here. And you are very right—she has suffered a great loss. And so, it is for her sake I am attempting to reform my character in polite society."

"Are you now? Reforming? How charming." Her dry tone conveyed her doubt, but still, she smiled. "Then of course, you must come in and begin your reformation at my ball, though I daresay the ladies would prefer your form just as it is. You have your father's look about you."

"Dear lady, you must promise not to hold that against me!"

"Ha ha! Yes, I have known him these many, many years, but I will tell you the comparison flatters you, my boy and not him. He used to attempt that sleepy-eyed look you've perfected. By all means use it, but use it wisely, upon the widows. Steer well clear of the young virgins or I shall find the country outside my ballroom doors all in an uproar. Can you behave yourself?"

"By all means, your ladyship. By all means."

Lady Harriet was generous, but not so generous as to introduce him where it might have done the most good, to her beautiful niece. Instead, she introduced him to some gentlemen of her generation, who were fond of their drink, their cards, and their horses in that order, and could laugh off the mention of his scandalous reputation.

Del stayed with the older gentlemen in the card room, where he was good-natured enough to lose some money, but he positioned himself as near the door as possible so he might observe Miss Burke.

He had badly misjudged their last encounter by putting a warning shot across her bow, but he had since fortified himself against her. He meant to win this war and defeat this enemy, so he must re-engage.

From the distance of the card room, she again seemed serene and remote. It was remarkable how little of her true self her appearance revealed, how effectively her intensity was cloaked in politeness. She had another young lady, a petite, vivacious blonde, at her elbow and seemed to be taking her around for introductions. But once she had made the introductions, she invariably stepped away quietly, hanging back from the group, not putting herself forward into the conversation. Yet, on closer observation, he could see she was not aloof exactly. She was engaged in what the others were saying, her eyes quick and wide, but solemn in her face. She simply kept her own counsel.

She was not the ice princess he had imagined, but now that he knew something of her, he was armed. He would be wise to her tricks. He would not be charmed by her aura of innocence, nor drawn in by her intoxicating scent.

He was the one seducing *her*.

Miss Burke reappeared at the head of the ballroom and he knew the time had come. He rose and went towards her. When the blond young lady took note of him, her blue eyes widening in surprise, and spoke into Miss Burke's ear, he stepped forward to intercept her.

He had prepared himself for all possibilities—for her to cut him, or attempt to avoid him, or give him some warning he was not to approach her in public. He had been prepared to pursue her to gain that moment of public acknowledgment.

He was astonished to find her immediately coming towards him.

She turned as if seeking him out, as if *she* had been looking for *him*. Despite the horrified gasp from her companion, Miss Burke let the other girl's restraining hand drop away and stepped towards him, directly into his path.

As if she wanted to meet. As if she wanted it to be unavoidable.

"Viscount Darling." She did not curtsy. Perhaps he had earned the insult.

He bowed deeply, his manners as fine as champagne. "Might I have a word, Miss Burke?"

"That depends, I suppose," she replied carefully. She did not smile, but spoke with the same quiet gravity as in their last encounter.

He hoped it wouldn't prove to be characteristic, this thoughtful, luminous presence she had. He wanted—*needed*—her to be the careless, heedless vixen of his mania. He could not *like* her, for God's sake.

She looked at him with steady seriousness for a moment. "It depends on what you plan to do with it once it's in your possession."

He searched her solemn, freckle-dusted face, looking for signs of flirting, the simpering knowledge of the coquette. With any other woman such an exchange of words would have been a declaration of, and an invitation to, flirtation. But her dark eyes held the same quiet gravity as her voice. He could not quite take her measure.

"What would you like me to do with it?"

She offered him a quick, humorless smile. "I should like you to be very careful with it."

And to be very careful with her. That was what she meant.

She understood exactly how rough he had been at their first meeting and she was acknowledging the power he had over her. How foolish to show him just how easily she could be wounded. The first had been but an opening salvo to test her range. She was making herself a very easy target.

"I give you my word, Miss Burke. I will be very, very careful with you indeed. In fact, I intend to give you an apology."

"Do you?" Her dark brows arched higher in surprise.

"Yes. I apologize for my less than polite behavior last evening. I can only say in my defense, you took me off guard." It was a dangerous thing to say to an enemy. It gave her information and power to use against him. But it was also useful as a test. Would she take advantage of it?

She did not. A momentary flicker of her eyebrow told him she was far too intelligent to buy his charm wholesale. "I must apologize as well. I should have sought out an introduction rather than take you unaware. I am not usually so dreadfully impulsive."

"No?"

"No." She made a firm little sideways shake of the head, before she looked him in the eye. "But I begin to see the advantage."

He pulled his body back from its natural inclination to lean towards her. "Indeed? Well, I am glad you did act impulsively. It was very good of you to speak to me of my sister."

Her brittle confidence seemed to ebb. "My lord, you must not praise me for common decency. I was longing to speak to you." Then she added with a little hesitation, "O-of her. Of Emily."

Interesting, the little stammer. Very effective. "Thank you. I think perhaps decency is becoming less and less common, which must account for my astonishment when you spoke to me so kindly. I have been too little among people of . . . open sensibilities."

"Indeed?" Her brows rose again as she regarded him

minutely, looking, he reckoned, for some sign of sarcasm. "I am very happy for a chance to speak about Emily. Your sister was very dear to me. As dear as a sister. I mourn her loss."

It was more difficult than he had anticipated, to have Emily spoken of by this woman. He needed to remind himself that while Miss Burke was not the ice princess he had made her out to be upon first sight, she had nevertheless betrayed Emily and her friendship and devotion. Del had read Emily's last letter again just that morning, so it would be fresh in his mind. He hardened his resolve anew.

"I thank you. Perhaps you would care to walk with me for a moment?"

She looked for a moment for her friend, who had disappeared. But she did not demure. "Yes."

"I am glad. I should like a chance to set things right. May I start again? Miss Burke"—he bowed correctly—"it is an honor to make your acquaintance. Rupert Delacorte, Viscount Darling, at your service. Am I making you uneasy, speaking so openly like this? But I should like to . . . further our acquaintance, if I may be so bold."

Miss Burke looked towards the dance floor.

God's balls. He could not stomach dancing with her. It was one thing to tarnish her reputation and ruin her by association, but he did not want what would amount to a public, legitimate announcement of interest in her, should he take her onto the dance floor. And he did not want to touch her. It was a strange, almost physical aversion. His gut clenched up tight as a grenade at the thought. No dancing.

"I am sorry, but I do not dance. My apologies. Perhaps we can walk, or you might meet me somewhere where we might exchange . . . a few words without the fear of being overheard. Or noticed. I fear being seen with me will do your reputation no good. But I should very much like the chance to talk to you about Emily." It was a useful little conceit, his concern for her reputation.

"Yes." She took the bait straightaway. She must feel very guilty indeed. "We must talk. But . . ."

She hesitated again. Indeed, she seemed full of hesitation, constantly appearing on the verge of stammering shyness. Emily's letters had never mentioned anything of the kind. They had been full of Miss Burke's eloquence and perfect way of addressing herself. The letters had sung her praises until—far from home and missing its half-forgotten comforts after years of rough living aboard ship—Del had imagined that he was in love with Celia Burke. He had been in love with what she represented: the open hearts of young English women who would not have to be paid in coin for their affection. She had been his ideal, his waking dream. Perhaps that was why he had felt her betrayal just as keenly as Emily. What a perfect little actress she was.

"My cousin's garden is very fine, with an arbor walk. It will be a more private place to talk, if that would suit. But we cannot be seen leaving together. If you would not mind going first, I shall follow in a few minutes. Should you like that?"

How sweet she seemed with all her deference.

He bowed deeply to take his leave. "I should like that very much indeed."

CHAPTER 6

Del got himself a drink and went outside, into the farthest reaches of the garden's darkness so he would not have to make polite conversation with anyone else. So he could keep talking himself into this folly that had seemed so logical, so necessary when he had set out from London. Within the confines of his mind, Celia Burke had seemed a perfect demon of a woman, an easy and necessary target for his wrath.

But as he waited and watched from the dark arbor, he was not so sure. He had made a career out of his ability to read men, to understand who they were and why they did the things they did. But his instincts were in constant and complete disagreement about Miss Burke. He simply could not take her measure.

Emily had been sure in her letters, and so heartbreakingly devastated over Celia Burke's betrayal, she had taken her own life. He could not allow himself to rest until he got to the bottom of what had happened between them.

He found the arbor walk running along the perimeter of the walled garden, and chose a spot closest to the house to wait for Miss Burke. She came out by a small door in the south wing, prudently trying to avoid notice. But she was not furtive. She walked collectedly, as if she had no hesitation in coming out to him. Foolish girl. He would have all the advantage.

She stopped just at the edge of the arbor where the spill from the house made a division of the darkness and light. It seemed fitting—or emblematic—that she be in the light, seemingly uncorrupted by the stain of sin, while he stayed in the darkness of the arbor.

Her simple chemise gown of pale, shining silk with a deep lace flounce around the neckline gave her an air of simple, unforced elegance and grace. Her hair was a contrasting, unadorned riot of loose curls tumbling about her face, creating a dark, glossy frame for the light porcelain of her skin and the dusty rose of her lips. The contrast between the untamed riot of the curls and the collected, restrained serenity of her face was almost shocking. It invited him to rake his hand through her hair and fist up those sinuous curls until he could pull her head back and kiss astonishment into those dark, watchful eyes and put a rush of color into those pale cheeks.

"Viscount Darling?"

He reminded himself he had the advantage. His eyes had already adjusted to the change from the blazing candlelight of the house to the perpetual half-dark twilight of English summer in the garden.

"I was not sure you would come." He did not approach her, but let his voice carry and beckon to her, and lead her deeper into the arbor.

"Of course I came. I said I would."

"You are true to your word then, although I am sure you would rather be back at the ball, dancing."

"No, not at all." She pulled off her gloves to pluck a leaf from the climbing vine and ease herself slowly into the deeper darkness.

He noticed at a glance, her fingers were bitten down to the

quick. Despite her serene appearance, Miss Burke was a worrier. Again, not what she appeared. And not what he expected.

"I'd rather be away from the ball," she continued. "I don't care for dancing, either."

That had to be a piece of flummery. What young lady didn't care for balls? Only the wallflowers, and The Ravishing Celia Burke was no wallflower. "What beautiful young woman does not care for dancing? You dance beautifully."

She did not make note of the fact he had been watching her. "I do like the dancing itself, sometimes, but I'm not very good with people. They're so invariably complicated and unpredictable. And I always say or do the wrong thing. Like when I met you. I should not have introduced myself to you. You did not care to have my acquaintance forced upon you."

How open and artless; grateful and generous at once. He responded in kind. "It was wrong of me to be so ungentle. I apologize." He clasped his hand over his heart and gave her his most winning smile.

Yet she remained immune to his charm, all solemn seriousness. "Thank you. I accept."

She ought to have been coy. Such a conversation with any of his female acquaintance in London would have been the opening salvo in a battle of flirtation. For God's sake, they were engaged in a secret meeting in a beautifully romantic, darkened garden on a balmy summer night. It was practically de rigeur to flirt. But try as he might, Darling could find no trace of the coquette in her voice, which was soft and lower than most females', but still entirely feminine. Her voice seemed . . . innocent.

No. That simply could not be. He would not allow it. He must think of Emily and all the things she would never do, and harden himself to this girl.

"How do you find Dartmouth, Viscount Darling? It must be very quiet and boring after your travels of the world."

Did she sound wistful? "Have you never traveled?"

"No. Not at all."

"Never? Have you never been away from Dartmouth? Been to London?"

"Only to Bath, to Miss Hadley's. I know I am hopelessly provincial after all your travels." Her tone was almost scornful.

"Not at all. I think you simply lack experience of the world. Of seeing a greater variety of people." He wasn't sure how he had come to be defending, or reassuring her.

"Oh, that is *certainly* true." She spoke with feeling as she leaned back against a column supporting the arbor. "But I fear a greater acquaintance with the world would only lead me to greater confusion and lesser understanding. I find people are simply hard to understand. A man like you is *impossible* to understand."

"You are too severe upon yourself. Yet, I find myself thankful for your lack of experience, else you would never talk to me. You would know a girl like you ought not to be talking to a man like me." He darkened his own voice with a bit of rueful wistfulness.

She turned to face him fully, and his eyes were drawn to her lips, red and chapped from being bitten. And to her eyes. It must be merely a trick of the light, but her eyes carried deeper shadows. When she looked at him thus, with those wide, solemn eyes, she appeared almost haunted.

As well she ought to be.

"Forgive me, Viscount Darling, but I should like to know to what purpose is this conversation?"

Her forthright question surprised him. "To what purpose? To improve our acquaintance. I had hoped we might even become friends. For Emily's sake."

"For Emily's sake," she echoed. "Viscount Darling, I hope I give no offense, but I was under the very strong impression that you do not like me. That you rather actively wish me ill."

He smiled to cover his surprise. Brilliant of her, of course, to make such a direct attack, when he had been guarding his metaphorical flanks. But he could lie as effectively as she.

"I do not wish you ill, Miss Burke. I wish most sincerely to become friends."

"Friends? Do you always make bets to seduce, ruin, and abandon your friends?"

Bolt after bolt, each surprising shot overthrew all his assumptions and all his plans. There was nothing, simply nothing he could say that would not condemn him. He braced himself for the onslaught of her condemnation, for the slap he knew he deserved, yet she remained calm and collected.

"That, Viscount Darling, is something I cannot understand. Would you care to explain it?" Her clear, quiet tone demanded an answer.

Oh, she was clever, a very worthy opponent.

"I see Commander McAlden has spoken with you first."

"You must not blame the Commander. I fancy he has done us both a favor, Viscount Darling. Although the Commander declined to take your bet, I intend to accept your challenge."

She could not have hit him any harder if she had slapped him. "You astonish me, Miss Burke."

"Thank you. I am glad. It evens us up a bit." She nodded, all steady purposefulness. "As we have both noted, I am shy of the world and lack experience. You, on the other hand, claim a surfeit. It seems the answer to both our difficulties lies in you giving me the benefit of your seduction. Then we will be even. Provided you are capable."

Oh, stupid girl to try to goad his pride. "You don't think I can do it?"

"I have no idea, really, but I hope you can. Seduce me without ever once touching me, that is. For I should not like to find myself bound to you in marriage. Can it be done?"

"It can," he answered carefully. "I have no desire to be trapped into a marriage either."

"Good, then we understand each other. You *may* seduce me"—she held up her hand in warning—"but you may not touch me."

"I may seduce you? It is not so straightforward, Miss Burke, this business of seduction. It is a dangerous business you undertake."

"Dangerous? How?"

"Because it must be based upon trust. You must trust that I will behave against my proven character. You must trust that my reputation is unearned. That I will not forget I was born a gentleman and I won't remember I've spent the better part of the past ten years working hard not to act like one. A very dangerous chance, Miss Burke. A very daring chance."

"No." She shook her head, still so solemn and determined. "I may be shy of the world, Viscount Darling, but I am not timid of purpose. I do not need to be afraid of you. I knew you, and I made up my mind to like you, indeed I did like you, long before I ever met you."

"Had you?" He could not stop his ridiculous smile. Despite his efforts to control himself, her words warmed a part of him he had encased in ice. "That was undoubtedly not wise, Miss Burke."

"Perhaps not. But I knew you." She looked at him fully for only a moment before she looked away, across the garden. Her voice became so soft, he had to take a step nearer to hear. "You were the man who left the comforts and assurances of home to prove himself to the world. You were the man who, through his own merit, became a respected officer. You were the man who wrote Emily of your concerns on behalf of your men. Of your quests for fairness and justice. Of your constant concern for their welfare." She hid her twisting hands behind her back, against the column. "You were the man who wrote openly to your younger sister of your love for her and your commitment to her happiness. You have no idea how I envied Emily such a brother."

She might as well have fired a pistol point-blank into his gut, such was the force of her quiet words and penetrating insight. In the course of less than a minute, she had presented him with a picture of his better self, of the man he had once prided himself on becoming. Before his descent into bitterness and despair. Before he had let himself become a cad, a libertine, and a debauched drunk. Before he had taught himself not to care. But a year of drunken excess, profligacy, and habituation to vice had not dulled the pain one whit.

The warmth of understanding, of *being understood*, filled him, softening him. He almost took another step nearer to her. Almost. But he could not. He could *not* touch her.

Instead, Del set his animal instinct, his natural, strong physical attraction to her, loose. He let his eyes range over the picture she presented.

She was pressed against the column, with her hands behind her back. Her elbows fanned out one to either side, rather like wings. The golden candlelight spilling from the tall windows and filtering down through the arbor dappled one side of the columns and left her gilded with the aura of an angel. An earthly reminder of moral failings.

But he didn't want to see her as anything approaching angelic. He didn't want to feel the pull of heaven-taught morality. She was not an angel—she was real. Her chest rose and fell with the same breath as every other being. Her dark, solemn eyes were alive. She was a beautiful, living, breathing woman. And he was a living, breathing man.

"I am many things, Miss Burke, but I am enough of a man to be very"—he let his voice drop lower, to a murmured growl—"very attracted to you."

He watched his words sink into her with a visible weight, her shoulders curling in to hold them close. Her face colored, a sweep of delicate rose washing across her cheeks. It was so easy, too easy, to give in to her attractions. She was everything beautiful and feminine. Everything he could have wanted. Before. Before Emily's death. Before the blackmail letter.

God almighty. He felt torn in half, anguished, his mind at war with his body.

He spoke, more to himself than to her. "Perhaps. I'm just enough of a gentleman to remember you are not at all for the likes of me. To know you are completely and utterly out of bounds. I ought not to sully you with any of my attentions."

"You don't sully me." The words tumbled out of her on a breathless exhalation.

"Don't I? Can you tell me you haven't been warned against me?"

"No, I can't." She looked down at her toes. "I have been warned. I have been expressly forbidden to have anything to do with you—to so much as speak with you."

He let a long silence stretch out between them until he drew her eyes back to his. "But?" he prompted gently.

"But. I may be shy of most people, Viscount Darling, but as I said, I do not suffer from timidity of purpose. I have always been resolute, but today I have decided to be daring."

Something within him, a wave of feeling, crested and cast him loose. "Daring? Will you be daring enough to meet with me despite your mother's prohibitions? Will you be daring enough to seek out the experience of the world you lack? Will you? Will you come with me? Into the dark?"

Celia Burke was under no illusions as to what Viscount Darling was asking. Despite the warning voices of her parents clamoring in her head, she wanted nothing more at this moment than to give in to the dark. To give in to him. Even in his present incarnation, she did not want to resist him and his dangerous, velvet-cloaked lures. Clearly, Viscount Darling was a man with great experience of the shifting shadows of desire and the pleasures to be had there.

She would take his devil's bargain. She would put herself into his power.

Viscount Darling. What a name. Lizzie would have said something entirely witty about *that*, but Lizzie wasn't there. Celia was quite alone and unequal to the wittiness needed to deal with such a name, or such a man. For the Viscount was without a doubt the most handsome, *darling* man she had ever laid eyes upon.

When he exerted himself to be pleasing he had the blond, blue-eyed good looks of a remorseful angel, the kind who would weep and still smile while smiting sinners. The smile seemed to hover just at the corner of his mouth, ready to pounce upon his lips at a moment's notice. Oh, and what a smile it was. Dazzling in its brilliance. And his lips, so strangely soft looking in such a hard face. A man ought not have such beautifully bow-shaped lips. Yet the whole of his face, even with his incongruously soft lips, was wholly masculine.

She ought not be thinking anything about the Viscount's lips or their lovely shape. No wonder her mother had warned her against him. He was already a bad influence on her wayward thoughts. How bad an influence he was to be upon her actions was yet to be proved.

"When you look at me like that, Miss Burke, I begin to be sorry I did not ask you to dance."

"Why? You said you did not care to dance."

He changed the cadence of his voice, whispering, creating an atmosphere of intimacy. "I begin to see the advantages it affords, for the opportunity to hold hands with a lovely young lady for a small length of time, without censure."

"Oh, yes. I see."

"Do you? Do you see I should have liked the opportunity to dance and hold hands with *you*, Miss Burke? But as you've been forbidden to speak to me, I can only assume you would have been forbidden to dance with me, as well."

Her silence served as confirmation.

"And yet"—his deep voice dropped to a murmur—"though we are not dancing, we are speaking, aren't we? Out here in the secluded dark. All alone."

"You must think me a coward—only willing to speak with you when I know my mother will not see." Her voice, so low and breathless, was unrecognizable to her.

"I think you prudent, for I know what my reputation would do to yours were we seen together publicly."

"Perhaps. But I think you have gone to great lengths to hide the nature of your true character from people."

"Oh, Miss Burke, never forget my unsavory reputation is well-earned. You must not forget that, even as you dare to meet with me. You must not forget, I was wanting to be able to dance with you, but not for the reasons you might suppose. Do you want to know why I want to dance with you?"

"Yes."

"I should have liked to hold out my hand to you and feel the weight of your palm in mine, like a gossamer alighting upon it."

Viscount Darling's voice vibrated through her, slow and warm, like honey melting into a hot drink of spirits. It flowed over her as intimate as a touch.

"Perhaps I would have left off my gloves, in the anticipation I might better feel the heat of your skin through your glove."

Celia almost looked down at her hand, to make sure it was still attached to her body, to make sure it was not nestled in his. The skin of her palm was warm and tingling, as if his bare, ungloved hand had caressed her.

"I would have contrived to put my hand in the slight indentation at the back of your spine as we moved through the figures or touch your waist to guide you down the line. You would have felt the heat and weight of my hand, even through the layers of your gown. Would you have liked that?"

The warm tightness deep in her belly was answer enough.

He did not wait for her answer, but went on. "And perhaps, if you might have given me the slightest hint you were not averse to my attentions, a look, a sigh, I would have contrived to take your elbow, as I led you back to your waiting mother, and my fingers would have found the soft, vulnerable skin of your inner arm just above the edge of your long evening glove, so I could discover, for one tiny moment, the silken texture of your warm flesh."

Celia felt all atremble, like when she had had a fever last spring. Hot and cold, shaking from the confusing and contradictory feelings jerking and swooping inside her chest like a tethered kite.

She put out her hand to stop him, to preserve her distance and her sanity, to keep him from coming any closer.

Yet he never approached. He stayed where he was, across the gap of ten feet, pressing his back against the opposite wall. The span might have been two hundred for all that he would not pass it. His hands were tucked behind his back, pressed flat against the brick wall, as hers were against the column, tracing the slight texture of the plaster in substitution for tracing his face.

"And I should have liked to know"—his low voice rumbled on—"if after that one tiny moment, my touch had made your breath tremble within your chest."

It was trembling now, even though he had never so much as moved an inch or a muscle. She tried to collect herself, to throw off this strange spell he had woven around her with his voice.

"Yes"—he gave her that slow, enigmatic smile—"I very much regret that I can never experience that dance with you, Miss Burke. It seems such an awful waste."

CHAPTER 7

"Viscount Darling." Her voice was breathless and low. She shook her head to clear it.

A noise, the sound of feet upon the gravel walks, had her turning her head. The musicians must have been taking a break, or it was late enough for the supper. She had no idea of the passage of time.

"I fear we are no longer alone, Miss Burke. You must step out."

Celia recognized Melissa Wainwright as one of the young ladies approaching on the gravel path. She stole a glance towards Viscount Darling, but he seemed to have disappeared into the darkened depths created by the vines and branches of the ancient, sweet-smelling climbing rose. She hadn't noticed it before. *Rosa damascena bifera.*

Celia schooled her expression to something she hoped approximated blandness and wandered slowly out onto the path, as if she had been walking the whole time.

"Oh, pardon me, Miss Burke. I don't mean to intrude, but I thought I saw you out here by yourself. You are all by yourself, are you not?"

Ah yes, ruination seemed to be available at each and every corner. "Yes, of course."

But Melissa was not convinced. "I thought I saw you come out with the Vile Viscount."

"I spoke to him to give my condolences on the death of his sister. You remember Emily Delacorte, do you not?"

"I . . . that is to say . . . I cannot recall."

"She was at Miss Hadley's with us. She died from a fever. No matter. I came out after, for some quiet and fresh air when I noticed I've a small rip—a very tiny, slight rip—in my flounce. It's small, but I fear another misstep could tear it further. I sent for my maid, Bains. I'm waiting for her now." Celia stepped away from the arbor and twirled herself around trying to get a look at the offending tear, making a deliberate spectacle of herself to divert Melissa's attention from the shadows behind her. "Mr. Percy Mandeville certainly has a lot to answer for. My advice would be to avoid dancing with him at all costs."

"That's easily enough accomplished, as I have not been introduced to Mr. Mandeville. You are lucky to have so very many admirers. But I don't remember seeing you dancing."

"Am I?" Celia chose the safer topic. "Yes, I'm sure I must be lucky. But the grass always does look greener from the other side of the fence, doesn't it."

Over Melissa's head, Viscount Darling slipped from the far end of the arbor to the shrubbery beyond. When he would have passed completely from sight, he stopped, silhouetted against the dark enveloping green of the hedge and looked at Celia, his endlessly bright eyes holding her gaze in invitation.

They were not done. He would be waiting for her. In the dark.

"You mean . . . you don't like it? All the attention." Clearly, Melissa could barely conceive of such a thing. Her mouth gaped open in astonishment.

"I assure you, Melissa, there is nothing I like less than being put in front of people. It makes me dreadfully uncomfortable. The process of a ball so very much resembles the auction of prize sheep at the fair, I can't like it."

"You don't like to dance, when all the gentlemen want nothing else *but* to dance with you? They all but fall at your feet, begging for the favor." Melissa looked at Celia with something more cynical than wide-eyed wonder. "You don't even like it, and all the young men are wild to dance with The Ravishing Miss Burke."

"Oh, please don't repeat that name. It's just silliness. There are a great many women in Dartmouth, not to mention the rest of the country, who are far more beautiful than I."

"But they're not here, are they?"

"Of course they are. You're here." Celia couldn't help herself—she reached out and touched Melissa's arm.

Melissa drew back in astonishment.

"I'm sorry, I've startled you." What on earth had prompted such behavior? Had Viscount Darling's intense words uncoiled within her the need to touch *something*? To *feel* something?

Melissa looked uneasy, shocked even.

Celia felt like such an awkward fool. She talked on to cover her embarrassment. "I'm sorry, if I am the first one to tell you, but you must know you are a very beautiful woman. Surely others, or your Mrs. Turbot, for instance, has told you that?"

"No. Why would she do so?"

Celia smiled at the strange, changeable nature of people. They defied classification, they made no sense. Why should everyone in Dartmouth tell her *she* was beautiful and no one tell Melissa Wainwright? "Because it's true. You haven't lacked for partners this evening, have you?"

"No. You've been very kind in introducing me to your acquaintance."

The words were correct, but there was an edge, a neediness to Melissa's tone Celia began to remember from school.

"Well, now they are your acquaintance. You may do as you wish with them, without any interference from me."

"Your cousin was kind enough to invite me, but others may

not receive me when they find I'm not like you. That I've no money and no connections to speak of."

"You have yourself, your conversation, your style. I hope you will not find Dartmouth society so high in the instep that they would behave so shallowly. I hope you believe *I* will not behave so shallowly."

"No, you will be kind to me. You always have been kind. I can only hope others will follow your example." Melissa tossed her chin up and put on a fierce smile, full of renewed purpose. "I will make myself a success."

Celia could only admire such determination. "Of course you will. You already are."

Melissa nodded, but didn't seem inclined to move away or end the conversation. Viscount Darling would not wait in the dark forever.

"Well, thank you for your assistance. I'll have to send again for my maid. I wonder where she could have gotten to?" Again, Celia performed her little dance of trying to look back over her shoulder to find the rip.

"If you'll pardon me—if I may—it's just here."

And there it was. A small rip to the hem of the flounced border. How bizarre. And how fortuitous. It was pleasant not to be lying.

"There it is. Well, I suppose I should be thankful it wasn't my toes. Although it was a very near run thing with Mr. Mandeville! I had hoped to escape unscathed."

"Only slightly scathed, I'm sure." Melissa's good humor was returning. "I'm sure I could repair it for you in a trice."

"Oh, I thank you very much for your offer, but I have already sent for Bains. I suppose I should go find her. Oh, look here she is. Thank you for keeping me company, Melissa."

"You're welcome, Celia."

Celia turned to Bains and Melissa moved away, back towards the ballroom doors. The musicians were launching into another quadrille.

"Where is it, miss?" Bains crouched down to inspect Celia's skirts.

"It's nothing really, just there—the trim on the hem." Celia waited until Melissa was well out of sight before she turned back to search the shadows of the arbor for signs of Viscount Darling's presence. "How did you know to come out?"

"Footman, that Timothy Middlecroft, come to find me in the servant's hall. You'll need to come in where there's better light."

"I'll come in, in a moment. You go get your needle and I'll meet you in the withdrawing room."

"Right, miss." Bains rose. "You coming?"

"In a moment, Bains. You get your needle case and meet me there."

"I don't like to leave you all alone out here, miss."

"I am perfectly fine on my own, Bains. Thank you for your concern."

"If you're sure, miss?"

"Bains. Just go. Please."

The maid reluctantly retreated across the garden and down the kitchen steps without another word, though she cast at least two glances back over her shoulder as she went.

Once she was gone from sight, Celia backed around the column and ran into the arbor, down the covered walk until it gave way to the shrubbery. She waited for her eyes to readjust to the greater darkness of the tall yew hedges that separated the garden from the expansive lawns beyond. *Taxus baccata,* she noted absently. The moonlight, which had filtered through the branches of the arbor, was absent. The darkness was as soft and thick as velvet. Even the playful evening breeze had given way to hushed, sweeping quiet.

She ducked silently around the hedge and stopped herself just short of running into the wall that was his chest. "Viscount Darling." Her voice was a rushed whisper. Up close, he was so much bigger, taller and broader than he had seemed when he kept to the shadows of the arbor. She began to feel over-whelmed, pulled into him as if he were a lodestone, as she had when he had filled the small book room.

"Miss Burke." He smiled at her, but backed away without touching her, though he kept his clear blue eyes locked on hers the entire way.

She followed, because she could not *not* follow him, but she schooled herself to walk more slowly, letting a prudent space open up between them.

"I'm glad you came," he began with a warming smile, and it was all she could do to stop herself from foolishly blurting out, *Me too*.

"We had not finished our conversation, had we? You had not yet decided if you would come with me."

"I'm here now, am I not?" It was all the admission she trusted herself to give.

"So you are." He smiled at her, a softening around his eyes, as if he were, for the first time she could discern, truly happy with her answer. "But it puts me in a bind, you see, Miss Burke."

"Normally, if I find myself alone with a beautiful young woman in a hushed and darkened shrubbery, I would be for-mulating plans and schemes to try and kiss her."

Did he not mean to kiss her? Was that not why he had in-vited her to this rendezvous? And was that not why she had come, so she could be kissed? It was not a flattering admission, but it was the truth. For all her declaration that he could not touch her, she was so near to him, and more than willing to have him do so.

"The difficulty lies in the fact that normally, I would never find myself with a beautiful young woman of good reputation and family in the first place. You are the first such young lady, brave enough, *daring* enough, to weather the storm of objec-tions against me."

Celia did not know whom she preferred, the tawny predator

or the man she knew lay somewhere beneath his wolf's cloth-ing. "Are they really necessary, my mother's warnings?"

"Oh, yes. Because you see, Miss Burke, I would like to kiss you. I would like nothing more. If you were some other woman, a barmaid or a widow or . . . but you're not. You're The Ravishing Miss Burke, granddaughter of the Duke of Shafton and niece to the Marquess of Widcombe. You are not for the likes of me."

Celia remained quiet, surprised by the fluttering of disap-pointment in her chest. She was not to be kissed after all. It was almost a pity. Her eyes lingered over the dichotomy of his mouth. The straight, almost stern line, surrounded by the al-most incongruously soft-looking lips.

"But I must be glad you're not for me. If you weren't so clearly out of bounds, I would move closer and inhale the scent of your perfume." He moved closer, but didn't entirely close the distance between them. His voice lowered again to an inti-mate rumble. "What is that you're wearing, Miss Burke?"

She looked down at her dress and slightly lifted the ma-terial of the skirt between her fingers. "Pale rose silk, my lord."

His eyes smiled as he shook his head. "I would have called it white, but it suits you very well. Just enough color to show off the cream of your skin and the dark silk of your hair."

"Thank you, my lord."

"But your scent, Miss Burke?"

She ducked her chin to find a moment away from the inten-sity of his clear blue eyes. "Just soap, my lord."

One corner of his mouth quirked up. "How straightforward you are, Miss Burke. No simpering, no flirting. May I tell you how refreshing I find such honesty?"

"No, my lord." Her voice was losing all substance, the same as her resolve.

"Shall I tell you?" He leaned in and inhaled the warm air at the base of her neck. "You smell like that arbor, of jasmine and roses."

"Damask rose. *Rosa damascena bifera.*"

"No Latin, Miss Burke. Just the summer scent of England and an English girl. But you've also got something else, something of the exotic East wafting about you. Incense and spices."

"How can you tell all that?"

"Because I can. That's how it is with you. I can find you in a garden full of fragrant, blossoming flowers, and I can find you in the midst of a pungent yew hedge. I could find you with my eyes blindfolded. In the dark."

Her claret red lips formed that lovely, entirely kissable, silent *oh* of surprise.

He closed his eyes to the sight of her pillow-soft lips and took another deep, satisfying breath. Turning away, he leaned his head into the hedge. He felt slightly dizzy, as if he were on an edge, teetering at the brink of some precipice. At the mythical perpetual, roaring waterfall at the edge of the world, dropping off into infinity. The infinity, the endless possibility of her.

"Just soap. From your bath. It's heavenly. You're heavenly. I'd like nothing more than to lay my cheek across the back of your neck and find that spot just behind your ear where the scent is strongest. But then I would be compelled to taste the warmth of your skin along the side of your neck, to press kisses down to your exquisite collarbone and the little hollow, right there. That sweet hollow, just waiting for me."

He opened his eyes to the sight of her in the moonlight, staring at him with dark eyes, enthralled by his words. Her mouth was open a tantalizing fraction that made him long to slip his tongue into her warmth. Her bitten lips were the dark color of Bordeaux and just as intoxicating.

"But then, once I had had that first taste of your flesh, I would need to know the feel of your lips beneath mine. To see if they could possibly feel as infinitely soft as they look. And I would need to fit my lips over yours and exert just enough pressure to feel the warmth of your flesh beneath mine."

Her breath left her body on a soft gasp and she was so still, pressing back into the hedge, he feared she had forgotten how to breathe. But her breasts were rising and falling with a rapidity that spoke of arousal. And she was not alone. His own breath was locking up tight in his chest, making him ache from the duality of what he was doing—arousing and denying all at the same time. It was having a decidedly erotic but chaotic effect upon his unruly body.

"I . . ." she whispered, and then tried again. "You seem to know my own thoughts before I do. I've never . . . My hands are tingling with the need to touch you. I want to touch your lips, to trace them with my fingers." She looked down at her hands as if they were foreign to her, and then rubbed them together. "It does no good. Still they tingle. And still I want to touch your lips."

She reached out and would have stroked along his bottom lip with one trembling finger. He felt himself leaning towards her, as desperate for the contact as she, when he stepped back. No. He was the one who was supposed to be seducing her. How could she, this untried, naive virgin have him aching and yearning for her simple touch?

"No." He filled his lungs with the moist night air. "We cannot. I dare not. Because if you touched me, Miss Burke, it would only be the beginning. It would give me license to take your mouth with mine." He closed his eyes, lost in the vision of his imagining. "Once I had kissed you, had tasted your lips and delved into the warmth of your unfathomably soft mouth, I would not be satisfied. I would not be happy until I peeled those silk clothes from your body and feasted my eyes upon your gloriously naked flesh. I would not be satisfied until I touched you. And once I had my hands upon the silk of your skin, I would not rest until I could bury my body in yours and feel the exquisite bliss of being inside you."

His breath was sawing in and out of his lungs as if he had run a great distance. He shook his head to clear the image of her sprawled out beneath him, her skin pink against the white of sheets, her dark hair spread in riotous abandon across his pillows.

But the reality of her appearance was no less arousing. Even in the dim moonlight, he could see her skin was aglow with suppressed passion, her hands were knotted into the sticky, prickly yew branches, and her breaths were labored.

"So, you see why you cannot touch me. Why we cannot touch each other. I beg you, Miss Burke. Do not tempt me with so addicting a drug. Do not tempt me to forget everything decent and right." He said it with more force than he ought, but he was in an agony of arousal. Thankfully, his last words had finally broken the spell he had cast around them.

She eased back away from him a pace or two.

"Forgive me, Miss Burke. You need not fear. You are quite safe with me. I am remembering, at long last, that I am a gentleman. For Emily's sake."

She nodded, a firm little dipping of her head. Her breath was still too fragmented to speak.

"You should go. Please." He needed her to go before he forgot all his fine words and noble-sounding, gentlemanly sentiments, and fucked her against a yew hedge. Because he was only kidding himself if he thought his actions of the past half hour were all about revenge or justice for Emily. He was deluding himself if he thought he was doing it for any reason other than that he wanted Celia Burke. He wanted her with a hunger that made a mockery of his self-control. A hunger that made a mockery of his gentlemanly behavior. And he knew if he didn't do something, he wasn't going to stop until he had her.

CHAPTER 8

Celia woke with a feeling of lightness she had not experienced in weeks. All would be fine. She was going to be fine. At the end of her road was still a lovely little cottage covered with fragrant climbing *Rosa bracteata*. When Viscount Darling's temporary fascination with her was through, she would still have her good name, her good sense, and her botanical work.

She had no doubt it was a temporary fascination. However she might try to remind him of his better self, he had shown her without question he was still a rake. And rakes always, always moved on to other pastures. Pastures full of widows and barmaids.

She felt so expansive she took Bains in tow before breakfast and set off across her father's estate to an old, unused stone granary where she had created her workshop.

"You're chipper as the larks this morning, miss."

"Yes, I am, Bains. I defy anyone to put me out of countenance this morning."

"You'll be out of countenance once we get to that cave of yours and you find one of your precious specimens has died since the last time we've been there."

"Not at all. I know where to get more!"

The workroom was more than a place to Celia, it was an idea. And an ideal. One she had nurtured from its inception in her brain until it was a physical place. A place where she could finally pursue her passion for botany without either interruption or interference. It was her sanctuary.

When they arrived at the tall stone barn, Celia and Bains climbed up the stairs to the loft and one by one threw open the heavy wooden shutters, flooding the room with bright summer sunlight. Beams of light slanted across the wide floor planks and filled the vaulted space with a golden glow.

All her money—all the money she might otherwise have had on hand to pay Viscount Darling, instead of becoming his willing partner in his game of seduction—had gone into this loft. In the dark days after she had come home from school, Celia had sought refuge in the great empty stone barn situated at the edge of the home farm, looking down over the mill creek.

Long ago, before her father had bought the manor as a wedding present for her mama, the barn had been a great granary, storing the harvest from the surrounding farms. But since her father's management of the estate had been mostly pastoral, rather than agricultural, and they no longer grew and cut much grain, the barn had fallen into disuse.

No one had seemed to mind when she had cobbled together the spare furnishings from the estate's castoffs. Once she set her mind upon creating a semblance of the laboratory they'd had at Miss Hadley's school, Celia had not rested until it was complete and she could take up her study as before. As she had told Viscount Darling, she was nothing if not resolute of purpose.

Only here was she entirely her own person. Only here, had she been able to order her time as she pleased. She had been able to make her own decisions about what plants to study, and how to go about the work of recording her finds. She had found her life's true purpose and dared to make her dreams a reality.

After opening the shutters, she checked on the previous session's drawings. She had completed a study of the carnivorous common bladderwort, *Utricularia vulgaris*. The microscopic inspection of the plant had revealed its submerged bladders had trapped water fleas and even a very small tadpole, all of which she had recorded in minute detail. The series of drawings were complete and dry. She took them down from the drying racks she'd improvised from baker's metal shelves and brought the last one she'd completed over to the light. The colors looked especially good. It had been difficult to achieve the bright intense yellow of the orchidlike blossoms and the vibrant soft green of the stem and root system. All in all, the *Utricularia vulgaris* series was a masterpiece.

It was a painstaking process she'd come up with, but in the absence of etching, which she knew nothing about, she had taken to drawing the plants first with pencil and then mixing watercolors to bring the drawings to vivid life. After the watercolor had dried, she traced over the pencil lines carefully with black India ink, to make the important outline of the plant fresh and crisp and easily discernible. Each drawing took days, but she did them in batches so every day she had several at different stages of development and completion on which to work.

As the current drawings were all dry, she collected them into a leather folio. There were by her last count three hundred and twenty-two full color drawings upon which her proposed masterwork, "A Survey of the Freshwater Plants of Devon," would be based.

While Bains sat at the table to work on her own drawings of designs for gowns, Celia changed her shoes into the sturdy leather boots she kept by the door. Her own halfboots would leak like an old rowboat, but the tall, oiled leather boots kept her nice and dry. She also took down from their pegs her long oiled canvas work apron and redingote.

It was the perfect day to collect the specimen of *Fontinalis antipyretica* she had seen growing in the stream below the millpond. She had just enough of the right color paint to capture the deep, verdant green of the slow-growing willow moss.

"I'm heading down to the creek, Bains." Celia picked up the empty wooden pails she kept for collecting and ducked out the door.

"Mind you wear your gloves," cautioned Bains. "Those rope handles will rough up your hands proper, if you're not careful. Then what'd Lady Caroline say, I ask you?"

"I have my gloves, Bains." Celia's poor mama never suspected why Celia went through so many pairs of riding gloves. "I'll be back within the hour. I know just where to get what I want. You work on your drawings until I come back. Mind you don't use up all that green. That pigment's expensive, Bains."

"Don't need you to tell me, miss. Now you be careful down that bank."

As Celia had been walking along the banks in question for more than fifteen summers, she paid Bains no mind, heading across the cart track and down the wooded hillside. It was the perfect day for a ramble in the woods, bright and clear. A glorious summer morning. Birdsong filled the wood, and soon the musical fall of water could be heard tumbling downstream over rocks and into pools. She had already mined most of this stretch of bank for aquatic plant life, but she followed the meandering line of the creek like an old friend, winding her way around horsetails, *Equisetum arvense*, and clumps of ferns, like *Pteridium aquilinum*—the poisonous effects of which, on grazing cattle and sheep, she had repeatedly warned her father and his steward—until all sound was drowned out by the roar of the millrace and the crank of the mechanical mill wheel.

Nobody paid Celia the slightest mind. She was a common enough sight along the local streams and riverbanks, but if anyone knew she was Lord Thomas Burke's daughter, they made no mention. She was certainly careful never to be recognized by anyone she knew, but Dartmouth society rarely made trips up to the mill and would never take note of mere peasants if they did. Celia went about her quiet business with buckets and nets, fishing bits of greenery out of the water without any ado.

She had reached a small pool, downstream from the larger millpond, when she saw him.

Viscount Darling was a quarter mile upstream, riding a powerful black hunter across the mill bridge and heading toward the lane that wound its way through the wood. He was attired in a black double-breasted redingote over a red waistcoat. His black felt round-brimmed hat nearly hid his wheatcolored mane. High upon the black horse he looked more handsome and remote than ever. An unattainable ideal.

She ducked her face down, careful to hide her features beneath the wide brim of her straw hat. From beneath the brim she could simply admire him from the distance. Much easier to look at him when he wasn't looking back at her with those azure blue eyes of his. They were the color of the sea and the sky, and spoke to her of all the wide-open, faraway places he had been. Places she would never see.

He turned and looked down the stream, directly at her.

It took every ounce of self-discipline she could muster not to bolt, but to stand still and hope his eyes would pass her by. She couldn't explain why, but after the intimacy, vulnerability, and excitement of their time together in the shrubbery, she could not let him catch her there, filthy dirty, hems six inches deep in water and mud. Not just because she looked like an urchin, but because she was engaged in the very thing his sister, and his letters to his sister, had inspired.

It had been hard enough to have him treat her with disdain in her uncle's book room, and to be so rude as to make a wager regarding her, but it would crush her, absolutely devastate her, if he were to show disregard, or worse, indifference to her work, to her one true attempt to find purpose.

She held still, like a deer in a wood, trying to take advantage of the camouflaging nature of her dull, earth-colored work clothing. It seemed for a moment as if he would go past, and keep riding in the grassy lane through the trees. Celia let out the breath she had been holding and relaxed her fear of being recognized.

But then he called out to her. "Miss Burke?"

Before she could admonish herself or even think about the folly she courted, her feet were moving across the millstream and she clambered into the densely wooded hillside as quickly as she could scramble.

The morning had begun with the promise of a beautiful day ahead. But what did one do for amusement in a provincial town like Dartmouth? It wasn't London, which after the past year Del was much more used to. He'd have to cultivate an entirely new set of habits now that he was in the country. One couldn't pursue seduction each and every waking moment.

That certainly had been what he had been pursuing, wasn't it? If he forced himself to be truthful, his time at the ball had been much more about pleasure than he had ever anticipated. The thought left him decidedly unsettled, and not a little amused. That he had thought Celia a worthy adversary had been enough to prick his interest. That she had instead become a worthy partner in seduction pricked more than that. Several other, much less intellectual parts of his body were unsuitably aroused.

After another long night, in which he had been plagued by erotic dreams of pale-skinned, dark-haired, naked women instead of the usual nightmares, Del had decided a bruising ride was just the thing. He had set off across the open, moorlike landscape at a hard pace, eventually taking the lane along the top of the ridge back towards Dartmouth. Nearer the town, he passed by the pillared gates with the bronze plaque announcing the lane to Fair Prospect, Lord Thomas Burke's estate.

Lord Thomas's property was clearly marked by the excellent state of the stone-walled hedgerows. Del rode on, compelled by a reason he could neither name nor understand, around the boundaries of the property, not daring to cross into the Burke estate. He had already trespassed upon the man's daughter. Somehow, he could not stomach trespassing upon his land.

He rode north, and then east, skirting the edges, cutting through unused pastures down towards the mill creek that fed into the Dart. At the mill, Del turned south and crossed the creek at the bridge.

As he crossed the stone bridge he saw a girl, a villager or a farmer's daughter he supposed, carrying a pail along the rock-strewn bank. At first glance, he could have sworn the girl jumping across the rocks looked just like Celia Burke.

Something like panic forked through him, like loose fingers of lightning, leaving a hot, metallic press of blood in his throat. He could not fathom his reaction. Damn his eyes, it was just a girl, not an enemy warship bearing down on him.

On a second look, though she was dressed in quite plain, earth-colored country clothes, Del was sure it was Miss Burke. It was Celia's profile, surely. No farmer's daughter had such pale, unlined skin. He urged his mount off the bridge and towards the bank to get a better look.

She was standing perfectly still on a rock next to the water, a little more than a quarter mile downstream. What on earth would The Ravishing Miss Burke be doing in the woods near the millstream? And dressed like a farmer's daughter? Anyone who had been at the ball and remarked upon her beauty would have laughed at the charge.

"Miss Burke? Hallo!" He tipped up his hat.

He was sure she looked up at him for a moment before she took off like a shot and scrambled back through the verdant undergrowth into the woods on the opposite side of the mill-stream.

"Miss Burke," he called again. Still, she did not stop. She tore up the hillside away from him, like a fey, half-wild creature.

What in bloody blazes was that all about? Del looked back to the spot where she had stood. Her pails were still there, abandoned on the rocks. His well-weathered heart had misfired when Celia had jumped over the slippery, irregularly shaped stones. All he could think of was Emily, her head bashed in by rocks just like those, falling insensible into the water. But Emily had not been walking along the bank. Emily had thrown herself off the bridge.

Del glanced at the single, arched span of the stone bridge. There was nothing he could put his finger on, no definitive connection. But his well-honed instinct—the instinct that had kept him alive for over eight years at sea—would not let the moment, or the feeling still sizzling through his body, go. It felt important, even though he could not fathom why.

Del could not follow the girl's progress through the dense bracken on the hillside. He had to turn his mount around and recross the bridge, by which time she would have disappeared from sight. But he was first and foremost a military man, still possessed of his Marine's experience and instinct. He was as good at reading the landscape as he was at reading a map.

All her father's land, her home, lay on the south side of the mill creek. The small wood on the other bank gave way to fields where she would find no cover. Farther downstream the creek widened and deepened where it fed into the Dart. She would not be able to ford the river there unless she decided to swim.

A mental image of Celia Burke, pale and naked, water glistening from her skin as she rose out of the water, seared into his brain.

He reined his horse sharply left and returned across the bridge to the mill. No matter which way she went, upstream or down, she would have to cross the river to follow the lane on the far side back up the hillside and onto her father's property. He dismounted, watered his horse at the pump in the mill yard, and sat down to wait.

It did not take long. Less than a quarter hour later she sprang into his vision, jumping across the water. Clever girl. She had waited for him to leave, then doubled back and retrieved her pails. Stealthily creeping upstream, under the bridge, she crossed when she thought it was safe. He mounted and followed, hanging back, staying out of sight and letting her go ahead unimpeded.

She moved quickly, with sure familiarity through the trees, and headed towards a stone building at the top of the hill. In another minute, she paused at a side door in the barn.

He could see her face, as she scanned the woods around her, her eyes wide and dark, her face pale with fright.

Why? He had told her she was safe from him. What could make her run? Del wound his way up to the crest of the hill. It seemed he was going to trespass on Lord Thomas's property after all.

Celia was red-faced and gasping for breath, from nerves and the climb, by the time she made it back to the barn. She dropped her buckets by the door and leaned against the wall.

"What's happened to you? You look done in. If that miller's boy's been giving you any trouble I'll box his—"

"Viscount Darling," she panted.

"Is giving you trouble? And him a Viscount! Isn't that always the way of it?"

Celia gulped in a breath. "No. He didn't give me trouble. Not exactly. He saw me. And I ran."

" 'Course you did. What with him being a libertine and all-around rotter. Your lady mother would have a fit to know he'd spoken to you. We'd best get straight home and come up with something, should he tell her. You get out of these wet things and—"

"Hello?" The Viscount's deep voice echoed up the stairs, vibrating through the frame timbers of the building and deep into Celia's chest.

"Oh, my God. The man's a bloody hound!" Celia's voice dropped to a whisper. "He's followed me." She flapped her hands at Bains. "Go! Get rid of him."

"What do you want me to do?"

"Go down, before he comes up, and pretend to lock up." She slapped the keys into Bains' hand. "Go! Before he comes up."

Bains mouthed something unintelligible, but went down. In another moment Celia heard her voice.

"Oh, sir. You startled me!"

"Your pardon, miss. I did call out," the Viscount said. "You work in the Burke household? Bains, isn't it?"

Celia tiptoed to the corner of the window to peek down.

"Yes, sir." Bains curtsyed.

"Ah yes, I collect you are Miss Burke's maid, are you not?"

"I don't discuss my mistress with anybody, sir." Bains lifted her chin and pulled the door closed behind her with a snap.

Viscount Darling heeded her subtle warning. "Very commendable, I'm sure. What is this place?"

"One of my master's barns, sir."

"Yes, I can see that. It appears to be something of an ancient granary. What is it used for?"

"I'm sure I don't know, sir." Bains' tone was just short of pert.

"Really?" Viscount Darling returned her an unflinching stare. "Just how do you find yourself out here?"

Bains folded her arms across her chest. "I do my master's business, sir. I'm told to clean out this old loft and that's what I do."

"Lord Thomas should have more care for his servants than to send them out alone, to do such a job of a morning."

"I was just locking up now, sir, if you'll be on your way."

"Here." Viscount Darling reached over and plucked the key from her hand. "Let me help you with this."

And before Celia's mouth could form a silent *no*, he was past Bains and treading up the stairs. Celia bolted for the only cover available, behind the stout door at the head of the stairs.

"Here now, sir. There's no call for you to go up there. That's my master's private room and you've no right to be here."

Viscount Darling took his time looking about the room. Celia inched her head over a fraction, until she was able to see him through the crack between the door and the jamb, as he strolled around the big central table. Some of Bains' sketches were scattered about, as well as some preliminary sketches Celia had made of the willow moss. Her master plant list, with all the projects she had planned, and those she had already completed, also lay on the work surface, at the end nearer her microscope.

It was too much to have him there, in her private, personal space. She had never felt so open and exposed, as if the room could reveal her most intimate secrets. It did, if he knew how to look. Everything there, every moment she had spent there, had been under his influence. Under the influence of his letters to his sister. Under the influence of his advice. His sense of merit. His daring and resolve. His purpose.

She had built this place out of her dreams. Her dreams of scholarly, botanical accomplishment and her dreams of him.

Viscount Darling's stroll took him down to the far end of the table where the double loft window let in a flood of light, illuminating the microscope, its brass gleaming brightly in the morning sunlight.

Celia felt the tension coil tight within her body. Her lungs felt rigid, frozen in her chest. Her stomach clenched up fast, as he began to inspect the instrument. Emily's microscope. Miss Hadley had sent the instrument to Celia after Emily's death, instructed by the family, she said, to put it to good use. Celia had been touched by Miss Hadley's thoughtfulness.

But the Viscount stared and frowned, and Celia held her breath. Did he know it was Emily's? How could he? He had been away at sea with His Majesty's Marines on a naval ship when Emily had purchased the instrument. Perhaps it was simply that a military man such as he had never seen such an instrument before. Oh Lord, she hoped he wouldn't fiddle with the knobs the way some careless girls at school had done. He might scratch or break the lens.

Celia remembered the excitement of the day when the wooden crate, stamped from MR. JOSIAH CULMER, MATHE-MATIC INSTRUMENT MAKER, WAPPING, LONDON arrived at Miss Hadley's. The poor porter, having no ready assistance besides two girls, whom he would never allow to help him, had had to manhandle the crate into the hallway outside the classrooms by himself. Emily's clever fingers had it pried open in a trice, and it had been a magical moment when she had pulled the gleaming brass instrument out of the straw.

The microscope, so vital to their study, was the only thing Celia had of Emily's, making it especially dear.

"I see your mistress is a scientific young woman, Bains."

Bains came to the side of the door, where Celia could see her. She looked uncomfortable but remained unforthcoming. "I'm sure I couldn't say, sir."

"Hmm. It is a beautiful instrument."

Bains was holding to her line. "If you say so, sir."

Celia pulled her eye away and pressed herself into the corner. She could hear Viscount Darling's booted footsteps as he prowled along the table. He stopped at the basket of lemons she kept to remove the ink and paint stains from her hands, picking one up to sniff at the rind.

"Citrus."

"Yes, sir." Bains managed to look affronted by even so innocuous a comment.

Viscount Darling said nothing more, but paced back down the length of the room, and then paused before the door with his back to her. Celia held her breath and closed her eyes. She fancied she could feel the heat of him through the slatted wood door.

And then she *could* feel him, as he leaned on the door, squashing her back against the rough stone wall.

"I saw your mistress this morning, Bains. Not too far from here. Down along the mill creek."

Celia could feel the rumble of his voice vibrate through her, through the wood of the door, a delicious, subtle tease.

"She looked quite lovely, in a sort of rumpled, country way. Fresh, with roses in her cheeks. That's what I think of, when I see her. Roses and jasmine. Even when I can't see her. Do you know, I sometimes imagine I can still smell the scent of her, as if she were in a room with me. Roses and jasmine. And citrus."

The Viscount leaned his full weight against the door, pushing her back against the wall behind, pinning her, trapping her breath in her chest as heat built in her body at his words, at the intimacy of his statement.

"I think you've had too much sun, sir." Bains was immune to his charm. "You ought to get yourself home."

"Then I'll see myself out. Good day to you, Bains. Please do give my kind regards to your mistress, The Ravishing Miss Burke."

CHAPTER 9

On Sunday morning, at the unfashionably early hour of ten o'clock, Del made his unhurried way over the threshold of St. Savior's Church. He felt the congregation's astonishment ripple over him as he walked up the center aisle in all his sartorial glory—his linen immaculate, his blue coat fitted like a glove, hat and prayer book in hand—as if he were quite used to attending divine services every day.

All he needed to finish his dramatic entrance to perfection was a requisite flash of lightning and a roaring clap of thunder.

The Gorgon, Lady Caroline Burke, noticed him first. Her flying eyebrows winged towards the rafters before she fixed him with a narrow, piercing scowl. The Burke family were seated in what looked to be their usual pew, to the left of the center aisle and two rows back from the front. Lady Caroline sat all the way to the outside of the pew, so by angling herself just enough, she appeared to be looking over her own family, when in reality, she had the greatest view over the rest of the congregation. Not a hat, a feather, nor a wayward smirk was going to escape her gimlet eye. There was no way for a rascal such as himself to go undetected.

Naturally, he bestowed upon her his sunniest, devil-may-care smile, and seated himself two rows back, directly behind her daughter.

When Miss Burke attempted to look around, The Gorgon gave her a hard pinch on the arm to keep her eyes decently facing front. She was left to lower her gaze demurely to her prayer book, the very picture of meek, modest, moral compliance, and leave the ogling of him to the more curious of her neighbors seated to the rear.

He wasn't sure what he had expected, other than to make Celia his subtle object. And to speak with her before too much time went by. He was getting impatient for answers. And just plain impatient. His dreams of late, never the most restful, had grown increasingly filled with her image. And decreasingly filled with her clothing.

But he was in church, where he knew he must be drawing far more than his fair share of attention. While some of the congregation made a show of ignoring him, a few hearty souls, like Lady Harriet Renning, acknowledged him. He was a greater object of curiosity than the rector's sermon, which he listened to with the appearance of clear-eyed attention. Likely half the congregation were waiting for him to be struck down at any moment by a tremendous lightning flash from a just and punitive God.

He was not struck down, and until such time as he felt the hot fork of the Devil in his back, he resolved to smile to everyone as serenely as if he were in a brothel.

But he was not in a brothel. St. Savior's was an ancient stone church, but the heat of July had managed to overwhelm even its thick stone walls. The air was thick and still as the rector's voice droned on like a bee, busy in a hedgerow. He ought to amuse himself by letting his gaze wander innocently over the magnificent medieval stained glass windows.

But Miss Burke had pinned her dark unruly curls up in defiance of fashion, and the back of her neck was long and white below the back rim of her hat. A single whorl of shining hair peaked from under the brim, dark silk against the vulnerable white of her neck.

Del wondered if any other man had ever noticed the way her hair grew in that swooping left-hand whorl. If any other man had even seen it or thought about placing his fingers there, to cup the back of her neck. The sight was strangely intimate, as if only a husband should or would know about such a place. As if only a man who had the *right* to touch her there and lift aside her glorious riot of hair or to press his lips to the sensitive skin at the top of her spine, should have discovered it.

God help him. What a strange, unwelcome thought, and yet he could not look away. He could not stop his mind from skimming around the bottom edge of the hat and mentally untying the ribbons to push the hat off, and give him unimpeded access to the long, delicate line of her jaw and the soft, vulnerable skin of her neck.

Vulnerable. No. He would not allow anything about her to be vulnerable to anything but his worst intentions. He very much hoped she would be vulnerable to him. He would do everything in his power to make it so.

He would tell her about kissing her neck. He would tell her he wanted nothing more than to slide his teeth down the sensitive tendon to the little hollow formed by her collarbone. He would tell her how her head would arch back and her mouth would fall open, ready, waiting, wanting him to kiss her and search out the sweet confines of her mouth with his tongue and teeth. How he would taste her honey, and she would taste him and melt into his arms.

He might be in a church, but she was likely as close to heaven as he would get.

That wasn't right. Her body would be heaven, what woman's would not? His response was as it would be with *any* beautiful woman. He wanted Celia Burke physically. He wanted to sink his aching cock into the tight, whisper-soft pillow of her body until he found his release—but he did not like the fact that he did.

He stayed in the pew after the closing—because he could not possibly stand up in his current, inappropriate state of arousal. He took the time to mark his place in the prayer book as if he had plans for further, detailed liturgical study. He let the rest of the exiting congregation pass him by, ignoring both the curious and the hungry stares.

He had prepared himself to receive fire and brimstone emanating from the Gorgon, and for her to lift away her skirts so they might not come in contact with the pollution of his pew. But as Lady Caroline Burke and her husband, Lord Thomas, passed by, abreast of Lord and Lady Renning, the entire foursome acknowledged him. Lord Thomas made a slight bow in his direction and his lady followed with a slight, but regal angling of her head.

Wonder of wonders, he was not to be cut. Dartmouth society appeared to be warming to the prodigal Viscount. Guilt threatened to swamp him at such fine treatment from Lord Thomas. Del had taken liberties with the man's daughter and had just daydreamed about taking even greater ones, while seated in church. He really did have no moral scruples.

As he stepped onto the wide stone steps, Del shook hands with the rector, Reverend Dr. Marlowe, and spoke politely to Lady Harriet Renning, who inquired after his mother's health. He might have approached Lord Thomas and Lady Caroline Burke had they not turned to speak with a neighbor and had not Miss Burke stepped a fraction apart.

He arrived by her side at the precise moment when she turned away from her conversation. He tipped his dove gray hat politely. "May I say I am pleased to see you this morning, Miss Burke."

"Good morning, Viscount Darling." She curtsyed demurely, keeping her eyes down, and would not look at him.

"Are you not going to say how surprised you are to see me here this morning?"

"Ought I to be surprised?"

"No, I suppose my attendance jibes quite nicely with that rather sunny, idealized version of my character to which you ascribe."

The faintest brewing of a smile appeared on her lips before she bit it back under control. "As you say, Viscount Darling."

"It is too beautiful a day for formality, is it not, Miss Burke? Please call me Darling. What did you think of the sermon?"

The momentary flash of panic on her face told him all—she had no idea what the sermon had been about. His presence had discommoded her so far as to disturb her perfect character. She could not truly remember. *Good.* At least he was not alone in this infernal hell of awareness he had created.

But Miss Burke was as clever as she was beautiful. She rallied. "The Reverend Marlowe is always most learned and eloquent when he speaks on God's infinite and merciful grace."

"I will have to take your word for it"—he smiled at her—"as I have not heard him before and was rather more interested in the beauties of the church."

She did not take his meaning. He really did have to teach her to flirt. It would make the whole process of seduction that much easier. But, he supposed, a great deal less interesting.

"Oh, yes, the windows are rather beautiful, are they not"—she turned to gaze upwards at the edifice—"and the architecture is Gothic, as I'm sure you know."

"Not at all. Never went to university and learned the niceties. Too busy killing Frenchies."

"Oh. I had not thought." And there was the blush, as if a paintbrush had been drawn across her cheek. "Do forgive me."

"I believe I shall." He gifted her with his breeziest, most charming smile.

She seemed to relax a bit, lowering the prayer book she had

clutched to her breast like armor. "Are you enjoying your stay in Dartmouth, Viscount Darling?"

"In a way. But I do not stay in Dartmouth. I am out on the coast, at Redlap Cove at the home of a friend."

"Of course!" She smiled, and transformed herself into the picture of genuine delight.

It surprised him that a young lady so conscious of her beauty as The Ravishing Miss Burke should ever crinkle up the corners of her eyes on purpose. No matter her skill at acting, he did not think any lady's vanity would have allowed such a purposeful defilement of her beauty. But then again, Miss Burke had been trudging around the countryside yesterday, dressed little better than a washerwoman. Perhaps beauty was not a hardened priority, for Miss Burke smiled away, giving her heretofore haunted eyes a merrier twinkle.

"Of course you are at Glass Cottage. How lovely. I should have realized. Do you find it to your liking?" Hers did not seem an idle, polite interest. She looked at him with expectation.

"Yes," he answered truthfully. "It is a pleasant, very comfortable house. I take it you know it?"

"Oh, yes. It belongs to my great friend Mrs. Marlowe, my Lizzie. I mean it belongs to Captain and Mrs. Marlowe. I take it you are acquainted?"

"With Captain Marlowe, yes. We sailed together for many a year, before I was brought home. From my knowledge of him, I can only suppose the house to be wholly hers. There is both wit and ease in the furnishings. I fancied it must show the hand of its mistress."

Nothing, it seemed, could have pleased Miss Burke more than such a compliment to her friend. He had not believed her capable of such loyalty.

"Why yes," she cried. "How perceptive of you. That is both Mrs. Marlowe and the house exactly—wit and ease. I admit, I envy Lizzie her lovely cottage."

"Really? You surprise me, Miss Burke. I would not have expected the granddaughter of a Duke and the niece of a Marquess to envy anybody a mere cottage."

"But there is nothing mere about Glass Cottage, is there? Such a happy, warm house and so beautifully situated, with the cove and the tide pools that form along the coast. There are several large streams that cut through her property. One marks the eastern boundary and comes right down to the shore to run into the sea, so full of excellent— Why it is just an excellent place."

She stopped abruptly, he thought, suddenly nervous in his presence again.

"But I am rambling on. Suffice it to say, I think it an excellent property, despite all the trouble they have had with the smuggling. I hope you enjoy your stay there."

"I thank you. I say, Miss Burke, I haven't a clue as to the etiquette of hosting a party at a house where we are merely guests, but I wonder if Commander McAlden and I might host an afternoon of some sort and have some people, perhaps you and your family, out for an afternoon by the shore?"

Miss Burke regarded him as if he had suddenly run mad. "I hardly know, Viscount Darling. You did say my whole family? My parents and my brothers and sister? I have three younger siblings." She pointed to two sooty-haired lads who looked as if mischief was their chief occupation.

"I collect you would be much easier in my presence if you were not going against the wishes of your family. So, if you are to spend time with me, your relations must be my friends as well. And I must be the one to befriend them." What was he doing? He *had* run barking mad.

"Would you really do that for me?" Her voice, low and breathless, was incredulous.

"I would."

She began to smile and bit her lip, as if to keep herself from hoping against hope that it could be so. "Well, I think you are already well acquainted with my mother's cousin, Lady Harriet Renning."

"I am. She happens to be a great friend in former days of my mother, the Countess of Cleeve."

"Ah. Well, if she were to aide you, I believe my parents might be more receptive to such an invitation."

"And you, Miss Burke?"

Her smile could no longer be contained and when it broke free, her radiance left him momentarily stunned. He felt as if he wanted nothing more in this world than to bask in the glow of her happiness. To spend a lifetime making her so radiantly happy.

"For myself, I should like nothing more than to accept if such an invitation were to be proffered, not the least for the pleasure of being at Glass Cottage again."

"So it would have nothing to do with the anticipation of the pleasure of each other's company? With the pleasures of being with *me*, Miss Burke?"

Color streaked across her face and she shot a furtive glance at her mother. "I must go, Viscount Darling." She bobbed a wobbly curtsy, her arms coming out to rest on the gate to steady herself. The sudden lack of grace looked out of place on her.

"Miss Burke, I have upset you. I apologize. Are you quite all right?" He put out his hand as if to steady her by the elbow, but it stayed in the middle of the space between them, waiting at the end of his arm, doing nothing.

She stared at his hand. At the fingers of the gray glove encasing his hand as if it had magically turned into an exotic lizard before her eyes.

"We may not touch. I must remember we may never touch," he said quietly.

She stepped back abruptly. "I must go."

"Of course. I will not detain you from your family. But might I ask one small question?"

"Yes?"

"What does a lovely young woman do for pleasure and exercise during the day here in Dartmouth?"

Miss Burke looked at him warily. She darted a glance at her mother, who was beginning to disapprove of the length of their conversation, but was not at a convenient distance to put an end to it.

"Shall you need to consult with your mother on your pastimes, Miss Burke?" he teased. "I thought you more daring than that. I confess, I am not as interested in her answer as I am in yours."

Again, the beautiful blush spread across her cheeks. The sort of blush the poets would have called artless. But she wasn't artless. She had betrayed Emily. He would do best to remember that and take no notice of her flushed flesh.

"No. I apologize. I do not need to seek my mother's opinion in order to give my own. Young people in Dartmouth engage in the usual country pursuits: walking, shooting, hunting, riding. I imagine our pursuits are very much like any other set of country people's. Any number of quaint, unexciting things."

"Tell me what you prefer. For instance, do you ride, Miss Burke?"

"I do, occasionally."

"I see. I was out riding myself, yesterday. But then you know that. You saw me. Just as I saw you."

She did not say anything, just pressed her teeth into her lip so hard, he feared she might draw blood. His overwhelming impulse was to ease her pain.

"Why did you run away?" he asked gently. "Why did you hide from me? You can't, you know. I told you I could find you in a room full of other people by your scent alone. How could you think I wouldn't find you when you were in the same room with me?"

She looked confused. Her forehead, under the upswept brim of her bonnet, pleated into tiny rows. And she was worry-

ing away at her lower lip. It was all he could do to keep himself from kissing her. Her answer was just above a whisper. "I
thought you would disapprove."

He felt his face twist into a scowl. "Disapprove? Of your
botanical studies? Why should I disapprove? *I* bought Emily
that microscope, Miss Burke. Did you not know that? Cost me
a fortune on a Marine colonel's wages. I hope it has proved to
be everything Mr. Culmer promised it would."

"Oh!" She covered her astonished mouth with her hand.
"Yes"—she nodded in answer—"it is a beautiful instrument.
It has been an honor and a privilege to have its use. If you
want it back, I'll be happy—"

"Good God, no. Your pardon, Miss Burke. No, I'd have no
bloody use for it. But I should have liked for you to show me
your work. Emily wrote at great lengths about it."

"You don't disapprove?" She watched him closely with
those solemn, dark eyes. The answer seemed vitally important to her, though he could not tell why.

"No, Miss Burke."

"And you won't tell"—she skated a glance at her mother—
"anyone?"

"No, Miss Burke," he repeated. "But as to riding? I was
rather hoping you might care to go riding with me. Say this afternoon?"

She drew an audible breath. "Viscount Darling, I am sensible of the honor of your invitation, but I—"

"Of course. You can't be seen out riding with a man your
parents have forbidden you to talk to, but I am working assiduously to change their opinion of me. I was thinking, if I
should just happen to come across an acquaintance while out
riding the fields to the west, I would be bound by the very narrow dictates of gentlemanly behavior to share my protection
with that acquaintance for the duration of the time our paths
lay in the same direction."

"I see." Another artless flush of color swept across her pale cheeks. "I do sometimes like to ride in the morning, before anyone else is up and about. Around seven in the morning, actually. I ride most often toward the village of Stoke Fleming, which lies a ways to the west."

"Ah. Perhaps I might see you out and about, though rumor has it we rakes never wake before the noon bell rings."

Finally her smile came back, somewhat subdued, but she was clearly happier and much more at ease. "Of course, you don't. How practical you are, Viscount Darling. Dartmouth society would be vastly disappointed if you did not live up to your scandalous reputation, at least a little."

"Ah." He made a self-deprecating little bow. "I had hoped to pass myself off with a degree of credit amongst strangers, but especially with you. For Emily's sake."

"For Emily's sake," she echoed.

"Then I will see you?"

The smile still hovered over those pitifully bitten lips. "Perhaps."

"Good enough. I give you good morning, Miss Burke."

"Good morning, Viscount Darling."

He touched his hat and left her staring at him in the sunshine.

CHAPTER 10

The invitation came early the next morning before Celia could even decide on the ride. A card from the Viscount Darling saying he and Commander McAlden had the pleasure of inviting the family for an afternoon picnic in the beautiful gardens at Glass Cottage. Lady Harriet Renning had been generous enough to consent to act as hostess, assuring the preparations would be all they ought to be.

Lady Caroline read the invitation with something between disapproval and admiration at their audacity. "Very clever, almost cunning, asking Harriet. She is a great friend of his mother, Countess of Cleeve, you know. Harriet does say Viscount Darling has pledged to reform himself for her sake. The Countess's not Harriet's. And he has behaved with perfect manners whilst he has been amongst us in Dartmouth."

Celia fought not to choke on her tea, but she was sure she had scalded the roof of her mouth.

Taking no notice, her mama tapped her teacup while she contemplated the invitation anew. "The whole family, and all your cousins from Widcombe have been invited. It is to be a family day. Informal. Harriet is no fool, so perhaps it will be conducted suitably, as it ought. I think I may safely rely upon her to make it so. And I admit, I am curious to see what your

Mrs. Marlowe has made of the place. Of course, her mother has exquisite taste. It was a famous place for parties in my grandmother's day. I know you have nothing but praises for Mrs. Marlowe, Celia, but she is your particular friend, so you see things with a friend's kindly eye—which is a lovely testament to your good nature, I'm sure. We do not want to be seen slighting Harriet, do we?"

"Well," was all Celia thought it prudent to say.

"We will go."

And so they did. Celia was a tangled skein of tension and loose ends. She knew Viscount Darling had done it for her and her alone. But had he done it in the hopes of being alone, of continuing their conversations? He had done it to give her the dark pleasure that blossomed within her like ripe fruit. *Fragaria vesca*. English strawberry.

Or had something else begun to happen? Had his reawakened better self begun to make inroads against the callous, blackmailing rake? It was too soon to know, but not too late to hope.

The carriage ride in the open barouche, with all the squirmings, muttering, and shrieks that younger brothers and sisters let out upon society for the day—like puppies spilled from a kennel—could make, only made the anticipation worse.

Their mother shushed and cuffed and lectured as they went. "This will not be a great day for you, I realize, Celia, as there will be only cousins present, but I would caution you, this occasion does not call for any deepening of acquaintance with our hosts. Particularly not with Commander McAlden. Sit still, Joseph. Don't look so at me, Celia. I've seen the way he looks at you. The way his eyes follow you. There is no reason for this alfresco party but to bring you into their sphere. He is not the kind of man who will make an acceptable husband. You must guard yourself."

Yes, from unworthy men. How ironic it had been Commander McAlden who had already given her the caution. But as her mother was unlikely to find any humor in the discovery, Celia kept the thought safely to herself.

As soon as they arrived, Lady Caroline commandeered the Commander for a tour of the house, and Celia was swept across the lawns with the children, who were more than ready for the gambol. Viscount Darling was there, along with Cousin Harriet and her family, and the Widcombe cousins, as well as the Glass Cottage staff, who already had the refreshments laid out on white, cloth-covered tables.

Walks through the gardens—which were still undergoing refurbishment, they were told—were the first order of the day. Celia found herself constantly called to by various relations who would ask after the identification of one plant or another. She gave her answers as loosely and commonly as possible— conscious of the Viscount, who always seemed to be standing at the periphery of the group—not quite ready to commit to the knowledge of the Latin species names.

No Latin, he had said that night. Even though he had since said he wanted to know more of her study, she was not quite ready to trust him with that. To trust him with her one true passion.

He made no attempt to speak to her, but walked with the group and, at turns, looked happy, then grave and concerned. To her, he did not seem himself, but then, neither did she in such a public place.

The afternoon wore on with predictability: polite, if stilted conversation at luncheon. Lady Caroline asked pointed questions about the Viscount's estranged relationship with his father. The Viscount parried her thrusts easily, with a lazy charm and a skilled ability to deflect the question. He politely abstained from making ripostes. Celia tried diligently to abstain from thinking he did so for her benefit. She wanted to dive under the table, or scream and stop it all, but she hadn't the courage.

At last, luncheon was done and Commander McAlden suggested a walk down the cliffs to the beach below, whereupon he delighted the boys by uncovering a smartly kept sailing dory and taking them out for a short sail about the bay. The more dignified of the adults remained above the cliffs, not braving the mildly treacherous walk down.

While the Commander and the Viscount were engaged in stepping the mast in the dory, Celia followed her sister, Julia, and a younger cousin, Hazel, over the rocks into the tide pools between them. Unobserved by the others, especially her mama, she peeled off her gloves and delighted in fishing bits of seaweed, winkles and whelks, empty shells and hermit crabs out of the shallow pools. She longed to tuck a piece of kelp into her pocket for later examination, but she knew from experience it would start to smell and dry out long before she had gotten it into a bowl.

"Miss Burke." Suddenly, Viscount Darling was beside her. Or at least he was close enough to speak to her directly.

"My lord?"

"Would you care to join me on the beach, Miss Burke?"

Julia and Hazel didn't notice. Without Celia to capture and pick up the slimy, moving, pinching bits, they soon lost interest and moved back to the sand near the water's edge to build a sand castle.

Celia followed him across the beach until they were a convenient distance from the children. He set his face to the sea, and the afternoon sunshine bounced off the water and gilded his skin with golden light. He was very much the lion, dressed in a tawny, golden brown coat and blazingly white linen. He had left off his hat in such an informal setting and his short hair ruffled in the breeze.

"Are you enjoying yourself, Miss Burke?"

"Yes, I thank you, my lord."

"Would you care to sit?"

She chose not to repeat her thanks, but simply spread her India patterned shawl on the warm sand and sat. But the Viscount didn't sit. He squatted down, easily balancing in a graceful crouch. "I've been waiting all afternoon to be able to speak to you. Finally, we are alone."

They were not, strictly speaking, alone. The children were ranged on the beach in front of them, but what he meant was that they were at a safe remove from all others. Their conversation, out in the open and still in sight of anyone who cared to look, could nevertheless be private.

Celia felt the sudden, hot singeing of her blood in anticipation. But the conversation began mundanely enough.

"How are you today?"

"Quite well, my lord," she lied. Her voice squeaked with tension. "And you?"

He nearly leveled her with the sudden blast of heat in his icy blue glance before he answered. "I am in hell, Miss Burke. I arranged an entire day just so I might be able to see you and I find that is all that I have been able to do—see you from a distance. I must accept it without complaint, knowing all the while, all I wanted was you. Knowing, even after you arrived, I must wait. I must play the host and bide my time. Knowing I would have to be a gentleman and keep my distance."

"Yes," was all she could say. It was enough to know she was not alone in her feelings, that he shared this yearning she could neither control nor govern. The only thing that could satisfy the yearning need was him—his smile, his charm, his presence, and his words.

"Lie down."

"I beg your—" She hesitated for a long moment, looking around at the others on the beach before she glanced back at him.

"They are well out of earshot," he assured her. His voice was full of a terse, tense energy that had been absent from their earlier . . . talks. "And I am six feet away from you."

She did as he asked. Her large brimmed straw bergère hat was crushed awkwardly at the back, so she unpinned the crown and tipped it forward to shade her face from the direct sun, and to keep her florid blushes hidden.

"Close your eyes. Go ahead. I'll keep watch."

She would have to trust him to keep her safe. It was a singularly daunting thought. Celia took one last look at his face, at his serious, tight-jawed expression, and closed her eyes. The moment she did, the sounds of the afternoon came alive in crystalline detail: the raucous cries of the gulls overhead, the gentle rhythmic lapping of the waves against the shore, the chattering of the children and the distant low hum of the grown-ups on the cliff tops above.

"Everyone else is so far away. And yet, I am as close as I can ever come to you." His voice had taken on the familiar low, seductive rumble.

Celia felt it vibrate through her, as if he had drawn a bow taut across her strings. She heard pain and regret in his voice, and knew it was the truth. No matter how attracted to him she was growing, he would never do. He was all she had ever wanted, but nothing she needed. And he had never talked of anything beyond these stolen, intoxicating moments of spoken intimacy.

Indeed, he had always indicated she was *not* for him. There was nothing for her, or for him, but what happened today, on this beach.

"Your mother is above on the cliffs, looking down at us, disapproving that I am so near, and yet seeing that I am far enough apart from you, she cannot object. I keep my eyes on the children at the water's edge, even though I would rather be looking at you. At the contours of your body as you are stretched out so beautifully in the sunlight."

Celia took a deep breath to calm the tumult of feelings darting about within her. She felt strangely exposed, though she was fully clothed and the skirts of her muslin dress covered her ankles and the tops of her kid halfboots. The sun pressed her down into the sand, turning her limbs to liquid heat.

"Tell me, is your skin as soft to the touch as it looks, Miss Burke?"

"I hardly know." She did not know if he could hear her whisper, but she could not bring herself to speak any louder without being able to see who heard.

He answered, "Then you must touch it, and feel it for me and let me know. You must put your hand along the skin of your cheek and tell me if it is softer than the silk of your gowns."

"It is . . . like cotton, not like silk."

"Ah, so soft. So warm and smooth. Familiar. I wish I could touch your cheek and feel your skin. I want to touch you everywhere and feel the soft warmth of your skin under my hands. Under my lips. And under my body."

A pulse moved across her skin as if he had touched her, a skittering sensation that ran down her neck and across her peaking breasts.

"I can see you shiver and tremble. My body shakes as well. With need."

His voice sounded closer and she felt the shifting of the sand as he moved nearer, but still stayed out of reach.

"Oh God, Celia." His voice was a low howl of pain. "I want you so badly, it's choking me."

His use of her name shivered a tart, sweet thrill through her. Pleasure, delight, and satisfaction blossomed within her, unfurling their petals downward through her body and into her soul.

"Celia, I . . . I never intended—"

He broke off and she turned her face towards him, under the wide brim of the hat, straining for the sound of his voice. Looking for something, anything to give her an indication of what he was thinking. And what he was feeling.

"No, please. Don't get up, don't move. I couldn't bear for this to end. For the day to be over and you to walk away, just when I have you to myself. Stay, a few moments longer, please. Stay."

She subsided, closing her eyes back under her hat. She could hear a movement of fabric, a sound as if he were chafing his palms along the thigh of his breeches. Awareness danced under the skin of her own hands.

"Your hand lies atop your dress, just out of my reach, over your smooth belly. If you press down, through the layers of fabric and material, what will you feel? The fabric of your muslin gown. And under that? The ribbing of your stays? Are they long or short, your stays? Do they dip down between your hips?"

Without moving her hands, Celia could feel the line of her corset, cut high over her hips, but flowing lower, in an inverted vee on her belly. She could feel, could picture the line it drew across her skin, accentuating and pointing lower, just as he had guessed, between her thighs to the center of her sex.

"If you were to move your hand and stroke lower, could you feel the soft press of your smooth white belly beneath? If it were my hand spanning your waist, instead of yours, would I feel the slight flexing of your soft flesh?"

Her hand seemed to flex of its own accord where it lay against the soft muslin of her gown. Heat and something more, something conversely hard and needy budded to life within her, flooding her belly. Between her thighs, a tightness gathered into a pleasurable ache.

"Yes. Please, Celia. Move your hand for me. Stroke along your hips. Follow the edge of your stays for me. Show me how far they go. How close they would take me to your sweet heat."

She couldn't. She couldn't move so much as a finger. She didn't think she could even breathe. She felt her body clench of its own accord, deep inside, a pulsing shaft of pleasure so strong and sweet, she heard herself gasp.

"Yes. I can't help it. I want my hands to be where yours are.

I want to stroke down to discover the soft petals of your flesh. I want to feel you open and blossom in my hands. And more than my hands. I want to taste you, lick you, and tongue you there."

She made a sound she had never heard, half cry, half plea.

"I shock you with my wants, with my needs. But it is true, Celia. I want to touch you. I want to taste you. I want all of you. Under your skirts, on top of your stays, gloriously naked. I want you in every way I can imagine."

She was nearly panting and bit down hard on her lip to still the sound, echoing in her ears beneath the enveloping brim of the hat.

Viscount Darling bit off a sudden oath. "I must stop. We must stop. The boat draws near. But promise me, in another moment, when you rise, promise me that later tonight when you undress yourself, and one by one take off all your clothes, and lie down in your bed, that you will think of me. And that you will stroke your hands along the topography of your body, beneath your covers, on your bare skin, and you will think of me. That you will think of my hand in place of yours and think of how I want to trace the swell of your breasts, and find the sweet buds of your nipples. And how I would stroke them so softly and so carefully they would pucker sweetly beneath my fingers, ready for my touch, and for my mouth.

She swallowed, and tried to calm her breathing. One hand crept up to cover her mouth, to silence the sounds of her gasps, and the other came up to clutch the brim of the hat to make sure she stayed hidden.

My God, she ached. Ached, lying prostrate before him, fully clothed but naked to the soul beneath his regard. Aching for everything he spoke of, every word he said.

"You will, won't you? You'll promise me, after you've cupped your breasts, you'll abandon them and slide your hands down your ribs, across your belly, lower, lower until you can reach there, between your thighs to your sex. And you'll cup yourself, cover your sweet mound, and know that is where I want my hand to be. Know I want to feel the whisper of your skin as I part your soft, delicate flesh myself, and find your pearl and slide myself into the blissful heat of your slick sheath. Oh, God yes. Promise me, Celia. Promise me."

And then she knew he was gone. She felt the loss of his presence, his warmth, his comfort, before she registered the crunch of his boots against the sand.

"Miss Burke? She is asleep, I think." His voice came from far away.

Then the ground pounded with smaller feet, and she was half up as her brothers flung themselves upon her.

"Did you see us, Celia, did you see us? We went ever so far."

"And so fast. Commander McAlden let *me* take the tiller.

"And he let me hold the sheet—that's the rope, Celia. Did you know that?"

They were in her arms, on top of her like puppies, thank God, and she could hold them to her and squeeze them, and ruffle their hair and let her feelings and her need exhaust itself on their behalf.

Another moment or two, another exciting revelation about the boat ride, and Commander McAlden, scowling heavily, and the Viscount, his face an inscrutable blank, were there to escort them all back up the path winding through the shrubbery up the cliff.

Viscount Darling carried Julia, who was hot and tired from too long in the sun, while the Commander kept pace with the two boys. Once they had reached the top, and Viscount Darling had released Julia into her nurse's care, he turned to Celia. "Your promise, Miss Burke?"

She glanced at him for a brief moment, to find the intensity of his clear blue eyes piercing hers. "Yes, Viscount Darling, I promise."

And he was gone.

*　*　*

"I saw you talking to him again!" Mama did not even wait until the coach was under way and rolling away from the door.

As Commander McAlden had not spoken one word to her, Celia could not pretend she did not understand to whom her mother was referring. "Everyone saw, Mama."

"*That* is my point."

"And also mine. Viscount Darling was our host. You spoke to him. Cousin Harriet spoke to him, and I spoke to him. Hardly food for scandal. Everyone, and any one of our relations could see our conversation was a brief chat. Nothing clandestine and hardly more than a few minutes long."

Celia's mother's keen instinct for trouble would not allow her to be satisfied by such a reasonable answer. It did not fit in with her plans for being right. "You were lying down on the sand."

"It was a picnic, Mama. I didn't even speak to him then. I had my bergère hat over my face and I was well away from him."

"He sat near you."

"Did he?"

"Yes. And watched Julia play."

"Oh. I imagine he was thinking of his sister."

"Hmm. And what, pray tell, did you talk about?"

"The usual things: the weather, the scenery, the luncheon. His sister." It was the first reasonable explanation that came to mind, since she couldn't very well say, "We talked about not touching." Because that wasn't exactly right either. He had talked. He had told her about what it might be like to touch and be touched. But they hadn't touched, or done anything but speak.

So why did her flesh tingle on the inside of her arm? And why was her stomach all knotted up with tension and guilt, as if she had?

Her mama was saying something. "Still? But the family is out of mourning. He could not be out in society otherwise."

"Yes, but I think his sister's death has been a heavy loss to bear."

Mama raised her eyebrows in consideration of such a strange idea, that a young handsome rake could have any emotional depth beyond that of a teacup. "I think it shows an emotionalism unbecoming in a gentleman."

"Oh, please! For heaven's sake, Mama." The idea that Viscount Darling was behaving in an emotional way, was giving vent to his personal feelings was contrary to every fiber of his character, his being. Contrary to his perfectly controlled, perfectly calibrated intent.

"Celia!" Though it was full summer, her mother's tone had frost on it. "What has come over you? I pray you will control your language and yourself."

Viscount Darling had come over her. Metaphorically speaking.

Celia had never spoken to her mother so frankly, without thinking, but she must be firm. She must be resolute, if she could not always be daring. "I apologize, Mama. What I meant was, it was not as if he was weeping and gnashing his teeth in hysterics. He just wanted to speak of her with someone who had known her for the period he was away. He last saw her when she was, I suppose, something around eight years old. About Julia's age."

Her mama was taking this change in Celia, the newfound daring to speak out, rather well, all things considered. She actually seemed to be listening. She made a little moue of her mouth as she considered Celia's words.

"I forgot that. He ran off so long ago. I understand even, that for a long time his family did not know if he was alive or dead. Then the fever took Lady Emily before he could see her again, I suppose. I thank God every day, it wasn't a putrid fever and that you never contracted it. Though perhaps that was because Miss Hadley acted so wisely and so quickly in closing the school and sending all the girls home."

"Yes, Mama." How easily everyone had swallowed the necessary lies.

What of Viscount Darling? What had his father, the Earl of Cleeve told him? It was all so terribly confusing, the tangled crossing of present and past. But Celia couldn't think of the Viscount. Not in front of her mama, who could usually see what Celia was thinking just as clearly as if it had been written across her face—unless Celia said and acted as she expected.

"It was a lovely afternoon, was it not? But if you don't mind, Mama, I'm rather tired and when we get home I'd like to rest before dinner."

"Of course, my dear. You need to get your rest. We've got the Bancroft soiree on Tuesday next, followed by . . ."

But Celia wasn't listening. She wanted to lie down upon her bed. And think of other things.

CHAPTER 11

It was a beautiful day. The bright morning air was growing warm and a light breeze was playing across her face. It was an easy day to destroy herself.

She was going to meet him.

She had dressed with greater care than an early morning ride had ever before warranted, donning a severely cut redingote riding habit of deep, saturated blue to give herself a greater air of authority and intelligence. An illusion of control. Oh, she pretended it was nothing to be up and dressed in her best habit well before eight o'clock in the morning, but Bains wasn't fooled.

"Well, you're a sight. Here, let me pin that hat—you've got the angle wrong. And let me set in a peacock feather. A dash of color against the stiff white of the straw will balance beautifully with the white blaze of the waistcoat peeping out below the cut-away of the jacket. There. Your Viscount Darling will find you quite irresistibly fetching."

"He is not my Viscount Darling."

"And I'm the Queen's cat."

"Bains."

"Don't you Bains me, miss. I've eyes in my head same as

anyone else, and I can see you're going out to meet someone, and I can see that Viscount's been talking you into being charmed. Dead sister, my fanny, if you don't mind my saying. He's doing you up right proper, he is."

"Bains!"

"You mind me well, miss. For all he looks like sunshine, that man is chock-full of dark trouble and wants nothing more than to lead you right into it. And nothing good, *nothing* e'er came of a girl walking out without her mother, especially *your* lady mother, knowing about it. No good a'tall."

Oh, but the lure of that dark was irresistible. "And that, my dear Bains, is why I am to go *riding*."

Despite her sassy words to Bains, Celia had never before approached her morning ride with so much trepidation. Not even in the days when she had most often ridden out with Lizzie, and never known what they might be getting into. But with Lizzie, she had always felt safe, because Lizzie was always up for whatever situation she might come across.

But Celia would have only herself to rely upon. Whatever confidence she had in her abilities to meet Viscount Darling with openness and honesty was undermined by her willingness to give in to his darkness, and the pleasures that awaited her. The low, familiar spiral of need coiled tight in her belly waiting for him to wind it tighter and at the same time give it ease.

About a mile past Jawbone Hill she saw him mounted on his huge hunter, but seated as comfortably as if he were in a library armchair. He appeared completely relaxed and at ease on his animal, a deep-chested Hanoverian. He was dressed in a dark forest green coat and fawn-colored breeches, which served to set off his golden complexion to perfection. His eyes looked bluer and clearer in the flat, gray light of the early morning. And he must have been bamming her about his schedule. He looked as fresh and cheerful as *Leucanthemum vulgare*, an oxeye daisy, as if he got up at the crack of dawn every day. No wonder he was considered a menace.

Her mouth had gone all cottony damp just looking at him. And yet, she was wearing her best blue redingote, sneaking out of the stables without an attendant groom, and placing herself in his trust.

"Well, good morning Miss Burke." He tipped his round-brimmed beaver hat to her. "What a delightful surprise to see you."

"Good morning, Viscount Darling. No need for subterfuge, I am quite alone."

"Are you really, Miss Burke? Do you think it wise? I assumed you would have ridden out with a groom, or I would not have suggested the outing. You ought to have a greater care for your personal safety." His words may have been cautionary, but his eyes were lit with mischievous delight.

"I thank you for your concern, Viscount Darling, but I have been riding alone over these lanes for well over ten years and not once has my personal safety ever been in jeopardy from anything but the occasional rainstorm. I am quite at home here."

He smiled, an enigmatic quirk of his lips that gave her little clue to what he was thinking but left her with the impression he was secretly amused. "Shall we? I thought we might ride out towards Dittisham, towards the ruins of the old Cistercian Abbey there. But I know you had spoken of Stoke Fleming."

"Oh, a ride to the ruins would be lovely. I've never been out to the site."

"Have you never been there before? It is only ten miles from Fair Prospect. I begin to understand the scope of your lack of experience of the world. We must remedy that."

"Viscount Darling. I thought we were in agreement that that is exactly what we are attempting to do." Her eyes skated across to him. "Within reason, of course."

"So straightforward." He shook his head at her. "Then I must be as well. I gave you my word, Miss Burke. I will not lay a hand on your person. You are quite safe with me."

Was she? She might be temporarily safe, but she was not safe from her own susceptibilities. She needed to remember herself with this man. What did Lizzie used to say? *Dear Celia—the wolf doesn't come to the door unless he is very, very hungry.*

The wolf turned his mount alongside her dappled gray mare. Celia thought they must look a picturesque pair: she on the gray, and so dark in coloring, and he, so light and bright on the black. They walked their horses sedately down the lane bordered by fieldstone walls for about a quarter mile before he spoke again.

"You were going along at a canter when I came upon you."

Did he think she had been anxious to see him? He would have been right. But she could not say so, of course.

"It was a good stretch of road for my mare. Mira prefers to run on the uphills."

"Miss Burke?" He frowned, shook his head, and smiled all at the same time. It was perfectly calibrated to charm. "Did you just roll your *R* when saying your horse's name?"

Celia felt a swath of heat scald its way across her cheeks and down her neck. "I'm sorry. She has got a more elegant name— Mirabula—it's from the Latin, *mirabula dictu*, which means . . . but I forgot. You don't care for Latin."

The Viscount smiled again and half closed his eyes.

It became, in a moment, difficult for her to swallow. Or breathe.

"I spoke from vanity. You must remember, I'm the sort of bounder who ran off from school before I could manage to achieve any competence in Latin."

Celia regarded him, with his leonine, sleepy-eyed gaze, for a long moment before she spoke. "You're not a bounder, Viscount Darling. I think you try very hard to let no one see behind the rather impressive fence of dissipation you've erected. Normally, people build a fence around their characters to keep people from being able to peer in, from seeing the nasty faults in their characters that actually exist. But you, Viscount Darling—I have the distinct impression you've erected your fence more as a stage upon which to advertise your dissipation, so no one might see over the fence and wonder at the steadfast character on the other side. But Emily never doubted that yours was a character of intelligence and loyalty, but above all, of truth."

It was the Viscount Darling's turn to be silent. He turned away towards the view so she could not read his expression. "Are you always so willfully kind, Miss Burke? You are making out my character to be rather better than it actually is, and I believe you do it as a kindness. You needn't."

"Yes I do need to remind you of who you are, for you seem to have forgotten. You have tried hard to forget. But as for myself, I do that, don't I? I want everything to be peaceful, everything to be at its best, everyone to be at their best and most good. It is a moral failing, this glossing, I know. I don't like to lie, but I give way to what you've called willful kindness, especially if the truth will cause unpleasantness." She looked down at her hands, spreading her fingers out palm up, as if she could still see the stains, the physical manifestation of her sins tattooed across her skin. "My only saving grace, if you can call it such, is that I am aware of my failing. I have not yet acquired the far deadlier habit of lying to myself. I know my faults well enough. I am only human."

Viscount Darling could only stare at her. At last, she had truly shocked him. Celia was glad. She had spoken too seriously, too truthfully, but she had nothing else with which to combat this man, except the truth. Her honesty, her openness must be her only defense to him.

"Is that enough, Miss Burke?" he finally asked, all traces of the devil-may-care bounder falling away. "Enough to know our faults to let ourselves forgive them?"

"I don't know. I do know other people are far more apt to forgive me than I deserve. I find it far harder to forgive myself than others seem to."

She saw it then, the sharpness in his eye that told her he was not going to be one of those people. Viscount Darling was a man who held people to account.

"Do you need forgiveness? Are there such faults in your character for which you must atone?"

"Yes." It frightened her to admit it to him, though she could not understand why. "But there are some faults for which no amount of atonement will ever suffice. For some wounds there is simply no balm."

He looked again off into the distance, either thinking about, or ignoring her words. She could not tell which. Then he turned to her, with the obvious design of making himself agreeable and charming. She had the impression a cloud had passed over the sun and the sky was clear again.

"You didn't say what it means—your mare's name."

"Oh. It means 'wonderful to say,' or something like that, but she also has some Spanish blood in her—Andalusian. The way she arches her neck up and seems to say, 'Look at me, look at me,' I rather thought the Spanish, *Mira, mira*, was more appropriate for her."

"Ingenious." He studied the mare for a moment. "Yes, I can see the Spanish influences in her confirmation. The strongly arched neck, and something almost delicate in the face. And I see what you mean. She seems to seek praise and attention as assiduously as you try to avoid them."

Compliments—they were his stock-in-trade. She felt heat prickle across her face. "Shall we let them run a bit?"

At his nod she eased her mare into an easy canter, and he

did the same, adjusting the huge black's pace to match her mount's. They spent a companionably silent mile before they drew the horses in to breeze and then to walk.

"Now tell me how is it a young lady of good family came to have such an extensive knowledge of Latin. It could not have been solely Miss Hadley's doing. I doubt my father would have approved of a course of study for young ladies that included Latin. As I recall from Emily's letters he was hesitant to let her go to school at all."

"Perhaps he felt he had already lost one child by sending him off to school. You left from school directly to enlist in the Marine Forces, did you not? But your father did not know you had done so. To him you were simply gone. Perhaps he did not want to endure the possibility of losing another."

He looked at her then—drew rein and halted, so he could peer at her—as if he could see through her, inside her head and read her thoughts. She wanted to throw up a hand to stop him, the way Bains did to avoid the evil eye. Only his eye wasn't evil, just too powerful for her comfort.

"How do you see things that way? How do you see me so clearly when I cannot divine my own thoughts with any accuracy? But you are very kind, willfully kind to consider my father in such a light."

"I am sorry if I intrude, but I was privileged to more of Emily's correspondence than just yours. You could not know it, but your father was very much interested, very much concerned, with you—and all his children, but you especially. Emily felt so anyway. She said he never stopped looking for you, even when he had told society he had given you up for lost. He never stopped looking, and in the end he found you, did he not?"

"He did. But it was too late for Emily by then. He did lose one of his children to school after all."

"Yes. I'm sorry, I had not considered that."

"But I did not bring you out riding on a beautiful summer day to talk of sad things, Miss Burke."

"You did not *bring* me out riding, Viscount Darling."

"Did I not? Did I not arrange to spend the morning riding with the most beautiful girl in Dartmouth?" The easy, effortless charm was back, as was the merry glint in his eye.

"You did not, because the most beautiful girl in Dartmouth is, if she has any sense, asleep in her bed at Number Four on the Undercliff Road at this time of day."

"You refer to your friend, Melissa Wainwright?"

"I do. Have you become acquainted with Miss Wainwright? Enough to know her direction?"

"Is that jealousy I hear, Miss Burke?"

"Is it? No, I don't intend . . . That is to say . . . I don't know." Her reaction to Viscount Darling's words had been purely instinctive. "I am not jealous of Miss Wainwright. Quite the opposite. I have been working to introduce her to Dartmouth society's notice."

"And by society, you mean the young men? Who cluster around *you* like moonstruck calves, I notice."

Was it his turn to be jealous? She did not think so.

"No. By society, I mean those young men's *mamas*, who will always have the greatest influence upon their sons, whether those sons care to admit it or not. It is their notice and approval Miss Wainwright must win before she will find herself an eligible parti."

"And you want her to be an eligible parti?"

"Yes, yes I do. Because that is what she wants. She longs to make a brilliant match."

"And what do you long for, Miss Burke?"

She kept her own counsel for a very long moment. "Anonymous notice. And a greater experience of the world."

"I begin to glimpse a secret bluestocking. That explains the Latin." His eyes told her he was teasing her.

"I admit I have made some study of Latin, but not a great deal. And my horse's name is just a quote from Virgil—the *Aeneid* is typical schoolboy study. And I might add, schoolgirl study as well, for despite your father's preferences, Miss Hadley's did have a course of classics study for girls who chose to take it. Emily was actually quite proficient—much more so than I—and she helped me quite a great deal. That was how we became friends—over *Robinia pseudoacacia umbraculifera*—that's the Latin name for false *Acacia*."

At the next turning of the lane, Viscount Darling directed them through the gap in the hedgerow. The low, stonewalled remnants of the abbey buildings came into view across the fields.

"You ride very well for a man who has spent his career on the water. But I recall in your letters, you said one of the things you missed about your life at sea was the horses and the riding. Emily commiserated with you quite keenly about that. I don't know if she told you in any of her letters, but we were not allowed to have horses at school. She always said she regretted not being able to explore the country around Bath properly, the way we could have if we had our horses. Of course, I did not have Mira then. But we walked a great deal. We enjoyed that."

"You are right. When I was aboard ship there was nary a horse to be found. I do remember Emily writing of her frustration at being without a mount as well. Though she did not say she longed to ride the country near Bath, I can easily imagine how she would have felt so. We grew up in Gloucestershire, north of Bath in the Cotswolds. It was beautiful countryside. Thank you for telling me that. It is nice to know she did not spend her entire time at school in misery."

Celia grew rather quiet at that. She hated, absolutely hated that she had not seen any sign of Emily's misery. Perhaps that is what he needed to hear?

"No, Viscount Darling. You should know Emily did not spend her days in misery. In fact, I cannot think of more than one other person in the whole world who had Emily's talent for being happy, for embracing life in all it's complicated, messy forms. I thought her happy. I know my friendship with her made *me* happy. If she was unhappy, she hid it well. It is a regret I shall carry with me always. I did not see her unhappiness, her despair, until it was far too late."

Darling looked for a moment as if she had struck a fist to his gut. "Then you know—do you?—how she died." His question held more the force of a statement.

"Yes." It was the barest whisper. Celia was astonished to find the hot clutch of pain welling in the back of her throat. No matter the passage of more than a year, sometimes the pain of Emily's death ached anew, like a deep wound that would not heal.

"And do you know why she threw herself off that bridge and smashed herself into the rocks below before she fell into the water?"

Celia could hear the rage bleeding into his voice. His horse jibed under him, shifting wide-eyed at the sudden tension emanating from the Viscount. He was fighting for control, both of the animal and of himself. She could feel his jagged emotions lash at her.

But she could not tell him. She could not bring herself to admit what she knew. It would change his view of Emily. It would change his view of *her*. Irrevocably.

She could *not* tell him.

"It pains me to say I don't know why, Viscount Darling. Emily was deeply troubled by something, but she had ceased to confide in me."

"Can you not imagine why that was, Miss Burke?" Viscount

Darling pulled to a halt, his eyes focusing on her with startling intensity.

"I have asked myself that question a thousand and one times since that April. I am sorry I cannot tell you more."

Del struggled to keep his equilibrium. He could feel black fury smoldering in his chest, threatening to erupt into violent rage. He reined his mount sharply away from her, and pitched himself from the saddle, lest he give in to the unholy urge to haul her up against him, crushing the pristine lace of her jabot in his fist, and shake the truth out of her. Before he wrapped his hand around her delicate neck, pressed down upon the fragile bones, and squeezed until she told him everything. Until she told him *why*.

"God damn your eyes." His jaw was clamped down so hard he gritted the words out through his teeth. "Tell me. Tell me the truth *now*, or so help me God, I'll—" He staggered down to a crouch, the monstrous rage growing into a ravenous pain in his gut.

She didn't—couldn't—speak. She stared at him, appalled at his language and the barely suppressed savagery in his voice, her eyes wide and all but rolling in fright.

But he would not, he could not relent. "Tell me, damn it," he ground at her. "Tell me why my sister, who was young and beautiful and good, should feel such a depth of misery and loneliness and devastation she would pitch herself off a bridge."

"I don't know," Celia cried. "Please. Don't you think I feel the same pain? I loved her, too. I loved her." She shouted, her words raw with anguish. "But she wouldn't confide in me. She told me nothing of her pain, or her misery. And I didn't see it. I'm sorry. I'm so sorry." She was crying, tears streaming down her face, her eyes burned red from the salt.

But he wouldn't soften, though pain clawed at his throat, raw and savage. It had to be said. "Were you her lover?"

Everything on her face spoke of shock—her eyes wide, her face pale, and her mouth open in a gasp. "Who told you that?" Her voice was the barest whisper. "No. No. I loved her like a sister."

"Emily did. Her letter to me, her last letter, said rumors had been put about concerning the two of you. That you were lovers. She was told you were the author of those rumors."

"Me! Emily thought *I*—? Oh my God." Her chest, which had been sobbing for breath, deflated as if the air had gone out of her sails. "No. No, Viscount Darling. I was not the author of such vile rumors. Who would make up such a lie about oneself?" Her voice was hollow and defeated, her innocence at a bitter end.

Del was not proud of himself for having accomplished the feat. He was torn between conflicting impulses—to press her for answers while she was so vulnerable—or to comfort her, and therefore himself, for their loss.

"Who would say something like that? Someone for whom it wasn't a lie."

"But it was—it is! Who would have told her that?"

"I don't know, Miss Burke. I simply don't know." He took a deep breath and picked up his hat, which had fallen, or he had inadvertently thrown, into the tall grass.

"Oh, my God. Poor, poor Emily."

Yes, poor Emily. And poor Miss Burke. She was still seated atop her mare, her face streaming wet with tears. She swiped the sleeve of her redingote across her nose. The gesture made her seem small and childish. Innocent. But she could not be. Not entirely.

"Did you know about the rumors?"

"Yes. Afterwards. When we read her note. It said—" She shook her head, unable, or unwilling to say what she must.

"You must tell me, Miss Burke. The time for willful kindness is past. The note?"

She looked at him with her red-rimmed eyes, as solemn and despairing as an angel. "Her suicide note."

It was remarkable how freshly he could feel anguish about something that had happened over a year ago. "I did not know she left one."

"She did. Otherwise we would not have known. I would have thought she had slipped and hit her head upon the rocks while she was out collecting plant specimens."

The image of Celia jumping across the rocks of the mill creek flashed through his mind. He remembered his surge of fright, his inexplicable mixture of rage and concern. He knew without a doubt it was because of Emily.

But Emily did not slip and fall. She had cast herself upon those rocks on purpose. "What did the note say?"

"That she killed herself because she was in love"—she firmed her wavering voice—"she was in love with me and could not live with me spurning her affections."

It came to him slowly, with the inexorable steadiness of a rising tide. Emily had wanted them to be lovers. They had more in common, he and Emily, than he could have ever thought. It was a painful truth, a physical ache so deep and so strong it spread throughout his body. He could not tell if it came from his head or his heart. He only knew it was so vast and so all consuming he could not think. It was like losing Emily all over again.

He had his answer, at last, but it brought him no peace. And Miss Burke looked anything but peaceful. She turned to stare back across the fields, the way they had come, as if unsure as to whether it was either safe, or preferable, to remain.

"Miss Burke, I owe you an apology."

She looked at him exactly the same way she had the first time he had apologized to her, solemn and still. "Did Emily truly believe I had started those rumors? Did you?"

"Emily's letters said she had been told by someone reliable, I assumed Miss Hadley, that you had been the source of the rumors. And I did. I did think you put them about, out of jealousy or . . . I don't know why. It doesn't matter why. I no longer believe it."

"It does matter. Is that the reason you decided to try and seduce me? So you could see if I was"—she searched for a word—"susceptible to you—to a man's words? A man's touch?"

He absolutely hated how stunningly perceptive she was. How she kept revealing truths about himself he had never recognized. He had never actively thought about the reason he had chosen to seduce Miss Burke as his revenge, but there it was.

She saw it on his face. "I'm going home." Her voice was ragged and weary. "I think our . . . association, for lack of a better term, is at an end. All bets are off. Isn't that what they say, Viscount Darling?"

"I am sorry. For my own sake, as well as Emily's. She would not like for us to part like this."

"Don't you *dare* use Emily's name again in that fashion. It's heartless. If what you say is true, if she truly thought so ill of me, she would *never* want us to even *speak* to each other." She reined her mare around. "Tell me one thing, Viscount Darling. Was any of it, was any part of what you said to me true?"

She wasn't referring to the current conversation, he knew. "We have both lied to each other."

"No. Every word *I* have spoken to you has been the truth. You just didn't believe it as such. While I took everything you said as the truth. And all of it has been lies."

"No. I wasn't lying when I said I was attracted to you. I wasn't lying when I said I wanted to touch you and kiss you and lie with you. I meant all of those things."

"Of course you did. *Every* man who says such things means it in that moment, Viscount Darling. But without—" She stopped herself. Then shook her head emphatically. "They mean nothing."

Del understood exactly what she was not saying. Something within him, a flicker of a flame, burst to life. But he had no time to consider it. If he did not stop her, she would go. And it was imperative, somehow, she not go.

"You didn't say you wanted *love*, Miss Burke. You said you wanted experience."

He stepped towards her to catch her rein, to keep her from flying from his side. "I can still give you that experience. I'd like to, if you will let me."

CHAPTER 12

"I may be provincial, Viscount Darling. But I am not stupid." Even through the pain she could feel anger brewing within her, dark and bitter. But perhaps not all of it should be directed at the Viscount. She had taken this ride, this journey with him, of her own accord.

You take a great chance I will remember I am a gentleman. She had been foolish, stupid even, to take such a chance. Yet even in the heat of the moment when she thought his boiling rage would spill over and scald them both, he had remembered he was a gentleman. He had acted as such. He had done nothing worse than scare the hairpins off her, and himself as well, with the uncomfortable truth.

It made such horrible sense. No wonder Emily would not speak to her of it. But even with such knowledge, the pain dulled not one whit. The guilt still ate at her, eroding her soul like acid.

But the Viscount Darling had behaved—in all but the swearing—as his better self. He had wrestled with his demons and mastered them. Perhaps she was not so foolish to trust her heart to make the right decision.

He looked up at her from her horse's head. "No, you're not

stupid at all. I also think you've liked the little experience we have shared thus far."

"Little?" Did he think it nothing, what they had shared? The feelings she had experienced?

"Oh, yes, my dear Miss Burke, very *little*. We have only scratched the surface of what lies between us, of the passions that lie dormant, waiting for us to awaken them."

Oh, he was good. Smooth. Impossibly handsome. Dangerous. Mostly that last, dangerous. Especially when she was emotionally exhausted, as limp as if she had been run through a mangle and hung out to dry.

"Please," he coaxed, "come walk with me. Nothing more. We'll tour the ruins, just as we ought."

"You're not going to . . . lose your temper again?"

"No. Not if you don't lose yours." His smile was gentle and reassuring.

"Perhaps." He *had* scared her earlier, even if he had controlled his rather impressive temper. "If you promise to remain a gentleman."

"Ah, but I'm not a gentleman, am I? That's what your mother has told you. And she's right, because if I were a gentleman I would never have noticed how perfectly your riding habit fits you. Nor would I let my gaze linger on the curve of your hip, or on the manifest curves of the rest of your body. If I were a gentleman, I would keep my eyes on your beautiful face and your beautiful, fathomless, dark eyes and I wouldn't let them linger on the delightfully full swell of your . . . habit."

His eyes flicked up to hers and then slowly slid down her body. She felt as if he had poured warm honey all over her. Celia pursed her lips together to keep her mouth from gaping open, but she could do nothing to calm the rapid tempo of her breath.

Oh, and he noticed that. He lowered his chin and looked at her with half-closed eyes, all drowsy, satisfied lion. She didn't know what to say, but she knew she wouldn't say anything to stop him. She had come to like it, this rush of sensation, this rush of heat pooling between her thighs. This heady feeling of wanting. It was exactly what she had come in search of. His words. His lovely words.

The heat in his eyes began to kindle a fire low inside her, deep in the place where sensation and emotion merged.

"Come, we can walk over there, between the walls to get out of the wind."

Celia dismounted and followed him at a slightly slower pace, walking the mare carefully over the uneven, wild grass.

"Perhaps," the Viscount asked over his shoulder, "before I open my mouth to reveal my inattentiveness in history as well as Latin, I should ask what you know about the Cistercians?"

Celia could not help the pleased smile curving her lips. It was the sort of offhand compliment perfectly calibrated to appeal to her. "I am no historian, either. I only remember the Dissolution of the Monasteries was sometime in the early sixteenth century. I assume that's what happened to this one. The monks driven out, the wealth and land confiscated and left empty. And the buildings falling little by little to the ravages of time, weather, and neglect."

"Well done." He took Mira's reins without touching Celia's hand and led the horses down the short bank. "I wonder, do you have any idea how perfectly your answer illustrates your character?"

"Please don't. I'm sure we've both had more than enough examination of characters for the day."

"A simple fact, a truth, told with imagination and empathy. More of your willful kindness."

"You did not seem to think it pleasing earlier."

"It grows on me." He gave her his tawny smile, all golden skin and flashing white teeth. He was doing his best to amuse and charm her. Silly that it was working so well.

He led the horses to the top of the slight rise, where the great buildings once stood, the low, stone-rubble walls marking the outline of the foundations. The wind, now that they were closer to the moorland, had picked up, tugging at her hat and whipping her skirts around her. Lest they be blown up over her head, Celia faced into the wind.

"How perfectly you appear thus."

"Buffeted?" Her laugh was nervous.

"Come then, down here," he directed, "out of the wind."

He found them a sunny spot between two buildings where enough of the walls remained to protect them from the wind.

"Oh, that's better." Celia put a hand up to reorient her tall round-brimmed hat.

"Yes." He tossed his own hat aside and leaned back against the wall.

She found a spot opposite him, careful to keep some distance between them. In the shelter of the walls, the sound of the wind gave way to quiet. The stones at her back were warm with the heat of the sun, and she leaned into them, as he had done. And as he had done, she removed her hat so she could tip her face up to the sun for a moment.

"I thought I liked you better up on the hill, with your skirts all pressed against you. But I like this better. You look all warm and tousled. Relaxed, as if you'd just come from bed. From my bed. Or perhaps," he smiled that wicked little grin that tipped up one corner of his mouth, "it's yours. Your virginal bed in your parents' home and I've snuck in, or climbed up through the window, to watch you and lay with you."

Celia put one hand out flat against the stone to anchor herself, to keep from floating away on such a romantic fantasy. She felt breathless and light, suspended almost, as if the earth had ceased to exert its pull upon her and had ceded all its gravity to Viscount Darling.

"May I, Miss Burke? May I speak to you like this?"

It was hard, even a little strange, to want to abandon herself to his pleasure, after all that had gone before. But he asked her with such polite, careful gravity, his attention, the promise of his focused regard, was like a balm.

"Yes." She swallowed and made her voice stronger. "Yes. Please."

He seemed to relax a little, the outline of his body softening, the lines of tension within him blurring a little. He filled his lungs with the fresh air and closed his own eyes for a moment. "I did like it when your skirts were pressed tight against your body. I could see you had legs." He smiled and opened his eyes to look at her again. "Will you? Will you gather your skirts up tight for me so I might see?" He swallowed and she was drawn by the strange vulnerability of his Adam's apple struggling in his neck.

She let her hat drop to the grass and began to gather up the fabric of the full skirts. Though his eyes appeared half closed, she saw in them an avid spark as she slowly fisted up the voluminous skirts. She was not the only one enthralled. She had the power to arouse him, just as thoroughly as he was arousing her, if she would but try. She wound her skirts around her wrist and tightened the fabric against the outline of her legs, slowly pulling the fabric taut.

"Yes." He didn't move, but pinned her against the wall with his lazy, intent stare as effectively as if he held her. "All I can think at the moment is how perfectly your body could be shaped by my hand."

He looked down to his open palm, as if amazed to still see it by his side, still empty. "How I'd like to put my hand at your waist and slowly move it upwards until I could shape the curve of your"—he hesitated and flicked his eyes away from her bodice and up to her eyes for only a moment before he swallowed hard—"breasts. Even through layers of fabric, through muslin and cotton and tanned leather gloves, I would be able to discern your shape. And imagine how you might look with that breast bared to my eyes and cupped by my hand."

Her hand came up to press against the hollow of her throat, as if her body already knew her pulse had begun to throb and pound under her skin. Her skin felt singed and prickly, exposed even under layers of covering fabric.

"My mind has gone further. It's racing ahead to count the number of buttons on the bodice of your riding jacket, and trying to figure out how best to undo each and every one of them."

Her gloved fingers clutched and tangled at the lace at her throat, to hold herself back, to keep from giving in to the yearning need to give herself wholly and unreservedly to him.

His voice dropped to a hoarse whisper. "Would you? Would you do it for me? Would you undo just one? Then I wouldn't have to wonder anymore how transparent the fabric of your chemisette underneath might be. If I could see the sliver of skin at your neckline? You always wear such demure gowns. Perhaps I might hope that a sporting costume might afford me a greater chance to see the beautiful curve of the hollow of your throat and the long delicate line of your collarbone, and the pearlescent gleam of your soft, white skin."

His words pierced her, body and soul, and she knew there was nothing she would not do if he asked her this way. Her breasts were already rising and falling with the shallow rapidity of her breath, her nipples pebbled hard against the inside of her stays. She looked down, away from his hungry lion's eyes, to her hands and began to pull off her tight leather riding gloves, until one after the other, she dropped them to the grass at her feet.

She closed her eyes and put her hand to the single closing button of the redingote jacket. It fell open easily, the large lapels catching and lifting in the breeze. Underneath was a silk waistcoat, with its line of double-breasted buttons. She undid only two, at the top, conscious of moving slowly so that her nervousness wouldn't show. But when her hand crept up to steady the lace of her jabot, tied in a demure bow at her throat, she could no longer pretend composure. Her hands—her entire body—trembled, pounding with excitement, yearning, and fear, as her fingers worked awkwardly to pull the lace away.

There was one small mother-of-pearl button at the close of the throat. With it finally undone, the soft, sheer batiste fell away from her collar, exposing only the hollow of her throat, though it felt as if it exposed much, much more. That small slide of flesh felt overly sensitive, scorched by the merest touch of the sunshine and whipped by the gentle breeze.

"More," he begged, his breath harsh in his throat.

Without taking her eyes from his face, from the intense, clear blue of his eyes as he watched her, she moved her shaking hands down to the next buttons. First one and then two were loose and undone, and the top of her stays was visible. Beneath, her breasts peaked, swollen and aching with need.

His eyes followed her hand, then looked her in the eyes to show her he wished there was a great deal more skin showing, before he tipped his head back against the wall.

"Show me, my Miss Burke. Show me the sweet flesh I can never have. Show me what I can only *dream* about at night. Every night."

"Please." Celia wasn't sure what she needed, except to make this neediness welling inside her go away. "I—"

"Put your small hand there—yes, there," his voice encouraged, "under your stays, feel the soft shape. Let your fingers find the tip, and put it between your finger and your thumb, squeeze it, just a little, just the barest bit, like I would. Oh, my God. Can you feel it? Does it feel good?"

"Yes." Her answer was a gasp.

"Celia." His breath was harsh and strained. "Pull the chemisette away. Let me see. Please."

She was as powerless to refuse his plea as he was to ask. She turned her head to the side and yanked the fabric wide. Her body felt on fire, hot and yearning for more. Every nerve, every feeling in her body was arching, reaching towards him.

"Yes, so pale and beautiful. Your breast fills your hand. Show me. Show me the sweet tip."

With one hand still holding the bunched linen tautly to the side, she arched her head back and offered her breast to his gaze.

"Celia. Oh, God, Celia. Look at me."

When she did, she was astonished at the gravity, the harsh sternness of his face. But he was not cold. His eyes blazed fire at her, a warmth she felt everywhere at once, until it coalesced in the sensitive, exposed flesh of her breast. She was astonished to find a tear sliding down her face.

"God, Celia. I'm sorry. Don't cry. Please, don't cry."

He didn't understand, he couldn't possibly understand the upwelling of emotion and need and desire. She had no words to explain.

He closed his eyes. "I'm no gentleman at all."

She pulled the loose sides of her shirt back together and held them there, clutching them closed, until there was not so much as a sliver of skin showing. "I don't believe you."

He opened his eyes, but for the first time, he looked away, unable to hold her gaze. "You ought to."

"No. Because if you weren't a gentleman, you wouldn't still be holding my horse, eight feet away from me. If you weren't a gentleman, we'd be rolling—" She couldn't bring herself to say the words. They created too vivid an image in her brain. A vivid, intimate picture of what might happen if the Viscount ever forgot himself enough to *do* all the things of which he spoke. To touch her and kiss her and stroke her. The things that made her feel daring and restless and wanting. Wanting to do more than just talk.

* * *

Del was stunned. There was no other word for how blindsided and nearly senseless he felt by the force of his need, his desire for her. For this woman he did not want, this girl he could not have.

He let his head fall back against the hard, uneven stones of the wall and rammed his thick skull hard against it, searching for the pain, seeking it even. Anything to keep him in place, anything to ground him to the spot where he stood. Anything to keep him from walking the five steps separating them and taking her bared breast into his hands and into his mouth and suckling her.

With a groan he turned, bracing one hand against the wall over his head, mooring himself there, keeping her from his sight and giving her a moment of privacy to restore her clothing to rights. He waited until he could no longer hear the rustling of fabric. "Are you all to rights?"

"Yes." Her voice was threadbare and too quiet.

He understood. He was, after all that, at a loss for words. "Thank you does not seem adequate for the occasion."

She smiled a little, with relief, he thought.

"We ought to go. I'll be missed."

She retrieved her mount and legged herself up into the saddle before he had collected himself to help her. In another moment she had the reins gathered in her hands, ready to move off. It was just as well. In his current state it was not safe for him to touch her, even something so innocuous as helping her into the saddle.

"Miss Burke." He stayed her with his voice, low and urgent. "May I see you again?" Even as he said the words, he wondered what exactly he was asking. What in hell, she would think he was asking. "I find I must—I want— Will you see me again?" *God's balls.* He'd been reduced to stammering entreaties.

"Yes." Typical, straightforward Celia. No more than one word, when just the one would suffice.

"Thank you, Miss Burke."

"Viscount Darling?"

"Yes?"

"Under the circumstances, don't you think . . . well, might you call me Celia? I think perhaps we've come a bit too far for Miss Burke."

"Yes." He smiled at her simple, sweet, straightforward logic. "I suppose we have come a bit far. But you see, while I may think of you as Celia, I may not call you that, else I might forget myself and slip and call you by your Christian name at the most inappropriate or inauspicious moment. Perhaps it can satisfy you to know you are Celia in my secret heart."

As soon as Del had escorted Celia as close as he dared to the gates of Fair Prospect, he turned and rode hell for leather back over the headland and home to Redlap Cove. He practically threw the reins to the stableboy, Jims, and made an immediate retreat into the sanctuary of the house. He was strung as taut as a halyard.

All because of a few hour's worth of privacy with Miss Burke.

Celia. Sweet God almighty, Celia.

He took the stairs two at a time, intent upon reaching the privacy of his bedchamber, though he was alone in the house. McAlden kept his own rooms in one of the secondary cottages on the property, but he had deemed Darling too august a guest to stay anywhere but in the spacious guest chambers of the main manor house. At the time, Del had thought it a ludicrous courtesy, but he was more than glad of the silence and privacy.

He slammed his way into the chamber, taking his frustration out on the inanimate doors when he had much rather be taking them out in another, far more carnal way.

Damn my eyes. Why did she have to be so beautiful? So god-damned beautiful it set his teeth on edge just looking at her? He knew deep in the empty, unused portions of his soul what he was doing was wrong, but was not able to stop himself.

God almighty, but he was a cad. He was bloody well able to stop himself. Trouble was, he didn't want to.

Not only was she beautiful, she was responsive. So sweetly responsive. And as she was, it seemed, so was he. Just the sight of her one day ago, on the sand, stretched before him in the hot, heavy sunshine like some pagan offering, had nearly done him in. And today. The mere thought of what she would look like when he had all her clothes off, naked and waiting beneath him, had him harder than a swivel gun and twice as likely to explode.

Del gritted his teeth and clenched his jaw hard, and still he could not withhold the surge of pleasure that brought his cock erect between his legs.

He leaned his head back against the door and closed his eyes, the better to envision her again. The bright sunlight of the morning had slanted across her face. It had highlighted the contrast of her pale, pink-tinged skin against the dusting of freckles and the dark sable of her hair blown across her face by the breeze. Her articulate hands had seemed so deceptively delicate as she peeled off her riding gloves. So slow and nimble at the buttons at her throat.

He couldn't withstand it any longer.

His own hand went unerringly down, his fingers making short work of the buttons at the flap of his breeches.

The memory of his first glimpse of her hidden flesh as the buttons of her habit came undone washed through him. She had quivered in anticipation as the tiny closures of her nearly translucent chemisette slipped apart to reveal the first sliver of soft white skin, her head tipping back against the wall at his words, exposing the long, long slide of her neck as it flowed down into the pale, glowing skin above her shift. Her throat working convulsively to swallow her fear and excitement as she let her fingers graze over her soft flesh and dip lower.

He took himself in hand and stroked up hard, pleasure coiling through him as he braced his legs apart and pushed his weight back into the stout panel of the door.

He could still envision the flush that began on her cheekbones when she closed her eyes and turned her face aside. The blush that spread slowly, like a smear of raspberry jam, across her chest as she slowly revealed one breast, uncovering it like a gift. Her beautiful naked breast, small and so perfectly round, held cradled by her quiescent fingers.

He stroked down, the friction of his fist tight on his cockstand, fierce and blissful. He reached down and palmed his balls. *God, yes.*

Her fingers so tentative as they searched out and found her nipple, and she felt the unexpected pleasure as she circled and then pinched the berry pink buds. The sound she had made as she plucked herself, the single note flying surprised from her open mouth, as if she had no idea. As if she'd never touched—

Aghh, God. The rapture spasmed through him as he rocked his hips and slammed back into the shivering door frame.

Celia. Sweet God, Celia.

CHAPTER 13

"Celia, where have you been? I expected you hours ago."
Her mama called out to her the minute Celia stepped into the back hallway.

How did she always, always, know?

"I was riding, Mama, and I lost track of the time." Celia did not stop, but kept walking towards the staircase.

"Celia." Lady Caroline's voice held all the cold and inexorable force of a glacier.

Celia came back to stand in the doorway.

"You did not take a groom with you."

"I went out early and wanted to be alone. I wanted time to myself."

Her mother looked at her in total silence for a long minute. "Pray, do not lie to me, Celia. Firstly, it is unbecoming in a lady and secondly, you do it poorly, for which, at this moment, I suppose I ought to be grateful."

Celia held her silence. There was no possible response.

"Were you with him?"

Celia didn't pretend to be evasive. Her mother was right—she wasn't very good at it. "I met Viscount Darling up on Jawbone Hill, if that's who you mean, and since I did not have a groom with me, he offered me his escort for the ride."

"I see."

"He was a perfect gentleman throughout."

"Really?"

"Yes." Celia felt the first welling of stubborn, irrational anger. "And I'm glad of it. I was glad of the opportunity to talk to him and get to know him better. I like him more as a friend than any twenty other young men whom you always seem so eager to promote. He was well-spoken and kind, and I don't know why you—"

"Of course you know why! He has made some efforts to re-pair his good name but he still has an unsavory reputation. A scandalous reputation. He drank to excess. He gambled. He consorted with all manner of—I will be blunt—reprobates, light-skirts, and criminals! Less than two weeks ago he was in-volved in a prize fight at a tavern on the waterfront. For years he had no regard for his family honor and he has, as yet, still not repaired his breech with them. And now it seems, out of all the rest of the world, he has developed a fascination for you. Can you tell me why?"

A fascination? Was that what it was? Whatever one called it, it was dark and needy and heady and confusing. And not something she could talk about with her mother.

"I don't know! Perhaps because I was his sister's friend. And because I have chosen to speak to him kindly about her."

"You cannot make me believe you spent an entire morning and afternoon riding about the countryside, doing nothing more than talking about a nineteen-year-old girl who suc-cumbed to a fever over a year ago."

"No. But while we did talk of other things, as well as his sis-ter, Emily, we did nothing else but talk. And I was glad for it. He was kind to me. He has lived a fascinating life."

Her mother took a deep fortifying breath before she went on. "Celia, you are nearly a woman grown. You are rapidly ap-proaching an age where your decisions will be all your own. I *beg* you to be cautious of this man. He ran away from his responsibilities to his family for years, abused his family's honor by taking up a profession unworthy of an heir and then, once he did come home, he spent all his time in idleness and dissipation."

"I disagree," Celia countered stubbornly. "He did not take up an unworthy profession. He was trying to earn his own reputation as an officer and a gentleman, rather than merely inherit it."

"Do you truly believe he has so quickly, in the space of less than a fortnight, reformed his character? He is not a fit companion for a gently bred young lady, no matter his fascination. Or perhaps, because of it."

"Mama, he has no fascination with me," Celia insisted, her voice rising in frustration. "He has not singled me out in any way. Our meeting was purely happenstance." She was lying. Twice in the space of one conversation with her mother. It was astonishing to realize how little she knew herself. Or how little control she seemed to have over herself. She could not stop the lies once they had flown from her mouth. They had already taken on a life of their own. "You make too much of nothing."

"Celia, I beg you. Do not lie to me and, please, for the love of God, do not take up the habit of lying to yourself."

For one monstrous moment, Celia did not know what to say or do. It was as if the words had come out of her own mouth, her own heart. Hadn't she said something nearly exactly the same to Viscount Darling?

Oh, God. Who had she become? What more of herself was she willing to give up for the bliss and the pleasure. The temporary pleasure he would give her only as long as his fascination lasted.

Before she could put any more lies into her mouth, Celia burst into tears.

"I'm so sorry, Mama." She had to speak around her gasping hiccups.

"My darling girl," her mother was there in a trice, enveloping her in her arms, "I understand, I do. I was young once. I can see he is a fascinating man. But he is also a dangerous man. If I cannot keep the danger from finding you, then I will do what I must. I will consult with your father, but I can see nothing for it, but a removal. I think it's time you had a season in London."

Celia had always protested any of her mother's plans to take her to London to show her off. If she must be bartered away like a prize ewe at the fair, Celia had always said, she'd much rather do so in the comfortable, secure environs of Devon and not in some dirty city.

Celia had never had a London season and at twenty, she felt a little old to be making a London come-out. But the city had many advantages, not the least of which was the residence of the Royal Society. Celia would also be able to pursue a number of publishers.

And Viscount Darling would not be there. She could put everything, the blackmail and the wager, behind her.

"Yes, please. Let us go to London."

Lady Caroline's eyes grew round with fresh worry. She had not expected compliance. "Oh my sweet child," she breathed. "It must be truly worse than I thought."

Lady Caroline and Celia settled into the Marquess and Marchioness of Widcombe's spacious town house at No. 51 Grosvenor Street in the heart of Mayfair. Lord Thomas was kept by pressing business from going with them. They took only Fells and Bains on the journey, and of course the coachman, Mr. Thaddeus Filberts, and a full complement of footmen. The journey was uneventful and enlivened only by the bickering between Mr. Filberts and Lady Caroline, who questioned and taxed the man with everything from his choice of roads to his decisions about when to change horses.

The entire reason for the discord could be laid to the single fact that Lady Caroline could not countenance a driver who was not named John Coachman. As Mr. Filberts had been with Lord Thomas since before Caroline became his lady wife, he had declined to force Mr. Filberts to go by a name not his own. Lady Caroline insisted, however, invariably calling him John Filberts Coachman, and he responded with all the appearance of due deference to Lady *Carlin*. It was such amicable disdain, and of such longstanding duration, they all regarded it as a comic relief from the tedium of driving.

Mr. Filberts, against the express wishes of Lady Caroline, chose to enter the city from the southwest, along Knightsbridge Road. To Celia, the city seemed to appear abruptly out of the fields. At Hyde Park Corner the noise and congestion, and the sheer amount of people was astonishing. Thousands and thousands were everywhere she looked. She saw horses and carriages of every shape and description. There was something new to see at every turn.

"Don't gawk, Celia dear." Mama chuckled.

But Celia could not stop herself. She had been right when she told Viscount Darling a greater experience of the world would probably only lead to greater confusion. How could so many different, strange people live cheek by jowl, without driving each other to utter distraction? And she hadn't yet even ventured out of the safe enclosure of the carriage!

Celia spent what daylight remained of their first day in London, and the greater part of the evening as well, ensconced in a window seat overlooking Grosvenor Street, watching everyone from the lamplighters to the housemaids go by. If she craned her neck hard, she could even catch a glimpse of Grosvenor Square at the corner. It was all so enormously diverting. Just what she needed to keep from thinking about leaving Viscount Darling and his icy-hot eyes behind.

But it did not exactly work. Thoughts of Viscount Darling,

his eyes—and especially his words—kept Celia up for more than one restless, sleepless night. Neither her mind nor her body would let go of their attachment to him. Under his influence her body had become a *terra incognita*, an unrecognizable landscape full of sensations and yearning needs she could neither control nor abate.

The Viscount might still be in Dartmouth, but her days were full of him. Everywhere she went, she scanned the crowd looking for his tall form. Every new thing she encountered, she wanted to tell him about. Every man she danced with, she wished was him. And so it was, only two days later, while she was out shopping with her mama and Bains on Oxford Street, she did not hear her name being called until someone touched her on the arm. When she did, her heart leapt against her ribs, like a bird in a cage.

"Why, Miss Burke, is that you? I called, but you did not answer."

"Oh, Melissa!" Celia put an involuntary hand to her chest to stem its pounding. "What an unexpected, but pleasant, surprise! What brings you to London? I thought you were quite settled in Dartmouth."

"I was about to ask the same of you, but it must be the same answer—society and fresh amusement! And shopping of course. Mrs. Turbot and I were just on our way into this drapers for some ribbon. You appear to be going there yourself."

"Yes, Mama is at the millinery shop just down the pavement, but Bains and I thought to look at some ribbon."

Celia accompanied Melissa and Bains inside, though she cared little about the merchandise.

Melissa cooed and billed over the various wares hung for their perusal. "Why look at this!" she called. "You must see this, Celia. It is the most perfect ribbon. The sherry color would be absolutely perfect for you. It so perfectly matches your eyes."

Celia smiled her thanks at the compliment. "You are too kind."

"In that width, you must have it to trim a bonnet, or even a gown—a sash perhaps. If they have it in a smaller width you must have it for a hair ribbon. Oh, it is so perfect, you must."

Celia could not join in Melissa's girlish enthusiasm. When had she outgrown gushing in rapture over ribbons? No she had not outgrown it at all. She had simply never indulged. Ribbons were hardly the things to give her raptures. And hardly the things for which she would part with her money.

Celia had been hoarding her pocket money in the hopes of being able to afford some short excursions to more scientific venues than a drapers. "I think not."

"Oh, come, I insist. It is too perfect to pass up."

"I'm afraid I must." Celia smiled politely and moved away, towards Bains.

Melissa would not let her go. "Why ever so?" she pouted. "There can be no reason you might not have it."

"There is a perfectly good reason. I have spent all my pocket monies for the quarter on other things, and so, I must practice the strictest economies."

From Melissa's look, Celia knew she did not believe her. How could it be Miss Burke, the daughter of Lady Caroline and Lord Thomas Burke, and the granddaughter of the Duke of Shafton, had less money than Melissa Wainwright, the natural daughter of somebody unknown, who had only a small independence?

Melissa was still eyeing Celia's reticule, as if she might snatch it to see for herself there were no coins within. "Well, I never. I could loan you the money."

Celia wasn't sure if she detected a hint of pleasure in Melissa's tone, but she could understand it. After all, Melissa would see their situations very differently. "No. I thank you, but I couldn't."

Was there hurt defiance in Melissa's eyes? Celia was res-olute. "Not only because I cannot know when I will be able to repay you, but also because it is my fault I have run through all my monies so foolishly and I must make myself feel my loss. You must make me feel it."

Melissa turned away, but she could not cover the vindictive triumph shining in her eyes at that moment. "All right. If you insist."

There were some things he could do, and things he could no longer do. Del found that he could no longer, with any sort of moral conscience, continue. He could not let himself spend another illicit minute alone with Celia Burke. His self-control was in tatters and his purpose in coming to Dartmouth had crumbled to dust at his feet.

But he couldn't stomach the thought of leaving, of quitting Dartmouth without some explanation on his part. He couldn't leave without seeing her and speaking to her once more. He owed her that much.

Perhaps he owed her more. Perhaps the reformation of his character he had announced in jest to Lady Harriet Renning wasn't as far-fetched as it had sounded when he had charmed his way into Celia's life. Perhaps it was time he meant it—for his own sake, not just Emily's.

Before he could talk himself into reconsidering the idea, or abandoning it altogether, Del took himself off to Dartmouth and up the lane to the door of Fair Prospect.

The butler, a younger man than he was accustomed to see-ing in so responsible a position, wasted no time in taking his card and showing him into Lord Thomas Burke's estate room. "Viscount Darling, my lord," the butler announced.

Lord Thomas Burke rose from behind his well-used desk, attired only in his shirtsleeves. "Thank you, Loring. Viscount Darling, forgive me for receiving you here so informally. I wasn't expecting visitors."

"Lord Thomas." Del bowed. "It is good of you to see me."

"A bit early to say that. It is, however, a surprise." Lord Thomas sat back down behind his desk and gestured to a chair. "What may I do for you?"

There was nothing for it. But the knot Del had expected to form in his throat was curiously absent. "I was hoping, my lord, you would do me the very great honor of permitting me to call upon your daughter."

"Call upon my daughter Celia?"

Del tried to keep a smile from curving his face. "Although Miss Julia is indeed a charming young lady, I believe Miss Burke is rather more appropriate for a man my age."

"Appropriateness, Viscount Darling, depends entirely upon one's point of view." Lord Thomas got up and silently poured himself a drink, though it was only one o'clock in the afternoon. He drank a portion of it and sat back down, giving Del a long, thorough look. "Did my daughter know of your plans to visit me?"

"No, sir. I thought it more appropriate"—the damn word lodged in his throat—"to secure your permission before I spoke to Miss Burke."

Lord Thomas kept his regard of Del steady while he took another meditative sip before he asked his next question. "Is my daughter aware of your regard, Viscount Darling?"

"I believe she is not unaware of it, sir."

Lord Thomas let out an inelegant snort. "I hadn't taken you for a politician. That was a very careful answer."

Del was losing confidence with every narrow stare. "My apologies, sir. I've never called upon a young lady's father before."

"No? At your age? Well, you're going on well enough. Care for a drink?" He gestured to the tray.

"I thank you, my lord, but no. I think it best to decline your offer."

"Another careful answer. You keep up this reformation of yours and your father will want you to stand for Parliament."

Del thought it best not to bring up his estrangement with his father, but Lord Thomas was proving himself to be as perceptive as his daughter. "That is a bit of a problem, isn't it?" He leaned back in his chair and regarded Del chillingly from under his brows. "I take it you are unaware that Miss Burke and Lady Caroline are currently away from home."

"I did not expect to be allowed the privilege of seeing Miss Burke solely on the strength of my request, my lord."

"They have left for an extended stay in London."

"London?" Del was flattened. She had gone to London? She, who had said she'd never been out of Dartmouth before. People would see her in London. Men—men he knew, men who had spent the past year carousing with him—would see her in London. His blood chilled another few degrees.

"Yes. Her mother, Lady Caroline, who can be counted an authority in these types of things, advised a removal to London. She detected in Celia the signs of a broken heart. Would you know anything about that, Viscount Darling?"

A pulse began to pound like a hammer along his temple. There was nothing prudent to say that would still be the truth. "Yes."

"Ah." Lord Thomas said nothing more, letting Del stew in the juices of his own conscience for a good long while.

"I apologize if I have indeed broken Miss Burke's heart through a misunderstanding. That was not my intention."

"Just what was your intention in coming to Dartmouth? I note you singled my daughter out rather quickly after your arrival."

"My intention was to find the girl who had been my sister's friend at school." That much, at least, was the truth.

"I see. Celia was deeply affected by your sister's death, Viscount Darling. Deeply grieved. Her letters home from school had been full of Lady Emily's praise, and she was so upset afterwards we feared for her health. She brooded, kept to herself, and when she did speak, she kept insisting, 'It makes no sense.' "

"I think we both found Emily's death particularly hard to bear."

"Yes. But as much as I may extend my sympathy for your loss, I cannot, and will not, countenance my daughter returning to the questionable health in which she came home from school a year and a half ago. Although Lady Caroline suspects only a lightly broken heart, I am of the opinion my Celia's distress runs deeper than a mere romantic misunderstanding. She has been deeply unhappy of late, and deeply secretive, neither of which are normally part of her character. I can only put it down to your influence."

"I see."

"I certainly hope you do, Viscount Darling, but to be clear, you may *not* call upon my daughter. Loring will show you out. Good day."

CHAPTER 14

London was improving upon Celia. Or rather, her opinion of London was improving with each new experience and each new opportunity, thanks to her mama having adopted town hours. After only one week of nightly social events—in Lady Caroline's opinion society was a bit thin at that time of year—her mother had taken to sleeping until at least noon.

That gave Celia more than enough time to explore all the places she chose, without her mother's infernal interference. With Bains at her side and the Marquess of Widcombe's town carriage at her disposal, every day brought a daring new adventure.

Celia hated the necessity of taking the emblazoned carriage, but she could hardly step out on Grosvenor Street and attempt to hire a hackney carriage without creating a scandal. But to make sure that no undue word got back to her mother about the rather scientific bent to her excursions, Celia felt obliged to engage in a little subterfuge. Bains—who was in high heaven riding through the streets of London in the elegant equipage with the tall glass windows, taking note of each and every fashionably dressed lady they passed—could be counted upon to suss out a shopping district or a warehouse, no matter where they went, and come home with a suitable purchase to thrill Lady Caroline.

Only the Royal Botanical Gardens, too far away at Kew, were beyond her reach. There was the collection of Sir Hans Sloane at Montague House, The Chelsea Physic Gardens and the Linnaean Society, but the best of all was the Royal Society, housed in Somerset House on the Strand.

At her first glimpse of the wide courtyard and imposing marble buildings of Somerset House, Celia nearly lost her courage to venture within such hallowed halls. The graveled courtyard, stretching towards the river, seemed enormous, the Society's offices at least a mile away across the expanse. The thought settled her—it would be a while still before they were actually there—she did not yet have to talk or explain herself. Bit by bit, meandering across the courtyard with Bains on her arm, Celia made it through the doors and into another world.

There was, she was ecstatic to find, that very afternoon a presentation by the famed astronomer Miss Caroline Herschel—whose work she had read in her uncle's copies of the *Philosophical Transactions of the Royal Society*—on her discovery of a comet. Even though she had no particular interest in astronomy, Celia chanced her mama's wrath and stayed, listening with rapt attention. However old and not handsome Miss Herschel might have been, she was greatly respected for the knowledge of her mind and the works she had authored. After listening to Miss Herschel's precise, German-accented account of her own late-in-life education and study, Celia felt emboldened. It really was possible to dare to try to take her place amongst scientists.

She had to wait an entire week before the next lecture, a discussion on botany. And so, when Friday finally brought the lecture by the Abbé Correa de Serra, the famed Portuguese botanist, who was to speak on the Fructification of Submersed Algae, Celia was prepared to be daring, and sat at the front of the hall, with her carefully packed portfolio of botanical drawings at her side.

The Abbé de Serra spoke knowledgeably, and at the end of his talk, he was happy to answer her questions regarding his observations and was enthusiastic when she offered her own.

Celia swallowed her burgeoning fears. "I have some drawings here, sir, my drawings of algae from Devon. Only freshwater species, you understand, but I have reason to believe they are quite different from the species you spoke of." Celia's fingers shook as she lifted her leather satchel and tried to pull out the correct sheet.

"Oh, how marvelous. You have drawings of your observations? Good, good. Put them up on the table, child, so I may look at them."

It was like a dream. Everything happened slowly like it was underwater and she was watching, except she was there, nearly jumping out of her skin with nervous excitement, feeling her clumsy, clammy fingers finally pull out the right sheet. "This is the drawing I thought you might want to see."

"Ahhh." The Abbé pushed his spectacles up on his forehead and squinted at her drawings, then pulled out his own notes to compare with them. Several other gentlemen at the table were looking as well, and one in particular picked up her drawings.

"Your pardon, sir." Celia didn't quite know what to do, but she didn't think she ought to snatch the drawings out of his hand.

"Oh, may I introduce you?" The Abbé waved his hand between them. "Senhora . . . ?"

"Oh, thank you, yes. Miss Celia Burke, of Dartmouth, Devon."

"I am the Abbé Correa de Serra, but you know that, and these gentlemen are Sir James Edward Smith—"

"Oh!" Celia dipped a rapid curtsy. "I have your *English*

Botany, Sir James. And of course Mr. William Hudson's *Flora Anglica*."

"Charmed, Miss Burke." He turned back to her drawings. "Interesting work."

"They are intended to be a survey of the freshwater plants of Devon, but I have only been collecting specimens for about one year, so far."

"A very good start, very good. Do you have accompanying text?"

"No, sir. My talent lies only in the drawings."

"And in the observing, I should think. Still, it is a good collection and a very valuable contribution. You have some algae here I think the Abbé will want a look at. Well drawn. Am I to understand this"—he pointed to one of the drawings—"is a drawing of the plant under microscopic inspection?"

"Yes, sir. The scale is just there."

"Have you shown these to a printer or a publisher?"

"No, Sir James. I-I hadn't any idea if they were any good. Or good enough to publish."

Sir James chuckled. "And now you know, Miss Burke. You might consider my publisher, Faulder on New Bond Street. He does a very credible job with good-colored plates like these. And knows just how to sell them to aristocratic libraries to pay for the expense of the printing."

Celia smiled but she could not make light of such libraries. Yes, they were often maintained and stocked for vanity's sake and the books never read, but where would she have been in her own education if not for the exceptionally well-stocked libraries of her father and uncles?

It was all so remarkable. She had spent years patiently and painstakingly preparing for this very moment. Now that it had arrived, she felt as if she would burst apart into a thousand shining pieces from the happiness welling within her.

Sir James was still looking through her work. "Yes, I would

advise you go see Faulder. I would be happy to send a letter of introduction with you by way of recommendation. But you must come to dine and meet some of the Fellows, if you are serious about your study."

"I thank you for the honor of the invitation, and I will see . . . That is, my father is not presently in London to accompany me, so I will need to defer to his . . ." She sounded like a child, not like the scientist she wanted to be. "I should very much like to meet more of the Fellows of the Society. I had the pleasure of hearing Sir Joseph Banks speak at the Linnaean Society meeting, on Tuesday last."

"Were you introduced to him?"

"No, Sir James."

"We must see to it."

"Sir James," the Abbé spoke up, "do look at this *Utricularia*. What do you call it?"

"Bladderwort, sir," Celia supplied.

"Yes, worts." He tried out the pronunciation. "A grouping of medicinal plants, yes? Just what I was saying about this misclassification, Sir James. Miss Burke, if I may be so bold, I should like to ask you to join me for a colloquium we shall be having soon on the relative merit of a strictly Linnaean system of classification. Are you familiar with the writing of Monsieur Jussieu . . ."

And thus, in the course of one afternoon, Celia was pleased to find herself, at last, a scientist.

Celia accompanied her mother to a musical evening at the home of Lady Edith Bancroft in such a good mood, nothing could possibly mar it. If mama noticed Celia's high spirits, and improved confidence, as certainly she must have, she made no remark and only congratulated herself on the success of her plan to bring Celia to London.

No sooner had they arrived than Celia saw a familiar figure.

Melissa Wainwright was present, already talking animatedly to a group of young people, clad in another lovely gown of rose silk similar to one of Celia's but in smaller proportions, and trimmed with lovely ivory ribbon and lace. It looked exceptionally like the one Bains had made in the chemise dress style out of stiff silk, with black trim.

Lady Caroline noticed too. "You must tell Bains of the compliment to her, with other young ladies copying your style of dress. She must have seen you in that gown in Dartmouth."

The more Celia looked, the more convinced she was that the dress, even trimmed in different colors, was not a copy. There was Bains' embroidery on the hem, her stock-in-trade, her calling card, cleverly disguised by the addition of bobbin lace.

Oh good Lord, had Melissa bought her cast-off dresses from the rag trader in Plymouth? Had Bains' sister even taken them that far? Was Melissa in such difficulty she was buying cast-off clothing? But what of her independence? What of her great show of having money that she could easily loan to Celia?

Celia pushed away the unpleasant thoughts. They felt too much like prying. Perhaps it was just a simple economy that Celia had never had the need, nor the wit, to utilize. But why did the sight of Melissa Wainwright wearing her cast-off clothing give her such a feeling of unease. She had gooseflesh up and down her arms, as if someone had walked over her grave.

Celia turned away from her mother to move into another room, away from Melissa when she caught sight of the familiar, stern face of Commander McAlden, splendidly handsome in his dress uniform of blue and gold braid. Celia realized he must be in London in some official capacity.

He came as soon as he saw them move beyond the reception line. Celia had an anxious flutter, wondering if her mother was going to snub the Commander, but after Lady Caroline shot a speaking glance at Celia, she gave him a curtsy.

Her mama needn't have worried. Celia was not altogether sure if Commander McAlden did not still scare her, despite the service he had performed for her. He was always so grim and determined looking, as if wherever he happened to be, was the last place he wanted to be, though she imagined he would look just as stern and ruthless on the deck of his ship.

"Commander McAlden," Lady Caroline said with one of her regal inclinations of her head.

"Lady Caroline. Miss Burke." He bowed to each one in turn. "I give you good evening."

"Good evening, Commander. What a pleasant surprise," Celia said.

"You honor me. I had not thought you in London."

"We arrived within the fortnight. I don't wonder why I should see you here tonight at a concert evening, where there will be no dancing."

"Is it so out of my nature to want to dance with a pretty girl?"

"Yes," she laughed. "Entirely out of your nature, I fear, but I do not say so to tax you with it."

"I thank you for not castigating me for it. Shall we sit?"

"Please." Celia took his arm as he led her into the next room, where the chairs were already set up for the concert. She was disappointed to find there was neither a thrill of anticipation nor the prickling awareness of him as a man. He might as well have been her father escorting her to her chair, for all the attraction she felt to him.

The truth was, she had never felt any attraction to Commander McAlden. Oh, he was handsome, in his tall, intimidating way. But she did not come alive when he was near—in fact until a few weeks ago, she had been hard-pressed to have more than a few words to say to him. She had rarely felt comfortable in his hard, unyielding presence. She felt wary of him.

He always appeared judgmental to her—always weighing out people's actions. Even though she had benefited from his judgment of his friend, Celia felt it would be a fearsome thing to disappoint Commander McAlden, and she did not want to be the woman who did.

The concert room was empty, with the exception of the musicians taking their places and warming up their instruments. She and the Commander sat—he one chair removed—in vacant chairs lined up along the wall.

"I feel it has been an age since I last saw you in Dartmouth, Commander. How long have you been in town?"

"Just over a fortnight. I was summoned from Dartmouth by the Admiralty on Navy business the evening of our picnic. What brings you here?"

"My mother brings me here, as indeed she brings me everywhere! A change of scenery and company, although I must say I much prefer the company of old friends." She smiled at him.

"Are we still old friends, Miss Burke? I feared our last conversation was uncomfortable for us both. Indeed, I feared the loss of two friends as a result."

"It may have been uncomfortable, but it was entirely necessary. And proved you a very good friend indeed."

"As Delacorte, that is Viscount Darling, has left the country as well, I see my fears were all for naught."

"I thank you. Thanks to you, I have survived my encounter with the dreaded Vile Viscount"—she smiled to show him she thought it a jest—"with my reputation intact." Yes, very much *virgo intacta*, though it might have been otherwise, if Viscount Darling had been the vile man he wanted them all to believe.

"Del has been my friend, my brother officer for many a year, Miss Burke. It pains me that such a temporary lapse in good behavior should form the whole of your opinion of him."

"Del?"

"Viscount Darling. His family name is Delacorte. We have

been . . . , that is, I have known him for a very long time. From his earliest time in the Marines, before he came into the title. It amuses both of us for me to call him by his name instead of his title."

"I know of his anonymous enlistment in the Marines and his working his way through the ranks to become an officer. I imagine he is justifiably proud to remember he was Colonel Delacorte entirely on his own merit."

"You see it exactly. That is what I mean by a temporary lapse. It is not in his true nature to be so cavalier with a person's honor. With either his own or yours."

"I understand, Commander, I do. You need not worry on the Viscount's account. I am sensible to the fact that he was under a great deal of duress regarding his sister's death. It was all a simple misunderstanding and it is done with now. You may rest easy."

The Commander's great chest heaved a sigh of relief. "Thank you. You are kindness itself, Miss Burke."

"You seemed surprised to see Commander McAlden this evening, but not unhappy."

Celia had grown used to her mother's recapping of the night's activities in the coach. At least she did so in the relative privacy of the carriage, instead of in the house, where every servant, however discrete, could hear.

"I did not know he had left Dartmouth. He said he was here at the behest of the Admiralty."

"You did not speak long."

"Commander McAlden is even worse at making idle conversation than I am. I don't think he is precisely shy, but he's not comfortable being social. It was kind of him—and correct—to greet us, for we are old acquaintances from Dartmouth." They had reached Widcombe house.

"Yes, quite correct," Mama agreed as the footman saw to the door. "How can one expect him to be comfortable? He was not born into society, but has had it thrust upon him as a result of his success at his profession."

"Do you think so?" Celia followed her mother up the short flight of steps.

"Undoubtedly. I have always said . . ."

Celia didn't hear the rest of it. She saw the folded letter waiting on the silver tray on top of the console table. And she knew.

She went cold, shivering in the summer heat, and remained in place, frozen to the spot, not daring to move any closer. But she must. Perhaps it was all in her head, this ridiculous foreboding, the dramatic notion of doom pounding in her chest.

She picked up the folded parchment and saw her name, MISS C. BURKE in a plain hand across the front. No direction. It must have been hand delivered.

Celia's hands shook as she broke the plain wax seal and unfolded the letter. It was almost exactly as the others.

> *To Miss C. Burke:*
>
> *Miss Burke, you cannot run away from your debts. If you do not wish the news of your illicit relationship with Emily Delacorte to forevermore mar your reputation, and if you do not want her decried as a suicide to your love, then you must pay for our silence. Time is running out. We have been patient with you. If the sum of FIVE hundred pounds is not delivered*

Five hundred pounds? Oh heavens above. How could he demand *more* when she hadn't had the last?

> *by Tuesday next at the following address—Powell's, George Alley—you will be ruined.*

He still wanted to see her ruined. Because she hadn't given him what he wanted, had she? She had run away from him and his ruinous seduction.

It had stopped being a game. She had come to trust him. She had come to think he trusted and cared for her. She had come to care for him too much. So much so, she had run away from him and from her feelings for him.

But he was back, to haunt and torment her again. God only knew what she was going to do.

CHAPTER 15

If doing the pretty in Dartmouth had been unpalatable, moving again in London society was nothing short of torture. Del had forgotten that among the ton, openness and honesty were lost arts. He had already spent a couple of fruitless nights haunting the ballrooms and ducking desperate mamas and equally incautious young married ladies, in search of Miss Celia Burke, damning his unsavory reputation that kept some doors closed to him.

He had discovered she stayed at her uncle's, the Marquess of Widcombe's house on Grosvenor Street, but he could hardly walk up and knock on the brass-plated door after Lord Thomas denied his permission. Del had been very clearly warned off the man's daughter. He would have to find Celia in a way that made it look entirely by chance.

He avoided examining his motive in this finding of Miss Burke. It was a compulsion, he knew, and an entirely illogical one. He had impulsively declared his intent to her father and been repulsed. If he continued to search her out, to press his suit, he had to understand what he was doing. He was making a legitimate offer for her, even though he'd already been turned down.

It made no sense, no matter how he looked at it. He shook

his head to better concentrate on his driving, before he drove up the back of a brewer's dray. Del had his pair of tall chestnuts under harness in an attempt to make his way across the busiest traffic in London. He was on his way to visit Gardiner's Saddlery in Long Acre for new equipage for the curricle. Alexander Gardiner was too good a saddler to pass over simply for the sin of keeping the patronage of Darling's estranged father. Not even Del's sense of resentment could run so deep as to deny himself the services of a superior craftsman. And it was a good day for driving. He and the horses were enjoying the seasonably cool breeze, when he saw Hugh McAlden, resplendent in his blues, walking away from the Admiralty Building in Whitehall towards Charing Cross.

"Hugh!" Del called and tooled his team to the curb. "Well met. What the devil have you been up to?"

McAlden gestured inelegantly to his uniform and hitched a thumb back at the Admiralty. "Waiting upon Sir Charles Middleton, who has yet another dicey proposition for me. But I might ask the same of you. What brings you to London? I thought you had gone off to drink your way through Gloucestershire."

"I decided to give London's charms another try."

"In July? You expect me to believe that?"

Del gave him a long, thorny look.

McAlden gave the thorn right back. "It had better not have anything to do with a certain charming young lady I had the pleasure of seeing last night."

The hackles Del didn't know he had rose along his spine. "I doubt it."

"Do you? It was charming how Miss Burke asked after all our mutual acquaintance in Dartmouth. With one notable exception. You." McAlden's brow arched into its own abbreviated version of a sneer. "Care to tell me why that might be?"

"No."

"Really, Del, you ought to have gotten over being such a

complete ass. But I suppose I should thank you for making me look so much more the gentleman to the lady as a result."

Del felt rather than heard the growl that came out of his throat. He was also halfway out of his seat in the curricle before he knew it. "Don't even think about it, Hugh."

"Why not, Del?"

Del wanted to wipe that superior, amused expression off Hugh's face with his fist. "None of your sodding business."

"I'm making it my business. Let's just say, I've decided to use my conscience to make up for your lack thereof, so I've made Miss Burke, and specifically your interest in her, my business. You're wrong about her, Del. Dead wrong."

"Not that it's any of your fucking business, McAlden, but I already know that."

"Do you?" McAlden stepped back a pace to regard Del anew.

"Just stay away from her, Hugh."

McAlden's smile dawned so slowly Del almost missed it. "So that's the way the wind blows, does it?"

Del could hear his friend's laughter all the way past Charing Cross.

It had become imperative Celia sell her drawings for a book. Even if, because she had no text to accompany the illustrations, she had to sell the drawings to a Fellow of the Royal Society, so he could publish his own book with her illustrations. Or perhaps she should be offering, for a fee, her service in making the drawings. Sir James Edward Smith had had his illustrations for *English Botany* made by Mr. Sowerby of the Linnaean Society. She ought to be able to find an arrangement similar to that.

Thus, the day was more important than ever. She dressed plainly, in her best redingote, to help combat the clammy grip of her awkwardness, the panicky feeling of shyness beginning to worm its way into her belly at the thought of speaking before so many people. Not that she knew how many people were likely to come to the colloquium, but if she did well, and impressed the assembled scholars, she might be able to find her way out of this nightmare. She might be able to pay Viscount Darling off and be done.

Lord, she had no time for the mixture of disappointment, regret, and anxiety at the mere thought of him. She would get over him. She would conquer this seemingly insurmountable difficulty, if she would but concentrate on one step at a time. First things first.

She and Bains took the Widcombe carriage as far as Beaufort Buildings, and got out to walk the rest of the way. Bains had picked up Celia's unease and could see her hesitation as they turned through the gates of Somerset House into the vast courtyard.

"I don't like it, miss. You do this, you go in there and talk all official like and you're sure to blow the gab. Your lady mother'll have it in her ears in no time."

"I know." Celia let out the breath she hadn't realized she was holding. "But I've no choice. Not that I want one. I want to do this, Bains. I want to be a renowned, published botanist, and this is what it's going to take, mother or no mother."

She tucked her head down and walked on resolutely. She would be resolute. She was even going to be daring.

The gray stone of the steps appeared before her eyes too quickly. She was there. It was time. There seemed to be an awful lot of people—men—brushing past, turning her this way and that, coattails flying by. She clutched her portfolio tighter.

"May I be of some assistance?" A soberly dressed porter stood next to his dais.

Celia took a deep breath. "I am here to take part in a colloquium on the merits of plant classification systems."

"Ah, Miss Burke?"

"Yes, Miss Celia Burke."

"Yes, Miss Burke, it is an honor. I've been expecting you. Welcome to the Royal Society." He bowed to her. "Right this way, please."

His business done at Gardiner's Saddlery, Del headed back down Drury Lane for the Strand, so he might take advantage of the relative fresh—and in London the term *fresh* was definitely relative—breeze off the river.

As he turned his horses and wove into the traffic on the Strand, he passed the gates of Somerset House. Something familiar, the flap of a jacket and skirt behind the long-legged stride of a countrywoman, caught his eye. He recognized Celia instantly by her dark blue redingote. By God, it would be a long time before he ever forgot that ensemble.

Miss Burke was in earnest conversation with her maid, who stood still for a moment while Miss Burke, glancing left and right in a furtive fashion, marched across the courtyard directly into Somerset House by the East Gate. An assignation? God's balls, it had taken her no time at all to forget him. But no, the maid was following, though reluctantly.

He drew the team to a halt and threw the reins to his tiger. "Walk them. I might be quite a while." To hell with his visit to the coffeehouse. He'd discovered this was a far more interesting development.

Del strode after Celia and her maid, keeping an eye on Bains as she trudged after Miss Burke, up the stairs and into the home of the Royal Society. Of course. The realization burst upon him like a thunderclap. Utterly stupid of him not to have looked there first.

It was not a place for clandestine trysts. The corridors were filled with an odd collection of middle-aged men, most of whom seemed to be headed to the east side of the building, where he was soon informed by the porter, an important scientific discussion was about to take place. The placard outside the hall read: A COLLOQUIUM ON THE COMPARATIVE MERITS OF CLASSIFICATION SYSTEMS OF PLANTS.

Del peered into the hall. It was filled with soberly dressed, and no doubt, learned Quaker gentlemen and their more finely dressed counterparts in the aristocracy, with a vicar sprinkled in here and there, all listening attentively as the scientist with the foreign accent standing at the front introduced his colleagues and his topic. Bains sat in a corner, looking unhappy and bored, holding Miss Burke's round-brimmed riding hat and gloves.

"The classification based solely on the Linnaean system is not sufficient . . . ," the foreigner droned on.

If he hadn't have been looking for her, Del might have missed her, she was so quiet and still. She sat at the front of the room, at the table of learned gentlemen. Miss Burke, the closet botanist. At the moment, not so closeted.

Del moved through the doorway and continued to watch Celia. She appeared as out of place amongst the men as a flamingo amongst crows. She was the youngest person present with the exception of one aristocrat's exotic page boy, and the only female.

Perhaps she wasn't such a flamingo. Not a hint of The Ravishing Miss Burke, great Local Beauty of Dartmouth could be seen. Behind the table, he could see none of the manifest curves the clever, tight tailoring of the jacket had revealed to him out on the moor. Her ensemble was dark in color, and severely masculine cut. She looked like the bluestockinged daughter of one of the sober, middle-class Quaker businessmen and not the granddaughter of a Duke and the niece of a Marquess.

She was giving the speaker her rapt attention. She brought to mind the look of the Renaissance painting of an enraptured Virgin Mary receiving the grace of God from the angel Gabriel. Her face was lit by an animation he had seen but rarely, the strange otherworldly glow of the true believer. And she was at a lecture, on the arcane nuances of plant classification.

"For an illustrative example of which I speak, I have the pleasure of introducing my talented colleague, Miss Burke, whose observational studies of the freshwater plants of Sussex, illustrate—"

There was his flamingo. Miss Burke turned an almost tropical color of pink as she leaned over to correct the speaker.

"Your pardon, Devon, the freshwater plants of Devon. As you can see here in this drawing of . . ."

And they were off again. Del wound his way into the back row and settled down to listen. His attention wandered, until the clear, low tones of Celia's alto could be heard clarifying some particular point of controversy or debate.

"As you can see by the microscopic examination of the bladder, although it is composed of a cell structure typical to plants, it acts more like a muscular organ . . ." She continued, calmly discussing "the different organs of reproduction present in both sexual and asexual reproduction . . ." Though her neck was covered with a lovely swath of color that disappeared under the lace of her chemisette.

He found it all devastatingly arousing.

It proved a strange, quick two hours, during which time he shifted frequently to ease the omnipresent tightness in his breeches, kept occasional track of Miss Burke's dozing maid, where she remained on her bench, and kept himself enormously entertained by imagining Miss Burke naked beneath him on that rather large polished table while she continued her low-voiced discussion about the organs of reproduction and the procreation of the species.

He did want to *procreate* with Miss Burke, didn't he? It was why he had called upon her father, and why he pursued her still, despite her father's pointed disapproval. Marriage.

At exactly two hours after the colloquium had begun, one of

the gentlemen at the table rang a little bell and the discussion came to an end. The doors opposite were opened by the porters and the assembly began to filter out, some talking in groups, still debating the merits of whatever side of the argument they favored. Del stood and planted himself in the middle of the corridor where she was sure to see him.

When Celia appeared, carried along like flotsam on the slowly moving tide of sober Quaker gentlemen and scientific lords, a beaming, beatific smile on her face, he felt her pleasure and pride in her accomplishment. She was, as Emily had insisted, an accomplished scientist. The clues to her passion had been there the whole time, from the first time he met her, that first night in the small cabinet room behind the library.

He pictured that room, the shelves behind her filled with vanilla-colored paper pamphlets—extracts, he would wager—which had all been published by the Royal Society.

And he thought of the barn with the tanks and the gleaming brass microscope, the intricate drawings and the bowl of lemons. He could picture her there, bent over her work, spending quiet hours absorbed in her tasks, then rising to wash her hands and rinse them in the juice of the lemons, scrubbing and rubbing them raw to remove the stain of the ink from her hands. It all made so much sense.

Del could feel the smile build across his face. She wasn't an actress at all, she was exactly as Emily had described: a shockingly well-educated, bluestocking scientist. The Ravishing Miss Burke, the future Viscountess Darling, was an eminent botanist.

Then she saw him.

"Miss Burke," he teased with a smile, "I rather think you have a lot to answer for."

The color and animation drained from her face in less time than it took him to reach her. She looked horrified—terrified—a metallic sheen of fear in her eyes.

He stepped forward and took her arm—aware of the fact

that it was the first time he had been able to do so, conscious of the very slight weight of her arm upon his. He could feel the tense tremors reverberate through her body. He put his other hand over hers to comfort her, and ease her shaking and show her she was in good hands. He stripped off his gloves to chafe and warm her skin, but her shaking grew rather than abated.

He led her out the backside of the building, where Somerset House faced the river, quickly taking her into a quiet, sunny spot where she could lean up against the wall, recover, and warm herself without his touching her. Though his hands prickled with the first feel of her hands beneath his, she did not seem to appreciate the experience, drawing her hands out of his at the first opportunity.

Del slowly backed away, giving her a foot or so of space between them. It seemed so far, when a week ago, he had felt it was barely room enough.

She would not look at him. "My maid is waiting at the entrance. She may grow worried if I don't appear."

"Of course. I won't keep you. But you need to recover yourself."

"Please, Viscount Darling. No one must know I'm here." She looked at him for the first time, her eyes shiny with fear.

How could she have come to be so afraid of him? She ought to know he loved her. She ought to have divined it with that remarkable insight of hers.

"I take it your parents do not know you're here?" he asked as gently as he could.

She shook her head mutely, growing more miserable and more guarded, if such a thing was possible. How had he ever thought she possessed a talent for subterfuge? Her neck was awash in nervous splotches of red. No actress, however skilled could fake such a level of genuine, wretched distress.

"My mother does not. Please, Viscount Darling, I can explain."

"Yes, I'm sure you can, though I doubt I will understand. What exactly was the topic today?"

She closed her eyes briefly. "The need for a system of morphological classification based on multiple biological characteristics."

Well. Clearly she was fully possessed of the necessary expertise. "How did you become involved in the colloquium? Without your mother's consent?"

She shrugged. "Because of my interest in botany."

Her whispered admission, more suitable to the confession of a secret addiction to opiates, or to murder, was so low he had to lean closer to hear her. Closer to her slight warmth, closer to her intoxicating scent.

He took her hand in his, turned it over to expose the fragile delicacy of her wrist, and raised it to his lips. Her skin was sweet, infinite softness. And lemons.

He could not stop his smile.

But she did not see it. "Please, Viscount Darling, please," she implored. "I don't have the money but I'll get it for you, I will. But I beg you not to tell anyone. Please."

How could he have thought her capable of such a grand deception when she clearly thought her life might be ruined if it were revealed she spent the afternoon with a roomful of learned Quakers? He shook his head at the thought. "How often do you come here?"

"Often. In the morning." Her eyes were still on her boots. Walking boots, not slippers. Such a countrywoman, even with her exquisite lace.

"Miss Burke. Celia." Something happened inside him at his use of her Christian name. In that moment she became his as she raised her face, her eyes red and shining with unshed tears. Not an elegant, picturesque weeper, his Celia. He wanted nothing more than to take her in his arms, hold her tight, and reassure her the world was not about to fall apart just because she had a scholarly interest in botany and had spoken in public about it. He was reminded they were still in public.

He stepped nearer, to shield her from the view of any passersby. Through the windows to the interior corridor he could see her maid anxiously peering through doorways.

"Your maid is looking for you. Here." He handed her a large handkerchief. "Mop up and off you go." He stifled all wants and desires, and settled for giving her shoulders a squeeze before turning her around and sending her off with a firm push between her shoulder blades.

"Please," she said over her shoulder, "promise me you won't tell anyone."

"Celia." How did she still have no idea how he felt about her? He would have to change that. "Go."

He drew back under an archway, away from the sunlight and out of sight of the window and watched her hurry away, vowing it would be the last time he sent her away from him. He would find a way around her father and his objections. He would make her happy, he would. He would find her that evening and tell her how he felt.

CHAPTER 16

Celia mumbled something to Bains about stepping out to speak to the Abbé and the dust swirling up from the courtyard, and blew her nose noisily into Viscount Darling's handkerchief to cover her distress.

They found the Widcombe coach at Exeter Change and Celia practically leapt in.

"What about the shopping, miss, so we'll have something to show?"

Celia was too upset and confused to think of logistics. "So we didn't find anything today. We can't be spending money every day." She shut her eyes to Bains' wounded countenance from her snappish tone. Oh Lord, but it was awful.

How had he found her? She had told no one, and she had begged the Abbé not to post her name anywhere, though he had chided her for being so easily swayed by society's opinion.

When had Viscount Darling come to London? She had heard nothing of it. She had been completely unprepared to see him standing in the doorway of the lecture hall. She had felt so proud, so happy, so full of accomplishment and pleasure at having earned her spot on the panel. She had thought of him, of his pride in having earned his rank as an officer in His Majesty's Marine Force and felt that she perfectly understood the need and the satisfaction in earning something completely on one's own, apart from any influence or assistance from family or relations.

And there he was, exactly as if she had conjured him. So tall and tawny in that room full of sober black, with his linen duster and his tan breeches. And that smile, so brilliant. And so knowing.

It was ludicrous, and unhelpful to her situation, that even now, when she was so badly embroiled with the man, she could not stop the direction of her wayward thoughts. Nor the reaction of her wayward body—to Viscount Darling, the man who continued to blackmail her. The man who had originally set out to purposefully torment and humiliate her. And now he had another piece of information with which to threaten her. To blackmail her.

She pressed the soft cotton handkerchief to her temple but she was instantly surrounded by the subtle scent of man. By his scent—horse and leather and spice. She let down the window and threw the hateful thing out the window as they turned the corner north onto Bond Street and into Mayfair.

"There now, miss," Bains said in conciliation. "You're looking the world better. Roses have come back to your cheeks. You looked so pale when you come out of that place, I thought for sure you'd come down with brain fever. Shut up with all that thinking and learning. Can't be good for a body. But now we've got you out, you look well enough."

"Thank you, Bains. I am sorry for my behavior, but I am quite fine now. You needn't fuss. And not a word to Lady Caroline, or we'll both have a flea in our ears and you'll be sent packing."

Bains took the warning in her stride. "No, miss. Never a word to Lady Caro. It's not worth my life to cross her."

"You're looking unnecessarily grim. This time I trust there won't be any threats of thrashings?" McAlden looked suitably formal in his blue full-dress uniform coat with the braid-edged white lapels.

"No." Del smiled. For the first time in a long time, he found himself missing his own scarlet officers' coat, which he had used to stand out in a crowd, like a badge of glory. Instead he was dressed in a somber double-breasted coat of black, with a subdued evening waistcoat of brocaded gold. "No thrashing. Nor dancing." He was reformed. He would be a model of decorum.

"Still averse? I find the activity grows on me, so don't bite my head off, or glower like some dog in the manger, when I ask Miss Burke to dance. She's the only one who doesn't make me feel like a fool. If you're too stubborn to dance with her, I don't see why I should have to follow suit."

"Agreed." Del put out his hand.

Hugh McAlden took it. "Agreed."

How apt Hugh had been. Del did feel very dog-in-the-manger, skulking about the edges of the emigré Contesse de l'Oise's ballroom, prowling in search of Celia. He didn't skulk, he—all right he was skulking, but like any good officer, he did it in the name of gathering intelligence. Her father *had* warned him off. It had to be careful going.

Del turned his back on the dance floor and moved towards the card room, an altogether safer haven for a man such as himself. He was there to make amends and promote himself with Celia's family and relations, not to fuel the fires of any other marriage-brokering mamas or their charges. He in particular wanted to avoid the notice of Celia's husband-hunting friend, that mercenary girl from Dartmouth, Miss Wainwright, who was holding court between him and the sanctuary of the card room.

As he passed just at the edge of earshot, he heard Miss Wainwright mention Celia's name, but her expression was not one of friendship or sympathy. There had been a satisfied, feline malice in her tiny little smile. He moved closer, edging backwards along the wall—skulking—until he could hear the snippets of conversation.

"Can't afford to be too choosy anymore, you know. She must get a husband. I had it from her myself only the other day."

He heard a murmur from one of the smaller tabbies.

"My dear, they're done up. Couldn't even buy a ribbon at the drapers. Must have sunk it all in one last desperate London push to see her married. She's been out in Dartmouth for years."

". . . so bad her father is not even here. They could only afford the two of them, and they stay by the charity of their relations at the Marquess of Widcombe's house."

"No!" chorused several attendees. They turned as one to see Celia, tense and white, dancing with Hugh.

"Even an officer, a professional man like Commander McAlden, is all she can hope for now. Unless of course, she traps some unsuspecting fellow. The Ravishing Miss Burke. Poor thing."

Del heard the delighted scorn in Melissa's voice and felt gutted. Her words had been like a knife to his hopes, his beliefs. But as he stood against the wall, struggling for equilibrium, it all began to make strange sense.

Lord Thomas had stayed in Dartmouth. Del had seen him there himself but not understood why. In his own pride, he had thought the man had stayed behind because they sought to remove Celia from his influence as soon as possible. And so they had, so she could come to London to be married.

But then why would Lord Thomas turn him off, when he had stated his honorable interest and intentions towards Celia? If she needed to be married off, why would they not marry her to him? He was certainly rich enough, if the Burkes were so desperate for money.

What had Celia said that afternoon, when he spoke to her at the Royal Society? *I don't have the money.*

What had she been admitting to? After all his doubts and

suspicions, had he been wrong about her? Had he been so drawn in by her, by her body and responsiveness, had he not known her words for lies? Jesus God. *She* could be his blackmailer. It was the perfect motive—she admitted she needed money.

God's balls. He had to get out of this place. He had to get out, where he could think.

Celia was not proud of herself. She had fallen apart under his scrutiny that afternoon. She had crumbled into a puddle of feminine tears instead of spitting in his eye. She had let him ruin her triumph.

It had to end. Celia could not, and would not spend another evening, or live another minute with the constant knot of worry eating away at her from the inside, draining all the life and happiness, all the purpose from her.

If he wanted her ruination, she would give it to him. She would go to him, and it would end.

She spent most of the endless night in meticulous, frightening preparation. The practical considerations nearly defeated her. She had never snuck out of her house in her life, even in Dartmouth, let alone in the middle of London and in the middle of the night. There had never been a need and she was not the type. She was not an adventurer. She had never so much as walked along a London street without an escort. And she was going to leave her home in the wee small hours of the morning, walk over half a mile without being detected, offer her body to her blackmailer, and somehow make it back before her absence was detected. *Oh, Lord.*

Celia would not give in to leg-weakening qualms. To the burning misery that would not abate. To despair.

First things first. She had to leave the house.

She briefly debated, and then rejected, the idea of enlisting Bains. She could not take her maid, or any other servant.

Should they be detected, she could bear the consequences for her own foolishness, but knew without a doubt, anyone caught helping her would be summarily sacked, without references. And Celia was anxious to ruin *only herself* in this hasty, ruinous endeavor.

At four o'clock in the morning, when the first faint stirrings of the summer dawn began to ease away the dark, Celia stole out. Dressed simply and covered entirely by a long, enveloping cloak, she let herself out the library window. She had a house key, but walking out the front door was too much of an advertisement of trouble, too bold. It seemed easier to slide the library window open and hop down the few feet to the narrow pavement between the houses. It also gave her a long moment, while her heart lodged itself in her throat, to adjust to the dim, mist-covered, early morning light and gather her courage.

She set off before she could think better of the plan. Up the few yards to the end of Grosvenor Street and then north along Grosvenor Square, where many of the mansions were still lit and people continued to socialize. Carriages rattled by, the beau monde on its drunken way home from balls, parties, and soirees.

She crossed back and forth across the street twice, to avoid groups of gentlemen strolling and carousing their way from one engagement to another, or making for the corners where hackney carriages might be found. Her footfalls echoed and kept time with the frantic beating of her heart.

Safely across, or rather around, since she kept to the outside of the park, and then a short block up North Audley, across Green Street to the chapel on the corner. Almost there. Another short block up Park Street, and finally she turned onto North Row and stood in front of Number Twenty-four.

The house was unattached, with walkways on either side going to the rear yard. It was not bright with lights, but neither did it still look shut up for the night. Celia scurried around to the back, looking at all the windows, hoping for one cracked to the breeze. But they were all let down from the top, and she could not reach them.

The half story below stairs had some minimal light. She went down the areaway stairs and peered through the window. The kitchens beyond the dim corridor were dark but she tried the knob. It opened silently under her hand.

The house was quiet, with no sound coming from any of the rooms, and no light from under the green baize door at the end of the hallway. She slipped inside cautiously, her heart pounding an erratic beat in her chest. After a long, frozen moment she found the courage to take first one step and then another and another, until she had eased herself quietly up the stairs to the entry hall. The steps creaked very little as she went up another two flights in the same painstaking fashion, until she found the bedchambers. She tried the door towards the back of the house and found a smallish, unadorned bedchamber, unoccupied. No Viscount Darling.

Oh, Lord, what if she found him with a woman in his bed?

For a long moment Celia wavered, her heart beating like a drum in her chest, and contemplated going back—giving up and going home before it was too late. But she was there. If she wanted some peace in her life, if she wanted her turmoil to end, she had to brazen it out. She had to be daring.

The next door she tried opened into a larger chamber and sitting room at the front of the house, facing North Row. Two deep leather armchairs sat near the hearth. In the adjoining room was a large bed with a very large body in it. A very large body with a very blond head. Viscount Darling.

Celia inched her way closer, each sound from her footfall, or rustle of her cloak amplified a hundredfold by the blood roaring in her ears. She heard a door shut downstairs, the first faint sounds of the house stirring to life. She had to do it now before it was too late.

"Viscount Darling?"

Then his voice came from the bed, gravelly and thick with sleep. "Bugger yourself, Gosling. It's too bloody early."

The whisper, normally just the sort of thing a man wanted to hear in the middle of the night, brought him reaching for the sword he no longer had at the ready. He felt even more naked without a weapon, but lack of clothing was the least of his worries. The voice, especially *that* voice, coming from his bedchamber, was wrong. All wrong.

"Who's there?" A slight rustle of cloth came from the other side of the bed. He waited while his eyes adjusted to the low light from the embers of the fire.

"Viscount Darling, it's Celia. Celia Burke."

As if he couldn't remember. As if he'd been busy seducing a hundred other chits by the name of Celia, had followed them across England, and might have trouble figuring out which one had crept into his bedchamber to stare at him naked in the wee small hours of the morning. As if she weren't standing less than four feet away. As if he couldn't smell her subtle fragrance from a mile away.

Del snatched up the sheets to cover his instantaneous reaction to her presence. "What are you doing here?" Other than staring rather fixedly at his sheets.

She swallowed and then nodded in her solemn way. "I've come to you."

"Come to me? What in God's name for? What is wrong?" He scrubbed a hand across his face and through his hair to bring himself fully awake. Celia Burke in his bedchamber, in the middle of the night was wrong. Very, very wrong. His mind hammered against his brain to get her out of there, while his body, still warm and relaxed from sleep, had a different scenario in mind.

His question was answered only by silence, and then the faint sound of fabric being arranged. No, disarranged.

"Jesus Christ. Stop." It was bad enough *he* had no clothes

on, but if she thought to put herself in a similar state . . . well it was more than he had bargained for. If he saw so much as a sliver of her soft, white skin— His mouth went dry at the thought. "I beg you, please stop."

He saw her white throat work as she swallowed. "I want it to end." Her hands were clenched into fists at her side. "It must end now." Tension and something worse, desperation, radiated out of her.

He heard her words and thought they were too much like Emily's. *I just want this pain to stop.*

Fear snaked through him like a lash. He held himself still though his eyes ranged over her. She had no weapon, no gun. A quick scan of the room proved the case atop the chest of drawers was still locked. He spoke quietly, almost gently. "You want what to end, Celia?"

"This. This standoff between us. This challenge, this bet. Your bet." She met his eyes steadily. "I've come to bargain the terms of my surrender."

His body relaxed enough to allow him to breathe again. "I don't understand."

"I am here to put an end to your threats. I will do this with you, I will lie with you, if you will promise me it will be the end of things between us. You can have your triumph. Then it will be over and we will never see or speak to each other again."

"No. That's not what I want at all."

"No? You've won. I don't have the money. I have no hopes of getting the money. But if you will promise, if you will swear on Emily's grave never to tell a soul, I will lie with you. I will let you ruin me in truth." Her voice sounded small and bitter. "After all the intimacies we have shared, I hardly think consummation will matter."

His brain latched fast to her words, knowing they were important, understanding they were vital, but she continued to loosen the neckline of her gown. The material bared a luminous swath of shoulder.

But it couldn't go on. He couldn't look at her. It was *not* right. "Who sent you? Who knows you're here?"

"No one. This is private, between you and me only. I'll do whatever you say. I'll give you whatever it is you want. I will trade you my body for the money. As long as you pledge, on your honor, that it will end tonight. I just want it to end."

She was saying the same thing over and over, but it wasn't making any sense. She pulled her arms out of the sleeves and pushed the gown down until it lay in a puddle at her feet. With the slightest shrug the translucent chemise would plummet to the floor, along with his chances for survival.

Damn his eyes. Already he could see the vivid pink outline of her nipples, peaked against the soft, sheer fabric of the chemise, beckoning him to taste and touch. Lower, along the slide of her belly, between the flare of her hips, a dark triangle. God help him.

He swallowed hard over the sudden dryness in his mouth, ignored the tightness in his belly, and willed his body to root itself to the bed so he could not move to her. "This isn't right. You shouldn't be here."

"I should. I want this ended."

It would end only in marriage. Or in tears. There was nothing else.

But what had she said? "What money? You'll trade your body for money?" Anger and disgust came at him like a slow, deliberate slap across his face. Then rage—black, towering rage, as abrupt and unruly as his arousal—erupted through him. "Have you sunk so low you'll whore yourself to me?" He threw the words at her, furious she would think so little of herself, and of him.

"If it will make you leave me alone, yes. I can't pay you any other way. Not even the drawings will bring enough." Her face was a pale oval of determination in the barely flickering light of the fire.

"Enough?"

"The five hundred pounds. All I can do is trade, but we both get what we want. You get my ruination, which you wanted from the start, and I get your silence."

Buying silence. It sounded all so bloody damned familiar. *God's balls.*

"Celia," he asked very carefully, tethering his anger on a very short, tight leash, "are you by any chance being black-mailed?"

"Of course I am!" She all but stamped her foot in frustration. "You know I am."

"I do now." The pieces slammed together in his brain, but they fit. God damn it, they fit. What a perfect, sodding mess. He had to get her out of there before the situation got any more complicated. Self-preservation made him look away and snatch up the raw silk banyan at the end of the bed. He whipped it around himself and moved quickly past her, to the window.

"How did you come?" Del pulled back the corner of the drape. The Marquess of Widcombe's carriage was not in the street. "Did you come alone?"

"I would hardly bring an entourage to an assignation, my lord." She crossed her arms under her breasts, stubbornly persistent.

"I am *not* your lord and this is *not* an assignation. Does anyone else know? Bains? Your coachman?"

"No, I did not advertise the fact I was planning to come here and offer you my virtue in exchange for my peace."

"How did you get here?"

"I walked."

He stopped. "You walked across Mayfair, by yourself at"— he glanced at the clock—"four o'clock in the morning? Are you mad, or do you think I am?" He gestured to the heap of fabric on the floor. "Put on your clothes. I'm taking you home."

"No." She shook her head stubbornly, yet he thought he could see a sheen of tears on her over-bright eyes. "No, I'm not going without your word."

"You have my word. I won't touch you. I'm taking you home. Put on your clothes. Please." He stalked over, scooped them up, and thrust them into her hands.

He dove into his dressing room and came up with suitable attire for prowling London's streets: dark breeches and old boots, linen shirt and a nondescript, baggy, long hunting coat. Nothing he could be seen in, but not being seen was of the essence. And just in case, he emptied the defensive contents of the wooden case on the chest of drawers into his pockets and waistband. Miss Burke may have been lucky on her trip to his door, but he wasn't the kind of man who relied upon luck.

He waited at the entrance to the dressing room. "Are you clothed?"

"Yes." It was a small whisper, but full of frustration.

He glanced out to make sure she was suitably covered before he opened the door to the corridor. "Gosling!"

Del picked up the voluminous cloak from the chair and wrapped it around her shoulders before he took her by the arm and steered her as quickly and quietly as possible, down the stairs.

Gosling appeared from the servants' rooms wearing a robe over his breeches. Celia pulled the cloak over her head and hid her face.

"May I be of any assistance, sir?"

"Yes, you can become deaf, dumb, and blind at this very moment, Gosling, but then I need you to look around and see if anyone followed her here."

"Done, sir." The butler's eyes never strayed towards Celia, remaining steadily on Del's face. "Will you require an unmarked carriage and a blind coachman, sir?"

"No. It will take too long and the fewer people who have to be struck with temporary blindness the better."

"Very good, sir."

"I'll wait in the kitchen for the all clear."

Celia glared at Del when he pushed her into a ladder-back chair in the kitchen. If he let himself touch her for too long, if he allowed himself any gentleness, he would be lost.

"How did you get in?"

"The door." She nodded at the areaway door behind him. "It wasn't locked."

"God's balls. Do you make a habit out of running about London by yourself in the middle of the night? You hardly seem the type." His anger should have been all for himself and his own carelessness, but all he could think was how small and how bitter she looked, closed off to him. He wanted to reach out and stroke the tangled curl that had fallen across her forehead out of her eye. And brush his fingers against the softness of her skin.

He sat on his hands.

She let out a mirthless wisp of a laugh. "No, I'm not the type, am I? But I did do it. I did climb out the library window and I did come all the way over here. Much good it did me. Here is the sum and total of my daring, at long last." She sighed.

"So you slid out Widcombe's library window alone? By yourself?" It was foolish daring, but daring, nonetheless.

"I told you." Her tone grew frustrated and impatient. "Yes, by myself."

Gosling came through the passageway. "All clear, sir. Though, I might recommend the back gate."

"My thoughts exactly." Del pulled Celia to her feet. "Let's get you home. Now."

He never let go of her arm as he hustled her through the darkened back garden, passed through the small mews, and headed down the alley. Dawn was broaching, making the streets less dangerous for them, but it was still deep darkness in the close confines of the alley.

Clever girl, she instinctively stayed close and he took her hand, small and cold, in his. He cut left halfway down the alley.

"No, it's this way." She tugged against his grip.

"I know where you live. We're going my way." He snagged her by the shoulder of her cloak and hauled her back beside him. He could feel the slight heat and smell the intoxicating scent of her body. They zigzagged their way across Mayfair in the early, blue-gray light of dawn. Every minute brought more light to see her face, to see the harsh circles under her eyes and see the bruised marks upon her lips. He wanted to tuck her up in bed, safe and sound. He wanted to tuck her up beneath him.

For half a moment he let himself picture what it would be like, what he would be doing right then, if he had simply thrown the covers back and taken her into his bed. If he had let her strip off the last barrier of her chemise and let him see the naked glory of her body. If he had her beneath him, pressed into those warm, rumpled sheets.

With his mind so occupied, he did not see them before it was almost too late.

"Well, looka here, mate. What a fine piece o' luck. Summ'uns a bit lost this fine morning."

CHAPTER 17

Del reeled Celia behind him as figures emerged from the purple mist. Two men, one hulking and the other whip lean, stepped forward from a side alley. He heard Celia's startled gasp, and felt her hands clutching at his arm and the back of his coat.

"Stay behind me," he instructed, keeping his eyes on the whippet, the one who had spoken, and letting the heady rush of violence, the need for a fight, sing into his veins. Then he smiled with his teeth, like the mad dog he was at that moment.

"I do believe you will live to regret this, gentlemen. *If* you live." He pulled the two pistols he'd shoved into his waistband clear and sighted on the leaner, more feral man, who had spoken. He was bound to be the brains of the operation.

The standoff, such as it was, lasted only a few more seconds. Del cocked back the hammers. "Oh, for fuck's sake. Run away. Now!" he roared at them.

They backed away and then turned to clatter down the alley, reabsorbed by the gray mist, disappearing as suddenly and silently as they had appeared.

Del shoved one of the pistols back into his waistband and turned for Celia.

She stepped away from him, stumbling on the back of her gown. Going down into a crouch, she held her hands out in front of her. Her eyes were huge in her face. She looked at him as if she'd only just come to realize he was truly dangerous. "I-I didn't know you had guns," she stammered.

"That's the whole point of having them. Come on." He pulled her up by the hand. "You don't belong in this alley."

"I wouldn't be in this alley if you hadn't led me here," she muttered through her teeth. Shock was wearing holes in her fright.

He kept her to his left and held the gun with his right, more careful of the turnings and cross alleys. They cut down Adams Mews, still locked up tight, its aristocratic patrons in their beds for the night, then dashed across Charles Street and into Bishop's Yard, behind Grosvenor Street. At the back of the yard, he stowed the second gun in the pocket of his big coat and jumped the brick wall, putting a hand down to hoist her up after him. She was strong and nimble enough to climb over easily. All that clambering about on hillsides and in streams, no doubt.

A line of shops and houses fronted Mount Row and the mews at the back of Grosvenor Street. Another fifty feet and they hauled up to the stable gate of Widcombe House.

It was a mercy the small gate set in the large stable door was unlocked. The coachmen must have stepped out for a pint or two.

Once he had her safely inside, Celia let go of his hand and leaned against the wall of the pass-through corridor to catch her breath. Del felt his own lungs expand with relief. At least if they were found on her uncle's property, it would be only a private scandal. *That* he could deal with.

"All right now? Come, I'll see you in."

"No." She straightened up and tried to draw herself together. "Are you planning on going back the same way, or shall I lead you out the front?'

"I'll see you in first. Then the front." He indicated the way forward with a toss of his head. The early summer light had begun to chase away the mist, though the garden was bathed in dim, flat white light. It was still quiet as they made their cautious way along the small walkway between the houses and came to a stop beneath the open library window.

"Lock it, once you're in."

"Yes. The gate's just there. There's a latch on this side." She stopped and indicated a wrought iron portal a few feet ahead.

"Right." He took a step towards the gate. He should have kept going through the gate, but he didn't. With all the blood-lust, the suppressed violence and hunger, the need, and God, the intoxicating smell of her roaring through his veins, he turned back to her, crowded her hard to the brick side of the house, and kissed her dead on the mouth.

The breath whooshed out of her lungs as her back hit the wall and his lips covered hers. He didn't touch her anywhere else. His hands were fisted into balls on either side of her head against the brick. He pressed his mouth to her lips. If it were the last time, if she really thought she wanted it ended between them, then he was going to take what he wanted and give her a taste of what she would always miss.

Her mouth was soft and cool, like a raindrop. Soft and liquid and open. He dove past her lips into the warmth, devouring her, falling, falling into her bliss. It was beyond a mere kiss. It was an exploration of her. He inhaled deeply, taking her essence deep into his lungs like a drug. He smelled lemons, in her hair and on her hands that came up to fist in his lapels. And something else, something deeper, exotic and homey at the same time. Something ravishing. He wanted to ravish *her*. He wanted to put his big hands along the slide of her slender neck, run them down her arms, and span her neat little waist.

He was falling. Her mouth was light and air, and she made a soft little moan of surrender before she began kissing him back, tentatively at first, then with more assurance. He knew if he put his hands on her he would not stop. He would not stop until he had her skirts above her waist and was buried to the hilt in her soft, slick warmth, fucking her for all he was worth.

Against the wall of the Marquess of Widcombe's town house. Out of which, she had snuck in the middle of the night. Out of which, at any moment, her angry uncle, the Marquess, or God forbid, her gorgon of a mother, might come storming after her wayward daughter.

He didn't want to find himself trapped into marriage with this enchanting woman, this strange closet botanist. He wanted her to bloody well *choose* him. The way he had chosen her.

Del forced himself to tear his lips away, to break off the kiss, but he was the one propping his arms against the wall, panting, his chest pumping like a bellows, his breath ruffling the loose hair that had fallen across her cheek.

And she wasn't unaffected. Her eyes were huge and shining in her face. One hand had risen up to cover her mouth, to touch those kiss-roughened lips.

"Well then, Miss Burke. Just so you know what you'll be missing." With that he took himself through the gate and back out into the night. With any luck he'd find that pair of foot-pads and get into a fight vicious enough to bruise the feeling of loss out of him.

When Celia saw the letter nested on the silver tray she felt no alarm. Well, perhaps a small bit of alarm, but she seemed to have become adjusted to the bolts of shock. Viscount Darling may not have been happy with her—he had been furious— but he was not unmoved. It was an interesting, but cautious, thought. So she was not at all prepared for the contents of the letter. Really, the damned paper *ought* to have been black.

> *Have a care for your reputation, Miss Burke, or there will be no saving it. Your name will be blackened all over town were it known to even a few in society you have been making clandestine assignations with a certain Vile Viscount. You try our patience, Miss Burke. The ton finds nothing half so entertaining as a downfall. The sum of one thousand pounds is now the figure that will buy your freedom. Tuesday next, Powell's, George Alley.*

Celia stared at the missive for a long moment and felt . . . nothing. No roiling in her belly. No icy clamminess in her palms. No feeling of cold goosebumps as if someone had walked over her grave. She felt curiously, strangely devoid of any emotion.

Perhaps it was from the growing regularity, the monotony of the event. How many blackmail notes could a girl get and still manufacture the same care? But most likely, the relief and pleasure she felt in *finally* knowing, beyond any sort of doubt, Viscount Darling was unequivocally *not* her blackmailer, had cancelled out all the anxiety she surely ought to have felt. Extraordinary.

Whatever the reason for her lack of desperation, she was glad of it. It left her free to think logically. Celia read the note again. Well, now, *they*—it was strange how quickly she had gone from *him* to *they*—they had done it. They had specifically mentioned her meeting with Viscount Darling, either in the wee hours of the night or at the Royal Society. They were now threatening not one, but two people she cared about—two Delacortes. She put the letter in her pocket.

She had a clear moral obligation to inform Viscount Darling of his involvement in the event. And she would bet five hundred pounds, that unlike her, with all his experience of the world, all his military prowess, and all his dangerous affinities, he would know exactly what to do.

There was also the rather important matter of the very large apology she owed him. For her clandestine appearance in his bedchamber—and for thinking he was her blackmailer in the first place. For ever doubting he was the man in Emily's letters she had first fallen in love with.

She wrote a note begging him to meet her immediately, on urgent business. She then dragged Bains out for a walk, ostensibly for a promenade around Grosvenor Square, but really to the corner of Oxford Road, where she found a crossing sweep eager to take her pennies in exchange for delivering a message to Number Twenty-four North Row, five blocks away. The sweep was back in less than five minutes with the answer.

Viscount Darling had written on a piece of paper a single word. *No.*

"No?" Celia wanted to stamp her foot on the sidewalk. "Well, that just tears it. Come along, Bains."

"Where are you— Oh no, miss," Bains called after her. "No means no."

"I find, my dear Bains, I am no longer willing to accept no for an answer. From anyone. Certainly not from Viscount Darling. It is for his own good."

And entirely necessary to her peace of mind. She simply had to see him. Despite her limited experience of physical intimacy, Celia was quite sure Viscount Darling had not kissed her like *that*—as if he were going to explode if he didn't put his lips upon hers—only to reject her. She felt a rush of heat as she relived the incendiary kiss again. She could still taste the salt of his skin, feel the roughness of his whiskers abrading her cheeks, and taste the dark spice of his mouth on hers. His was a kiss well worth fighting for.

Celia marched herself right up his front steps and banged the knocker down hard. The door was answered immediately by Gosling, who looked at her with incredulous alarm when Viscount Darling came into the corridor.

"God's balls. I just got you—" Del whipped out his arm and yanked her inside, leaving Bains to scurry in behind her. "What are you thinking, coming here in the middle of the morning? I told you *no*. No means no."

The damn fool girl's maid muttered, " 'Swhat I said."

They were still standing in his entry hall. He didn't dare invite her into his drawing room. He didn't want her staying that long.

She held out the note crushed in her fist. "You can't send me a note like this and expect me to do nothing. I had to see you. It's important."

"God's balls, Celia. *You* sent *me* the note, if you'll recall. Which I answered, refusing to meet with you in a compromising manner. If you had just waited, I would have been able to sort out something more suitable than this." He pushed the door closed behind her. "You can't be seen here, for God's sake. I realize you are purposefully trying to be ruined, but I'm beginning to believe I'm not the man for the job after all."

"It's too late for that!"

"So I see." She was becoming a tenacious, persistent little thing. She looked marvelous, all flushed with indignation, pink-cheeked and vibrant. But there were still those damned dark smudges under her eyes.

Del stomped down the hall to his office. She followed reluctantly, as if her bravado had only carried her so far and was faltering at a deeper incursion into his lair. It hadn't gone so well last time, had it? But she followed him anyway. Leaving the door open behind him he moved to put his desk between them.

"Now"—he focused on the letter she still clutched in her hand—"what is this all about?"

"I received another letter. A blackmail letter, only it was

about you!" She pulled it from her pocket and thrust the paper at him.

He pulled it out of her grasp and scanned the contents. It was strikingly all too familiar. The cold of deep abiding anger tunneled through him. Pernicious bastards. But something was thawing the cold. Satisfaction. He knew, without a doubt, he was going to catch them. They'd given a different address. "You said 'another.' "

"Yes. But I thought you sent the two others."

Everything began to slowly fall into place, like the tumblers falling in a lock. All that time, they'd been playing against each other, instead of against the real blackmailer.

"I can tell you, without a shadow of a doubt, my dear Miss Burke, I did not write this, nor did I write the two others." He took his paper out of his drawer and held it out to her.

"Oh, my God in heaven. It's nearly the same."

"Yes, but you'll note, I hope, that it is addressed to me."

She turned the letter over and stared.

"So I hope you will acquit me of blackmailing you, while I'm being blackmailed as well."

"Oh, bloody . . . gracious. This is awful." She sat abruptly, a little heap of muslin in his study chair, the wind completely gone from her sails. "How much did they . . . ? Five thousand pounds?" Her voice was an incredulous squeak. "My God, I don't know if I should feel thankful or insulted they only asked me for a thousand."

"Have you paid them?"

"Nothing yet. It was three hundred at first, then five, then one thousand. But I thought it was you. I thought you would give up the money in lieu of . . . And they still want it and I've . . ." She covered her face with her hands.

"Celia. I am not your blackmailer. And I was not attempting to coerce you into intimacies with me in lieu of the black-mail money. I wouldn't do that to you." Del pushed his unruly hair out of his eyes. The whole damn affair just kept getting more complicated. Except that it was also getting simpler.

"Celia, there is much more to this and we must talk, but not here, not now. You cannot be seen entering or, God's balls, leaving my house during the day. We've got to get you out."

"But if you're not the blackmailer, who is? Nobody but Miss Hadley knew what . . . happened to Emily, and she would never do this. I'm quite sure of it. Oh, my God, do you think they are blackmailing her as well?"

Clever Celia. "I mean to find out."

"What do you plan to do?"

"At the moment? Nothing, except get you home. Again."

Celia's mouth gaped open in amazement. She was deflated and incredulously irate, all at the same time, his lovely complicated girl. "Nothing? But they will ruin Emily's reputation. They will say she was a suicide."

"She was. Emily is already dead. Nothing else can harm her now. Only my family's reputation will be harmed, and I hardly care about that now, do I?" He laughed ruefully. "But your reputation is another thing entirely."

She regarded him solemnly for a very long moment. "Is it really?"

"I think it must be so. You must go."

"No! I'm not going to go until—"

He reached across the desk and placed a finger against her mouth. God almighty, but her lips were soft.

"Celia, we will figure this out and put a stop to it. But this is not the time. If you had a greater experience of the world, or perhaps if you weren't so stubborn, so bloody resolute, you'd have listened to your mother when she told you, young ladies never visit the home of a single man, no matter the time of day and no matter their business. And young, unmarried ladies have no business at all at the home of a rake. Now you will go. Gosling!"

"My lord." Gosling was in the hallway. "With respect, my

lord, I thought it best Miss Burke's departure should be public. Cook will escort her out and we will put it about that you are not at home, sir."

"Yes, all right. Good thinking." He turned Celia by the shoulder to face him. That little taste of her had opened the floodwaters within him and he could not keep himself from leaning down and covering her lips with his. He fell into her softness, into the honeyed warmth of her mouth. She almost pulled back when he slipped past her lips to let his tongue taste her. He couldn't let her go—his need was so great. He stabbed his hand through the soft mass of her curls to cup the nape of her neck and hold her to him, to keep her open to his ravishment of her mouth.

"My lord." Gosling, the chaperone, spoke.

"We are not done, Celia. We will talk. I will arrange something. But be patient. Please, for God's sake, promise me you won't do anything stupid like this again."

"Yes, but I had to."

"Promise me."

"All right."

He squeezed her hand in farewell and put her into Gosling's care, after which he retreated behind the library drapes to watch the theatricals.

In another minute, the cook, Mrs. Bobbins, led Celia by the hand up the kitchen stairwell with one arm around her waist and her other clutching a large flag of a handkerchief. There was much hand patting, bowing, and fond good-byeing, whilst Celia's maid took her arm, and Bobbins and Gosling stood in the street waving her away.

Del noticed the housekeeper from next door, ostensibly with her market basket and a kitchen maid in tow, approach Mrs. Bobbins with a slight curtsy.

Mrs. Bobbins gesticulated dramatically and loudly. ". . . the lovely young lady just left. How nice it was to see her again, though I hadn't seen her in many a year. Called to see me though I have not worked in her mother's kitchen for many a year. She were always just the sweetest thing you ever did see and wasn't that just handsome behavior. Oh, as long as I live, I'll never forget this moment—all the way across Marylebone to see me. Well, I never. But I've a pie in the oven for the Viscount when he gets back. You have a lovely day."

Mrs. Bobbins. Formerly of the Haymarket Theatre, London and currently of the household of his Lordship, the Viscount Darling.

CHAPTER 18

Three days went by. Three long, boring, anxiety-filled days, in which she attended a number of amusements, danced mechanically with a number of unremarkable and un-remembered gentlemen at a number of unimportant balls, and in the process made herself quite miserable looking for Viscount Darling, who, true to his word, did not come or ap-proach her once. The first day had passed in nervous expecta-tion of word from him, but when two more days passed with no sight of him, she began to relax into her disappointment.

The evening's purgatory was being held at the Dowager Duchess Lucan's huge mansion facing Green Park. Although the house was huge, it scarcely seemed capable of holding the immense crush of the Mid-Summer Ball. Celia had attended a number of mid-summer balls in Dartmouth and had always as-sociated them with country pursuits: bonfires, village dances, and sing-alongs. Although the house was packed to the rafters, the evening held no such innocent promise.

Mr. Philip Haythornthwaite led her off the dance floor and she chanced to see Commander McAlden standing nearby. She left Haythornthwaite for her friend.

"Good evening, Commander."

"I hope it will prove to be a good evening, Miss Burke. Delighted to see you. I wonder if I might escort you to the refreshment table?"

She agreed, glad to be free of Mr. Haythornthwaite and his detailed account of cattle breeding in the midlands. When they went out the passage, the Commander let go of her arm and stepped back.

"Celia." Viscount Darling loomed out of an alcove.

At last. "Viscount Darling, I *must* speak to you."

"*Must?*" His smile fished up the corner of his mouth. "You look very serious, Miss Burke. Might I offer you some refreshment?" When she shook her head, he continued on grimly. "Well, at least paste a smile of some sort on your face, unless you want people to notice how vexed with me you appear to be."

"Oh, yes. How do you do, Viscount Darling." She curtsyed. "I had not heard you were in town."

He bowed. "Good, and now we will walk out to the terrace, where we will part, and you will linger for a few moments before wandering down the garden path towards the mews. There is a cloak on a bench just down the path. Gosling will meet you and conduct you through. How long can you be gone?"

"It is a crush. Upwards of an hour, I should think."

"We'll aim for less. Count to one hundred slowly, then off you go."

"Where do you go?"

"Out the front. Publicly. I'll meet you in the carriage." Then he bowed and moved away from her.

Celia closed her eyes so she wouldn't follow his departure with her gaze, and began counting. It was impossible to go slowly, when every minute, every moment she was away from her mother was being wasted. She walked with as measured a pace as possible toward the back of the huge garden and took up the beautiful taffeta cloak with the huge, enveloping hood waiting for her on a bench. When she found the back gate

Gosling was there to conduct her anonymously through the mews and across carriage-clogged Brick Street.

"This way, miss."

The curtains had been drawn, and the carriage lit before Gosling handed her in. They were away in a trice, onto Piccadilly along Green Park. In another few blocks, the carriage slowed to a walk and Viscount Darling jumped aboard. Instantly, the once spacious carriage became immeasurably smaller. He took the backward seat and tossed his hat and evening gloves beside him. "All right? Everything went smoothly?"

"Yes. Where are we going?"

"Nowhere. In circles around Green Park. This was the best I could come up with for someplace private to talk. We'll go round the park until it's time to get you back." He ran his hand through his hair, making shocks of it stick up straight. It made him look younger and much less intimidating. But she needed him to be worldly and experienced, did she not? That was why she had gone to him, for his help and experience in dealing with the blackmail.

"Thank you for taking all this trouble."

"It's no trouble. Comparatively speaking." He smiled at her, a smile of such quick brightness and almost boyish chagrin, she had to laugh with him.

"It is quite ridiculous, isn't it? Victims of the same blackmailer, spending all our time blaming one another. I'm quite ashamed of myself for it."

"Don't be, Celia. For if you are ashamed, then I must be also and we'll waste all our time on apologies when we could be comparing our notes, so to speak. They were good assumptions, although false."

She was warmed through by his use of her Christian name. They'd come a rather long way, hadn't they? "Yes, all right. So what do we do?"

"I've had a Bow Street Runner, with the improbable name

of Mr. Henry Younghusband, under consultation since I received the first letter back in May."

"You made that up."

"His name? I assure you, I did not." He smiled as he angled himself into the corner and leaned back, making himself more comfortable. "To add insult to injury, the poor man is neither young nor married, as far as I can tell."

It felt good to laugh. It felt especially good to laugh with Viscount Darling. They had had so much mistrust between them.

"He is very good at his job, and has traced the payment of the first note to an address in Bath. To Jonstone's Tobaccanists."

"In Bridewell Lane?" Celia was practically out of her seat. "That is the shop where Emily received your letters!"

"And you accompanied her. It is how Mr. Younghusband was given your description. And how *I* came to find you."

"Oh, I see."

"So, I thought I had found the blackmailer when the trail led to Dartmouth. Until I got this letter." He pulled the missive out of his interior breast coat pocket and offered it to her. "You'll remember, it differs from yours."

"Yes, they ask for a monstrous amount of money, for one thing. Oh, and they say it is to keep you from having to marry me."

"Yes, but that is not the point. The point is that they have given you a different address for payment. Now I can set Mr. Younghusband to the task of watching both Powell's bookshop in George Alley and this address in Robin Hood Court. And making comparisons from what we learned in Bath."

"I don't even know where George Alley is. But I don't have the money to pay anyway. That was the whole reason—"

"Yes. I don't know whether to be flattered you offered, or furious with you for trying to sell yourself so cheap."

"Cheap?" Celia felt heat blossom on her face. "I thought it was a monstrous load of money."

"And so it is." He smiled his tawny, sleepy lion smile. "Beauty is in the eyes of the beholder."

"I don't understand."

"Meaning, I should have been very glad to pay a thousand pounds for the pleasure of having you, Miss Burke." It was his lion voice, low and purring, full of leashed menace and dark promises. He crossed his booted legs on the plush upholstery of her bench.

Celia felt heat blossom everywhere, down her neck and in the valley between her breasts. "But you didn't. You didn't want me." Her voice sounded as thin as her confidence.

"Now, that is not correct. I did want you. I still do want you. I simply could not have you. Not under those circumstances. Not as things stood between us at that point."

"Oh. And where do things stand between us?"

"Unsettled and unfinished." He looked grim and unhappy for a moment before he lifted his brows. "But back to your question—George Alley is in Fleet Street and I will put up the thousand. I have every expectation of getting it back."

Celia swallowed what little pride she had left. "I wish I could protest and say I won't let you, say I'll think of something. But the truth is, I can't think of anything and I should be very grateful to you for it."

"I like grateful. But we needn't give the whole. I think it best to start out with the original three, and ask them for more time—a few days only. It will give us another chance to catch them out."

"Oh, yes, that sounds very logical."

"Do you think you can do it? Take the Marquess of Widcombe's town carriage up to Fleet Street and drop your package off at Powell's by yourself? Mr. Younghusband and I shall be watching."

"May I take Bains with me?"

"Yes, of course."

"All right then. It's settled."

The coach went round a bend and hit a rut. Celia grabbed for the hanging straps. Viscount Darling brought one of his booted legs off the bench and across her as a brace to steady her. For half a moment his leg was against her thigh. "Your pardon, Miss Burke."

So he was back to "Miss Burke." She let her fingers slide off his boot and he lowered his feet back down, flat onto the floor of the carriage.

"How shall we arrange for the money?"

"I have it here." He took a small stack of fifty-pound bank-notes out of his breast coat pocket. "Do you have a reticule?"

She held up empty hands. "I'm sorry, no."

"Pockets?"

"Not in this gown." It was one of Bains' superb creations, a chemise dress style, made up of silk under lace.

"Very beautiful, but not altogether practical for our purposes. Well." He shifted back in his seat, crossing one booted leg over his knee. The faint stirring of a grin began to curve the edge of his lips. "That leaves the old-fashioned method."

"Old-fashioned?" She wrinkled up her nose. "What do you mean?"

The grin spread up toward his half-closed, sleepy eyes. "I mean, my dear Miss Burke, you will need to secure the notes"—he lifted his brows and nodded at her chest—"down your bodice."

Her hand rose of its own volition to cover her chest where it showed above the lace edging of her gown. But she knew he was right. There was nowhere else.

"Will you turn around?"

"I should, shouldn't I? A gentleman would turn around. But, I think we both know, Miss Burke"—he sat up and one at a time, placed his booted feet on the bench on either side of her, penning her between his legs—"I am, at heart, *not* a gentleman. *Not* in this area of endeavor, and *not* with you."

The intensity of his look, his singular focus on her was unnerving and exhilarating. Her skin warmed under his gaze and her breasts began to feel full within the tight confines of her stays. She remembered the last time they had been together alone, what she had done for him. What she had done for herself.

Viscount Darling leaned forward and rested his forearms upon his knees. Placing a kiss upon the packet of banknotes, he slowly, smiling that tawny lion smile the whole while, slowly passed them to her.

"Handsomely now, Miss Burke. Slowly. Ease it down until it rests snug against the underside of your lovely round breast. There now."

She knew she must be scarlet with heat as she pulled her fingers back out of her bodice.

"Well done, Miss Burke. Although I am tempted to . . ." He rubbed his thumb along his bottom lip.

She was predictably enthralled by the sight of his calloused thumb passing back and forth along his improbable, bow-shaped lips. "Tempted?"

"To make sure it is well secured. After all, it is a *monstrous* load of money," he teased. "I am tempted to put my hands on your shoulders and push you back against the squabs, and run my finger"—he held up a single index finger—"down that fascinating line of your neck, and brush aside your lace so I could feel the soft slide of your skin. Down until it disappeared into your bodice and I could dip my fingers inside your always so-modest bodice and delve down until I could feel the tightly ruched peaks of your beautiful, sweet breasts. Then I'd tweak each pink tip, roll them between my thumb and forefinger until you cried out with pleasure. You would cry out, wouldn't you? You would cry out for me because you're so wonderfully responsive. Under all that demure packaging, wildly passionate. You're responding right now, aren't you? Your breasts feel tight and sensitive, just waiting for the bliss of my touch."

God, yes, she felt it just as if he'd done it. Pleasure, warm and greedy, blossomed where his words touched her. Her body was arching towards him, helpless not to want what he offered. He played her as if she was his instrument, tuned only to his touch. But he was not unaffected. His breath was coming just as shallow and fast as hers.

"But you are only tempted, Viscount Darling?"

"Alas, my sweet Celia, I dare not touch what I am not yet allowed to have."

Not yet? That sounded immensely hopeful. "What about me, Viscount Darling. What if *I* dare? You say *you* cannot, and will not, touch me because you fear, with your experience of the bliss to come, you could not stop. But I have not your experience, have I? And therefore none of your fear."

She placed her hands on top of his knees as he straddled her. She felt the instant change from lazy pleasure to coiled tension, as if loose electricity had jumped through his body.

"Celia." His voice was a harsh warning, and also, perhaps, just enough of a plea.

"It's hardly fair, Viscount Darling, for you to toy with my feelings and fill me with such sensations and such longing, without giving me the chance to play as well."

"I hardly—"

He broke off when she moved her hands, massaging and kneading the thick muscles of his thighs.

"I don't have your experience and knowledge, so I'll have to guess. You'll have to help me. Does this feel good?" She circled her thumbs on the inside of his thighs.

"Yes," he bit off.

"But you don't sound pleased." Celia copied the words he had used with her. "Perhaps if I ran my hands along the length of your inner thigh, like this, you would like it more?"

In response, he put his hands out to either side of the carriage walls to brace his arms, and she suspected, to keep from touching her. But his body's instinctive response to her was obvious. The fabric at the apex of his thighs tented.

Celia felt a surge of power and satisfaction she had never experienced before. It was singularly heady. She looked into his clear blue eyes. "I'll take that as a yes, Viscount Darling." Her hands massaged and kneaded him through the satin fabric of his breeches, and she could feel the hardened strength of his deeply corded muscles beneath her palms. "I can feel the strength of your legs. But that's not where you really want my hands, is it? You want them here, on your—" She touched him lightly.

He seemed to wince and he sucked air in between his tightly clenched teeth.

"I'm afraid, Viscount Darling, I don't know what to call it."

He looked at her, a stare of such heat and nakedness she felt it within her, pulsating at her core.

"My cock, Celia, my cock."

"Your cock." Her whisper did not sound at all as sure as she had wished. "If I was more experienced, would I touch it? Would you like me to?"

"Yes." He said it through clenched teeth, as if he were bracing himself for pain. He closed his eyes and let his head fall back against the leather squabs.

Celia let her fingers play lightly over the material along the length of his member, his cock. "And how would I touch you? Softly, as you have told me I should like to be touched, or differently, perhaps more firmly?"

"Harder."

"Yes then, harder." She pressed along the length of him. "Like this? Tell me how you want me to touch you harder."

"Wrap your hand around." His jaw worked as he spoke.

She did as he directed, wrapping her hand fully around the erect length of his cock through the interfering layers of his breeches. "I would imagine this would be so much better, so much more enjoyable for you, as well as for me, if I were touching your warm flesh instead of the cool satin of your breeches." She kept one hand encircling him while the other sought out the buttons of the flap of his breeches. "If my hand were directly on your . . . cock."

In a flash his hand came down hard over her wrists and in another moment she was lifted, pushed back against the bench, her wrists pinioned against the squabs. He held her there for a long moment as he struggled to calm his breath.

"Don't," he said quietly. "Do not play with fire, Miss Burke, unless you are quite prepared to be badly burned." He loosened his grip on her wrists and slid slowly away from her. Then he banged on the roof of the carriage, drawing it to an abrupt halt.

"I will have to beg your pardon, Miss Burke. Gosling will see you safely back." With that Viscount Darling left the carriage and departed into the night.

CHAPTER 19

Tuesday at precisely ten-fifteen in the morning, Celia alighted from the Marquess of Widcombe's grand town carriage onto the crowded pavement of Fleet Street. The coachman would go no farther. He did not want to risk his equipage nor his cattle on the close confines of George Alley.

Powell's was a bookseller halfway down the block. With Bains clutching her arm, Celia went straight to the counter. Best to get it over with directly.

"I should like to leave this package here."

The clerk glanced at the sealed envelope, supremely disinterested in her little drama. "For the post, miss? You'll need the direction."

"No, not for the post. For picking up, here." How awkward. She hadn't imagined dithering over how to leave her blackmail payment.

"Still, miss, it will need a name."

Celia glanced at Bains for a moment, then leaned forward to say quietly, "I don't have the name."

"Like that, is it? Don't suppose you'll want to leave your name?"

"I couldn't—"

"Right then, initials top right corner. Left by one well-dressed, cautious young lady. Fee to be paid by whoever picks it up. Will that be all, miss?"

Celia knew she had gone scarlet with embarrassment. "Yes, thank you." She excused herself, only to bump into the customer directly behind her, a civil middle-aged businessman, who tipped his hat politely.

"Your pardon, miss."

"Not at all, sir. If you'll excuse me—"

"Oh, miss, you've dropped your reticule." Before Celia could protest she had none, he pressed one into her hand with another tip of his hat. "Mr. Henry Younghusband at your service, miss."

Viscount Darling's runner. She thanked him with a quick curtsy and hurried to the coach with Bains. As soon as they were tucked inside the carriage, Celia pulled out Viscount Darling's note.

> *I watch from the coffeehouse opposite, Younghusband from inside the bookstore, though it may be some time, even days before we know the outcome, if at all. I will be in touch. Do not try to contact me.*

She would have to leave the business to him and hope for the best. Celia directed the driver to return immediately to Grosvenor Street. Her father had come up from Dartmouth and she would need to be more circumspect in her activities. He might not talk and lecture like her mama, but he was no less sharp for it. And he did not sleep till noon.

For the second time during her stay in London, the time wore heavily on Celia. She had no work of her own, no microscope nor specimens, though she did have correspondence with both the Abbé de Serra and Sir James, as well as with the printer, Mr. Faulder. Correspondence could only take up a fraction of the day. The rest must belong to her mama, shopping, and social events, none of which she could enjoy while her fate still hung in the balance.

More days passed, there was no word from Viscount Darling. There was simply no Viscount Darling. She had not seen him since the morning in George Alley. Strictly speaking, even then she had not seen him—she had only his note. He had not sent another. Celia had, of course, sent Bains over to visit with Mrs. Bobbins, but she came back empty-handed, with no news. It was supremely frustrating. Despite her attempts to see him, and speak with him, Viscount Darling remained resolutely uninvolved. There had been no attempt to arrange the sort of intimate conversations they had once shared. He was avoiding her at all costs. Presumably he had left or was planning to leave the rest of the money—the two hundred pounds—on his own, without her involvement. Or he had decided not to put up the rest of the money, choosing to cut his losses and leave her to deal with the rest of the mess by herself.

If that were to happen, she would have no choice but to tell her father. As it was, she was overdue to have a conversation with him regarding the Royal Society. She didn't want him to hear it from anybody else.

In the meantime, she must smile and curtsy and dance as little as possible in the Dowager Duchess of Fenmore's opulent ballroom. Celia had first danced again with Mr. Haythornthwaite and his breeding program, then retreated to sit quietly in a chair at the side of the ballroom.

She was unprepared when Viscount Darling suddenly asked in her ear. "Miss Burke, do you know who that woman is, there?"

She hadn't even known he was at the ball. Indeed he hung back, at the division of the wall, as if he didn't want to be seen with her. She sat only a foot from him, but felt none of his attention. His mind was elsewhere. Whatever fascination he'd had with her had run its course, as she knew it must. But knowledge could not fill the hollow empty space inside her. She looked along the wall of chairs as he gestured with his drink. "Mrs. Turbot?"

"The lady in the blue, old-fashioned gown with the white lace cap."

"She is Mrs. Turbot, Melissa Wainwright's companion."

Viscount Darling made a guttural sound, like the snapping of a twig. "Melissa Wainwright."

Celia felt an entirely unwelcome stab of jealousy, which left a sour, unpleasant taste in her mouth, as if she had swallowed a toad. Melissa was quite beautiful. Perhaps her petite, blond beauty would be a perfect match for Viscount Darling's own gilded looks. "Have you not been introduced? I thought you had made her acquaintance in Dartmouth?"

"Dartmouth. And Bath." But Viscount Darling was no longer having an idle conversation with her. Everything about him, his posture, the controlled tension on his face, had changed.

"Yes, from school. We spoke of her, if you remember, of me introducing her to influential ladies."

"It will therefore come as a surprise to you that Mrs. Turbot was at Powell's Booksellers Tuesday last and retrieved your packet. She took a hackney to a house on the outskirts of Marylebone."

Celia's stomach turned to water. Thank God she was already sitting. "I don't know if that is where Melissa lives."

"The same lady retrieved my letter at Robin Hood Court on Wednesday. I had assumed she was a servant. I might not have recognized her but . . ." He let the thought lapse.

"Does Melissa know?"

"That I suspect her, or that her servant retrieved the money?"

Celia shrugged hopelessly. The realization, the pain, crept through her slowly, a crawling numbness that somehow ached.

"I think it very likely Miss Wainwright knows everything. Mrs. Turbot is merely a servant in her household. Do you happen to know when she joined Miss Wainwright's employ?"

"Shortly before Melissa came to Dartmouth, I thought."

"That places Miss Wainwright at Miss Hadley's School in Bath, in Dartmouth, and now in London. All three places from which the letters have come."

"But she is my friend." Misery stole Celia's voice. "Oh, I hate people. I shall never understand them, ever. They are so lying and deceitful and hateful."

"No one can betray like a friend, Celia. I think you need to get used to the idea Miss Wainwright was never truly your friend." He added in an undertone, "The library at the end of the next set." Then he bowed and stepped away. "Your servant, Miss Burke."

"Celia?" Her mama's smile was like a snowbank, blinding and icy. "You will excuse my daughter, my lord." She inclined her head to Viscount Darling, took Celia's arm, and led her away. "My dear child, you need not talk to the man if he upsets you so much. You look peaked and unhappy. We are at a ball. Smile. Here is Lord Monaton, asking for an introduction and to dance with you. This is my daughter, Lord Monaton. Celia, may I introduce Lord Monaton to you? My daughter, Miss Celia Burke."

"Delighted, Miss Burke. Would you do me the honor . . ."

Lord Monaton was destined to be deeply disappointed in The Ravishing Miss Burke. She had absolutely no conversation for him. Her mind was elsewhere.

She could think of only two things. One, Melissa Wainwright had betrayed not only her, but Emily Delacorte as well, and deeply so. Two, if her blackmailer was Melissa Wainwright, then she and Viscount Darling had come to the end of their journey together. If they had finally solved the riddle that vexed them, they no longer had any excuse for seeing each other.

"I understand you have some knowledge of plants, Miss Burke." Lord Monaton was talking at her as they stood at the head of the dance. "My own interest lies with roses. I have had some small success with crossbreeding a new species of China rose, from stock lately brought from China, you know."

Was it wrong to pray it was not Melissa, just to prolong her acquaintance with Viscount Darling? What if she never saw him again? She would go back to Dartmouth and he might never visit there again. Or worse, if he did visit and brought some other woman, his wife with him. No, it would be better never to see him again.

So why did she feel like crying?

"I fear you did not enjoy the dance, Miss Burke. I will leave you with your father." The lordling bowed to Celia and nodded to her father. "Lord Thomas."

"Celia? Did you not enjoy meeting Lord Monaton? I had to cage the young man twice to get him to attend. I know he is a rosarian, but he shares your former interest in botany. The fellow is just about the only man under the age of thirty who will at once fit your criteria, my expectations, and your mother's standards."

A rosarian. A botanist. And she couldn't even remember, two minutes after their dance, exactly what he looked like. Viscount Darling was right. All those weeks ago when he had made his bet. He had ruined her for all other men without once touching her.

According to her father, Lord Monaton was the one man she would have been happy to marry one month ago. He was young and handsome—and a lord. But she didn't want him. She wanted what she could not have. What she could not stop herself from wanting.

"Celia, are you unwell?"

"No, Papa. I am only upset with some dreadful news I had of a friend. Someone I thought was a friend."

"Viscount Darling?"

"No, no. Melissa Wainwright. She is not what she appears to be, it seems."

"Is that because she is now dancing with Viscount Darling?"

"Is she?" Dancing with Melissa as he had never danced with Celia? "I daresay, he is exactly what she deserves." She could only hope Viscount Darling would make sure of that. "Your pardon, Papa. If you will excuse me, I should like to repair to the ladies withdrawing room for a moment."

Instead, she went directly across the house to the small library, the Dowager not being much of a reader, and made herself as inconspicuous as possible in a window alcove. She did not have long to wait.

Viscount Darling escorted Melissa in and closed the door behind them.

Melissa was speaking, "—and I cannot stay above a minute, I'm afraid, for it would be thought quite wrong of me to speak to you alone."

"Really?" Viscount Darling had invested his voice with bored haughteur. "I should have thought being alone with a man like me would be very much to your desire, Miss Wainwright."

"You mistake me, I—"

"Oh, I do not mistake you, Miss Wainwright. I think it only fair to warn you I have had you under investigation by a runner from the Bow Street Magistrate's office. After all, I've already paid you twice. What could be better or more desirable for you than to have another opportunity to blackmail me."

Melissa waited too long before she spoke. "I have no idea what you are talking about."

"The Bow Street Magistrate's office says you do know. I am

inclined to agree with them, because they have proof. They will implicate your companion, Mrs. Turbot, as well. They, if they decide to take you into custody, have very harsh penalties."

There was tension and anger in Melissa's voice. "I begin to see why people have called you the Vile Viscount."

"You have no idea, Miss Wainwright, of what I am capable. Shall I tell you? Shall I describe what I will say to others, to my friends, my fellow officers, when I leave this room after being closeted in here with you?"

There was a sharp intake of breath. "You bastard."

"Exactly. I am just the sort of bastard who would ruin you, right now, here on Lady Home's carpet, without a second thought, and tell everyone I had pleasure in doing so and to hell with your accusations. You should have checked more thoroughly into my character before you decided to blackmail me."

Melissa backed away from him, wary and nervous, but he was between her and the door.

"Frightened you now, have I, Miss Wainwright? Good. It shouldn't take more than a word here or there among my associates in His Majesty's Marine Forces, to have it said you're easy goods. That you'll spread your legs for anyone in a barracks, as long as they've the ready cash."

"You unmitigated, filthy—"

"Yes, we've covered that, Miss Wainwright."

"You have no proof, because none exists. You're just trying to frighten me with your accusations. But I can make accusations as well. I can scream this room down around you in a minute and accuse you."

"You could. But then, I just might make an offer to marry you, and then you'd have to choose between your ruinations— mine or society's. An unpalatable choice, I should think."

Celia's heart was in her throat, stuck there, stoppering her breath.

"I *will* scream. I—"

"You go right ahead. For here we have Miss Burke, your friend, whom you asked to meet you here, as a witness. She will say you are taken in an hysterical fit. What say you, Miss Burke?"

Melissa whirled around as Celia stepped from the shadow of the window. The girl's face was as mobile as a clockwork, moving, ticking along until she found the appropriate time. "Celia, my dear friend. Thank God you're here."

"It's true, isn't it, Melissa? It was you. You started those vile rumors that sent Emily to her death."

For a moment Celia thought she was going to continue to bluster and deny. Then Melissa tossed her blond curls and tried to look down her nose at Celia. "Don't be so naive. The rumors were no more than you earned and deserved, being so secretive, scurrying about in your woods, whispering to each other all the time. People were already thinking it."

"Why? Why did you do it?"

"Why not? I needed the money, but I don't suppose you, with all your wealth and privilege and relations, would understand that." Her tone was scathing. "I must live, Celia, and to do so, I must have money. But to get money, I must marry. But to marry, I must have money, to buy clothes and a house and respectability, so I can meet a rich eligible young man to marry. So I can have money. All those young men falling at your feet. All those men whom you—you who have everything—disdain. Well, I want them and there is no reason I shouldn't have them."

"No reason except it was simply wrong. It is all founded on lies and deceit."

"Of course you would think so, which is why I had such pleasure in blackmailing you, so full of scruples and moral surety. Well, I can't afford your scruples, Miss Burke. As for the lies and deceit, the Bank of England works on lies and deceit—why should I be any different?"

Celia had never felt such cold, hollow disillusion.

"Oh, you needn't look so affronted. It wasn't personal."

"Of course it was personal, Melissa. Your own jealous words have just proven it. You want what you think I have. You feel entitled to it."

Melissa quirked her lips and raised her eyebrow in a sneering fashion, but gave no answer.

"Now," Viscount Darling broke the silence, "we come to the conclusion, in which I tell you, Miss Wainwright, in no uncertain terms, to stop. If one word—one further breath of trouble comes to Miss Burke or myself about any of these matters—I will ruin you. I will see you hounded out of this country. Your letters warned us particularly to remember how fickle the ton is, how much they love to see a spotless reputation being dragged through the mud. Nothing half so entertaining as a downfall. Wasn't that what you said?"

Melissa had no answer.

"Go away, quickly and quietly, or you shall find yourself a victim of your own practice. Do you understand? Do you agree?"

"What choice do I have in the mat—"

"*Do you agree?*"

Melissa swallowed, finally intimidated by the barely leashed force of the Viscount's anger. "Yes."

"Then you may go. And do not come back. Your days in the ton are over." He unlocked the door and held it open.

Melissa picked up her skirts and stalked out with all the vitriol and dignity of an exiled queen.

"Well." Celia had to work to draw enough breath back into her lungs. "That, I can only hope, is the end of that. Thank you, Viscount Darling. I am grateful."

"I like grateful."

Celia, despite the growing pain in her chest, would make it easy for him. She owed him that much. "We have accomplished our goal and we can part as friends."

"Friends." He said the word as if tasting it for the first time, as if he hadn't been the one to say it all those weeks ago. "I don't think I've ever been friends with a young lady before. Certainly not with one I have tried to seduce."

She felt the predictable heated flush flare up her neck.

"We have been strangely intimate for friends," he said.

"Yes, we have been intimate friends, but we have not been lovers. At your insistence."

"It wouldn't have been right. There was too much misunder-standing—"

"I know. So let us part as friends." She put out her hand for him to shake.

Del took her hand, his palm eclipsing hers. He moved his fingers ever so slightly, so he could feel the pulse in her wrist, strong and constant. That's what she was beneath her decep-tive exterior of beauty—strong and constant. Resolute.

He raised her hand up slowly and pressed a kiss to the top of her gloved hand, and then to the turn of her wrist. Her scent rose again, floral and exotic, laced with citrus. With lemon. He wanted to peel off every layer of her clothes and search her body for those warm pulse points of scent. "We cannot part as friends. Because, you and I, Miss Burke, have unfinished business."

Her mouth fell open, her lips parted in surprise. Without thinking he pulled her toward him and lowered his mouth to hers. She turned her head at the last moment, and his kiss landed gently on the soft skin of her cheek. Her skin, against his, was so deeply, intoxicatingly soft. A slight pillow of a cheek, whispering its balm across the incipient roughness of his beard.

His eyes shuttered closed and he inhaled deeply, drawing her scent, her essence into him.

She drew away.

He let her go, bemused, startled even, by his almost spiri-tual reaction to her. His mind went back to that first moment, when he had been so full of hate, so willing to believe the worst of her, and yet his body had recognized her immediately.

This one. This one alone will do. This is what I want.

She almost stepped back, and then she moved, as light, erratic, and unpredictable as a butterfly and alit, with the same sense of delicate discovery, upon his mouth. Her lips were soft, so soft, softer than he remembered. He did not have adequate feelings for the fathoms of sensation when her lips settled so sweetly and tentatively upon his.

He could not stop himself from at last, at long last, taking her face in his hands and cradling the fragile strength of her jaw between his palms, angling her head to draw her deeper to him. Every nerve in his body stretched towards her, anxious to catalogue every sensation, every nuance he had denied himself. His tongue explored the texture of her lips and when he pressed a small kiss to the corner of her mouth she opened to him. The sweetness of her mouth flooded him. He delved deeper, again and again, starved for the taste and feel of her. His hand crept up to the nape of her neck to entwine in her dark silken curls.

He wanted to kiss her everywhere, to taste each and every inch of her skin. His mouth slid along her cheek and he was startled to taste the damp salt of tears.

"Don't," he murmured as he thumbed the tears away. "Please, love, don't."

"Exactly the word I was thinking. *Don't.*" A father's enraged voice, followed by the firm closing of a door. "Now step away from my daughter."

Even as Del's arms reached instinctively to pull her behind him, even as he leaned towards her to give her the protection of his body, she jumped in front of him. As if she, this exquisite piece of human frailty, thought she needed to protect him from her father.

"We were saying good-bye, Papa, the Viscount and I. So you may take me home now, please."

"I don't think so, Celia. That is not what good-bye looks like. That looked very much like hello. As in, hello, Viscount Darling. I am Lord Thomas Burke, Celia's father, and I shall expect you to attend me tomorrow morning. Do I make myself clear?"

"I shall deem it an honor to wait upon you, my lord."

"No," Celia gasped. "This is entirely unnecessary, Papa. You misunderstand."

"No." Her father's voice was more than firm, it was unyielding. "It is you who do not understand, Celia. This is not a discussion. Your mutual lack of discretion has ended that possibility. You are being talked about. You will return to your mother now."

"Papa. Viscount Darling—"

"Now."

As soon as Celia went through the door, she understood what her father had said. Any number of people loitered casually in the hallway, which only minutes ago had been entirely deserted. She felt her face flame.

But she drew on composure like a cloak. She used her high color and made it her camouflage. She forced herself to achieve a brilliant, almost intoxicated smile, as if there were nothing going on behind the library doors she didn't think was perfectly wonderful. She would get through the rest of the evening without anyone being the wiser.

Her mother made only the slightest of double takes when Celia went to her. "Papa desires to go, Mama. He has gone to collect the carriage."

Her mama's nostrils flared slightly—she had always been able to smell a lie—but she gave nothing else away. She made unhurried good-byes while Celia stood radiantly by.

Celia continued to smile her way around the ballroom. She

followed the linked chain of whispers until it came to moor upon Melissa Wainwright, who had clearly not quit the ball-room. Oh, she was pleased with herself, Miss Wainwright was. It was clear from the look of triumph curving her lips into a smug smile, she had orchestrated this. Yes, even now, one of Celia's acquaintance was speaking from behind her fan into Melissa's ears.

Spite, pure and crystalline, and as sharp as a blade, lanced through Celia. It was natural that she should feel such an emotion and she shook off the impulse to suppress it. Miss Wainwright had done nothing for months but try to harm Celia. It was time Melissa took a dose of her own bitter med-icine.

"Oh, Miss Wainwright. Allow me to say good evening to you."

Melissa's smug smile held for another moment or two as Celia advanced upon her.

"Going so soon, Miss Burke? You poor dear. There seemed to be such a dreadful commotion in the library."

Celia allowed her brows to rise and she turned to look back at the hallway from whence she had come. "A commotion?" Easy enough to refute as there had been none.

"Why yes. I was told quite distinctly that you were alone with Viscount Darling. The Vile Viscount."

"Yes, yes I was. I find his character has been quite wrongly maligned. Don't you, Miss Wainwright? After Viscount Dar-ling was so kind to help you out of your *dreadful* trouble?"

Melissa tried to brazen it out. "You admit that you were quite alone with him?"

"Oh, yes. We had a lovely conversation, Miss Wainwright. About you."

All conversation in the vicinity had stopped. Mouths had fallen agape and every ear was turned to catch the byplay between them, but at least as many people had turned to scrutinize Miss Wainwright as were looking at Celia. Good.

Let Melissa taste what she had so stupidly and callously begun.

Out of the corner of her eye Celia could see her mother advancing with the stately confidence of a ship of the line. "But here is my mama, come to bid you good-bye, for I doubt we shall ever see you here again."

Celia took her mother's arm and out they sailed, smiling as if nothing in the world could possibly be wrong.

CHAPTER 20

Del arrived at Widcombe House on foot. Gosling, who knew everything about how one ought to conduct such things, had advised using the town coach with the addition of the family coat of arms emblazoned on the side. Del didn't think anything was going to impress Lord Thomas Burke. And it took less time to walk. If Celia could do it in the middle of the night, surely he could do it in the middle of the day.

When he knocked, Del was shown directly to a small book room, at one end of a larger library. As he entered, Lord Thomas did not get up. Del was sensible of the subtle signal, and did his future father-in-law the courtesy of letting the man intimidate him. Del remained standing in front of Lord Thomas's desk.

"My lord." He bowed. "I thank you for agreeing to see me today. I have come to request the honor of your daughter's hand in marriage."

Lord Thomas did not invite him to sit. "It gives me great pain, Viscount Darling, to inflict you upon my daughter as a husband. You are not at all what I would have chosen for her. Nor are you in any way what she would have chosen for herself, were she still free to do so. Your actions have robbed her of that opportunity."

The accusation that Celia would not have chosen him stung. But he wouldn't degrade himself further by asking what her father thought she did want. It was enough to know she *had* wanted him bloody well enough to sneak across Mayfair and practically strip herself naked in his bedchamber.

"I will do everything in my power to see your daughter wants for nothing."

Lord Thomas was not impressed by Del's declaration. "Yes, but will you be able to make her happy? Do you have *any* idea what makes her happy?"

Del would bet long odds he knew a thing or two, about which Miss Burke's father had no earthly idea. Only one would he voice in public. "Botany."

"Ah. Very good. You surprise me, Viscount Darling." Though Lord Thomas was not as surprised as Darling would have thought.

"As do you. I had not thought her parents knew of her interests."

"Good Lord, man," Lord Thomas scoffed. "She has a work room in an old barn on my property and an assortment of equipment for specimen collection, not to mention she corresponds regularly with other botanists and lately with members of the Royal Society. Do you really think all that could go on if I were unaware of it? If I had not given my tacit permission?"

"Then you approve?"

"Obviously. She could not have pursued her studies otherwise. But the more important question at this juncture is whether you approve? Or even understand?"

"I foresee no reason why I might interfere with her interest."

"Can you not? Then I think you have not thought seriously about marriage and what it will entail. But of course"—Lord Thomas let out a sound of disgust—"you would not have thought of marriage at all, were your hand not forced."

There was no point in answering. Del's reputation alone was enough to suppose he had never thought seriously of marriage.

"A small word, *interest*." Lord Thomas continued to eye him with something less than affection. "Have you seen her work?"

"Just once, though I was not sure at the time, it was hers."

"Typical of her. Do you know enough about it to know it is good? Very good. And that it is a serious, scholarly undertaking?"

"I know she has ambitions for fellowship in the Royal Society."

"She told you that? She must trust you a good deal more than I thought, to share that information."

"She does. I accompanied her to a colloquium of the Royal Society in which she was an invited speaker." It was stretching the truth, but he wanted to prove to Lord Thomas he knew a thing or two about his daughter even her father did not know. He knew a lot of things about his daughter that the man did not know, but then again, this was hardly the time.

"Has she indicated she would welcome a marriage with you?"

Other than stripping naked in his bedroom, no. But the discussion that night had not touched upon marriage. "I have not had the honor of asking Miss Burke yet."

"No, you haven't. You were too busy taking the honor of putting your tongue down my daughter's throat to ask if she'd welcome your suit."

Del felt his face heat at such plain speaking. "I will not deny I find your daughter exceptionally attractive. That is why I should like the honor of marrying her at your earliest convenience."

"Yes, it must be done. There is nothing else for it." Lord Thomas passed a hand over his eyes. "You will procure a special license. And you will act the besotted bridegroom for all the world to see."

"Yes, sir."

Lord Thomas let out a long, unhappy exhalation. "Have you come prepared to apprise me of your finances and hammer out the marriage settlement?"

"I have instructed my man of business to wait upon your pleasure at your earliest convenience."

"I have no *pleasure* in this, but we'll have him for a start. As you are heir to your father, you will need the Earl of Cleeve, and his man of business, to be a party to the settlement."

"I will inform him of your request, sir."

"I shall expect you to attend as well, Viscount Darling. You can't get out of this so easily."

Del clenched his jaw. "It is well known my father and I are estranged."

"Is that what you call it? Ha. Well, the time has come for you to be un-estranged. You will not take my daughter into a house divided by the petty quarrels of a rebellious son."

Del could not even fight for his pride. Still Lord Thomas sat behind his desk, poking him like a bear in a cage.

"Well, best get on with it. Go to your father's house—he's in town by the by. He'll be expecting you. Send me word directly when you both might next attend me to finish the financial arrangements."

"Yes, sir. May I also be allowed a moment to speak to your daughter privately?"

"No. Get your father here and then we'll see."

Del did not do as Lord Thomas asked, and wait upon his father. Instead, they met for the first time in over a year on the pavement outside Widcombe House before their appointment with Lord Thomas Burke. Del had again walked from North Row, and it appeared his father had done the same from the family residence only one and a half blocks away on Grosvenor Square. What tidy neighbors they all were.

He bowed to his father and waited for him to speak.

"Rupert," his father acknowledged him. "Hell of a fix you've gotten yourself into. You look well. Your mother will be pleased. You will call on her this afternoon if you can remember where the house is." The Earl of Cleeve turned and gestured in the direction of the family mansion with his walking stick, just to make his point.

"Your servant, sir."

"Good." The Earl turned for the door. "Let us proceed."

The portal was opened immediately and they were shown into the Marquess of Widcombe's library, where Lord Thomas Burke waited.

The butler announced, "My lord, the Earl of Cleeve and Viscount Darling to see you."

The Earl of Cleeve walked in without ceremony and straightaway gave his hand to Celia's father. "Thomas."

Lord Thomas shook it grimly. "Barney.

Del nearly choked. He didn't think he had ever heard his father referred to so familiarly, but then again, they *had* spent the better part of the past ten years apart. He kept towards the back of the room as the others took their places—his father and Lord Thomas seated in chairs facing each other in front of the large mahogany desk, and each of their men of business at the book table in the center of the room.

"So." The Earl of Cleeve settled comfortably into an armchair. "I find my son is to marry your daughter."

"He is. There's no help for it. Found him with his tongue down her throat. Takes after his father."

Cleeve inclined his head at Lord Thomas with what Del could only describe as a mischievous, schoolboy grin. "Naturally. I understand Miss Burke is an exceptionally beautiful young woman."

"She takes after her mother."

"Naturally. The delightful Lady Caroline. I trust your lady is in good health?"

"The best. She would not countenance otherwise."

That response gained a bigger smile from Del's father. "Of course."

Clearly, there was history between these men, and perhaps even Lady Caroline, Del knew nothing about.

"And your lady," Lord Thomas returned, "the Countess?"

"She gets on better and better, thank you, and will continue apace, now that her son is home." He shot Del a potent glance before saying, "This is her first trip back to London."

He did not say, *since Emily's death and our year of mourning,* but Del felt the words even unsaid.

"Thank you for letting me know so quickly we were needed"—the earl shot another glance at his son—"to celebrate."

Del was annoyed with the clubbiness of their banter. They were making a joke of him. "My lord, shall we get on with it?" he asked without finesse.

"By all means," his father answered.

Lord Thomas scowled. "Yes, then speak up and tell us, Viscount Darling, what you have to offer."

It seemed to take hours. The Viscount, his father, and their men of business had arrived at eleven o'clock in the morning. The clock was nearing two in the afternoon when at last the butler came to ask Celia to attend her father in his study.

When she went downstairs Viscount Darling was by himself. Since the awful night at Fenmore House she had seen nothing of him but the glance she had of him walking up Grosvenor Street. She'd watched from her third-floor bedchamber window, whence she had been banished while the situation was settled between gentlemen.

"Viscount Darling."

He bowed correctly. "Miss Burke."

They stood awkwardly for a long moment. At least she felt awkward. It didn't help that he stood there assessing her, saying nothing.

"I am very sorry for all this trouble."

"As am I." He was solemn and clearly very, very unhappy with the state of events.

"I tried to explain to Papa we wouldn't suit." It was all her fault. If only she hadn't kissed him. If only she'd done the right thing and not given in to the impulse to touch him one last time. She didn't want to regret the kiss. She didn't want to know one impetuous, glorious, lovely kiss had led to this awful state of affairs. She didn't want to know she had trapped him with her incaution. She had trapped herself as well.

She wanted to remember the bittersweet tenderness of the kiss. It was only her third. Though they had all come from the same man, they had been nothing alike. The first had been all rough possession, heated and thrilling, the second over almost as soon as it began, while the third kiss, the one that had sealed their fate, had pierced her soul with its generosity and shocking affection.

Celia tried to latch on to that thought. He must have *some* affection for her. He would never have consented to taking her for a wife otherwise.

"Why won't we suit, Miss Burke?" His voice was quiet and low.

She was back to being Miss Burke, when only two days ago she had been Celia. "You are very much a man of the world, so obviously at home in London, where you have a great deal of acquaintance. I wish only for quiet country living, where I can continue my studies. I would always be uncomfortable here, in your world."

"I own a house in the country. You will be comfortable there."

She noted very precisely he made no mention of himself. She must accustom herself to it. "Oh. Thank you. Where will you live?"

He tipped his head back slowly, so he might regard her with patronizing haughtiness the way he had that first night, in Widcombe's book room. "Wherever my business takes me."

"I see. Your family's house is in Gloucestershire, I believe?" What a horrible conversation they were having.

"Yes, my family's house is in Gloucestershire."

"So you see we will not suit, for I had hoped not to leave Devon. My work is there."

He regarded her silently, his deep blue eyes narrowed in displeasure for a very long time before he spoke. "But we must marry. There is no going around it or putting it off, I am told. Not even for your work."

The silence in the room was like the morning fog, entirely impenetrable. Celia had no skill, no charm to deal with the wall that was his discontent. "I am sorry, Viscount Darling."

"Yes, Miss Burke. So am I." He bowed and took his leave.

They were married two days later at the fashionable St. George's Church in Hanover Square. The high-toned church was a sop to Lady Caroline, who, robbed of the fashionable wedding she would have preferred for her daughter, had to settle instead for a fashionable church.

The ceremony seemed fast and nearly intelligible. Celia was quite at sea over his names, there were so many. Rupert James Edmund Walter Charles. She was only Celia Augusta.

She longed for the familiar confines of St. Savior's and the comfort of friends. She longed for Lizzie, for her advice and sensible disdain for pomp and rank. The guests were all so exhaustively elevated and grand. Dukes, Marquesses and Earls, Commanders and Lieutenants. Such a plethora of names and titles, Celia wasn't sure she could keep them straight, until she reminded herself how very much like Latin plant names they were, rather a human system of classification. She herself was to be classified as a Viscountess—Viscountess Darling. One day, she would be Countess of Cleeve. It was all unbelievable. And so unnecessary.

Clearly Viscount Darling thought so. He looked as miserable as he did magnificent. He had chosen to wear his scarlet Marine Forces uniform, with its silver epaulettes and buttons, and wide red sash over his white waistcoat. But the brilliant color could not animate the impenetrable mask of his carefully blank face. He made no expression to give her any idea of what he was thinking or feeling. He made no intonation as he repeated his vows and handed her a small signet ring to put on her own finger.

They left immediately following a short, uneventful breakfast where everyone was cordial, but no one was happy. It was all very English.

The Viscount handed her into the Earl of Cleeve's richly appointed traveling carriage but sat next to her for only the time it took them to pull out of sight of the house, whereupon he stopped the coach, disembarked, and mounted his black Hanoverian.

"Viscount Darling?" Celia had no idea what she was meant to call him. "May I ask how far we are to go?" She had not packed any bags, nor had she instructed Bains to do so.

"As far as we can." And he was gone.

They left the city through the Tyburn Toll Gate and headed west by northwest on the Oxford Road. Exhausted from the tension, tired and bored, Celia fell asleep midafternoon and slept until Viscount Darling woke her late in the long summer evening.

They were at an inn. She stood transfixed, squinting upward with her hand raised to shade her eyes, by the sign swinging over the yard—a vibrantly painted depiction of a prancing dog wearing a scarlet doublet. "The Dog in a Doublet. How intriguing."

"It's just an expression." He scowled. "It refers to a sort of daring, resolute fellow."

"Yes, I know." How extraordinary. Perhaps it was a sign—an omen, not just an advertisement—a sign she had done the right thing after all. She had been daring and resolute, and look where it had gotten her. Married to Viscount Darling.

But he did not appreciate her remark. "Ah. I had momentarily forgotten how shockingly well-educated you are."

Celia kept quiet after that rebuke. She didn't inquire about her accommodations, or his, for that matter. She was so astonished to be shown into a bedchamber and find Bains already there, waiting with all her baggage, Celia ran into her arms and promptly burst into tears.

"Miss Celia. There, there. Bains has you. You'll be just fine now, my lamb. Your Bains has you now."

He wanted to get drunk. He wanted not to give a damn. He wanted his wife not to address him as an object, a thing. He wanted a lot of damn things he was bloody unlikely to get.

But he could get drunk. It had been a long time since he'd indulged in the pleasure of oblivion. If he wasn't to get it in the preferred form from his weeping bride, he could find it in a glass. Or a tankard. Several tankards.

The taproom of the Dog in a Doublet, where he began, appropriately enough, with a pint of bitters, was full of jovial fellows ready to drink to his health and help him pass his time and his money. Del was also pleased to find there was to be an impromptu prizefight held in the stable yard later in the evening. An ostler of the inn had been challenged by another man—a brawny footman from a traveling carriage, according to one source, or the son of the local blacksmith from another, equally unreliable report.

Here was sport to warm a man's blood. Just the sort of thing he liked—violent, bloody, and straightforward. And no damn weeping.

Del wondered idly if the footman was one of his. He wandered out to the yard with a pitcher of ale and found his father's driver, Bibbs, making good book. "How's it running, Bibbs?"

"Four to one for the ostler. Mick's his name. Big Irish kid. Good lad. Strong and quick. Good for a heavy mill."

"And the challenger? One of yours?"

Bibbs shook his jowls. "Blacksmith's apprentice from the village. I'm after thinking there's history between them two. Wouldn't be surprised to find there's a woman in it."

"I'll put ten on the challenger."

"Ha ha. You were always bloody-minded, even as a boy. But I'll be happy to relieve you of your money, your lordship."

He might have been bloody-minded as a lad, but he was more so that night, drunk and antagonistic. He almost wished he were going to be the one Mick the Ostler would mill into the ground. Anything would be better than his current state. Anything to bruise the bloody care out of him.

The fight was to be staged in the yard, in a fairly level area of the cobbles marked off by chalk. Del did have the presence of mind to note the ring was nearly under the "very best room" the innkeeper had allotted them, the room where his sobbing bride slept. But with this throng, she wouldn't sleep for long. He almost thought of going up and warning her. Almost. But he was drunk and she was beautiful. It didn't seem like a smart combination. And he was a little unsure of his ability to successfully navigate the narrow stairs. So instead, he took another drink and elbowed his way to the edge of the ring.

The two men stripped to their breeches and stepped in. The blacksmith's lad was a long way from his last bath and stank of coal fire. And they hadn't even broken a sweat. Someone, a small fellow with yellow teeth and a stentorian voice, called out the match under London Prize Rules, and the mill was on.

Mick the Ostler was a rangy fellow with a long reach, and he took his opponent's measure with a few lightning quick jabs with his left. Bill the Smithy moved slowly and took both hits without making a stab of his own. Then Mick the Ostler simply let loose a cannon of a right and the smithy was down like a gunner. And stayed down.

The crowd shifted and surged in disgust and discontent. One of the lads from the stable threw a bucket of water on the smithy. Nothing. The man was out cold. The fight was over almost as soon as it had begun.

Deprived of their sport, the crowd began to get ugly and abusive, hurling invectives at Yellow Teeth and pushing and shoving at each other. In another minute the event would erupt into an out-and-out melee. Not that Del would mind in the least. A good brawl would finish his day off nicely.

With that thought fresh in his lushy head, Del stepped forward and said, "I'll give him some sport," and proceeded to strip off his coat and clothing.

Bibbs, knowing a thing or two about working the odds in a nasty crowd, appeared by his side and bawled, "May I hold yer coat for ya, Colonel, yer lordship?"

"Good man, Bibbs," Del drawled. "We'll have a go of it, shall we?"

The crowd erupted in rude pleasure at the thought of witnessing the thrashing of an aristocrat.

"Sure you want to be in my corner, Bibbs?"

Bibbs tipped him a wink. "You were always a dab hand with yer fives as a lad. Have ya kept it up?"

"I was four years a bullock in the Marines before I became an officer, Bibbs. What do you think?"

"Ah, ha ha. I think we'll have a fine go of it, so we will." Bibbs turned to address the crowd. "Who'll lay me money against his lordship, the Viscount?" There was a surge of takers, fists of money were thrust under Bibbs' nose.

Yellow Teeth sidled up and informed Del, "This ain't Gentleman Jackson's here, yer lordship. If you can't take it no more, you've to cry off. Yeh ken?"

"I ken." Del stripped off his shirt and stepped in. "I'll give him a fair brawl."

The crowd's mood, though improved, was still restive. They were ravenous for blood.

"Mill the bastard, Micko," and, "Serve that cull out," were some of the less obscene calls. Del smiled. It was going to be a proper cat scrawl. He stepped into the ring, put up his hands, and they were at it. There was no easing in, no finesse. Mick came at him with the punishing right, but Del was fast and looking for it. He blocked him high and came under with a hook to soften up his insides. The lad took it with a hard grunt and came back with a rounder of a left that glanced along Del's jaw and sent shards of pain cracking through him like grapeshot, clearing out his brains. *God, that felt good.*

The crowd surged and backed around them, a living sea of oaths and obscene encouragement. "Tip the cove a muzzler, Mick!"

The lad swung out again with the right, but Del was already in with a straight shot that cracked hard against Mick's mouth. Blood began to seep from his lip.

"There's a proper muzzler," Bibbs cried in response, right before Mick the Ostler laid Del out like an undertaker. It was a bruising cross from his left that came out of nowhere. Del's knees hit the cobbles first, before he went down hard, landing on his shoulder. Pain lodged against his ribs and began to radiate down his side. But now he was fully awake. And he was all for it. The screaming and shouting was like a wall of noise closing him in, narrowing the world and all he wanted from it to these ten feet of pavement.

He surged to his feet, turned back upon Mick, and let the world explode from the end of his arm.

CHAPTER 21

Celia woke with a start to find herself still crunched uncomfortably in an armchair. She had not been able to bring herself to lie down upon the bed. It seemed too . . . definite, too . . . Oh, she could not even put to words the discomfort and disquiet she felt around him. Any ease she had ever felt with Viscount Darling had vanished with the distant, almost cold tone of his conduct at the church.

The fire had burned low and the sky had gone dark with night. But the shadows and lights from the inn yard played across the low-beamed ceiling. She had neglected to close the curtains. It seemed as if it ought to be the dead of night, but a veritable tumult was rising from the yard. Celia crossed to the window. The low firelight from within and the wavering torchlight from without made it hard to see through the mullioned windows what was happening outside. She opened the casement and peered cautiously out.

Men were everywhere, milling about, talking and laughing and calling at the top of their lungs. Beneath her window, money and ale were changing hands freely, and she went on her tiptoes to look farther. *Oh, good gracious.* The crowd encircled two men, who were stripped to the waist and pummeling the stuffing out of each other.

It was a fight—a bare-knuckle boxing match—of some sort. Celia's stomach tightened. How appalling, the idea of two men pummeling each other for entertainment and profit.

There was something about the bare skin of one man, gilded by the torchlight, golden like a pagan idol. *Oh, good God.*

Celia nearly tipped herself out the window, craning her head to see. It was *him*. It was Viscount Darling, her husband. She clamped a hand across her mouth to keep from crying out. He had shed all his clothes except his boots and breeches. No matter her opinion of the spectacle, she could not take her eyes off him. Light shone off the skin of his strong forearms and there was a glimmering of the fine hairs on his arm. He was taller than most of the men who crowded around him shouting and swearing and gesturing. The man fighting him was just as tall, but dark headed, and appeared to be pummeling her husband to a bloody pulp. Blood streaked down one side of his beautiful face and oozed from his mouth and several spots along his ribs.

Celia bit down hard on her lip to keep from making a sound. Darling's body shone pale in the torchlight, like something out of Montague House—a marble statue of a Greek god, all sleek white skin and carved muscle. She could see the contours of his broad shoulders and the sculpted length of his arms as the muscles bunched and whipped out to strike.

He turned, following his opponent, who, now that she could see him, was as bloody as Viscount Darling, his split lip oozing blood down his chin. She watched as Darling's arm lashed out and cracked the man hard across his nose, snapping his head back before he fell backward into the arms of the throng.

A roar rose up from the surging crowd as blood gushed from the dark-haired man's nose. The men tried to push him back towards Viscount Darling, but he was unsteady and stumbled.

Darling caught him before he fell, and they staggered and slipped slowly towards the cobbles together.

The spectators pressed forward, and for a long moment Celia couldn't see anything. Then a huzzah went up and Viscount Darling and the other fellow were hoisted on shoulders and paraded around the throng. Men were patting each other and the two fighters on the backs and giving them drinks of ale. Viscount Darling tossed back a tankard and roared with laughter. When they let him down he shook hands with his fellow fighter and ambled unsteadily out of their midst back to Gosling and the driver Bibbs, who handed him his clothes. But he didn't put any of it back on. The Viscount swiped the blood from his face and lips with the back of his arm, and tipped his head up to laugh and drink down another throatful of ale from a dripping jug.

His eyes, already swelling and growing black from the beating, met hers. She wanted to call out. Her instinct was to ask him if he was all right, to see if he was hurt, but he just stared at her. It was a look of such black, almost violent intent, she recoiled.

Darling laughed and started into the building, clearly intent upon gaining their room. Celia could hear his heavy, booted tread on the stairs, moving unsteadily up to her.

She tasted the acid pulse of fear in her mouth and without thinking, she flew across the room to the door and jammed the bar down, locking the door. The treads of his uneven footsteps sounded in the corridor and came to a halt outside her door. She could hear and feel him thumb the latch, and lean his weight into the door. He rattled it once.

"Celia," his voice was a low, hushed growl that raised the fine hair on her neck. "I know you're in there. Let me in."

She held her breath and covered her mouth with her hand, lest her will give way before her good sense. She held her other hand over the latch, holding it firmly in place.

"Damn it to hell, Celia." He rattled the latch once more, then turned and stomped down the passage and down the stairway.

She had never, even at the beginning of their acquaintance, let herself believe he was anything but what Emily had believed. She had never let herself consider that his reputation, although earned by bad behavior, was who he was. But she was no longer sure. She was afraid. Afraid of what her rash behavior had made her become.

Darling slept off the worst of his evening's excess in a pile of hay in the stable. Not exactly the most salubrious of accommodations, but he'd had many worse. When Gosling awoke him, the ingenious man had somehow contrived to have hot water, shaving gear, and a fresh press of clothes at the ready. By the time he sent for his wife, Del was every inch the tailored aristocrat—with an enormous quantity of vivid, swollen bruises.

But even dressed flawlessly, he was surprised to find uncertainty making mush of his insides. He was not looking forward to the coming interview with his wife. While he had slept off most of his irrational anger at her barring the door to him—he agreed her actions had been prudent, given his state of inebriation and his general level of bloodlust—he was in no shape for a lecture. After all, it had been partially her fault his violently conflicted feelings for her had sent him in search of a brawl in the first place.

But there was no lecture, nor even so much as a reproachful look. She was the very picture of martyred, bashful timidity.

"My lord," was all she said. She did not look him in the eye as he handed her into the carriage, and immediately took the backward facing seat, sliding to the far side of the upholstered bench.

"Good morning, madam." He followed her in and sat in the

middle of the forward facing seat, where she should have been.

Why would she assume he would not treat her with the most simple courtesy? Did she think him such an animal, so unmannerly, so ungentlemanly and savage not to know what was due her? God's balls but martyrdom would get old very, very fast. He could not keep the mocking bite from his tone. "I trust you slept well."

Her head snapped towards him at that, and he was surprised again—strange how he was not yet used to her surprising him at almost every turn—by what he saw in her eyes. She was afraid. Of him.

Del swallowed that piece of information as readily as a jagged shard of glass. He had only once before seen the same kind of fear shining in her eyes—in the alley on the way back from North Row that night. *Damn my eyes.*

She was afraid, but at least she was honest. "I-I did not sleep well." She managed to look him in the eye fleetingly as she answered. "I think you know that. The noise and the . . . violence—"

"I'm sorry," he replied, though he hadn't been sorry for the fight, not at all. He had instigated it, for Christ's sake, looking for a way to bruise the bloody, frustrated hunger out of him. And he wasn't sorry she'd seen. It had given him a thrill of almost savage, animal pride to see her watching him, to know that her eyes were on his body. But he had not counted on the violence making her afraid.

"Are you . . . are you very much hurt?" She was looking at his gloriously blackened eye. Gosling's hand mirror had revealed a deep wash of purples and greens under his puffy skin.

"No." He lifted one side—the unsplit side—of his mouth and gave her what he hoped was a cocky grin, although the effect lost something when he winced. "You should see the other fellow."

"I did. He had blood all over his face and chest." She shivered a little, pushing herself farther into her corner.

"Must have broken his nose. Bleed rather a lot, noses do. So do cuts of any kind to the head. Even this little one here"—he pointed to the plastered slit under his eye—"bled like a river. But they don't hurt much."

She nodded thoughtfully as if she were cataloguing that particular piece of information somewhere in the recesses of her scientific mind. At least they were talking, though she was still cramped up in that corner. They bounced hard from the rutted roads over the Cotswold Hills and she grabbed at the strap to keep herself steady.

"The fog is lifting. There should be some spectacular scenery. Why don't you sit here, so you'll have a better view?" He slid over in the seat, making ample room for her on the upholstered bench.

"No I-I wouldn't want to bump into you. Your . . . ribs. They were all red and bruised, all smashed last night."

So she had noticed.

"They're purple this morning, though I daresay, they'll keep. We've hours to go yet, and I doubt the roads will improve. You'd best come over."

"I am fine here, thank you."

"Suit yourself," he growled. *God's balls, but she makes it easy to be irritated with her.* He pulled his tall hat down over his eyes, folded his arms across his chest, stretched his long booted legs across on top of the middle of the other seat, and closed his eyes. He would be comfortable even if she chose not to be. Let her cower in her corner. He did not want her. He did not like her. He was not in love with her.

The motion of the carriage was unsteady, and when they hit

a particularly jolting rut, she flung out her hand and grabbed his leg to steady herself.

And he knew it was all a lie, his protestation. He knew, because a shot of pure, unadulterated lust bolted up his leg straight to his groin at the feel of her hand clutching the inside of his knee. *Damn her.* He widened his stance, shoving his leg up next to her, bracing her into the corner. And still she hung on to his leg. He never lifted his eyes, but he could feel that hand. He could feel his nerves stretching taut towards the pressure of her fingers, sorting out each and every individual sensation they engendered, each and every tentative caress and flex of her fingers along the sensitive inside of his knee.

He learned something about himself then, about his own body. He, who had taught mistresses in a dozen languages, who had prided himself on his prowess as a cocksman, learned something about himself from this naive, terrified virgin.

It seemed the inside of his knee was a remarkably sensitive place. Had he ever been asked to name an area pertinent to arousal, he would not have thought to mention that small patch of his bodily real estate, but it seemed the whole world, every tactile sensation worth feeling, was concentrated there, where her hand gripped his leg. Even through the layers of his breeches and smallclothes. Even over the cotton of his stockinged leg.

He braced his legs wider still, snugging up against her, fencing her in tight with the weight of his body. And she didn't protest. She clutched him tighter as they climbed into the rutted Cotswold Hills.

She had not been so timid the last time she had held his leg in a carriage, had she? Then she had looked at him with those wide eyes of hers and offered to fondle his aching cock. That would be a definite improvement upon the present circumstances. Del eyed her from under the low brim of his hat. What would it take for him to finish what they had started that night in the carriage? They were married now. He could do with her as he liked.

But she would not spare even a glance towards him. She was so resolutely stiff and anxious, despite her clutch of his knee, his pride would not let him relent. He'd be damned before he was going to extend an ounce of energy seducing her into a better humor. He turned his head away and closed his eyes again.

He thought of his small, snug house. It wasn't large, by his way of thinking. It was nothing on the scale of his father's seat, Cleeve Abbey, where he had grown up, or even Fair Prospect. It was just a manor house, but Del liked to call it his navy house—the property he had purchased with his hard-won prize money. It was his and his alone, something apart from the vast Delacorte holdings of which he would one day have to become the owner.

His house was not vast. It was small and private—a perfect retreat while he figured out what in the bloody world he was going to do with his reluctant bride.

Finally, in the early afternoon they pulled up the lane in front of a lovely, picturesque, moated manor house of the last century. "What a pretty house."

Viscount Darling made no response, just handed Celia out of the carriage and walked her to the steps where an older couple waited.

"Mr. and Mrs. Level, this is my wife, Viscountess Darling. Mrs. Level is my housekeeper and Level is my steward."

"Welcome, my lady," Mrs. Level made a deep curtsy, and welcomed Celia with a sunny, open smile.

Celia returned her smile as best she could. "Thank you."

Mrs. Level led her in. Although old-fashioned in layout, the house was scrupulously clean, with large, sashed windows in every room. "How very pretty." Celia felt very conscious of making a good impression despite her discomfort in being so closely watched. She kept a smile pinned resolutely to her face. "And well kept. Is there other staff I might meet?"

"I get three girls from the village, days, when his lordship is here, and Level will get some boys for the stable if those carriages are to stay. Will you need a girl, my lady?"

"No, thank you. My maid, Bains, follows with the baggage. She's been with me in Dartmouth, so she's a countrywoman. I hope you'll like her." There was a clattering and jangling of brass and leather as the second carriage drove into sight. "Here she is."

Bains disembarked directly. "If I might ask, my lady, how long are we to be here, so I might get up the bags."

"I don't know. I shall have to ask Viscount Darling."

He still stood by the door, stripping of his gloves. "This, madame, will be your home."

Celia nodded and moved away, anxious to conceal the film of heat in her eyes, but Bains seemed oblivious to the tension between them.

"Right then, my lady. If you'll show me where am I to take my lady's things?" Bains asked Mrs. Level, who turned to Viscount Darling.

"Suit yourself." He shrugged and walked away.

Celia felt her face scorch with embarrassment. His disdain, especially in front of their servants, was completely humiliating. He might as well have posted a notice—they were not to be intimate in any way.

She was offered tea, either in the drawing room or in the sunny central hall, but Celia asked if she might take it upstairs in her new room. She had no desire to take tea alone and she'd much rather be busy with Bains than fall into purposeless self-pity as she began the task of settling into her new home. It would keep her from wondering if Viscount Darling had any plans to make it his home as well.

Bains' back soon grew sore from lifting, and there were more trunks to bring up from the pile in the forecourt. Without any footmen on hand to help Bains shift the heavy baggage it was slow going.

"Bains, you just concentrate on that lot. I'll get the rest."

"My lady—"

"Stop, Bains. I've carried heavier buckets up from the river, you know I have."

"That's not the point, miss. He should have—I mean you're mistress here now, and you should have staff provided for you, so you don't have to do such things."

"Please don't, Bains." Celia might think the same thing, but she would not give in to self-pity, nor let Bains be disrespectful to Viscount Darling. They had enough trouble as it was without borrowing more. "I don't mind, truly. You leave me to it."

When she had managed to heft one middling-size chest onto her back and drag another small one alongside, Viscount Darling reemerged from whatever lair he'd crawled into. Striding angrily down the steps to stop her, he growled, "What in hell do you think you are doing?" He pulled the larger of the two out of her grip and hoisted it himself.

"I'm baking a cake. Obviously."

The Viscount was predictably unamused. "If that was an attempt at humor, my lady—"

Anger burst out of her like hail from a cloud, pelting down icy bits of cold resentment. "It was not an attempt at humor, my lord. It was an attempt at sarcasm. Something with which you are all too familiar."

He cocked his head back at that.

Good. He wasn't the only one who could be curt and surly. It kept her from examining the pain that radiated from her heart whenever she was in his uninterested presence.

"Madam, I am only trying to keep you from getting yourself hurt."

"Then, my lord, you are several days too late." With that

she turned around and slammed her way into the house. She would not cry. She would not. She had not endured a black-mailer and seduction and spite just to turn into a watering pot because Viscount Darling still found her too skinny a Christ-ian to bother eating. She would not cry.

But it was hard to stay hurt and resentful in such beautiful surroundings. She went out the doors that led to the moated grass terrace at the back of the house. The constant sound of the flowing water was a balm. Beyond, on the other side of the moat were lovely naturally planted gardens, which gave way to lawns and woods. On the lawn was a sweeping view down the hill toward the wide river Severn. It was magnificently, serenely beautiful.

Celia could no more stay away from the water than could a duck. Algae and plants were rooted in the brick walls of the moat channel, but not a large variety, from what she could see. She crossed the moat carefully by the small removable foot-bridge, which was little more than a reinforced plank, and fol-lowed the water upstream until she was following along the banks of the stream that fed water into the channels. It was, much to her delight, teeming with aquatic plant life.

She may have been deprived of finishing her survey of Devon plant life, but she would have ample time to begin anew there. Once Viscount Darling was gone off, she could do as she liked with her time. She would have to see if there was suitable space for a workroom in one of the outbuildings along the stable courtyard. If Viscount Darling was to abandon her, she could order the house as she liked. She could even have her own study and book room. What a brilliant idea!

Celia turned back to the house with fresh eyes. She did not know enough about architecture to know the name of the style of building, but she knew the house appealed to some-thing within her, something that recognized a need for bal-ance and harmony. Lord knew, she would find little enough of

it in her marriage. At least she would find it in her surroundings. The manor house was perfectly symmetrical, in the
shape of a shallow *H*, though the land inside the moat was
roughly rectangular in shape. How serendipitous that Viscount
Darling should bring her to a house so shaped by the course of
water.

She had wandered out of doors without the benefit of either
shawl or bonnet, and soon enough she felt the lack of a hat.
After the gray of the morning, the sun shone down in all its
summer fierceness. Her fair skin would be reddened and
freckled in no time.

She wandered slowly back towards the south side of the
house, and the attached, walled stable yard and gardens. The
stable yard was still busy with the housing of two coaches and
nine animals, so she went on to the kitchen garden, a large
plot with herbs and vegetables all neatly set out in rows behind low boxed knot hedges. Her favorite herbs were lined up
like friends ready to be greeted. They warmed her as only
friends could.

A step led up, out of the walled stable court back into the
house. The kitchens, where she could hear Mrs. Level clattering away at dinner were down to the right, but to the left was
a study. She was astonished to find it completely filled with
books!

Celia stepped towards the entry. With all his stories of being
mad to leave school for the Marines, she had never imagined
Viscount Darling as a reading man. But such a room, filled to
the brim with books packed tight on the shelves and scattered
in piles on the large central table!

She would have stepped in, but she saw him then, Viscount
Darling, seated at a large desk between the windows at the far
side of the room, scribbling away at some important document
or other. She pulled back into the shadow of the corridor and
watched him surreptitiously. He had removed his coat and was

clad in his loose, unbuttoned linen shirt and waistcoat. Now that she had seen him stripped of his veneer of civility, his mask of civilized gentleman, she knew hardened flesh and sinew lay beneath. Sculpted chest and broad shoulders. Pale gleaming skin. Bunched muscles along his abdomen, and lower where the trail of gleaming blond hair disappeared into the waist of his breeches.

She turned away from the doorway, pressed herself flat against the wall of the house, and clenched her thighs to dispel the startling ache deep in her belly.

This would not do. She could not spend the rest of her life yearning and panting after a man who found her so utterly and deeply uninteresting and unappealing, he was prepared to leave her behind in this house while he went back out into the world.

There were only two things she could do. She must either learn to live without him, or make him want to stay.

After Celia's very clear warning, Del stayed away from her for the rest of the day and throughout the evening. He took dinner in his study and was informed his wife took hers on a tray upstairs. Yet, his thoughts, though he tried to busy himself with work, were with her constantly. He had only to look outside his window, and there she had been, trying to haul boxes heavier than her entire body weight up two flights of stairs, arguing with him in the courtyard, lying flat on her stomach on the lawn to search the moat for plant life or examining the herb beds, rattling off Latin names like incantations. Perhaps she was muttering incantations and casting spells against him. What had she said? *I hate people. They are so lying and deceitful and hateful.* She might as well have been describing him. Perhaps she was.

But he was hopelessly spellbound. Despite all his injunctions to the contrary, he couldn't stop himself from looking.

And wanting. Wanting to hold her and soothe her spiky anger, ease away the fears that lurked behind her haunted eyes. Perhaps it had to do with how alike she seemed to Emily. Except what he felt for Celia wasn't the least bit brotherly. It was barely civilized.

It was compelling—compelling him to quit his study and wander through the gardens in the bright moonlight, letting the constant sound of the water soothe the misbegotten tension out of him. But as soon as he returned to the quiet of the house, he was compelled to seek her out, to prowl through the empty, darkened rooms, climb the creaking staircase and seek out her door. Compelling him to try the handle.

It turned silently in his hand. She had not locked him out. Was it relief or resolve that flowed through him?

Del waited until his eyes adjusted to the pale moonlight streaming through the open windows. She was asleep, though she was not a peaceful sleeper, his Celia. The bedcovers and linens were a complete tangle. She was turned over onto her belly and her nightclothes had slipped off her shoulder to reveal the pale triangle of her shoulder blade. Her feet were spread apart, separated, one bare foot and ankle defiantly projecting out from beneath the covers, over the side of the bed. Oh, God, it was strangely beautiful, the arc of her calf. It rose from the scoop at the back of her foot in an elegant swoop of muscle and sinew.

How ridiculous. Young ladies didn't have muscle and sinew. They were all pillowed softness and heady, drugging scent. And gracefully toned calves.

As he watched, she stirred, turning first one way and tossing the other, pulling the nightdress taut against the outline of one perfect breast. Del felt an instant flood of pure arousal. But he moved no closer. He had no doubt he could wake her with kisses and ease her into his arms. But he couldn't do it. It was too important. She had to choose. He could only pray she would choose him.

Del dropped down into an upholstered chair and kept his eyes on her, on the beautiful, rumpled, delectable image she presented, letting lust wash through his body like the warmth of the night breeze. He wouldn't think about why he felt such desire or what he was going to do about it. He wouldn't think at all. Because he would find it damned inconvenient, not to mention bloody-minded, to desire and be aroused by a girl he had once pledged to hate and never touch.

CHAPTER 22

Del watched Celia wake slowly as the bright morning sun streamed in the east windows and fell across the bed. She stretched and blinked at him, rubbing at her face as if the cobwebs of her dreams still clung to her.

"Did I dream you?" she breathed.

No hysterics. No protests. No coldness. She radiated warm, curious interest.

"It isn't a dream. I'm here."

He could hear the sounds of the house stirring to life below—Mrs. Level in the kitchens and Bains climbing the north stair with an uneven, burdened gate, likely hauling up Celia's morning water. He could not linger.

"I've been here all night, but I must go." He stood.

"Wait," she protested and threw the covers off, revealing those pale wondrous calves and bare feet. There was something erotically intimate about the sight of her long elegant feet, as she padded silently across the floor towards her dressing room, looking for a robe. As she passed near him he could see one shoulder beautifully revealed and the peaks of her nipples visible through the cotton of her nightdress as the morning's chill air reached her body.

"Come riding with me. I'm going out. Come with me." He hadn't meant it to sound like a command.

She stopped and turned, and the morning sunlight backlit the translucent cotton of her nightdress so he could see the exquisite silhouette of her naked body beneath. God's balls, he was instantly hard. She hugged herself against the morning air, folding her arms across her body, around the middle, but the move only seemed to accentuate the press of the thin fabric against her breasts. The sweet rose of her nipples stood out starkly, begging for his touch. He took a step towards her.

But she had already turned for the dressing room, yawning and raking a hand through the riot of her curls. "I'll come. I'll come. Let me get changed." Bains was at the dressing room door, giving him a disapproving look before the two of them disappeared behind closed doors.

He swallowed and shifted slightly to ease the tightness of his cock against his breeches. Why had he not taken her? Why did he persist in torturing himself?

Because as much as he wanted her, he wanted her to be willing. No, more than willing. Eager. He wanted Celia to need and want him just as much as he needed and wanted her. To love him just as much as he loved her.

Nothing else was good enough. Nothing else mattered.

He took less than a quarter of an hour to wash, scrape the beard from his face, and change his clothes before he was in the yard. He had just realized Celia was going to have to ride one of the carriage horses, when he heard her quick footsteps. He kept his hat low over his eyes and tried to hide his hunger at the sight of her running out of the house and across the stable yard towards him, flushed and breathless, so obviously anxious not to keep him waiting.

She was dressed in a different riding habit from their outing in Dartmouth—a bright, matching green jacket and waistcoat, fitting snugly across her chest and arms, over a lighter-colored, country skirt—though she wore the same lace fichu secured with a knot at her neck, covering any view of her flesh.

A few minutes saw them off. Del led them across the bridge and into the fields to the west, towards the Severn, down the gentle hillside to a wooded path along the river.

When they reached the river she spoke. "Thank you for bringing me out. It is a pleasure to explore the countryside hereabouts with someone who knows the area. I missed this."

"Riding?"

"Yes. I didn't ride at all in London. But mostly, I missed being in the countryside. If I try hard enough, I can imagine I'm still in Dartmouth. I'm very glad there's a river. And the stream and moat."

"Did you not like London?"

"It was exciting. And different. The Royal Society was beyond my expectation. But I fear I am a countrywoman at heart. This is excellent country."

She was looking with interest at the river, no doubt picturing the various pieces of interesting glop she would fish out to draw. There were still dark smudges under her eyes, but they were sparkling with curiosity and light.

"I have no idea, of course, but I imagine it will be possible for you to find specimens for your drawings here, although the water is somewhat more brackish than along the Devon coast."

"Oh, my study has been of only freshwater plants, not the coastal." She looked away to avoid giving full answers.

Del could not quite understand her. She seemed at turns anxious to please and drawing away, at odds with herself. Or him. What a pair, they were—neither of them knew their own mind well enough to be other than confused and confusing. But he would not give up.

"Will the stream by itself provide enough subjects of interest for your study?"

"I suppose. It depends." Her manner was hesitant, and when he looked at her face, he could see the lines of confusion pleating her brow.

"Do you not plan to take up your study anew here?"

At his question she took a deep breath and asked, "Will you let me?"

"Let you?" He was her husband, not her keeper. But it stung, she should think so little of him. After all they had been through, after all they had spoken of, she ought to know him better. She ought to remember. *He* had been the one to buy the bloody microscope. How could she have forgotten? "I had thought a dedicated scientist would simply insist. But I suppose you're not the insisting type, are you?"

"No." She swallowed and kept her eyes away, hiding herself from him. Retreating into obedient passivity.

His carefully forgotten anger of the previous day boiled to the surface. "Is there anything you're going to insist upon in this misbegotten marriage?" Frustration colored his voice but he didn't wish the words back. It seemed as good a time as any to have it out, once and for all. He had to know.

But Celia didn't seem inclined to row with him. She squinted over the vista of the estuary and answered with her own question. "Why were you in my room this morning?" Her voice trembled slightly, but there was nothing accusatory in her tone. She projected a quiet, if slightly anxious curiosity. It seemed there were things she had to know as well.

Del felt the bluster pass out of him. "Honestly? I meant to show you there would be no locked doors between us. Ever again."

She nodded, more in acceptance, he thought, than agreement. "I'm sorry. I should not have done so at the inn. You were injured and bleeding and I should have let you in, but I was . . ."

"Afraid. You were afraid of me."

She nodded, keeping her eyes down. The answer was the barest whisper. "Yes."

He realized she was not angry, or still afraid. She was ashamed. Ashamed of being afraid. As ashamed as he was for frightening her. "You needn't be afraid. That's why I stayed in your room last night. To show you I am not a ravening animal. I slept in the chair all night because it seemed the best way to prove you can trust me."

She looked at him fully. "You've always been trustworthy. Even when you said I shouldn't trust you, I always could. I should have remembered that."

The knowledge of his fault lanced through him. He had not always been trustworthy. He had thought the worst of her. He had acted badly towards her. "I called it willful kindness, this way you have, but now I know its true name: generosity. You are very generous to me."

She blushed, the sunlight beaming down on her face. The wash of pink across her cheeks brought out the scattering of freckles across her nose. "I was dreaming of you, this morning, and then—there you were. It seemed as if I had conjured you out of the dream."

"What did you dream?"

"I was thinking of you when I went to bed. I couldn't sleep, because I owed you an apology for my rude behavior." A frown pinched lines between her brows. "It had gotten late. The house was quiet. Everyone else was already abed, I suppose. But I like that time best, when everything is quiet and still and washed in moonlight. I went down to your study, looking for you. But you weren't there, so I took a glass of brandy. Or cognac. I'm not sure I know the difference."

It was a charming, if contradictory, picture she painted. "I didn't think you touched spirits."

"Oh, I am not so completely naive or green as that, Viscount Darling. I have had wine and sherry. But not brandy." She glanced up at him from under the brim of her hat as she spoke. "You will think I'm foolish, but I thought the brandy smelled like you. I thought if I drank a bit of it, it would taste like you."

Del felt the pulse of arousal fill his veins, a low kindling of heat from deep in his gut, spreading slowly throughout his body, warming him. But desire was not the only thing he felt. There was something else. The tightness in his chest began to ease, to be replaced by a feeling of lightness, of buoyancy. It felt very much like hope. "And did it? Taste like me?"

She was still looking at him with her brow puckered into a small frown. "I don't know, do I? I can only imagine. You stay away from me so assiduously. You are very angry with me."

Her manner wasn't flirtatious, neither was it an invitation to prove her wrong. He could see the etching of hurt in the corners of her eyes. She was looking for an answer. Scientifically. Honestly. Courageously.

He needed to be equally courageous, equally daring. "I am not angry at you. I—"

"But you do not wish to be married to me. You regret the necessity."

He regretted it only for her sake. He regretted they had been forced. Because he selfishly wanted to be chosen for himself alone. "Celia, nothing in the world could have forced me to marry you if I did not wish to do so."

She shrugged and hitched up her shoulders, a twisting, defensive posture. "Yet, you take no pleasure in it. I am quite sure you do not want me to feel any of the pleasure I feel in your company."

The seed of hope in his chest expanded into life. She took pleasure in his company—despite the fact that of late he had not been fit company at all. Willfully kind. Generous.

"Did you like the brandy? The taste?"

"It was very strong. I'm not sure I actually liked it—or that I'd go so far as to say I liked it, but I did like the way it made me feel afterwards. All . . . pleasant and warm. I can see why gentlemen like it. All the cares of the world seemed to slowly dissolve away."

"Why, Viscountess, I think you got a bit foxed. I'm sorry I missed that." He smiled at her to show he was teasing.

"I don't know," she said politely, not understanding him. "I didn't feel intoxicated, foxed as you say. I didn't want to sing bawdy songs or wander through the house, or cast up my accounts in the shrubbery. I just felt . . . happy, or happier at least."

But her tone was anything but happy or satisfied. She was confused. She was disappointed. In him.

They'd arrived back at the house, and Level was in the yard, waiting. "Ostler's here for the horses, sir."

"Yes, just a moment." Del dismounted and practically ran to Celia's side to help her down before she could accomplish it on her own. He would have kept his hands on her waist. He would have picked her up and carried her inside. He should have. But she stepped back.

"Thank you for escorting me. "I've—" She stopped herself.

It was obvious to him she really hadn't enjoyed herself. She was just trying to be polite but couldn't bring herself to outright lie.

He wouldn't make her. He did the only noble, trustworthy thing he could think of. He bowed to her and let her walk away.

Del was determined to charm her anew. He had done it once before and could do it again. He asked Mrs. Level to serve them a luncheon, as they had had no breakfast, in the more intimate confines of his study, where Celia had come looking for him. And had taken a drink. To taste him.

They ate at the small worktable. He cleared off the haphazard piles of books as Mrs. Level laid everything out.

Celia was looking at a framed architectural plan of the house. "Was it really designed by Sir Christopher Wren?"

"This house? I honestly don't know. It was advertised to me as 'very likely by Wren' when I bought it, but it has never been confirmed. I just think of it as my 'navy house'—bought and paid for with my prize monies. What do you think of it?"

"It is very pretty. I like it very much."

Del took a chance. "Shall you be happy here?" he asked quietly.

She stopped and looked up at him. Her answer was careful, and he thought, a little bit hopeful. "I shall try. What about you?"

"I shall try as well." He was quite determined. "Come and sit down." He held out a chair for her.

She smiled, a slow, tentative lighting of her face. He was struck anew with how fresh and pretty she was up close, how real she appeared, with her brandy-colored eyes, dusting of freckles, and ripe, bitten lips. But he wanted more than just proximity—he wanted intimacy.

"Tell me something about you, something no one in the whole world knows about you."

She wrinkled up her freckled nose. "A secret?"

"Yes, right now. Right off the top of your head."

"I can't swim." She bit her bottom lip.

"What?" She kept surprising him, again and again. "You're joking. A woman who spends as much time around water as you, and you can't swim? And I've put you in a house surrounded by water. Oh, Christ. We'll have to change that. I'll have to teach you straightaway."

"Will you?"

"Yes. I can't have you here, of all places— There's a pond just across the bridge and over that way." He twisted to point out the window to the east. Images of her floated across his brain, wet and clinging to him.

"Will you tell me something no one knows about *you?*" She was still smiling, wanting her share of the secrets. "Not even Emily, or Commander McAlden."

Del would much rather stick to the thought of her naked, or as close to naked as he could get her, lying in his arms in the water. Sodden bliss. "I adore chocolate gateau."

She laughed at that. He felt a smoldering of pleasure at the sound, and at her smile beaming across the table. His eyes dropped to her mouth, still bitten and chapped. He wanted to stop her worrying at her lips with his own mouth, covering hers, soothing away the anxiety and tension.

"So did Emily. Adore gateau. Did you know that? But you must have had a family cook who made excellent cake when you were little children, for you both to have such a preference."

They had, hadn't they? A tall, rather string-beanish woman, who—though she was called Mrs. Cook, as every good, English Head of Kitchen must be—was no one's image of a typical, apple-cheeked butterball. But what Mrs. Cook lacked in personal excess, she more than made up for in the excess and excellence of the sweets. However she had routinely turned out innumerable, perfectly adequate joints of roast beef and lamb to his father's bland specifications, she had been brilliant at baking. Cakes, pastries, scones, fruit tarts, and, oh God, the chocolate. He began to salivate, just thinking about it.

Funny how Celia could have strung such an accurate conjecture out of nothing more than air and insight. "You've very insightful."

"Not at all." Her smile faded slowly. "I don't seem to have any insight into you. Or what you want, Viscount Darling."

He wanted to touch her. He wanted to inhale her, devour her, take her. She was his wife. He was her husband. Perhaps she did not love him, but he could make her desire him. That was at least a place to start, wasn't it?

"What I would like, Celia, is for you to stop calling me Viscount Darling, as if we've never met before. We are married."

She swallowed. "Yes. I am sorry." She shifted back in her seat and fidgeted with the serving cloths. "This is wretched, isn't it? I seem to be terribly awkward around you again."

He rose and poured a tumbler of brandy. It was too early for alcohol, but she had wondered what he would taste like, and he meant to let her find out. "I daresay, you never thought to find yourself married. Especially not to me."

"Well, I did expect to marry, eventually, but no, not to you. I imagined doing other things with you, but not getting married," she admitted with an embarrassed laugh.

Ah. This he understood. This he could use to his advantage. "What other things did you imagine?"

"Oh. Well . . ." Two spots of high color bloomed on her cheeks.

"Celia?"

She sprang up from the table and paced away and back. "The things you had talked about. But you needn't be concerned. I understand now, it was just talk. I understand now, you don't even like to touch me."

"Is that what you thought?" He hadn't planned for his voice to move that low, or take on that rasp. It just happened.

It brought her to a near shocked standstill in the middle of a shaft of sunlight pouring over the rug. "Yes," she whispered.

"Can you not think of an alternative reason I might have kept my hands from touching you?"

She was as still as a deer in the forest. "No."

"Ah, well. You are very wrong. There is an altogether different reason." But he made no move to show her the error of her ways, or otherwise prove her wrong. He took a slow swallow of brandy. And he watched her.

One hand went up to her throat and he could see the beginnings of a magnificent flush flare up along the side of her long neck. She cast about for a distraction and found one—the tray, where she went to busy herself. Poor girl, she'd find no refuge in a dish of tea. He was in his own home, and he was married to The Ravishing Miss Burke and he meant, finally, after all his bloody dithering, to have her. To ravish her.

And he knew exactly how to do it.

He rose as well. "Yes, very wrong. Because my aversion, as you think of it, is due to the fact that if I touched you, I would not stop there. I not only want to touch you, but I am going to touch you. Now. I'm going to make love to you, Celia. I'm going to fuck you."

The teacup, a piece of fine bone china, hand painted with intricate designs in gold leaf, leapt like a live thing from her suddenly graceless hands and smashed unceremoniously into the assorted plates and pots on the tray. Hot tea and other things—honey and icing, he thought—clattered and spilled to the floor, spattering the front of her dress. There was a dash of the sticky stuff on the skin along her jawbone, just begging to be licked off. He'd get to that later.

Bains came rushing in. "Miss! I mean, my lady, what has happened? Are you hurt?"

"Your mistress has only dropped her teacup in surprise, Bains. You may go."

"But my lady's gown, sir, will stain."

"Why don't you go up and prepare a change of clothes for her? You may go."

Bains departed but Del never took his eyes from Celia's face while he spoke. The heat that had crept across her skin like sunrise had vanished, replaced by an almost porcelain pale demeanor.

"You shouldn't say . . ." Celia's words were barely a whisper.

He finished for her. "Such filthy things to my wife? I shouldn't shock you? But I wanted to shock you, Celia. I

wanted to let you know my intentions. I wanted you to be prepared. For what's to come."

"To come?"

"Yes, definitely to come." He sat back down in his leather
wingback armchair and took another drink, enjoying his private little joke.

"When?"

"That all depends upon you, I suppose."

She swallowed hard before she attempted to answer. She
was beginning to understand, or at least she felt it—the dark
almost inexorable tide of desire between them. All he had to
do was fan the flames and they would both ignite.

He let the thrill of anticipation begin to fill him. He took
another drink with the satisfaction of knowing his wait—
God's balls, but he had waited such a long, long time to have
her—was at an end. He was finally going to peel the layers of
clothing and undergarments from her body until she was
naked before him and he could lay her down and do unspeak-
ably blissful things to both their bodies.

Celia stood rooted to the same spot as if she were planted
there.

He helped her on. "It all depends upon how you want it to
go. Do you want it to happen quickly, or slowly, your seduction?"

"Slowly," she answered instantly. There was no hesitation,
only breathless wonder.

Del smiled with a relief he had not known he would feel.

He leaned over to place his drink on a nearby table and
turned so he was facing her fully. Then he sat back, stretching
out and crossing his booted legs negligibly, like a man intent
on making his wife see him as clearly and lustfully as he was
seeing her.

"Ah, that is the scientist in you, no doubt, wanting to do
everything—and I do intend to do everything—in its correct

order. Thoroughly. With great attention to detail and a minute observation of the results. Yes, I can see how you would prefer that. I confess, I think I shall like it, too. Very much."

"But I don't—"

"Don't you? But I do. I most fervently do."

"Then why do you not touch me? Why do you sit all the way over there, looking at me like that, like some awful, all-powerful despot? Like the sultan waiting to tell Scheherazade if he was going to cut off her head," she cried, frustration and confusion coloring her voice.

Her lips were parted and he could hear her breath begin to shorten and tighten within her chest, which rose and fell with percussive—or punctual—regularity, pushing the front of her stays against the flimsy confinement of her muslin gown.

"Shall you be my Scheherazade? My favorite harem girl, my *houri*? I confess, the images that spring to mind and the sensations that accompany the thought of you dancing naked before me, your tall, pale body gleaming as you turn and twirl in the sunlight, brings me great pleasure."

She gasped at him.

"Or perhaps, I should prefer to be your Scheherazade? Perhaps I should promise to tell you things that will keep you up until the sunrise? I think I should begin by telling you how pleasing it is for me to look upon you. To see the innate loveliness of your face, the architecture of your beauty, you once said. But it is more than arched brows and large eyes, your beauty. It is who you are when you look at me."

Her lips parted on an exhalation and it was all he could do to keep from leaping upon her, from taking that full lower lip into his mouth.

"I want to map that architecture with my hands and my mouth and my tongue as well as my eyes. I want to feel the curve of your cheek under my palm and taste the curve of your lip. I want to part your lips and delve deep into your sweetness with my tongue." He smiled at her again through half-closed, lazy eyes. "Perhaps you won't be sweet at all. Perhaps you'll be tart and piquant like tropical fruit, but I want to know. I want to know everything about you, everything about your body."

Her breath rose and fell rapidly. He let his gaze linger on her breasts, caressing her with his eyes, until he could watch her reaction. Her nostrils flared delicately and her eyes became lidded and heavy.

"Oh, yes. Contrary to your assertion, I do like to look at your body. I like to watch you move, to see the flowing lines and the graceful economy of everything you do. How you react. How susceptible you are to my words. Oh, yes, I like to look at your body. And at you."

She kept her eyes fastened to his with a concentrated focus that spoke of anticipation.

He did not mean to disappoint her. "After all this time, after all this looking, I still have to wonder what glories lie hidden beneath all that delightful sprigged muslin and petticoats. But I'll know soon enough, when I take them off you. I'll know what your stays look like. Most likely they will be plain and unadorned, as I always thought—practical, with a short, plain busk, with no carvings or secret messages from lovers. I know you haven't had any other lover. Apart from me. And we have shared only three kisses and exactly one real touch of your hand in mine. Though you have had your hands on the clothes covering my body."

Her hands were twisted into a tight little knot in front of her.

"But you may surprise me with some very well-hidden bit of feminine vanity, by having beautifully made stays with satin lacings. Maybe you'd look so enchanting in lacy things that I shall have some made for you to my order. I really can't say, can I, until I peel that dress off you?"

He rose and she took an involuntary step back, poised on the threshold of her desire.

"Then I'll have a much better idea. A better idea of exactly what your body will look like, naked and moving with the pleasure I will give you with my hands, and my mouth, and my body, while we fuck."

"Don't say that." She staggered a bit from the impact of his words. She put a hand out to the back of a chair to steady herself, but it only served to give him more ideas. Ideas about bending her forward over the back of the chair. Ideas of watching her hands flex to find purchase in the upholstery. To anchor herself, as he dragged up her skirts and filled his hands with the perfect roundness of her bottom and took her from behind, sliding his cock deep inside her heat.

But he was getting ahead of himself.

Another filthy, private joke. God, he was a bastard. He kept his laugh inside his head. The last thing he needed to do was scare her. Not when he was so close. "Don't say 'fuck'? But I like it. It's a good Anglo-Saxon word, visceral and real. As real as you are. As real as what we're going to do. As real as the pleasure we will feel."

But Celia wasn't being so easily led. Her voice was light, and a little shaky, but she held to her purpose. "I don't want to think and talk and dream and hear about it any more! I want to . . ." Courage failed her, or perhaps she didn't have adequate vocabulary to express the feelings careening through her body.

"You want to experience. You want to feel. To touch and be touched. To kiss and be kissed."

"Yes," she admitted, "but—"

"Then go."

Her eyes darted across the room and back to his face. "Where?"

"Upstairs. Before I'm tempted to toss your skirts over your

head and fuck you senseless on my study floor. But make no mistake, Celia, I do mean to fuck you senseless."

He advanced towards her, heedless of the puddles of tea and sugar pooling on the floor. She edged around the wreck of the tray as he came forward.

"Go," he instructed.

She had one last question. "Are you coming?"

CHAPTER 23

He smiled at her, a full flash of his teeth. He smiled at her the way a lion must smile at a gazelle he encounters at the waterhole. "Oh, absolutely. I promise."

Celia would have reached for him, to take his hand, to reassure herself he meant what he said, that he wasn't just playing another sensual game with her, but he moved around her and held the study door open for her.

She tried to walk calmly across the hall and to the stairs, but she could feel the heat of his body behind her, just out of touch, a coiled, magnetic presence pulling her back and urging her on. She hurried upwards.

She turned at the top of the stairs towards her rooms, but he stopped her with nothing more than his voice.

"My room."

"But I'll need . . . I need Bains."

"No."

But Bains had been waiting for her and, indeed, had already heard her voice, for she opened the door to Celia's rooms and said, "I've everything laid out, my lady."

"No. You may go, Bains," Viscount Darling repeated in a quiet but implacable tone. "My room."

Celia moved slowly down the hallway without even looking

at Bains. She was far too embarrassed. She didn't wait for him, but opened the door herself, determined not to let him lead her everywhere, not to be a puppet on his string.

"You didn't have to say that. She'll think—"

"Yes." He closed the door behind them and leaned back against the portal. "She'll think we're making love. In fact, she won't just think it, she'll know we're up here, in my chamber, on my bed, taking our clothes off and fucking each other until we scream with pleasure. Everyone in the house will know. Because I'm not going to bother to hide my pleasure. I'm going to yell out loud when I finally taste you and see you and take you. And I'm going to make very sure you scream my name in ecstasy when I bring you to the peak of your bliss."

Her hand rose up to cover her mouth, to stop such unmannerly thoughts from making equally unmannerly sounds. Because she knew he meant to do everything he said. And she knew, without a doubt, that she deeply, desperately, wanted him to make her scream his name with shock and delight.

He pushed off the door and prowled closer, so close he could have touched her, but he didn't. She swayed towards him, helpless with wanting.

And still he made her wait. "It's going to take a long, long time to make that happen. We're going to be panting with want. Loudly. Calling out each other's names. Loudly. I'm going to enjoy each and every sound, every sigh and every moment." He held up his index finger and pointed it right at her. "Now take that gown off."

She fumbled with the tie of her fichu as he stripped off his coat and laid it carefully across the back of a chair. It struck her as polite, even a bit housebroken. Such a strangely domestic description of Viscount Darling, when at all other times he reminded her of nothing so much as a huge predator, a large, sleek jungle cat, like the angry animal in the cage in the traveling menagerie. And like the cat he was, he watched her.

Dressed only in his shirtsleeves and waistcoat he managed

to look even taller and broader, more masculine than ever. Except for that time in his house in London, when he had been naked. She jerked the fichu away.

He stripped off his cravat and her eye was attracted to the golden skin below his neck where the button of his shirt had come undone. She tore her gaze away and knelt down to unlace her halfboots and roll down her stockings while she figured out how she was to deal with the lacings of her gown.

"I like that. You have no idea how erotic a sight your bare feet are."

She peeked up at him. His hands were undoing his cuffs, then the buttons of his waistcoat, which soon followed his coat jacket over the back of the chair. He pulled the tail of his linen shirt free of the waist of his breeches before he paused.

"You're falling behind." He reached back and stripped the shirt off over his head.

He was so . . . naked. So golden and sleek, muscled and broad. And covered along the lines of his bones—his ribs, shoulders, and jaw—with deep purple bruises and cuts. He looked raw, savage, and animalistic. She thought again of that avenging angel, but without the civilizing camouflage of clothes he seemed altogether too pagan, the kind of Christian who was half lion.

And such an expanse of bare flesh, even though he was still in his breeches and boots. Like he had been in the inn yard. Flushed with exertion and the sheen of his own sweat and blood. A fierce wave of excitement shivered through her. *Oh, God.* Something was wrong with her, to have been so excited by that sight. To be so aroused by the memory. Even the sight of his bruises and welts caused her skin to feel on fire.

"Now, Celia."

"The laces." She swallowed and tried to calm her stammering voice. "I can't reach the laces."

He lowered his head to regard her through half-closed eyes as he stalked nearer. He stood close, so close she could feel the heat radiating off his chest in waves and smell the subtle male scent of his body. His breath, laced with the pungent fumes of brandy, warmed the sensitive side of her neck and he leaned his head close to hers. "Turn around."

She did so, very slowly, reveling in the sensations caused by the passing of the heat from the furnace of his chest, warming first her front, and then her back. Her skin felt nearly blistered by his heat. Celia bent her head forward and closed her eyes. "The laces tie off at the top. Bains always does them like that."

She felt the weight of his hand press into the small of her back before he slowly stroked one long finger up the seam to her neckline, leaving a path of prickling sensation in its wake. Then his long, clever fingers delved between her shoulder blades to fish out the lace ends.

"Thank you, Celia." His voice was a soft growl in her ear. "Perhaps I shouldn't tell you I know very well how to unlace a lady's gown, but shameful as that prior knowledge may seem, now that I'm married, I aim to put it to very good use."

She ought to have felt disgusted by the thought of all the women he must have slept with before. But all she could manage to feel was grateful for his skill at seduction and happy for the promise in his statement. She felt a sharp tug or two as he undid the knots, but he didn't immediately take it off. Instead, he fisted up the loosened material, pulling the bodice taut over her chest.

"Why, Celia, you've been holding out on me, with your modest gowns and full-cut styles."

She was a tall girl, but he was taller, and loomed over her from behind. She felt small, almost powerless when he pulled her back against his chest. He traced his fingers over the exposed skin at the side of her neck and then down, over her collarbone. Her skin came alive, shimmering with liquid heat under his touch.

His hand moved lower, and she watched with gasping antic-ipation as he traced the swell of her breast through the fabric of her gown, over the layers of stays and chemise. She could feel the scorching pleasure as her nipples peaked tight be-neath the weight of his hand. He could feel it, too. He thumbed her through the fabric, plucking her, making her arch and push herself into his hand, as pleasure burst under her skin with each caress.

"I want to see you naked and spread out before me," he whispered over her shoulder, into her ear. He let go of the gown from the back, and all of it, bodice and stays, sagged off her. She pulled her arms free and turned to him.

"I've only had glimpses, tantalizing glimpses, of your sweet flesh. Do you remember? Do you remember how you bared yourself for me? I want you to do it again."

Her fingers went to the drawstring of her chemise and she loosened it with a tug. She could feel her breasts firm and swell, yearning for his gaze and his touch as the fabric slid down across the tightly furled, aching peaks, baring her to him.

"Yes." He swallowed. "The skirts."

Celia found the tapes of the skirts and petticoats and let them go. They puddled to her feet on the floor. She stepped out and bent to pick them up.

"Leave them." He pulled her back against the furnace of his chest. "I want you to touch yourself for me, the way you promised. Do you remember, Celia? Do you?"

His whispers shivered down the side of her neck.

"Did you do it? Did you touch yourself for me?"

"Yes."

"Show me." He watched from above and behind her shoul-der. She could hear and feel him go at his own clothes, at the flap of his breeches, with a heedless disregard for their care, popping the buttons in his haste. They skittered unheeded across the floor. He kept his eyes focused on her. On her body. "Show me," he begged, his voice full of urgency. "Touch yourself for me. I want you to hold your breasts for me."

She did, running her palm around her middle and up, over her ribs until she cradled herself in her hand. She felt hot, and aware, but the sensation was empty. She wanted his hand there. His fingers stroking across her flesh. She tried to tell him. "I want—" The words died in her throat.

He let her go and kicked his boot tree roughly into place, levering his legs out of his tight-fitting boots. In another moment he had shucked his breeches and was over her, pushing her back on the bed, coming on top of her all at once, as if he could not wait. As if he had finally exhausted his seemingly endless well of patience and self-control.

He was everywhere, his hands at her face and her hair, kissing her, his body pressing her down into the mattress. Her senses were overwhelmed by him, by the brandy-laced probe of his tongue, by the soft firmness of his lips, by the sharp edge of his teeth as he took her lower lip and worried at it. By the rasp of his afternoon beard against the skin of her neck and chest, by the press of his hands against her breast and by the abrasion of the hair on his legs.

He kissed his way along her jaw and down along her collarbone and her mouth fell open. He dipped his tongue into the hollow at her throat and she felt her pulse leap. He had said he would do that one day, hadn't he? Finally he was with her, as she felt those things, sharing her need.

He slid lower on her body. His hands slipped down her neck and around to press her shoulders into the mattress. His lips traced a molten path across her skin to her breasts, licking and sucking her, shooting sparks of pleasure across her belly and lower, between her tightly clenched thighs.

She wrapped her arms around his head, holding him to her and raking her hands through his hair, fisting up the short golden strands. She arched into him, pressing, wanting, needing, taking everything he could give her and holding it tight.

He levered himself off her, knelt over her legs and ran his eyes and his hands over her body, from her tightly peaked nipples down to dip into the sensitive indentation of her navel. Her skin felt taut and alive, as if it came to life for just this moment, just these heady, intoxicating sensations.

"My God, look at you."

She couldn't. She arched her head back and closed her eyes, letting him do as he wished, letting the pleasure of his praise unfurl within her.

He raked his hands through the curls on her mound, pulling and teasing, looking, making her want to scream and beg and plead with him to please, dear God, please touch her there and ease the burning ache he had created with his hands, his tongue, and his words.

Then he did, slipping first one long finger, and then another inside her. He stroked, sending wave after wave of greedy need spiraling higher. She was flying away, leaving behind everything but the pleasure and desire for him. He turned his wrist, and his thumb joined his clever fingers, parting the folds of her flesh and finding a spot, a place from which bliss and heat and pleasure burst forth, shooting rockets of sensation through her.

A startled sound of ecstasy flew out of her throat.

"Yes, there. Your quim. Where you're wet and ready for me."

He stroked again and she bucked up into his hand, searching for more, for more of the friction and strong bliss of his clever fingers.

"I'm going to put myself, my cock inside you. Inside your beautiful, wet quim."

She had no pride. She had nothing but need, urgent, intense need. "Please."

He kneed her legs apart and positioned his body at her entrance. She felt her legs bow and her body arch up towards him, ready and wanting.

"You're mine, Celia. You always have been. Mine." Del couldn't wait any longer. He shoved himself fully inside her slick heat.

He was catapulted by the dizzying rush of satisfaction and unadulterated bliss. He knew he was on a bed, and Celia was in his arms, but the world fell away from him until there was nothing but the sweet, lush confines of her body against his.

A sound of anguish and disappointment tore from her throat, piercing the haze of his relentless need. He should have gone slower. He should have taken greater care. But he couldn't regret the blissful feeling of being inside her lush, tight cunny. There were no words, no thoughts adequate to describe the bone-deep satisfaction, the rightness of having Celia in his arms, beneath him.

"Hush." He kissed her softly on her tightly gritted mouth, and on the freckle just next to her lip. Light, sweet, balming kisses to show her, to teach her. "It's done, sweet." And he moved his hand up from where he had pinioned her hipbones to the mattress, so he could frame her face and coax her back into pleasure. "It will be better soon. I'll make it better. Much better."

She stared up at him with those wide, dark, trusting eyes and he wanted to fall into her, into her sweetness and her light. He let his body relax into her and let his body weight ease down into her softness as he angled her jaw more to his liking, luring her into opening her mouth to the probe of his tongue.

When she did, he kept kissing her and exploring the honey sweet taste of her, until she joined him in the dance, until her tongue chased and sucked at his in hot, open-mouthed, carnal kisses. When she was gasping with want, he left her lips and slid his teeth down the side of her neck along the sensitive tendon.

She let out an inarticulate groan of encouragement and turned to allow him greater access. He rose above her, on his elbows, so he could look at her and turn his attention to her exquisite breasts. How had he ever thought them small? They were exquisite, perfectly rounded. Made for his touch.

He levered himself fully off her so he could fill his hands with her. But as he did so he brought more weight to bear lower, where their bodies were so intimately joined. She let out a low sound of pleasure.

He ran his thumbs across the tightly furled peaks of her breasts and nudged his cock deep within her at the same time.

"Yes. Please." Her voice was all needy plea.

"Ah, yes, your pearl. Have I taught you about your pearl? Did I tell you how to find the pearl hidden in your quim? How it likes to be stroked so lightly, how you can bring yourself pleasure with your own touch? But I haven't taught you what my body can do for you. How you would want me to grind down into you and make you moan with pleasure." He suited action to words and as he worked to bring her pleasure, a wave of scorching heat crashed over him. "Do you like that, Celia?

"Yes." Her gasp was full of wonder.

He moved again, angling his pelvis to bring just enough pressure, just enough friction to appease the greedy, clawing need and bring them both wave after wave of pleasure. "Say my name, Celia."

"Viscount Darling."

He laughed at the same time he surged into her. "No. My name, Celia. Say my name." The need was like a live thing crashing about inside him.

"Del."

"Yes." He surged again, drenched in heat and pleasure. "Again."

"Del. Please, Del, please."

"Yes." He raised her hips up and tilted her hips just so, and rocked into her core. He felt fused to her, bound to her body and yet, falling away, carried away by the nearly unbearable pleasure. He reached his hand down to her slick quim, fondling and searching, even as his body rocked and surged into hers.

And then he found it—the place within her that would make pleasure explode behind her eyelids. He flicked her ever so gently and she erupted. She twisted up beneath him in one last vault of blissful friction and let out a high keen of surrender.

All he heard, as she flew away, was Celia crooning his name as he took her by the hips one last time and rammed himself home, following her over the edge into oblivion.

CHAPTER 24

Celia woke slowly and, little by little, registered her husband's presence in her bed. Or rather, she was still in his bed. And they had . . . she'd let him . . . so many times she'd lost count. Finally they had fallen asleep from complete and utter exhaustion.

He was stretched across the greater portion of the bed, facedown on the mattress, with his arm thrown over her, hugging her to him, even in his sleep.

Celia wondered vaguely if there was a protocol for waking up with one's husband. Was she to wake him, or wait until he came awake of his own accord? But if she did not leave the bed soon, and repair to the privacy of her dressing room, she would soon be in some distress.

She eased out of bed, only to rediscover she was achingly sore and entirely naked. There was nothing but the sheet in which she might clothe herself. Her clothes were in heaps on the other side of the bed, and the sheet was tangled under Viscount—under Del's lovely, sleeping body. Celia dashed on tiptoes through the connecting door, through Del's dressing room to her own, where Bains was already waiting for her.

"I've a hot bath ready for you, miss." The maid kept her

eyes down, but her voice was full of resigned indignation. "I've no doubt you'll need one."

Celia tried to conceal what felt like a furious blush, by ducking behind the screen to fish out a dressing gown and use the necessary. "Thank you, Bains."

Bains was a dear, with all her fussing and mixing of jugs of water, but what Celia really wanted was to be alone while she sorted out her feelings and soaked away the newfound aches. And scrubbed the smear of blood from her inner thigh. She hadn't felt this tender since Lizzie had tried to teach her to ride astride.

"That will be all, Bains. You may go." He had come so quietly she had not heard him until his voice vibrated through the screen.

"Yes, sir." Bains quickly excused herself.

"Celia?"

There was that tone, that intent. Celia felt desire and expectation leap in her blood. How quickly and easily she had been trained to his hand.

"Are you hiding?"

"No," she lied, and stepped cautiously around the screen. "Good morning." She had almost added Viscount Darling out of habit. Almost. But now there was no thought of anything but her Del.

He was clad only in his small clothes, completely naked from the waist up. Poor Bains—no wonder she'd fled. Celia herself had only marginally more time to become accustomed to it.

But the truth was Celia didn't want Bains looking at Viscount Darling's near naked splendor. He was hers now, as she was his. Hers to look at and hers to marvel over. Her great tawny cat to try and train to her hand.

He crouched carefully next to the tub, favoring his ribs, she thought. It made her feel better and less anxious to know, despite his strength and commanding presence, he was as human and as sore from their exertions as she.

He trailed his hands through the water. "Why don't you get in before it cools?"

"You don't have to stay. You look tired. I'm sure you've better things to—" She broke off at his look—a lazy, heated smile.

"I *don't* have better things to do." He smiled. "I haven't had better things to do than look at you naked for a long time. Come." He held out his hand to assist her into the small tub.

She climbed carefully in, holding the dressing gown out around the edge of the rim like a curtain, and managed to almost sit down before divesting herself of the protective piece of apparel. It was silly to be so nervous and awkward after all they had done, but he didn't seem to take notice.

He knelt by the tub, absorbed in giving her an intense, rather proprietary perusal. He reached through the water to the dissipating smear of blood on her thigh. "Are you all right? Are you hurt? Or sore?"

With that small gesture, it came clear to her just how much everything between them had changed. There was nothing about her, about her body that was not his concern. She had become fully his.

Heat chased across her face and down her neck. "A little." But was he also hers in the same proprietary way? She looked at the green and purplish tinge of the bruises still streaked across his ribs and eye. "What about you?"

"Yes, I'm sore, too. But happily so." He laughed and took up a soft sponge. "Lie back. Let me." He took up the bar of soap Bains had left on the stool and put it to his nose. "Yes. Jasmine and roses. But not quite. It needs to be combined with you for the correct effect."

"And the correct effect is for you to soap me like a nursemaid?" It felt strange to allow him to cosset her so.

"No. I don't think I shall do it at all like your nursemaid. You see, I want to use it as an excuse to run my hands all over you and get you slick and wet and ready for my touch again. So we can make love again." He ran the sponge up the length of her inner arm slowly, and then along the line of her collarbone. "I like having you all naked and bare before me. No clothes to strip off. No tantalizing glimpses, no wondering if anything I'm saying to you is having the desired effect. With you so very naked and bare, I can see your nipples are pink and tight and waiting for me.

She was ready for his touch. With only his words and his gaze, she was already aching for him, breathless and wanting. Her breasts felt full and sensitive, nerves skittering and skating under the surface of her skin in anticipation. And lower, between her thighs, in her center, the place he called her quim, she could feel a low throb as awareness and need began to fill her. She arched her back and let her head lean against the lip of the slipper tub, opening her arms to him, letting him look and touch his fill, giving herself over to the warmth radiating from his gaze. She clenched her inner muscles together and felt the stabbing rush of pleasure, the prelude to coming bliss.

Del ran the sponge down and around each breast, moving in slow circles until at last the fibrous material of the sponge dragged across the sensitive peaks. She heard her own exhalation of pleasure.

"Yes," he encouraged, and she opened her eyes to watch him as he looked at her. His eyes roved over her avidly, heating and touching the skin his hands did not. He turned his wrist and the rough, toughened skin of his knuckles abraded her nipples, sending bursts of blissful heat radiating across her body.

He leaned in and took her breast between his lips and teeth, sucking her and sending her higher and higher with every stroke, while his hand searched lower, over the rising curve of her hips and down, delving between her tightly clenched thighs. He dragged the sponge back and forth across her mound, teasing and arousing her, even as he left to sit back and watch the play of arousal chase across her skin.

He reached his long arm beneath the water to retrieve her foot. He brought it out of the water and crooked it over the edge of the tub, running his hands and the soapy sponge all around the high arch, rubbing and pushing his thumbs into the ball of her foot. It was heavenly torture.

He gave her one of his sleepy smiles, all drowsy satisfied eyes. But he held her gaze as he lifted out the other leg, draping her apart, opening her for his perusal.

He looked at her, his eyes ranging down one leg and then the other slowly. He held her there for a long moment, each of his hands on the inside of her ankles, exerting just enough pressure, drawing out the anticipation just enough so she was breathless with want.

She wanted him breathless as well. "I like looking at you, too. I like looking at your body. I like touching it more."

He stood at the foot of the tub and in one swift motion, shucked his drawers completely and, stepped out of them. He stood before her in all his erect glory. God, he was beautiful, so golden and strong, so sleekly muscled everywhere. Especially where that curious ridge of muscle separated his hips from the taut line of his belly. She smiled. "It's so curious and so beautifully strange, your cock."

"Don't say that." He laughed as he reached down for her. "You can't imagine what it does to me."

"I don't need to imagine. I can see."

He lifted her clear of the tub and pulled her against him, the water from her body cascading down and soaking them both. "How scientific of you, observing and cataloguing." He kissed her lightly on the mouth. "Perhaps I ought to teach you something new. Something where you can't observe at all. Something where you can only feel."

His voice had dipped and darkened, sending chords of awareness strumming through her. He picked her up and kissed her hard and deep, filling her mouth with the taste of him as he carried her back to his bed and eased her down.

"What—"

He lay a finger across her lips. "No questions. No talking. No words at all. Just feelings. All your senses stretching out to understand, all on your own, without me to tell you. Close your eyes."

He was smiling at her, that lazy, sleepy smile that both aroused and calmed her. She did as he bid. He leaned down and kissed her on her mouth, a lingering kiss full of easy promise, and then rolled her over onto her belly.

"Del?"

"Hush."

She opened her eyes and turned her head to the side to see, but couldn't see him behind her. Sunlight poured in through the windows, filling the room with bright, blinding light. She felt the bed dip from his weight, but still he didn't touch her, coming to sit, she thought, on the side away from where she was facing. He laced his fingers through her hair, drawing it out, letting the tousled curls fall through his fingers, tugging gently at her scalp. The effect was soothing and invigorating at the same time. And redolent with anticipation.

He spread her hair out across her back, then swept it aside to put his hands on her shoulders and began to massage. His strong hands dug deep, easing out each knot of tension, coming around her shoulders and tugging just enough on the skin of her upper chest that she felt the awareness blossom in her breasts even though they were pushed into the mattress by her weight.

And then Del's big hand skimmed down her back, tracing

the line of her spine, down and back up, until his hand came to rest in the small of her back, heavy and possessive.

Celia found herself straining for his voice. She had grown so accustomed to it, she needed it to lead her, to push her higher and higher into her arousal. And there was nothing. Nothing but the muted sound of the shifting sheets as he moved and pressed his hands at her back. Her nerves, all her senses, were straining towards him.

He took a single, long finger and traced the cleft of her bottom, all the way down, and then up, the backs of his fingers dragging along the soft, exposed flesh, sending flashes of exquisite anticipation shafting through her. She wanted to squirm and move, but the weight of his other hand, still pressing her firmly into the mattress, kept her still. She could feel her muscles clench and pulse deep within the place he had been inside her. In the place where she wanted him now.

But it was too much, this need, this void. This emptiness she had carried within her that only he could fill. She crossed her ankles, pressing her thighs tightly together, to ease the tremor within. Though she heard no sound, Del must have laughed at her feeble attempts to close herself to him. She felt the vibration of his amusement echo through her as he ran his palms down the backs of her legs. Then his hands closed upon her ankles and pulled her legs slowly, inexorably, apart, spreading and opening her.

She felt vulnerable and not a little scared, unsure of herself and him. But he did nothing to allay her fears. He didn't speak or let her see him. She had only the sound of his escalating breath to gauge his arousal. And the possessive, authoritative press of his hands as he arranged her for his pleasure.

He wanted her this way—hot and tense and quaking inside, aroused by the idea he was looking at her even as he held her ankles apart. Looking at her body, and arousing himself with the sight.

She closed her eyes tight, clenching her whole body taut with a need, a yearning so fierce her muscles ached. Even her arms were pulled in tight, fisted up at her sides, holding her together lest she fly into a million pieces.

He shifted behind her, kneeling between her outspread thighs. His hands slid down to the inside of her thighs to knead and arouse, his thumbs pressing inward and circling slowly, moving closer and closer to her core, to the center of her need. She felt her body lifting and arcing towards him, toward the promise of his touch.

Then his touch was on her, at her center, one long finger sliding into her, stroking and playing her, as if she were an instrument tuned to his touch. But as he plucked and played she felt the greedy coil of need spiral tighter, twisting and turning within, until her body began to twist and turn in earnest, reaching and pushing back against his hands.

At that, he left her and she heard her own needy cry of disappointment. But he shifted again, and she felt his weight settle upon her, long and heavy. Dominant. He was everywhere, above and around her, surrounding her with his heat and his intent. She could feel his purpose in the strength of his body, and the caress of his chest as it moved against her back, in the way he nosed aside her hair and kissed her, his teeth scoring the sensitive tendon along the side of her neck. She felt caged and restless, pushing back against him, felt his belly snug against her bottom. Felt the blunt, velvet probe of his body pushing into hers, stretching and filling her, and then, he flexed his hips and sheathed himself to the hilt within her.

"Celia." He said her name like a prayer.

She felt heat and pleasure spilling together, tumbling her over and over like a wave. He moved above her, back and forth like the tide, pushing and ebbing, only to return again, with another wave, another thundering crash of sensation.

A sound like a groan reverberated through his chest and she was glad he felt it, too—need so fierce and so blissful she could not even articulate it.

He reached for her tightly fisted hands and drew them out to the side, lacing his fingers with hers. Something within her unfurled at the gesture, so possessive and yet protective. She felt safe, literally in his hands. She was where she belonged, with him, body and soul.

He pushed up, taking his weight onto his arms, and air rushed over her, cooling her skin, and she breathed it in. She missed the reassurance, the solidity and comfort of his weight upon her, tethering her to the earth. But the position brought his hips more snugly against her bottom, and changed his angle. When he rocked into her again, she felt him all the way to her core. He pushed up, leveraging his hips, changing the angle once more. And she found herself following, pushing back into him, wanting more of his body against hers, wanting more of the friction of his taut belly against her backside.

His arms came around her and he gathered her up to kneel before him, between his powerful, flexing thighs. She leaned back against his heat and let her head fall against his shoulder, opening herself, displaying herself for his eyes and his touch. His big hands searched and stoked upwards, cupping her breasts, fondling and playing. His clever fingers found her nipples tight and ready. He pressed the delicate pink tips between his fingers, each tweak, each pluck sending a note of needy pleasure cascading through her bones. His other hand roved down, splaying across the flat of her belly, and lower, tangling in the curls covering her mound. He stroked her, parting her flesh, brushing a featherlight touch across that place, her pearl. Sensations burst and beckoned.

"Yes," she sobbed. "Yes, Del, please."

"Celia. I can't wait. I need—Celia!" And he gripped her

hard against him and exploded into her, and she went careening over the edge.

She was flying, untethered to earth, aloft on gust after gust of searing sensation, blown from bliss to bliss by his breath, his touch. His love.

Two hours later, Celia could barely look at Del for the heat in her face, as he perused her from across the breakfast table, all lazy, knowing smiles. If he kept looking at her like that, she was going to dissolve into a puddle on the floor. She needed to find some purpose. Other than climbing back into his bed. "May I put my books in your library?"

"Celia, this your house, too. You needn't ask permission."

His laughing tone was just short of patronizing. "I wasn't asking for permission. I was asking for your consent. I wouldn't like it if someone came and rearranged my library to their whim without at least consulting me. It is only polite to do so." But it seemed everything she did this morning was destined to amuse him. "I was simply giving you the courtesy of warning you. I'm taking over your study. Good day, sir."

His laughter followed her down the corridor and across the house.

Mr. Level had put the heavy trunks containing her collection of books in the middle of the floor. The problem, she soon saw, was that there was no room on the shelves. Nor did the books seem to be in any particular order. They were stacked on the shelves haphazardly, novels mixed in with histories, poetry with social commentary. Her orderly, classifying, assorting brain began to rebel. She would never be able to find what she needed.

It wouldn't do. Everything must be sorted. Even the stacks on the table. Celia crossed to the desk to draw out writing paper and found the desk drawer to the right filled with old letters, tossed in no particular order. She immediately recognized the handwriting. It was Emily's.

Before she could question the rightness of her actions, she began to read, sorting them chronologically as she went. Some of them were written before she had known Emily, before she had arrived at school, but for most she had been there, very often in same the room with Emily when she had written them. Emily had often read her letters aloud and they had laughed and joked and exclaimed together over one witticism or another.

Celia had spent upwards of an hour by the time she finally got to the letters near the end, written in the weeks before Emily's death. It was so hard to read those last few. To feel anew Emily's doubts and torment caused by the rumors. Celia could well understand Del's pain, his thirst for revenge. It was awful to read of those ugly, taunting rumors and know Melissa Wainwright had started them.

She was lost to her sorrow, her face wet with tears and her nose beginning to run, when he walked in.

"Celia," he gathered her into his arms. "Don't cry, love."

"Oh, Del." She put her arm around his middle burying her face in his lovely, broad, warm, solid chest. "I should have asked first, but I had to read them. It's still so sad. So horribly sad."

"Hush. It's all right." He held her to him and stroked her hair. "Don't cry."

"I was with her when she wrote most of these. I remember everything we were doing and oh, it just makes me so sad. But I want to read them all, even the ones at the end." Celia looked up at him. "You need a secretary, by the way. You're shockingly disorganized." She blew her nose into the handkerchief he handed her.

"Coming from the weeping woman without a handkerchief." He looked down at the paper in her hand and he pulled a worn parchment out of his breast coat pocket. "*This* is the last one. I was coming to put it back with the others."

Celia looked again at the date on the letter in her hand. "No. This one is dated just six days before she . . . died. Six days. She would have written at least two more letters. She was nothing if not punctual and organized"—she looked around at the library with its haphazard piles of books—"unlike you."

"Yes, very unlike me. Do you mean to say, you *know* she wrote more letters nearer to the date of her death?'

"I don't know, but I think it very likely. Perhaps she did not get a chance to post them. Or by the time they had reached wherever you were supposed to be, you had already come back and missed them?"

He looked away, out the window. "That's possible. Probable even. Could have gone off on some other ship and missed me completely."

"Where would the letters have gone, in either instance? If she didn't post them or if they never got to you?"

Del's mouth turned down at the corner. "To Cleeve, I suppose. They would have taken all her possessions home to Cleeve Abbey."

"Perhaps you could write them. Or we could go there."

He closed up like a fist. "No. Why dig up the past? It won't bring Emily back."

She agreed. "But I feel as if I'm missing something. Something important. Reading the letters again, it just strikes me as . . ." She frowned, trying to adequately identify the emotion. "These letters say Emily originally thought I was the source of the rumors—which I didn't know about until after—until I had read her suicide note. Why did that note say she was killing herself for love of me? She never said so in these letters. She was shocked by the rumors, as shocked as I was. It's simply wrong."

"Perhaps she didn't have the courage to tell me her true feelings."

"No, that can't be right, either. She wasn't like that. She was straightforward and courageous. She told you the truth about everything else important in her life, didn't she?"

He nodded slowly. "Yes."

"I would like to see those last letters if they exist. I wish I'd saved the note—her . . . last note." She shook her head, wishing she could shake away the empty feelings just as easily. "Del, it just makes no sense."

He nodded grimly. "You're right. We need to go to Cleeve."

CHAPTER 25

It took a day's hard ride to cover the fifty miles to Cleeve Abbey. Celia was buoyant and hopeful throughout the long day—she shared none of Del's trepidation. He had seen the place only once in the past nine and a half years, when his father had brought him home from the Marines after Emily's death.

When he had received Emily's last letter, he had become so concerned he had petitioned straightaway for leave to go to her. He had transferred within days to a ship making for Portsmouth. It had been an interminable two weeks' sail, buffeted by bad weather and indifferent winds.

When he had at last lowered anchor in Portsmouth, his father, having found his direction through Emily's letters, had been waiting for him on the quay, with the news he was too late. Emily was already dead.

Del had gone home with his cold, withdrawn, silent father in the family coach only long enough to see her grave, before he left for London. He couldn't stay at Cleeve Abbey. Even with all its balance and symmetry, it had seemed strict and confining. Even a house that big could not contain all the rage and frustration he felt. Nothing could.

His father had thought to control him by denying the funds to finance his fall into disrepute, but Del had his own independent fortune, earned through prize monies. Indeed, he was still living on prize money. The damned settlements he had worked with Lord Thomas Burke had specified it. He would take no money from Cleeve.

They rode into the forecourt in the late afternoon. He had forgotten the abbey's easy, lush beauty. Summer brought a softness and warmth that had been noticeably lacking on his last visit. It had seemed to rain incessantly that spring. Or perhaps he remembered only the rain, an outward sign of his inner misery.

Cleeve Abbey, despite its medieval name, was a massive hall in the classical style, monumental in its scale. As a child, Del had often thought it seemed more of a museum than a home. But in all its Palladian grandness, the house was softened by the lush green of a Cotswold summer. Nevertheless, when they rode across the huge lawn of the forecourt, troops of liveried footmen decamped from the central door on the ground floor beneath the cascading terrace steps and the *piano nobili* above.

Del helped Celia from her horse, and they were immediately shown up to the large central hall, where the Countess awaited them.

"Rupert, darling, how like you not to send word of your visit." She turned her pale cheek for a kiss. "Have you no luggage?"

"Good evening, Mama. It follows."

"Lovely." She squeezed his hand in affection. "How nice you could visit so soon after your wedding. My dear"—she embraced Celia—"welcome to Cleeve Abbey. Should you like to retire, or may I offer you some refreshment?"

"I confess, your ladyship"—Celia curtsyed to his mother—"a dish of tea seems just the thing."

"Then you shall have it." She smiled and nodded at the butler in confirmation of her request. "The yellow drawing room."

They were shown into to the Countess's private sitting room. It was nothing as he remembered, all done up in bright, sunny colors and exquisite textures of light silk. When the Countess took her seat, she held out her hand to him, so he kissed his mother's cheek again before he retreated to stand apart at the mantelpiece. It astonished him, the warmth and genuine pleasure of her welcome, her incredible lack of resentment at his incommunicative treatment of his family in the past years. She kept looking at him as if she needed to repeatedly reassure herself he was real and standing in her room. It was humbling.

"My dear." Lady Cleeve greeted Celia in the same way, with a kiss to her cheek. "I am so glad you have come. We did not get a chance to speak at your wedding, or before. Rupert seems to have been in an abominable rush to marry, though now that I have you before me, it is obvious why. You are very lovely."

His mother was so small and dainty next to Celia, whom he realized once again was really rather tall. She didn't always seem so to him, because of course she was smaller than he, but compared to the rest of the world, she was a veritable Diana. She stood a full head taller than his mother.

The Countess of Cleeve was easing into middle age with all the appearance of grace. Yet, he could see she had been wearied by her sorrow, as if her pain had marked itself into the lines visible on her face. It was as Lady Renning had said— Emily's death had been a great loss for his mother. He had been alone in his rage, but not in his pain.

How could he not have seen that?

But his mother conducted herself with all her usual warmth, always a striking contrast to his dictatorial father.

"You are too kind, your ladyship," Celia answered and an arc of color spread across her cheeks.

"Not at all. You will think me sentimental, but I am glad to have a daughter in the house again. Especially you, for I felt I already knew you and loved you, through my dear Emily's letters."

Celia impulsively covered the Countess's hand with her own. "I am honored, my lady, and I do not think you sentimental. I understand you completely, because I feel quite the same. I knew you all, and loved you all, but especially Viscount Darling, before I met any of you."

"Yes, their letters." The Countess looked away, pained by the memory. "We did not know they wrote, you see. It was hard. We had been deprived of him for so long, and she kept his whereabouts a secret from his father and me, but I console myself at least *she* had him for the time leading up to her death. It is a comfort to know that."

"I am sorry you were deprived of him, but I must be happy for myself, for if Emily had not read me his letters, I could not have fallen in love with him. So you see, it was Emily who brought us together and I must be always grateful for that."

"Then so am I, my dear, so am I."

"But also, ma'am," Celia interposed gently, "it is in search of those very letters we come. Viscount Darling is missing, or never received, some letters I am sure Emily wrote to him. We were hoping that such letters were either returned here with her things, or were forwarded here for him."

"I do not know. Rupert?" She turned to her son. "Your father took care of all those things. He went to the school in Bath to . . . take care of everything. You shall have to apply to him."

"Thank you, ma'am, I will."

Del excused himself. He thought of going for a walk to reacquaint himself with the abbey grounds, to put off the inevitable conversation with his father, but his better self would not allow it. At this time of day the Earl was to be found in his estate office, working with his secretary. Del did not especially want to beard the Lion of Cleeve in his own den, but Colonel Delacorte would never have put off an unpleasant dressing-down from a superior officer. He would have done it straight-away with fatalistic good humor.

At his knock, his father bade him enter and Del stepped back in time into his father's meticulously kept estate office. It was one in a suite of rooms from which the Earl presided over his vast holdings. The estate office was nearer the back of the house, where there was a small vestibule for people with busi-ness with him to be received. Beyond the office lay the Earl's private book room, a place where he read, kept his personal correspondence, smoked, and took his leisure. Beyond that was the more public room of the library, a magnificent oak-paneled chamber of two stories with a small balcony ringing the second floor. It housed the abbey's magnificent collection of books, some of which dated to the period more than two hundred and fifty years earlier when the abbey had been dis-solved during the reign of King Henry VIII. They were rooms that spoke of rank and responsibility, and of duty. Duty to Cleeve.

"Forgive me for the intrusion, sir. May I speak to you?"

The Earl of Cleeve leaned back in his chair to consider his request. He showed no surprise that his son should have sud-denly appeared before him after years and years away—pre-sumably a servant had informed him of Del and Celia's arrival. Behind his desk, in the seat of his power, the Lion of Cleeve was just as Del had remembered and expected. His piercing blue eyes were still quick and penetrating, even predatory, tracking Del as he stepped into the room, trespassing into the Earl's territory. But there were changes too. The leonine mane of ginger blond hair was liberally streaked with white, and there were lines etched across his handsome, tanned face, wrought by care or worry or simply age. Cleeve had always seemed so all-knowing, all-powerful, and even invincible, Del was startled by this aspect of humanity and mortality in his father. Time passed and changed all of them.

But the Lion of Cleeve was far from feeble. He waved off his secretary, and regarded his son down the impressive length of his aquiline nose. "Be so good as to give us a moment, Sands—"

"There's no need, sir," Del interrupted, determined to keep the interview as short as possible. "This task will undoubtedly fall to Sands. I have just now spoken to Mother about the dispensation of Emily's things from school. Mother indicated you were the one to bring all of Emily's effects back from Bath. I thought you might have some record."

"Of course I do." His father was nothing if not a prodigious record keeper. "May I ask why you are suddenly so interested in something which took place over a year ago?"

"It is not a sudden impulse, sir." Del tried to keep to the tone he would have used with a commanding officer. "I have had this matter under consideration for some time, though it may prove to be nothing. I am looking for more of Emily's letters—letters I never received. I had hoped they might be amongst Emily's possessions, if they still exist."

"What do you hope to find in these letters you did not receive?" His father's tone was mildly curious.

Del hated having to justify himself to his father, like a child, especially as he was not yet ready to reveal their suspicions. Too much was at stake. And he wanted to do it on his own. It was his mission, his mania, to get to the bottom of Emily's death. He did not want his father's help or interference. "I am not exactly sure, sir. But I hope to afford both myself and Miss Burke—that is, my wife—more clarity of understanding regarding Emily's death."

"I see. It has been my experience some things are beyond understanding, Rupert. However, Sands will know where to find the record of the inventory."

"Yes, my lord." The secretary spoke up on cue. "That would have been April of the year ninety-three?" Mr. Sands rose and went unerringly to the place on the shelf where the appropriate ledger was housed. "Would you care to read it now, my lord?"

"Thank you, Sands. I'll take it into the library, if I may. But also, I might ask if the items listed in the inventory still exist, are they here?" Del could think of no less awkward way to ask. "What happened to the things listed in your meticulous inventory?"

"They were delivered here, for your mother to see, or not see, as she chose in her grief. Grief which, I will note, you neither shared nor witnessed." His father spoke gruffly.

Del would not argue with his father. There was nothing to be gained for any of them in a row over his actions. Emily was dead, and he still did not know the reason.

"If your mother did not order them distributed to the parish, I imagine your sister's things to still be in trunks, either in her former room or recently transferred to storage at the end of the year's mourning period. Mrs. Starling would know."

"Thank you." He bowed to his father. "I will consult with the housekeeper."

"One moment. Thank you, Sands."

The secretary bowed himself out of the room as quietly and efficiently as he did everything else.

The Earl wasted no time coming to his point. "Well, Rupert, I am glad you have seen fit to visit your mother. She has been anxious to see you and celebrate your marriage, and get to know your bride."

"Yes, sir. I left them together."

"Good. She seems an amiable girl."

"She is. And particularly intelligent."

A strange smile played at the corner of his father's mouth. "Yes, an admirable quality. She was your sister's friend, as I recall." He shifted in his seat and regarded his papers for a long moment before he spoke. "I do not pretend to understand your reasons for looking among Emily's things, but I will *ask*— because I have learned *insisting* will do no good with you—I will ask you not to upset your mother with whatever quest you have currently set for yourself."

"I would never set out to—"

"No, you never set out to hurt her, but you *have*, nonetheless. With your absence and your distance."

Del could not bring himself to openly concur, although he knew it to be true.

"I pray, however," his father went on, "you do not willfully misunderstand me. I am glad you are come home. I have waited a very long time—patiently I have thought, though you may not find it so—to have my son back."

Ah, yes, the inevitable reckoning. His father loved nothing so much as reminding Del of his failures to his duty. "I am here, at your disposal."

His father raised his eyes to the ceiling and chuckled. "You, my son, have never been at my disposal. Not when you were a lad, and certainly not now. You have not even been under my influence since some time in the spring of the year of our Lord seventeen hundred and eighty-five. Nor, in the time since your arrival back in England, have I asked you to be. Can you imagine why that might be, Rupert?"

Because his father did not like anything he could not control, had always been Del's opinion. But there was no answer to give that would not insult them both.

"It is because you are your own man. You set yourself out to be, ten years ago, wholly outside of my influence or interference. Once I knew what you had done—joined His Majesty's Marine Forces rather than merely run away or having been carried off by some miscreant, as we imagined—I thought you had done it to prove yourself worthy and capable, on your own terms, of the power and privilege that had come to you by right of birth. Was I wrong?"

It was a good thing Celia had him so accustomed to shocks. "No, sir. You are not wrong."

"Yet *you* have not been satisfied. You have not come back to Cleeve ready or willing to take on any of the responsibilities for which you have proven yourself so immensely capable. This I do not understand. I cannot comprehend why, after nine years of meritorious, courageous service, you should have spent the past year wasting everything for which you labored, throwing off every characteristic you set out to earn."

His father rose out of his chair in his agitation and paced behind his desk. "So I can only wait until you are satisfied, and pray that day will not come at my death."

Del swallowed hard, his misconceptions a bitter pill lodging in his throat. That his father understood his motives, and perhaps even approved of them, had never, ever occurred to him. That he should be waiting, *waiting* patiently for Del to come back on his own, was astounding and remarkable. And wholly new.

His defiance, his refusal to even attempt to see the world from his father's side of that desk, began to seem childish and ultimately, simply wrong.

"I take your point, sir. And I . . . apologize. I am ready to take up my responsibilities to you and to Cleeve in the very near future. But I have one last task to complete—this business about Emily—I need to finish before I can be at your disposal."

That his father was surprised was evident in the utterly blank look on his face and in the abrupt way he resumed his seat. "It cannot be that easy." His father frowned at him. "I finally avail myself of the opportunity to speak to you on the subject and it simply comes to an end? Great God. I would have spoken to you a year ago, had I known it could be so easy."

Del shrugged sheepishly. "Perhaps it is simply time."

His father's wry smile showed he thought it well past time, but Del was surprised to note his father refrained from voicing his sentiments, and said only, "However it comes to pass, I am glad for it. Finish whatever business you have about Emily— but kindly do remember to spare your mother any greater heartache—and come back to us as soon as you can. I should be very glad to have you for my own sake, but also for your mother's and your brothers'."

Del took up the ledger and moved through the suite to the library, warming with the pleasure of being understood. Then, the first person who had introduced him to that pleasure came in the door. Celia wore a worried smile.

"The footman told me I could find you in here. How did it go with the Earl? What did you find?"

"Nothing yet. This ledger contains the inventory of Emily's things brought home from school."

Celia's brow puckered even as she peered at the page. "A formal inventory?"

"My father has something of a penchant for record keeping."

"Oh." Her face cleared as she considered that. "I can see why he might, with so many properties to keep track of and so many people under his care and responsibility."

So eminently reasonable. Of course she would see it as such. But even with his newfound understanding of his father, Del discovered he was not yet ready to give over all his resentments. "I don't know, perhaps he might accomplish it by actually knowing the people involved and listening to them. Then he might remember things instead of having to rely upon his neat little ticks and numbers in ledgers. People ought not to be reduced to neat, tidy columns. Dead daughters should not be reduced to a list of durable goods. Life is too precious, though it is generally neither tidy nor neat."

Celia stared at him with her wide, startled eyes and then she simply put her arms around his middle and hugged him. He slowly put his arms around her, and felt the fragile strength of her body. "Thank you. Come, let us look at the lists."

They poured over them together, side by side, her rich sable head bent close to his. Celia pointed to a particular entry. "I think this means there are, or at least *were*, three sets of letters. How do we get them?"

Del immediately called for Mrs. Starling, Cleeve's housekeeper, who informed them she would have the items brought down from storage within a half hour.

The footman delivered three meticulously labeled leather boxes, dusted and cleaned before they were brought downstairs from whatever attic in which they had been found. The first box contained the Countess's letters to her daughter, still bound in blue ribbon. The letters shouldn't have surprised Del. After all, Emily had been an active correspondent with him, why should it surprise him she had also been writing to her mother? It was just that he had never imagined it. He had thought of his tie to Emily as so wholly private, he did not consider she might have had other familial ties as well.

The second box knocked him over the head with the wrongness of his assumptions. For there, also carefully banded with ribbons, were letters from his father, the Earl of Cleeve, to his beloved daughter. Del picked one up to assure himself they were real. They were written, not in Mr. Sands' clean, elegant hand, but in his father's more crabbed, intense style. They were many in number, at least two letters a week for the entire two-year period she spent at school. And they were signed, one and all, not by the Earl of Cleeve, or even Cleeve, but by *your loving Papa*.

Del read another and another. They were full, not just of the social events their mother had detailed, but of personal concerns and inquiries. Did she have enough pin money, was the school warm enough, did she like her classes, could he send anything for her comfort?

That his father was a cold, demanding man, withdrawn from his family, had been one of Del's longest-held beliefs. And it was simply not true. Or at least it was not true for Emily.

Celia had somehow followed the direction of his thoughts. "Del, why did you leave?"

"I didn't leave. Not in the beginning. I was sent away, as most boys are, to school. And then, later, I simply went on an adventure."

She frowned at him. Clearly, a longer, better answer was in order.

"When I went away to school, I loved it. I was freed, at least temporarily, from the restrictions of being the heir. I could play and talk with boys my own age, and my own station in life. And others who were not. I fell in with a group of boys who were younger sons—they called themselves the Ready Seconds. I came to admire them. They had more pluck and substance, more ability to do things for themselves than I did. As younger sons, they were more used to doing things, achieving their ends by their own merit. I resolved to be like them. I used Delacorte as a name—not Darling. As the time came to leave school, most of them were destined for the military. So I signed up, too. But lacking my father's approval and patronage, I could not buy a commission, so I simply enlisted in his Majesty's Marine Forces. I took the king's shilling and off I went from Portsmouth."

"How extraordinary."

"Only for someone born an heir. For almost every other man I encountered in my years of service, such a story is all too ordinary."

"I see." She nodded, then held something out to him. "Here they are."

The last two of Emily's letters. Written, he could see, a day apart, starting three days before her death. They were still sealed. No one had ever read them. Del took them to the window and sat down to read them. His fingers were shaking. Celia stayed where she was, alternately biting her lips and the nail of her thumb. He could do nothing for the moment to relieve her anxiety. Because he shared it.

He broke the seal and read. When he finished he looked up at Celia. "Emily was being blackmailed—with the rumor of your supposed illicit relationship." It was so close to their own circumstance, Del had no doubt he knew the name of her blackmailer. He broke open the second letter.

Celia rose. She could not keep still. She lifted her hand to cover her mouth.

He scanned the second letter, then spoke. "It was Melissa Wainwright. Emily confirms it. She states her intention of confronting Melissa, who, I'm quoting from the letter, *somehow knows the exact amount of guineas I have in my possession. Almost as if she had counted them herself. But she has counted far less than I know I ought to have, for they are quite regular in arriving, but not in being spent. I can only suspect she has been stealing them and now wants to get ahold of the whole lot free and clear without being accused of stealing.*"

Del looked up at Celia. "It took her far less time to figure it out than either one of us."

"Will your father have a record of what monies he sent Emily?"

"No doubt."

"We can cross-check against this inventory." She ran back to the table to scan the ledger they had brought up from the library. "No monies recorded as being amongst her possessions. Are you sure she did not intend to pay Melissa?"

Del turned back to the letters. "Quite sure."

"Then Melissa is quite possibly a thief as well as a blackmailer. I remember Emily used to be a little cavalier about the money—saying it was always more than she could ever

spend. I think she thought your father spoiled her in that regard."

"I'm glad if he did."

"And shall you tell him so?"

He grinned at Celia, with her incredible insights. "Yes,
Celia, I think I shall."

Del found his father in his book room.

"Did you find what you were looking for?"

"Yes, we did. I must tell you, Emily was being blackmailed
over a supposed liaison." He kept the nature of the rumor to
himself. It would only serve to embarrass Celia. "I know the
identity of the blackmailer, and I intend to bring her to justice."

His father hid his surprise, but not his outrage. Del could
see his jaw flex hard before he spoke. "How? On what sort of a
charge?"

"Theft, if nothing else. It is my belief this person, Melissa
Wainwright, stole considerable monies from Emily. All the pin
money you had sent her during the time she was there. I wonder if you could have Sands confirm the number for me?"

"Of course. But I know myself what I sent to her—four
guineas a month. It seemed little enough."

"Celia's memory was that Emily rarely spent the money, so
even if she spent some, that still leaves well over two hundred
pounds. People are transported for far less."

"But how shall you prove it?"

"I am not yet sure, but I will need to leave immediately, before I lose track of Miss Wainwright."

"Then I will wish you Godspeed."

"Thank you, sir." Del lingered another moment.

"Was there something else?"

"Yes, I wanted to thank you for keeping such good records,
and for keeping all the letters. They were invaluable."

"I'm glad."

"So am I." Del swallowed his pride. "But I am also angry."

The Earl's head came up. "Why should you be angry?"

"Because those letters, so meticulously kept, showed me a side of you I had not the wit nor the maturity to think even existed. I am angry I denied it to myself."

His father was completely, utterly still for a very long moment. "As it happens, I owe you an apology as well. Because if you had not run off, if you had not gone off to make your own way, I might not have felt the loss so heavily. I am sorry it took your leaving to make me a better father."

Del could not believe there was heat welling in his throat.

"Will you not stay? At least for a short time? It would mean a great deal to your mother."

Del swallowed over the knot in his throat at the thought of his mother's welcome and generosity. "I will come back, but this business of Emily's death is unfinished. I have reason to believe . . . I no longer feel confident Emily's death was a suicide."

"Because of the theft? Perhaps Miss Wainwright was simply being an opportunist after Emily's death. Rupert, it is a bitter truth to swallow, but I have her note. The note she wrote just before she killed herself."

Without moving from his chair, his father opened a locked drawer of his desk and drew out a folded note.

A pain, which could only have been his heart breaking, knocked the breath from Del's lungs. "You kept it."

His father gave a rueful smile. "You have noted my record-keeping tendencies. But this isn't a record this is . . . a reminder. As I said, some truths are too bitter to swallow all at once."

"May I see it?"

"Yes, of course."

CHAPTER 26

Cleeve Abbey fell away as the Earl's traveling coach headed southeast, back to London. Back toward Melissa Wainwright. Del and Celia sat side by side on the forward-facing seat. He held her hand tightly in his lap but did not say anything for miles and miles, disquieted, Celia thought, from his conversation with his father.

"Did you mean that?" he asked at last. "What you said to my mother? That you had already fallen in love with me long before you met me, or did you just say it to ease her mind?"

"I told you when I first met you, I had made up my mind to like you long before I ever met you. And that was why. I was abominably in love with you."

He reached across and lifted her clear off the seat and onto his lap. She folded herself into his warmth and comfort. "How very intelligent you were to do so."

"It was not particularly intelligent. It was *daring*."

He kissed her, gently at first, but what began in sweetness and gratitude soon became something more, something hungry and yearning. His lips, his lovely, firm, bow-shaped lips pressed into hers again and again. His hands left her waist to skim along her jaw and angle her mouth for his opening. His tongue stroked and licked at her, kindling the fire between them with each blissful sear. Everything within her, every nerve, every fiber of her being reached out to him, with heat and urgency.

She slid her hands along the strong line of his jaw, marveling at the strength inherent in each and every part of him. Marveling at the difference between the rasp of his clean-shaven skin and the opulent softness of his firm lips. Such a dichotomy, such contradiction, all within one man.

His mouth left hers to kiss his way down her neck. She arched her neck to give him greater access even as she ran her own hands through his soft, shining hair and pulled herself closer to him, closer to his heat and his warmth. Closer to his love.

Then his gloved hands were at her bodice, quickly stripping away her buttons, parting her short redingote and waistcoat, pulling apart her chemisette, until he bared her to her stays. His mouth was on her skin above the line of her shift and she was arching and throwing back her head to help him, to show him what she wanted. To show him her love.

Del was as intent, as ravenous as she—kissing and pushing away fabric, layer by layer, and working the laces of her stays until he freed her breasts, so he could ravage her with his eyes, his mouth, and his tongue. She held him to her, her hands tangling in his hair, as he sucked and tongued her over and over, moving from one tightly furled peak to the other, leaving a trail of fire from her breasts to deep within, to her womb.

He let her go, lifting his mouth from her body. He picked her up off him and pressed her into the seat opposite, leaving her there, bared to the waist, gasping and panting with need, while he divested himself of unneeded clothing.

Del pushed his hat away and stripped off his gloves, throwing them onto the seat without even looking. He unbuttoned and shrugged his way out of his coat, and flung away his cravat. He looked at her with such heat and intent, it knocked the breath from her and she was in pain, aching without being

touched. She thought he would lift her to him to kiss and fondle. But he reached down and raised her legs to either side of
him, resting them on the opposite seat.

Celia's heart began to pound. She remembered only too
well the night they had been in the carriage together and his
feet had been set high on the seat, surrounding her. "Del?"

"Brace yourself, Celia." He flipped up her skirts and ran his
hands up and down her legs, over her stockings to the edge of
her garters.

"No." She was shocked at the openness, the sheer carnality
of his intentions.

He grinned and nodded in the affirmative. "Oh, yes."

"Del, you can't—"

Del slid to his knees in front of her. "I can. I will."

"But the curtains. Someone could see."

"Only you. If you pull your bodice back into order no one
will know, will they? They'll just see a lady sitting, oh so very
primly in her carriage, and they'll never suspect that I'm
under your skirts, licking your quim and making you come
into my mouth."

She was shocked by his raw carnality but helpless to resist
him and his sleepy-eyed intensity. Celia felt heat flash under
her skin, and her head felt light, faint with anticipation and
need. Del put his hands upon her legs and pushed them
wider. He lowered his head to feather kisses inside her thighs
and she felt herself come undone, inch by tantalizing inch.

Oh, God, yes, he could. Celia nearly shrieked at the first warm,
wet lick of his tongue across her. But the sound that came out
of her mouth was all animal pleasure.

"Mmm," he agreed, and she could feel his voice vibrate
through her as he tongued and probed her. She was afloat,
warm and languid, buoyed along on a current of soft, infinitely
pleasant sensation.

With a precise touch she could never have prepared herself
for, he kissed her *there*. On that spot, on the place from which

her desire arose. Her pearl, he had called it and she felt like a pearl—smooth, flowing with liquid light. A craving, a hungry yearning, rose within her and her hands tangled in his hair, pulling him to her, pressing his lips, his beautiful clever lips against that most sensitive place. She felt feverish with the relentlessly gentle onslaught of his tongue against the center of her very being.

Her fingers curled and dug into the upholstery, frantic to hold herself down, anxious to bind herself to him, but she was falling away, upward, carried aloft by his strength and his gentleness.

Her unruly, daring body was still rooted upon the earth, writhing upon the seat, twisting and turning until, with one precise elegant touch she flew, blinded by the explosion of light and heat behind her eyelids.

She had time to rest in the afterglow of her release. While she was still wet and still shaking from the outrageous force of his love, Del wasted no time. He unbuttoned the flap on his breeches, lifted her up like a rag doll and just as easily lowered and impaled her upon his ready cock.

And they burst into flame.

Celia woke with a headache, something she was normally unaccustomed to. She told herself it was due to the distress and tension of the whole affair, the hideous apprehension that Melissa's "independence" might actually have come from Emily's stolen guineas.

It might also have been due to the fact she woke up alone. Instead of her husband's shining head, there was a note on the pillow beside her.

> *My dear, forgive me. I thought it best to get this business out of the way and done with. Younghusband goes with me, as does a magistrate from the Bow Street Court. I hope to bring you news by this afternoon.*

The clock had not yet struck seven. Celia pelted out of bed and grabbed up the first garment she could find to cover her nakedness, her husband's elegant silk banyan.

"Del? Del!" Her words echoed in the corridor as she pelted down the stairs towards the back of the house. "Don't you dare be gone. Del!"

Celia went down the servants' stairs into the kitchen, where she found only Mrs. Bobbins. "Where is everyone?"

"My lady." The cook bobbed a quick half-curtsy, moving a pot easily from the stove to the table. "Gone off early, they all did. Gosling with my lord. And your girl Bains, she's gone off to get me some eggs. We had no word you were coming back so soon, and Bains didn't think you'd be up this early, else she'd be here to see to you."

"Yes, of course, that's fine. How long ago did they leave? The Viscount, that is?"

"Couldn't say, as they didn't take any breakfast. Shall I get you your chocolate, then, my lady?"

Celia didn't answer and ran back up the stairs to poke her head through the drawing room curtains and scan North Row. Empty. She was too late—Del must have left at dawn. She didn't even have Melissa's direction—only that she was somewhere in Marylebone.

She would have to wait.

By the time she stomped barefooted back down to the breakfast room, muttering vile imprecations against overprotective husbands, Mrs. Bobbins had brought a lovely pot of chocolate. "You just start on that and I'll have the rest up in a tic, sure as Sundays."

Celia sat down, poured herself a cup, and was in the midst of contemplating whether or not she had better take the cup back upstairs to attempt to dress when Mrs. Turbot, towing Melissa Wainwright by the hand, appeared in the corridor. At first glance, Celia had the impression of a governess hauling along a reluctant, naughty pupil. Had Mrs. Turbot brought Melissa there, to her, for a reckoning? But where was Del? It seemed so . . . wrong.

She stood when Mrs. Turbot sighted her and came straight for the breakfast room. There was no other way out of the room. "Mrs. Turbot, Melissa, to what do I owe the honor?" Her voice was thin and quavering, and could not carry it off with any aplomb.

"Honor," Mrs. Turbot sneered. "I've had more than enough of your honor, thank you very much. You and your husband, both."

"I beg your pardon?"

"You may beg all you like. In fact, by the time we're through, my lady, I'll wager you're going to beg whether you like it or not."

Gooseflesh prickled across Celia's skin. She did not know what to do, but she knew she had to do *something*. "Mrs. Turbot, you appear greatly agitated. Let me get you a dish of tea."

"No farther," the woman cried, and pulled out a small pistol from the pocket of her gown.

Celia almost laughed. The gun, however tiny, looked entirely ridiculous in the hands of Mrs. Turbot, with her lace mobcap perched atop her head like a large white toadstool. Celia slid slowly into the chair, and tried to employ the sort of voice Del used upon her, hypnotic and soothing.

"I fear you are greatly overset, Mrs. Turbot. Perhaps you and Melissa might sit down to recover yourself." She glanced at Melissa, who looked positively green. "Melissa looks like she could particularly use a cup of tea."

"I am not overset. And I'll be damned before I let you and that bloody Viscount Darling ruin everything we've worked for."

"I told you we never should have—" Melissa stopped at a murderous look from Mrs. Turbot.

The aim of the gun in the woman's hand wavered only momentarily before settling back on Celia. "Get up and come with us. You're going to be our guarantee of safe passage. I've got a hackney carriage outside. Get up and come."

Celia kept her eyes on the gun shaking in Mrs. Turbot's hand and knew if she left the protection of her husband's house—where her husband would, at some point, return and where someone surely could be called upon for assistance—if she went out into the streets with this woman, her chances of survival would diminish exponentially with every step away. She had to stay put. She had to be resolute.

"And how am I to do so? I would be happy to accompany you, but I am not at all dressed. If you will but give me—"

"No!" The gun wavered again. "You will go nowhere."

"But surely if we are to leave in a hackney carriage, I must have clothes, or someone will notice. You cannot drag a half-naked woman through the streets of London without drawing attention."

"Ma—"

"Melissa!" Mrs. Turbot cut her charge off. "Take that"— she motioned to the silk curtain ties—"and bind her hands."

"How's she to write the letter to Viscount Darling with her hands tied?" Melissa asked.

"It doesn't matter who writes it, as long as he knows we've got her."

"I think Melissa might be better employed in getting me a plain gown from my chamber, so I might be suitably covered when we leave." Celia knew she was grasping at cobwebs, try-ing to come up with some way to stall for time, to get them separated. There was already friction between the two women. Perhaps she could exploit it to her benefit. "My dressing room is the last door on the left. The green should do very well."

"No! Stay where you are, Melissa, and bind her."

Melissa was half rebellion, half petulance, but she began to do as she was bid, unwinding the cord from the drapery.

"Don't do it, Melissa. People are transported for stealing

handkerchiefs. Imagine what a judge will do to someone who stole more than a hundred pounds from the Earl of Cleeve's daughter. Not to mention blackmailing a peer."

From her place at the window, Melissa's nervous eyes darted to Mrs. Turbot.

"You should have listened when Viscount Darling warned you the first time, Melissa." Celia kept at her. "You should have run when you had a chance." Celia stepped toward her.

"That's exactly what we aim to do now. Get away from her, before I have to shoot you where you stand. Don't think I won't! The Earl of Cleeve's stubborn daughter died easy enough and if you don't do exactly as I say, you're next."

Celia felt her heart stutter to a painful, lurching stop. "You killed Emily Delacorte?"

"That's right," snarled Mrs. Turbot at the same time Melissa blurted, "It was an accident."

Celia looked from one to the other and knew that the truth lay somewhere in between. "Tell me what happened."

"We don't have time for this," Mrs. Turbot fumed. "Melissa hit her to keep from peaching on us and I finished her off. Just as I'll finish you off, if you don't do as I say right now." She motioned with the barrel of the gun. "Bind her, Melissa."

Upon which, Mrs. Bobbins bustled in with a tray laden with food and hot beverages. "I heard you had visitors, my lady, so I brought more chocolate and coffee." She stopped abruptly. "Here, now, wot's this?"

For a long moment no one, certainly not Celia, seemed to know what to do. Mrs. Bobbins frowned at Mrs. Turbot, her face as disapproving as a prune. Mrs. Turbot swung the gun back and forth between the two of them, uncertain as to who was the greater threat. And then, improbably, Mrs. Bobbins smiled and turned back to the tray.

"Lord, didn't know it was *you!* Janey Wainwright, as I live and breathe. I didn't know her ladyship was interested in the plays. His lordship don't care for 'em. Still, I haven't seen you in a whore's age, Janey. Beg your pardon, your ladyship. Well, Janey"—Mrs. Bobbins straightened up with one hand on her ample hips—"how've you been keeping yourself?"

Celia looked from Mrs. Bobbins and her extraordinary speech, to Mrs. Turbot, who had turned the pasty white color of her namesake fish.

"I don't know what you're talking about." The gun was on Mrs. Bobbins now, and Celia wrapped her hands around the back of the chair, ready to throw it whenever the opportunity arose.

"Well, that's a fine way to greet an old friend. It's your old Fanny Bobbins, it is, Janey. We worked together at the Haymarket Theatre, we did, back in the day, 'till she got a bellyful. Here's your pot, ma'am," she informed Celia, handing her another pot of steaming hot chocolate, though the one on the table was still nearly full. She turned back to "Janey." "So what are you working on now? Melodrama, is it? And who's this with you? Oh, she's the spit of you, she is."

Janey Wainwright Turbot swung the gun wildly back and forth between the two women in front of her, before she settled again on Celia. "I'll shoot the Viscountess."

"Oh, that's famous, that is," Mrs. Bobbins crowed and clapped. "Bill would love this. Great one for the melodrama and the panto, is Bill." She flapped her hand at Mrs. Turbot and turned away to the door. "Bill," she bawled down the corridor, "you've gotta see this." She came back to stand by the tea tray, the picture of happy anticipation.

Bill? Did she mean Gosling? But he was gone with Del. Celia had no idea if Mrs. Bobbins was truly mad or just crazy like a fox, but she noticed the cook had the lid off the coffeepot. Steam—scalding steam—rose in graceful, purposeful arabesques. Bless her ample heart, Fanny Bobbins was as daring as they came.

Her heart beating a wild tattoo in her chest, Celia followed suit, letting go of the chair and holding the pot of chocolate, ready to pitch it at Melissa.

Footsteps rang out on the servants' stair and everything happened in a blur.

As soon as Mrs. Turbot swung the gun around to face whoever was coming to the breakfast room door, Mrs. Bobbins emptied the entire coffeepot of scalding liquid onto Mrs. Turbot's hand.

Mrs. Turbot screamed, "You bitch," and dropped the gun. Mrs. Bobbins, who Celia thought had fallen down in an apoplexy, but who had really grasped the corner of the carpet runner, quite literally pulled the rug out from under Mrs. Turbot. The woman crashed against the wall and the gun skidded across the floor.

Mrs. Bobbins picked it up and said, "Stupid cow, you never could act. Mrs. Turbot was my character, you cow." She looked with disgust at the gun. "Bad stage prop—doesn't even have a hammer."

The house was then full of the sounds of running feet and doors bursting open, and the breakfast room was filled with men holding real guns, drawn and at the ready.

"Del! You came."

"To save the day. Except it had already been saved." Del looked at Celia. "You saved yourself. Are you all right? Are you hurt?"

"No, I'm fine. Thanks to your Mrs. Bobbins—wherever did you get her?" Celia turned to the cook. "You were magnificent."

He crushed Celia to his chest, even as he leveled his gun upon Janey Wainwright, still stunned and prone, upon the floor.

"You wouldn't shoot a defenseless woman," she begged.

"Shut up, Janey," Mrs. Bobbins instructed. "You're quite welcome, my lady. Don't get much of a chance to play to the balcony these days. By any roads, I couldn't let Janey have the stage to herself, could I? Poor daft cow."

"I think she's Melissa's mother, by the way, Mrs. Turbot is. Except she's not Mrs. Turbot, who turns out to be a character from a play. According to your Mrs. Bobbins, she's Jane Wainwright, an actress, formerly of the Haymarket Theatre, which she left, pregnant some eighteen and a half years ago, if I understand Mrs. Bobbins' cant."

"You've the right of it, my lady."

"Thank you, Mrs. Bobbins. I can't thank you enough. My God, Celia, when I realized what I'd done, how I'd left you alone—and when we discovered they had flown, but only just—God's balls, I don't ever want to go through another half hour like that again. Took ten years off me."

Celia pushed his hair out of his eyes. "Are you sure you're all right? You're breathing awful hard."

"I ran. I couldn't wait for the carriage in all that traffic. So I ran to come back to you." He pulled her hard against him. "Am I squashing you?"

"No." Del was holding her very close, as if he would never let her go. Celia rather liked the feeling of being squashed up against his waistcoat, while he tucked her under his chin and kissed her forehead. Celia snuggled against Del's chest for another moment while Mr. Younghusband and his constables had Melissa and her mother by the arms and were escorting them away.

"What will happen to her, to them?"

"Transportation if they're lucky. Hanging if they are not. And all for bloody money." His disgust was apparent.

"Yes, money, you bastard," spat Jane Wainwright. "Only people who don't need money can afford to sneer at it."

"Madam, do not so much as tempt me to spare the King's Bench the trouble of your accommodation."

She scoffed. "Even you wouldn't shoot an unarmed woman."

"Women are never unarmed, madam. You forced your way into my home. I've shot strangers for less, and none of them killed my sister or threatened my wife. Take them away."

Celia found her eyes hot with unshed tears.

"Don't cry for them, Celia. They are not worth your tears."

"I can't help but feel sorry for them. We're not all like you, Del. We can't all just take the king's shilling and go off and win our fortunes. They had to have something to live on, too."

"That's more of your willful kindness, Celia, my darling."

"That's what I'm supposed to call you."

"Are you?"

"Yes. My darling Viscount Darling."

"Am I your darling?"

She smiled at him and felt his golden strength flow through her. "My darling Del. Do you know, it is not even eight o'clock in the morning? May we please go upstairs and go back to bed?"

"My Ravishing Viscountess, I should like nothing better."

If you liked this book,
try Katherine Irons' SEABORNE,
in stores now . . .

M organ watched from the surf. Spending so long out of water this afternoon had taxed his strength, both in the energy needed to maintain the illusion that he was a human and the strain it took for him to breathe on land. He felt an overwhelming weariness of body and spirit.

Being in such close contact with the human woman should have dissolved the odd attraction he felt for her. Despite her quick wit and obvious intelligence, she was damaged, her health even more frail than the average land dweller's. Although he couldn't assess her physical condition without examining her, he guessed that she was paralyzed from the waist down.

Not that it would have been a problem if she weren't human. Atlanteans had virtually no physical handicaps and possessed superhealing abilities. Short of the impossibility of replacing a missing limb that had been cut off in battle or eaten by a shark, almost any injury would heal in a matter of hours. They suffered from none of the viruses, heart disease, cancers, and various illnesses that plagued humans.

Leaving the cradle of life, the sea, brought with it many challenges for the human race. The earth's force of gravity and the constant assault on the earth's surface from radiation put constant pressure on the human species. Atlanteans, who had remained in the water, were both superior intellectual and sexual beings.

The sexual part was the problem. Unfortunately, heightened sensuality was one weakness that Atlanteans suffered from, both males and females. Although some couples mated for life and remained faithful to each other, the majority, like him, took sexual pleasure where they found it. Since his kind were bound by none of the artificial human rules of morality, adults finding pleasure whenever and wherever they pleased with other adults was the norm.

Morgan reasoned that he had acquired a desire for a woman that he was forbidden to touch. It was a rare occurrence, one that he personally had never experienced, although he'd heard tales of other Atlanteans struck by this same fever in the blood. Inflamed by the unsatisfied lust for a certain object of desire—even a human one—brought weakness and both mental and physical pain.

Claire was so human that he didn't understand how he could be attracted to her. He should have felt pity for her. Instead, he wanted to take her in his arms. He wanted to touch her skin, to taste it, to nibble his way from her delicate eyelids to the tips of her toes . . . to lave every square inch of her body with his tongue. He wanted to inhale her scent until he was intoxicated by it, to run his fingers through her hair, suck her nipples until they hardened to tight buds, and cradle her in his arms. Even now, watching her at a distance, Morgan could feel his groin tightening with need. He wanted her as he hadn't wanted a female in three hundred years . . . perhaps five.

And she had been equally attracted to him. He had read the invitation in her eyes. Naturally, most sexually mature humans desired his kind. There were legends of those who walked the earth, breathed air, yet lived on the blood of their fellow humans. Vampires, they were called. It was said that vampires possessed the ability to bewitch humans with their sexuality, but the power of these bloodsuckers—if they truly existed—would be nothing compared to the sensual lure of the Atlantean race.

He sank under the waves, reveling in the powerful surge of the tide, savoring the tangy feel of the salt on his skin. This was his element; this was where he belonged. Venturing on dry land, even for a few hours, was dangerous in more ways than he could count.

But the pounding in his head and the pressure in his groin remained as strong as ever. He seemed tangled in a web of sorcery. No matter how much reason told him to leave this place, to forget her, he was incapable of doing so. He had to find a way to end this connection before it was too late.

Perhaps the only way to rid himself of his attraction was to make love to her. It would be risky. The laws against Atlanteans and humans sharing sexual favors were rigid and strictly enforced. If he was caught, he could be severely punished.

The thought that he already could have been caught watching Claire by his greatest enemy came to him. But he didn't think Caddoc had seen him spying on the woman. It was more likely that his half brother had witnessed the near drowning of the boy. If Caddoc knew about Claire, he would have taunted him about it. Caddoc never had the self-control to hold his tongue. The offense, having romantic contact with a human, would be even greater than rescuing one from drowning.

Morgan clenched his jaw. Tonight, he would go to Claire. But this time, he would take her into his element. Once they were beneath the ocean, he could use his healing powers to temporarily give her back the use of her legs. She would be able to respond to his seduction, to feel his mouth on her body, to enjoy each shared sensation. And he knew he would satisfy her more than any human male she'd ever been intimate with. But then, sadly, he'd have to wipe away her memory of the evening.

He told himself that if she came willingly, it wasn't really abduction, and if she didn't resist, what they did together would harm no one. The argument was as full of holes as the *Titanic*, but he was in no mood to be rational. As impossible as it was to believe, Claire had become an immovable obstruction. If he was to complete his mission and return to defend himself in front of the High Court, he'd have to shatter the ancient laws and seduce her first.

And try THE SHADOW GUARD,
new from Diane Whiteside,
out this month from Brava . . .

M urder cases frequently felt like a messy ball of string. But he'd always known where to find a loose end to pull for clues.

Forty-eight hours into the case—the grace period when he could usually at least guess where to look—every lead had led nowhere. And the public was giving him mountains more stuff to track down every minute.

He cursed under his breath and drained his latte. Dammit, maybe if he looked online he could find a lead. The coroner's preliminary report might have something useful in it.

His cell phone buzzed against his hip, and he ignored it.

He frowned. How many people had the number to his personal cell? His brother Logan and . . .

The distinctive triple pattern sounded again.

He grabbed his phone and flipped it open.

Message from Andromache.

A slow smile spread across his face despite everything else demanding his attention. They'd played *Argos* together on the same server since the game had started six years ago. Now they were members of the same guild. He was a mage, who specialized in blasting bad guys with spectacularly efficient spells, which removed them faster than any court system. She was a very sneaky, barbarian warrior, notable for her boobs, black braids, and flying axes according to her online avatar.

He couldn't count the number of quests they'd gone on. He wouldn't have as many points if they didn't game together so often.

> *Hey there,* he texted back to her.
> *Hi. Gaming tonight?*
> *Sorry. Big case here eating up my time.*

He kicked back in his chair, certain she wouldn't want to chat about his job any more than he would hers. She'd probably figured out he was a cop, based on his responses to some very illegal suggestions on *Argos* boards. But she'd never said so specifically and she sure as hell had never been interested in any crimes.

> *The Belhaven knifing victim?*

A cold wave rippled across Jake's skin, faster than a trout rising for air. The number of people who knew exactly how small-mouth the mystery lady had died were fewer than he had fingers on his phone's keys.

Why? he asked and wondered how fast he could subpoena Andromache's cell phone records, if she didn't tell him.

There was a long pause.

An e-mail announced that the coroner's preliminary report was available for review. Nothing helpful there; that doughty old broad had already phoned him with the results.

Jake started to compose a stronger demand for Andromache.

> *Do you have ANY leads to the killer?*

His thumbs hung over the keypad and he gaped at the small screen like a stranded trout. Why the emphasis? Did she know how unusually hard this case was?

A million questions clamored in his head but he couldn't send any of them on an open line. He settled for the simplest.

Why do you ask?

Seconds ticked past before an answer came, every letter emblazoned on a yellow flag like a giant warning sign.

I can help.
What do you mean???

Her answer shot back faster than the freight trains barreling into town.

Where can we talk? PRIVATELY.

Jake stood up so abruptly that his keyboard bounced onto the carpeted floor. Heads turned to stare and he glowered their owners back to their own business.

He could take her into an interrogation room but that would be recorded. Years of friendship demanded better treatment, at least until he knew whether she was willing to tell the truth.

He chose every Belhaven cop's favorite hangout.

Duffy's Tavern in an hour?
Sure. See ya then.

She disappeared without asking how to find Duffy's. Only the trail of golden balloons and text across his phone's screen confirmed she just might have something helpful to say.

He blew out a breath and shoved his phone back into its holster.

The pile of message slips seemed to sneer at him, all spurious innocence in its demand for his attention.

Dammit, his brain would rather race through a thousand labyrinths in a quest to discover Andromache's secrets. Starting with what the hell she looked like.

His computer chimed. A small, orange square began to flash on his monitor's corner.

Jake gave it the same narrow-eyed look he'd grant an open door in a drug dealer's hideout. Then he clicked on it.

Hammond, I need you in my office now. The FBI is here. Over.

All of Jake's previous arrogance about the Feds faded into cold mush at the bottom of his stomach, together with every other stupid boast he'd ever made. What the hell could they do for his case except slow it down?

He gritted his teeth and typed. *Roger that.*

Maybe he'd catch a break, the second one of the day, and they'd only want to talk guard duty. Yeah, right.

"Hammond, these are Special Agents Fisher and Murphy of the FBI." Andrews' body looked more relaxed than Jake expected and yet his eyes were more perplexed. Around him, photographs of him with foreign and national dignitaries radiated confidence. Highly polished examples of every rifle the department had owned for the past two centuries conveyed lethal competence.

Jake shook hands with the two pin-striped strangers and tried to hide his wariness. Their well-tailored suits couldn't disguise the weapons belts at their hips nor their direct assessment of him.

"Gentlemen, this is Sergeant Jake Hammond. He's the head of our Homicide Unit and is personally leading the investigation into Saturday night's murder case. He was the first detective on the scene."

"Very glad to meet you, Hammond," said Murphy, the taller of the two and a woman. "We'll be working closely with you on Division Director Williams's murder."

"Division Director? Williams?" Shock thudded through Jake's system and deepened his voice. "May I ask who you're talking about?"

"Melinda Williams is a GSA division director who was reported missing in North Carolina five days ago," Murphy answered quietly, her cool, black eyes measuring Jake like a surveyor's sextant.

"Five days? If she drove directly back here, then three days in the water—" The calendar arranged itself in front of his eyes, dates sturdy as soldiers standing to be counted.

"And two days in the coroner's office. Yes, the timeline fits neatly." Murphy sipped her coffee as precisely as she'd folded the scarf at her neck. "Miss Williams took a rental car to Elizabeth City, since flights aren't readily available there, unlike Raleigh."

"But she was reported missing in North Carolina, not here." Jake doggedly pursued the victim's footprints.

"Because she didn't tell her office or her family that she was returning. When she didn't phone in, the search started at her North Carolina long-term rental apartment."

Chief Andrews watched them silently, his fingers steepled like a rack of guns ready to go to war.

"Why do you think it's her?" Jake pushed harder, determined to find all the secrets in the FBI's arsenal.

"Miss Williams is very distinctive physically." Fisher spoke up for the first time, his deep voice shadowing the room. "Height, weight"—his eyes met Jake's and they shared a moment's masculine response to those statistics—"and a small zodiac tattoo on the small of her back all matched your victim.

Her fingerprints came back positive just before Murphy and I arrived here."

"Good to know," Jake murmured. They'd probably rushed the tests through. "She worked for GSA, you said. The General Services Administration, right?"

He kept his tongue, and hopefully his tone, away from dismissing them as the bureaucrats' bureaucrats.

"Correct. She was in the Public Building Service, where Uncle Sam is the government's landlord." Fisher and Murphy's utter relaxation confirmed that they, too, considered Williams and her group to be just ordinary public servants, not critical to the country's protection.

"Report said that she was knifed, which is why we came over," Murphy added.

"Since she's a federal employee and disappeared while she was working, her death might be related to her job, making it an FBI issue." Fisher peered into his mug's depths, then unhappily swirled the dregs. "I never expected to find a vanilla latte with soy at a police station. Can we have another round of coffee, please, before we talk about today's real problem—the upcoming arraignment of those terrorists?"

"Sure thing." Jake pushed back his chair. He too could use a good drink.

Triumph flickered through the chief's eyes for an instant. He swore gourmet coffee won more interrogations and political negotiations than any other bribe.

"Once we nail that down, we can chat about how to conduct a joint investigation into Miss Williams's death. It shouldn't take more than a few minutes to make sure we cover all the basics."

Jake nodded politely and headed for the best stash of coffee fixings in the building. He'd need all the help he could get to wash down the FBI's ideas of partnership.

Then get out in time to meet Andromache.

There's nothing sexier than a BIG BAD BEAST. Keep an eye out for Shelly Laurenston's latest, coming next month!

U lrich Van Holtz turned over and snuggled closer to the denim-clad thigh resting by his head. Then he remembered that he'd gone to bed alone last night.

Forcing one eye open, he gazed at the face grinning down at him.

"Mornin', supermodel."

He hated when she called him that. The dismissive tone of it grated on his nerves. Especially his sensitive *morning* nerves. She might as well say, "Mornin', you who serve no purpose."

"Dee-Ann." He glanced around, trying to figure out what was going on. "What time is it?"

"Dawn-ish."

"Dawn-*ish*?"

"Not quite dawn, no longer night."

"And is there a reason you're in my bed at dawn-ish . . . fully clothed? Because I'm pretty sure you'd be much more comfortable naked."

Her lips curved slightly. "Look at you, Van Holtz. Trying to sweet talk me."

"If it'll get you naked . . ."

"You're my boss."

"I'm your supervisor."

"If you can fire me, you're my boss. Didn't they teach you that in your fancy college?"

"My fancy college was a culinary school and I spent most of my classes trying to understand my French instructors. So if they mentioned that boss-supervisor distinction, I probably missed it."

"You're still holding my thigh, boss."

"You're still in my bed. And you're still not naked."

"Me naked is like me dressed. Still covered in scars and willing to kill."

"Now you're just trying to turn me on." Ric yawned, reluctantly unwrapping his arms from Dee's scrumptious thigh and using the move to get a good look at her.

She'd let her dark brown hair grow out a bit in recent months so that the heavy, wavy strands rested below her ears, framing a square jaw that sported a five-inch scar from her military days and a more recent bruise he was guessing had happened last night. She had a typical Smith nose—a bit long and rather wide at the tip—and the proud, high forehead. But it was those eyes that disturbed most of the populace because they were the one part of her that never shifted. They stayed the same color and shape no matter what form she was in. Many people called the color "dog yellow" but Ric thought of it as a canine gold. And Ric didn't find those eyes off-putting. No, he found them entrancing. Just like the woman.

Ric had only known the She-wolf about seven months but since the first time he'd laid eyes on her, he'd been madly, deeply in lust. Then, over time, he'd gotten to know her, and he'd come to fall madly, deeply in love. There was just one problem with them becoming mates and living happily ever after—and that problem's name was Dee-Ann Smith.

"So is there a reason you're here, in my bed, not naked,

around dawn-*ish* that doesn't involve us forgetting the idiotic limits of business protocol so that you can ravish my more-than-willing body?"

"Yep."

When she said nothing else, Ric sat up and offered, "Let me guess. The tellin' will be easier if it's around some waffles and bacon."

"Those words are true, but faking that accent ain't endearing you to my Confederate heart."

"I bet adding blueberries to those waffles will."

"Canned or fresh?"

Mouth open, Ric glared at her over his shoulder.

"It's a fair question."

"Out." He pointed at his bedroom door. "If you're going to question whether I'd use *canned* anything in my food while sitting on my bed *not* naked, then you can just get the hell out of my bedroom . . . and sit in my kitchen, quietly, until I arrive."

"Will you be in a better mood?"

"Will you be naked?"

"Like a wolf with a bone," she muttered, and told him, "Not likely."

"Then I guess you have your answer."

"Oh, come on. Can I at least sit here and watch you strut into the bathroom bare-ass naked?"

"No, you may not." He threw his legs over the side of the bed. "However, you may look over your shoulder longingly while I, in a very manly way, walk purposely into the bathroom bare-ass naked. Because I'm not here for your entertainment, Ms. Smith."

"It's Miss. Nice Southern girls use Miss."

"Then I guess that still makes you a Ms."

Dee-Ann Smith sat at Van Holtz's kitchen table, her fingers tracing the lines in the marble. His kitchen table was real marble, too, the legs made of the finest wood. Not like her parents' Formica table that still had the crack in it from when Rory Reed's big head drunkenly slammed into it after they'd had too many beers the night of their junior year homecoming game.

Then again, everything about Van Holtz's apartment spoke of money and the finest of everything. Yet his place somehow managed to be comfortable, not like some spots in the city where everything was so fancy Dee didn't know who'd want to visit or sit on a damn thing. Of course, Van Holtz didn't come off like some spoiled rich kid that she'd want to slap around when he got mouthy. She'd thought he'd be that way, but since meeting him a few months back, he'd proven that he wasn't like that at all.

Shame she couldn't say that for several of his family members. She'd met his daddy only a few times and each time was a little worse than the last. And his older brother wasn't much better. To be honest, she didn't know why Van Holtz didn't challenge them both and take the Alpha position from the mean old bastard. That's how they did it among the Smiths, and it was a way of life that had worked for them for at least three centuries.

Hair dripping wet from the shower, Van Holtz walked into his kitchen. He wore black sweatpants and was pulling a black T-shirt over his head, giving Dee an oh-too-brief glimpse at an absolutely superb set of abs and narrow hips. No, he wasn't as big a wolf as Dee was used to—in fact, they were the same six-two height and nearly the same width—but good Lord, the man had an amazing body. It must be all the things he did during the day. Executive chef at the Fifth Avenue Van Holtz restaurant; a goalie for the shifter-only pro team he owned, the Carnivores; and one of the supervisors for the Group. A position that, although he didn't spend as much time in the field as Dee-Ann and her team, did force him to keep in excellent shape.

Giving another yawn, Van Holtz pushed his wet, dark blond hair off his face, brown eyes trying to focus while he scanned the kitchen.

"Coffee's in the pot," she said.

Some men, they simply couldn't function without their morning coffee, and that was Van Holtz.

"Thank you," he sighed, grabbing the mug she'd taken out for him and filling it up. If he minded that she'd become quite familiar with his kitchen and his apartment in general, after months of coming and going as she pleased, he never showed it.

Dee waited until he'd had a few sips and finally turned to her with a smile.

"Good morning."

She returned that smile, something she normally didn't bother to do with most, and replied, "Morning."

"I promised you waffles with *fresh* blueberries." He sniffed in disgust. "Canned. As if I'd ever."

"I know. I know. Sacrilege."

"Exactly!"

Dee-Ann sat patiently at the kitchen table while Van Holtz whipped up a full breakfast for her the way most people whipped up a couple of pieces of toast.

"So, Dee . . ." Van Holtz placed perfectly made waffles and bacon in front of her with warmed syrup in a bowl and a small dish of butter right behind it. "What brings you here?"

He sat down on the chair across from her with his own plate of food.

"Cats irritate me."

Van Holtz nodded, chewing on a bite of food. "And yet you work so well with them on a day-to-day basis."

"Not when they get in my way."

"Is there a possibility you can be more specific on what your complaint is?"

"But it's fun to watch you so confused."

"Only one cup of coffee, Dee-Ann. Only one cup."

She laughed a little, always amused when Van Holtz got a bit cranky.

"We went to raid a hybrid fight last night—not only was there no fight, but there were felines already there."

"Which felines?"

"KZS."

"Oh." He took another bite of bacon. "*Those* felines. Well, maybe they're trying to—"

"Those felines ain't gonna help mutts, Van Holtz, you know that."

"Can't you just call me Ric? You know, like everyone else." And since the man had more cousins than should legally be allowed, all with the last name Van Holtz, perhaps that would be a bit easier for all concerned.

"Fine. They're not going to help, *Ric*."

"And yet it seems as if they are—or at least trying."

"They're doing something—and I don't like it. I don't like when anyone gets in my way." Especially particular felines who had wicked right crosses that Dee's jaw was still feeling several hours later.

"All right," he said. "I'll deal with it."

"Just like that?"

"Yep. Just like that. Orange juice?" She nodded and he poured freshly squeezed orange juice into her glass.

"You don't want to talk to the team first?"

"I talked to you. What's the team going to tell me that you haven't? Except they'll probably use more syllables and keep the antifeline sentiment out of it."

She nodded and watched him eat. Pretty. The man was just . . . pretty. Not girly—although she was sure her daddy and uncles would think so—but pretty. Handsome and gorgeous might be the more acceptable terms when talking about men, but those words did not fit him.

"Is something wrong with your food?" he asked, noticing that she hadn't started eating.

She glanced down at the expertly prepared waffle, big fresh blueberries throughout, powdered sugar sprinkled over it. In bowls he'd also put out more fresh blueberries, along with strawberries and peaches. He'd given her a linen napkin to use and heavy, expensive-looking flatware to eat with. And he'd set all this up in about thirty minutes.

The whole meal was, in a word, perfection, which was why Dee replied, "It's all right . . . I guess."

A dark eyebrow peaked. "You guess?"

"Haven't tried it yet, now have I? Can't tell you if I like it if I haven't tried it."

"Only one cup of coffee, Dee. Only one."

"Maybe it's time you had another."

"Eat and tell me my food is amazing or I'm going to get cranky again."

"If you're going to be pushy . . ." She took a bite, letting the flavors burst against her taste buds. Damn, but the man could cook. Didn't seem right, did it? Pretty and a good cook.

"Well?"

"Do I really need to tell you how good it is?"

"Yes. Although I'm enjoying your orgasm face."

She smirked. "Darlin', you don't know my orgasm face."

"Yet, I'm ever hopeful."

"Keepin' the dream alive."

"Someone has to." He winked at her and went back to his food. "I'll see what I can find out about what's going on with KZS and get back to you." He looked up at her and smiled. "Don't worry, Dee-Ann. I've got your back."

She knew that. She knew he would come through as

promised. As hard as it was to believe, she was learning to trust the one breed of wolf her daddy told her never to trust.

Then again . . . her daddy had never tasted the man's blueberry waffles.

"But do me a favor, Dee," he said. "Until I get this straightened out, don't get into it with the cats."

Dee stared at him and asked with all honesty, "What makes you think I would?"